AFTER: THE NEW EARTH II

Journey to the Jungle City

Keith R. Mueller

WALDORF PUBLISHING

Published by Waldorf Publishing
2140 Hall Johnson Road
#102-345
Grapevine, Texas 76051

www.WaldorfPublishing.com

After: The New Earth II
Journey to the Jungle City

ISBN: 978-1-64136-969-5
Library of Congress Control Number: 2018933208

DEDICATION

I would like to dedicate this book to those fighting to stop human trafficking and child prostitution. And to those who come after—those who work to lead the abused back into the Light.

CHAPTER 1

The city was quiet. Kel and Lyria stood in the darkened office with Tom Leatham, editor and owner of the Los Angeles Journal. They quietly looked out the second floor office window into the gas lit streets below them. A mule-drawn wagon, twin lanterns gently swaying from poles on either side of the driver's seat, made its way slowly down the dark street on some errand, carrying its dim oasis of pale yellow light with it. The driver sat slumped forward as though already asleep.

Los Angeles, the Black City of the West, was huge; its size almost impossible to comprehend, especially for someone like Kel. Neither he nor Lyria had ever been in any cities before. Kel had seen them in his mind's eye, as he'd read the books in the small library his father owned. His father had insisted he learn to read, and while he'd fought against it in his youth, he now saw the value in the written word—especially the words written in this newspaper regarding the predations of the Bishop and his minions.

Sprawling for many miles in all directions, Los Angeles was home to tens of millions, and more were arriving daily. Fleeing the slowly advancing glaciers still far to the north, some came in fear, and others came for the adventure. Sometimes a young member of one of the free tribes, in the city on a trading mission, would run away from his family and stay in the city, lured by the lights, fast life, women, and the seemingly endless opportunities that lay all about, just for the taking.

Some found success in various business ventures, while others found nothing but depravity in stinking bars and even filthier flophouses. Their lives were short, ended too soon by the knife, gun, or that most seductive of enemies, narcotic drugs.

* * * *

In the darkness, Tom and Kel watched the sinister green, purple, and red flickering of the Aurora—what the free tribes called the 'ice lights'—barely visible far to the north. It was a constant reminder of what lay out there in the darkness far beyond the city: a frozen, uncompromising death.

Kel sighed. "It is beautiful—is it not—in its own way?"

Tom laughed in response. "So is the giant anaconda serpent as it wraps its beautiful coils about you and suffocates you."

Kel nodded and laughed. "The city can suffocate you as well, if you allow it."

"That is true; there are times I've felt that way."

"How do you control that feeling?"

"It's simple, Kel. I just look out at the Northern Lights and it reminds me that things could be much worse."

Kel stared in disbelief, and Tom laughed. They all looked out again at the dim flickering of the Aurora.

* * * *

The all-pervasive glaciers had been advancing slowly for many thousands of years, but it had been of no great concern to the ancient civilizations until the ice wall, a mile high, finally reached the citadels of men and began destroying their shining cities of glass and marble. They tried to stop the advance of the glaciers, but all of their mighty machines of iron and steam, their giant reflecting mirrors, and advanced sciences so useful for man in claiming the earth and trying to claim the very heavens above them, failed to stop the ice.

Though they were able to gaze into the vast realm of stars with their sky windows, as the ancient legends called them, and though they had been able to send their rockets high enough into the sky that they could not return, they could not stop the threat that was right in front of them: the age of ice.

In time, all of the northernmost cities of the ancient 'city builders,' as the free tribes referred to them, were gone, possibly buried forever beneath the wall of ice. Once, these mighty civilizations had spread throughout the temperate regions of the Earth, but warfare between the civilizations across the sea and the ones on this landmass, plus the oncoming ice, brought the shining promise of a free civilization to an end.

Then came the final terror—something that affected the cities and the tribes. It was a deadly pandemic influenza that had finally ended it. The disease spread quickly, killing eighty percent of the human population of the earth in less than two years before it had finally run its course.

Civilization, as the city builders had known it, was dead; buried in cities void of humanity that were for many years nothing more than pest holes populated by rats and insects feeding on the millions of unburied dead—for who could bury the dead when there was no one alive? The deaths had come so quickly and overwhelmingly that nothing could be done. People fled the cities, seeking safety in the wilderness. But the disease found them nonetheless.

Eventually, in a few hundred years, some of the cities were cleared out, rebuilt and repopulated by the survivors, but the concept of any kind of central government was finished. Gigantic cities, each a nation unto itself, became the norm. In the vast wildernesses between the city-states, the free tribes roamed in the company of cave bears, mammoths, dire wolves, and saber-toothed tigers.

* * * *

Tom turned to the desk, and poured wine into the waiting glasses. Even if his friends didn't need it, he did.

His two solemn friends joined him. He looked each of them in their eyes, then raised his glass and smiled.

"A toast," he said, "to the success of your mission, and the freedom and rescue of your friends and compatriots."

Kel smiled, lifting his glass as well. "To Tom Leatham—a warrior of words, exposing evil and corruption in a way that allows others to see it, and take action against it."

"And to the successful completion of our journey—the freeing of our shamans, and the bright blood of the Bishop upon my blade," Lyria raised her glass and said with a grin.

"You've always had such a way with words, my love," Kel laughed.

"Kel, you knew falling in love with me would be a dangerous job."

"I cannot deny that," he replied, "but I would live my life with no other, save you."

"Nor I," she responded softly.

Tom filled their glasses one more time, raising his again. "To love, no matter how dangerous it may be."

They all laughed, friends enjoying a last night together before parting ways, perhaps forever.

* * * *

Kel was young, barely nineteen summers. He was tall and very fit, as were all the peoples of the free tribes who lived by hunting, agriculture, and barter. He'd been an apprentice shaman of great promise in his isolated tribe on the far side of the mountains that lay east of the city. He and Lyria should have been married by this time, but something had happened.

While he was away from the village on a hunting trip, a black zeppelin visited one night. The airship had dispersed a white cloud that put everyone quickly to sleep. When they awoke a day later, the airship was gone, and so was Garn, the tribe's shaman—Kel's grandfather and mentor.

Kel had one last obligation to fulfill before he could become a full shaman—a man of knowledge. Until he completed that obligation, tribal custom forbade his marriage—his marriage to his childhood love. His last ritual, something his grandfather had called the Shadow Walk, needed to happen. Kel had no idea what this ritual might entail; his grandfather had been his instructor in the ways of Spirit, and had not told him the nature of the Shadow Walk.

And now, Garn had been whisked away into the night sky; kidnapped by the cowardly crew of an airship who would not meet in face-to-face combat. They were cowards who attacked in the night, and killed babies and the old. He had to discover what happened, and why. With the help of his grandmother Pela, and Lyria, who knew how to use the sacred drum, he'd taken a journey between the worlds.

There, in the guise of his spirit totem, Hawk, he discovered that shamans from other villages were also being carried off into the night. Although no one could understand what the Black City might want with these men of knowledge and magic, everyone knew from stories of raids by the black ships from years past that they came from Los Angeles. And so, it was into the West that Kel decided to go in search of his grandfather, to find answers, and perhaps vengeance.

* * * *

Lyria stood holding Kel's hand as she gazed out once more into the dim haze that seemed to float in the street far below them. A steam lorry whizzed by on some unknown mission, the green canvas covering the cargo compartment flapping crazily in the speed-induced wind. The driver was moving fast in the belief there were no other vehicles on the road in front of him at this late hour. Lyria thought of the mule cart that had just plodded its way passed, and she hoped the animals and driver would be safe and out of reach of the speeding van.

Kel looked at Lyria. "It seems peaceful, does it not?"

Lyria whispered, "It may simply be that the darkness hides the darkness inside itself."

Tom laughed. "I never thought of it in those terms; I might have to use that in a story sometime."

"It is yours to use," the young woman said, looking at Tom with bright blue eyes. She smiled.

"Thank you," he responded, lifting his glass in her direction, "I believe I shall!"

They all drained their glasses.

* * * *

Lyria, a young woman of eighteen summers, was now a member of the same tribe as Kel. It was one of the tribes in a loose confederation of tribes that called themselves the Mastodon Clan. But it had not always been so. As a young child she'd been gifted to Garn in the hope that he might be able to help her. Her tribe's shaman had not been able to figure out what was wrong with the girl—why she would behave strangely and sometimes even violently.

Working with Garn and Pela, Lyria discovered her totem, the fierce saber-toothed tiger they called Ice Tigers. They would come to her spontaneously and literally possess her. Once she gained the required self-control and learned the disciplines of the warrior spirit, she understood this mighty gift and how to use it. This was never more apparent, or necessary, than the night of an attack by bandits on their village a number of years ago.

One of the bandits had decided to rape a pretty young woman with blue eyes and dark hair. He pulled her forward from the circle of captives, and then struck her, which turned out to be a fatal mistake.

From out of nowhere, Lyria's Ice Tiger took her. In mere seconds, her eyes suddenly turned an uncanny green instead of their natural blue, and she singlehandedly killed five bandits using their own spears and heavy daggers. The remaining bandits, seeing what had happened to their compatriots, fled into the night. The village's possessions and the young girl's life had been saved, and for Lyria it was a defining moment.

From that point on she dedicated herself to the way of the warrior. In her former tribe, all of the women were warriors, and now in her new home, she was following in that tradition. And when her betrothed, Kel, journeyed to the Black City, she went with him.

* * * *

"It's been a couple days now," Tom said thoughtfully, "and there have been no further killings."

"I heard the police captured the killer," Kel offered. "Some drunken man who confessed is what I have heard."

"I wrote that story," Tom said grimly, "but it is not the truth."

"What?" Lyria was shocked.

"If it was not true, why did you print it?"

Tom glanced at Kel, then at Lyria, and laughed once more. "I printed the story we received from one Sergeant Jinks of the Los Angeles Police Department to protect one of the magician's most valuable contacts."

"Won't that lead the people of this city into unawareness? Is that wise?"

Tom looked at Kel again, a slight grin playing across his face. "Do you mean even more unaware than they are ordinarily? This is very big city, Kel, and the people want to stay anonymous; hardly anyone knows their neighbor. Even if we were to publish every gruesome detail of the so-called 'vampire killings,' do you really think any of the people would begin to be more careful?"

Kel thought about this. "In a city of so many, I suppose the terrible deaths of a few are…far removed; each person knows they couldn't possibly be the next victim—why would they be? Among millions, their chances of being chosen by this or any other criminal act would be very small. Also, if they did not know any of the dead personally, how could it possibly affect them?"

Tom smiled. "You're sounding more and more like a city dweller every day!"

"Then maybe it is a good thing that we leave this place in the morning," Lyria said. Tom and Kel both looked at her. It was very possible she'd spoken the truth.

Somewhere within the city, a dangerously deranged woman was hunting and killing, taking trophies of hair cuttings, drinking her victims' blood, and on two occasions at least, she'd eaten parts of their internal organs. The Bishop and the priesthood of the Cathedral knew who she was, for they'd brought Adria to the city.

Though they didn't realize it, Kel and Lyria both knew the woman too; she'd been a member of their tribe, long before she became a killer—they knew her as a romantic challenge to Lyria and Kel's relationship. In fact, they didn't know she was in the city.

Adria had been a girl of the same tribe as Kel. She'd been in shamanic training along with him until it was discovered that she couldn't control herself between the worlds. She would inadvertently call scorpions and centipedes, and one night they'd almost killed her. She was a danger to herself and probably to others—certainly not one for the ways of magic.

When Garn ended her training, she was certain it was Lyria's fault. Lyria had come to her tribe, an outsider, and had stolen Kel's heart—a heart she was certain belonged only to her. And so she waited, and planned.

During one summer festival, Adria met a strange man who was reputed to be a sorcerer and shape-shifter. He'd told her many things; among them that power could be taken by force if one was willing to pay the price. Adria listened intently. This man was telling her things about herself she'd always suspected: she could become divine if she was willing to pay the price.

The zeppelin attack and Garn's kidnapping had been the catalyst she'd sought. Using the milk of the poppy seed she'd stolen from the shaman's own home, and the venom of scorpions, she'd murdered her parents. She was told it was the price she had to pay for power, to become the divine Scorpion Queen.

Close on the heels of the kidnapping, another airship arrived; this was a white craft carrying only a small crew and one priest. Father

Woods spoke to the leaders of the tribes who had gathered to discuss the possibility of war with the Black City, telling them not to attack. He told them that the priests were now looking for the kidnapped shamans. His lies were met with some skepticism, which enraged Adria; in her mind she believed this priest loved her—and that he was her betrothed.

That night Adria followed four shamans into the woods. There the shamans traveled between the worlds and discovered the priest's lies. Adria was furious. How dare they accuse the handsome and wealthy priest, her betrothed, of such vile things! In a silent attack as they slept, she killed them all, returning to her village where she attacked and almost killed Pela.

She then fled the village and stowed away on the zeppelin. Eventually she was discovered and taken to the Black City where she was indoctrinated into the world of prostitution and heroin addiction. But in the end, she couldn't control her killer instincts and in a violent attack, she slew a wealthy industrialist and his son—she had been sent to the man's home and told to sexually 'entertain' in exchange for weapons.

Once more she was on the run, hiding and killing as she went. She eventually found herself in one of the large city parks where she befriended several young girls who had run away from an orphan's home and now considered themselves to be 'wild' and a tribe of their own. Adria had plans for such weak naivety.

* * * *

Kel nodded. "I understand. It appears then that this Sergeant Jinks is actually helping the Cathedral cover up the killings, or rather who the killer is. Though why this should be, I cannot imagine—killing an innocent person to accomplish his goal…"

"I cannot explain it either," Tom responded. "All we know is that a prostitute who also works as a spy for the magician had…an encounter with Sergeant Jinks the same night the man died in his jail cell. He told her as part of his sex play that he'd set up the supposedly guilty man—an old school friend of his who'd been a drunkard for years.

He didn't tell the hooker why he'd do such a thing, but the woman indicated that he was quite proud of himself. My supposition, and that of the magician, is simply that Sergeant Jinks is a devoted follower of the Book of the Prophets and that he is in the thrall of the Bishop.

Being a prostitute, she hears many things that none else would hear. It is supremely important that we protect her identity and thereby her life, even if it means publishing stories we know are not true."

Again, Kel just shook his head. How depraved could a so-called 'civilization' get? He longed to return to his tribe, along with his grandfather and his betrothed—to return to the simple life of truths clearly spoken, and obligations always met.

He thought back to his first meeting with the magician.

The magician, it turned out, was a strange fellow. Kel had first met him in a seedy tavern called the Green Hyena where he performed various feats of stage magic and mental deception using mild hallucinogenic herbs secreted into the drinks of the patrons. It was there that he took their money and listened to their drink-loosened words. In this manner he was able to gather a large amount of intelligence for the secret society, the resistance movement attempting to undermine the work and power of the Church of the Redeemed God.

This resistance group within the Black City of the West was working tirelessly against all the interests of the Cathedral and its sinister and dangerous leader—a man known only as 'The Bishop.'

CHAPTER 2

The Bishop's past was shrouded in mystery. Years ago, he had suddenly appeared in the city—a priest, it was said, from the far away city-state of Atlanta—though there was really no proof of that. In a surprisingly short time he was elevated to the position of Bishop of the Church of the Redeemed God—in ages past, called the Liberated God.

Once a very popular religion, it had in recent years fallen out of favor in the eyes of the people of the city-state of Los Angeles, which was in no small measure thanks to the work of the resistance and its members—one of which was Tom Leatham, another was Lyria and Kel's friend Dan Hendricks. But the real reason for the church's decline in popularity lie mostly with the Bishop himself, primarily in the ways he changed the fundamental beliefs and behaviors of his faithful followers.

Most of the religions of the world recognized the simple truth that for balance to exist, and therefore life, two forces were needed to work in harmony. These two forces could be plainly seen anywhere on the Earth: day and night, light and dark, man and woman, life and death. And so the population of the Earth worshipped a God and Goddess. The religion of the Redeemed God taught that God became angry when He discovered the Goddess had created useless, trivial, and distracting things such as love, sex, and beauty. These things would clearly distract the people from adoring God. So in righteous anger, he ensnared the Goddess, binding and blindfolding her as She slept.

Now only God could rule and create, and be deserving of worship. For this reason, He was first called The Liberated God, and later, The Redeemed God. The altar images of this religion were a male Divine being standing with one foot triumphantly placed on a supine, bound, and gagged female figure—the Goddess was finally put in Her rightful place where She could do no more harm.

The original basic teaching of this faith, beyond the usual ones of all religions involving worship of the Divine and church services, was that women, created by the Goddess, were just as inferior as She. It was for this reason women were supposed to subjugate themselves to the males in their lives. Women were expected to have their husband's dinner on the table when he arrived home at the end of the day, and then to willingly service him wantonly in bed at night at his whim.

But with the arrival of the Bishop, things changed. Suddenly, women and girls were merely slaves—pack animals and breeders to produce more male children. To finance the Cathedral and all the various enterprises the Bishop was involved in, women and girl children of church members were told they had to submit to an even lower level. They were told they had to prostitute themselves for the honor and glory of God, to save their miserable souls from a burning place the Bishop named 'Hell.'

This was done willingly by the thoroughly indoctrinated male membership. But the Bishop wanted more; greed is never happy with just a little. Kidnapping, forced narcotics addiction, and gang rape was used to turn innocent children and women, not even of his faith, into prostitutes for his financial gain. Once that fact was revealed to the population of the city, the Church of the Redeemed God was looked upon with fear and distrust.

Because of this, the Bishop had constructed another city far to the south in a part of the world men called 'Green Hell' or simply 'The Green.' This vast jungle continent, shrouded in legends of death and terror, was said to be inhospitable to city-bred folk and so the ancient city builders had avoided it with a fear it justly deserved.

In this wild land the Bishop was building cities, quietly moving the faithful south. His plans were many and diverse. The plans were something the resistance had only heard about in vague, tavern-whispered rumors. These plans, the Bishop believed, if they were to come to fruition, would make him the undisputed ruler of Los Angeles, and eventually ruler of the world—a title he thought he clearly deserved.

But he has yet another scheme, one undreamed of by the small group of friends standing in the darkened offices of the Los Angeles Journal; another conspiracy known only to a chosen few. This secret is the Bishop's end game, his ultimate goal. It is something unspoken and unknown even to the most ingenious spies of the resistance. He has high hopes this ultimate plan will change the world forever, and bring it to its knees before his might.

* * * *

There is also another force beyond the resistance working against him—a child he'd himself raped repeatedly. To the Bishop, she was just another of many kidnapping victims of his greed and lust, made a prostitute by force and fear. But the captive girl had suddenly escaped his clutches in a most unusual way, and though he sees himself becoming god-like, he is not omniscient. Even now he cannot see the power that is building against him and his kind. It is a power carried by a young girl who was once Noria, and is now called Raven.

By accident or perhaps intervention, Lyria and Kel were taken to where nine-year-old Noria was about to be gang-raped again by priests of the Cathedral. A pimp, believing Kel to be a priest because he was dressed in a priest's garb, intercepted him as he was leaving the Green Hyena after having talked with the magician. The pimp took Kel and Lyria to a nearby apartment building so that Kel could use the girl too—for a fee, of course.

Inside, they found a beautiful child bound to the bed and three men drawing lots for the privilege of being the first. The girl looked to Lyria and begged to be killed. Then in anger and disgust, some 'Divine Other' took control of Lyria and the three priests were flung into the sky, seventy-seven floors above the ground. By the time the three hit the cobblestone street below, all that remained of them was raven-picked skeletons.

The 'Other' called to Noria and told her that her name now was Raven and that She, the Great Raven, Goddess of war, is her totem and protector and that she will become a force in the Earth the likes of which has not been seen in an age.

Kel, Lyria, and Raven then fled the building and made their escape, eventually reuniting with other friends they'd made along the way. Raven's peculiar gift of 'seeing' was gradually made apparent to them—she was both psychic and clairvoyant.

Next they learned that the Bishop had a plan for Green Hell, and that the kidnapped shamans they sought were no longer in Los Angeles. They had been taken into the southern jungle by the priesthood for some inscrutable purpose—a purpose that must involve magic, and their ability to communicate with animal spirits.

And so the three of them must travel south as well, into that hot, moist land known to Kel only from mysterious dreams of another black city being built by slaves and hovered over by black zeppelins. In his dream Kel had heard something that terrified him. It was an animal cry coming from very far away, a cry that was shockingly ancient and alien.

* * * *

Another steam vehicle passed on the street below. This one was moving slowly; coal oil lanterns focused with thick lenses probed the darkness along sidewalks and into alleys and storefronts with bright, searching beams. It was a police car, still looking for a killer that was supposedly already dead, hanged in his cell by his own hand even before he could be tried.

It was obvious that not everyone believed the story Sergeant Jinks had told. The three of them watched the car cruise past in silence. Kel shivered; he recalled the words of the child now called Raven, who was asleep in the adjoining room.

"The darkness has legs, you know," she'd said, "it bites."

There was a low moan from behind the closed door; Raven was dreaming. Lyria and Kel moved quietly but quickly into the darkened, secret room—they'd learned that even in her sleep, the beautiful and strange little girl would sometimes see. Raven was mumbling now, barely audible. Kel leaned close, listening.

"The fireflies will end it," she whispered cryptically, "and the birds." And then the child was once again silent, sleeping peacefully with a slight smile on her lips. Lyria looked quizzically at Kel, who could only shrug. It was just like the last time she'd mentioned fireflies when she first found out they were heading south.

She'd said, "Birds and fireflies; I'm going home."

They both knew that in the morning the girl would have no memory of this dream, and what it might have meant. In fact, if they were to awaken her right now, that would still be the case.

The night was late, and the wine was taking its toll. Lyria and Kel were sleepy. They'd have a big day tomorrow for they were journeying to The Green in the morning aboard a crystal ship. Kel smiled worriedly. Though he was intrigued by the concept of a crystal ship, the thought of being on the wide sea was…intimidating. Lyria leaned over and kissed him, squeezing his hand.

"Everything will be fine," she whispered.

"I hope so," Kel responded. "We'd just started learning our way around this city with the help of Dan and his friends, and now we find ourselves moving again."

"If we keep moving, they cannot catch us," Lyria responded with a slight laugh. "It is the bison who lingers at the watering hole that falls to the dire wolf."

Kel squeezed her hand and smiled.

CHAPTER 3

Traveling through the dark sky well south of the city, a black zeppelin cruised steadily in a southerly direction. All eight of the hydrogen-fueled engines were humming smoothly. The engine master glanced over his gauges in the dim glow of the cabin's shielded lanterns; the light reflecting from the polished brass and glass twinkled almost like stars. There were no problems. He sighed, allowing himself to recline into his seat, putting his hands behind his head, smiling and staring out into the blackness that surrounded them.

This was going to be a very long journey, but already three days were behind them—as were the cities of civilized men. That last outpost, San Diego, was well behind them as well. There were still a few cities ahead—Acapulco and Mexico City, among the larger. But they were not like the cities of the north—not as modern nor as populous. Still, they had a loyal following among some of these people, though none of them had been invited south.

With such a very important passenger aboard, now was not the time to let down his guard. The engine master looked over to where the Bishop slept peacefully in the cot folded down from the wall in the crew's darkened sleeping quarters. Across from him on another cot, the Bishop's servant, Harold, lay on his back, snoring softly. Beyond them, six members of the flight crew slept as well; at dawn they'd be awakened to take command of the airship.

The engine master's eyes then traveled to the large, canvas covered bundles secured to the deck with heavy cord and bronze hooks at the very back of the crew's sleeping quarters. It was pretty dark back there, especially at night, but this mountain of possessions was clearly visible. Of course there were the usual items of travel one would expect to see on such a long journey: iron-banded steamer trunks with formidable looking locking hasps and a valise or two. These items were dominated by the very large one secured in the center of the mound. The engine master heard the commander snicker, and turned to him with a grin. He was watching where the engine master was looking. "It's hard to believe he had to take his desk, of all the damn things!"

The engine master nodded in agreement. "Aye, sir—especially since we're headed to a place that might well be the place the Redeemed God first created wood."

The commander snorted. "That's a good way to put it."

"Well, if you think about it, sir, Green Hell has more wood free for the taking than any place I've ever heard of. Thousands of miles of trees and other resources in all directions, just sitting there, waiting for civilized man to come and take it."

"True. That would be the last place I'd think to take even more wood."

The engine master laughed softly. "The Bishop is going to be the king of wood in a few days—trees as far as the eye can see, and well beyond—all of it there for his taking."

"Well, everyone has their own eccentricities, I suppose. He can be the king of wood if he wishes; I'd rather be the king of all women."

"Yeah, I could go along with that. By the way, if that works out for you and you decide you need a prince of women…just let me know!"

The commander laughed.

The engine master glanced again into the rear of the ship's gondola. "I wonder what it would be like to be the Bishop's servant."

The commander laughed again. "I don't think that's something I'd be interested in finding out. I'm rather used to being the one in charge!"

They both snickered, and the commander returned to the pilothouse—somebody had to make sure the Bishop's damn desk arrived in one piece.

* * * *

Adria was not asleep that night either. She lay in the darkness of the park, thinking. Although she felt no urge to kill at this moment, she knew she needed to have money if she was going to continue to live in the city; the city ran on money, it seemed.

She still mourned the loss of the jewels and gold coins she'd stolen from the home of the wealthy arms manufacturer after she'd killed him and his son. The jewelry and gold belonged to her—she thought it was her divine right.

Somehow the coppers had found her apartment and now all her money and jewelry was gone. Someone must have told them where she lived—but who? She supposed it didn't really matter; done is done, as they say.

Still, the scorpion spirit had made sure she was out of the building when they'd come calling. It always watched out for her, which was more than her parents, tribe, and friends had ever done. She looked with some malice at the sleeping children. Were they her friends? Would they betray her like everyone else had?

Most devastating of all was the loss of the hair trophies she'd taken after each kill. The coppers had taken those, too. Why would they take her trophies? What use could they have for hanks of cut hair? The answer was obvious: malice. They were jealous and frightened of her power. They also had her very first trophy, taken from a woman with whom she'd lived for a short time. She'd been looking forward to making a skirt of her sacrifices' hair to wear under her dress. Again she imagined all that delightful hair—nice long hair rubbing gently against her thighs as she walked, rubbing against her everywhere. Well, she reasoned, shaking her head to clear it, there were lots of people in the Black City, and she'd be able to kill many more.

The killing and blood drinking were necessary. She'd discovered in a dream that the evil woman Lyria had put a curse on her that would cause her blood to dry up right in her veins and kill her—the jealous bitch! The only way she could stay alive was by replenishing her blood with new blood. To her surprise, using her fantastic abilities at reading minds, she realized that many people were willing to die for her; that she, a Divinity in the making, was worth dying for. They pleaded with her mind to be allowed to die that she may live. She knew it was true, she'd heard the begging and the scorpions told her it was so as well.

When her inner scorpion was not telling her to find people willing to sacrifice themselves to her that she might take their blood, she would on occasion fall back on her original profession here in the Black City—the oldest profession. Money had been unknown in her tribal life before coming to the city with her betrothed, the handsome and wealthy Father Woods. How she longed to return to him, triumphant! Here money was vital. She needed it for food and for the narcotics she craved. The beautiful heroin and what she called the Sting of the Scorpion—what her connections on the street simply referred to as mescaline.

She rose, quietly leaving the small, impromptu shack made of scrap lumber and fallen branches. She left the younger girls asleep in the park; there would be time enough to introduce them to this most easy way to make money. She grinned to herself; she could be their pimp! She knew there were some men who would pay a lot of money to be the first in a young girl's life. It would happen to them sooner or later anyway, wouldn't it? Why shouldn't she be the one who made the money from their young bodies—from their virginity? The voices kept telling her how special she was; how close to godhead she was getting. Everyone would naturally serve her in any way she deemed fit, even these young girls. The world was hers; all she had to do was take it.

She came out of her reverie to find she was approaching the corner where she'd seen the police cars that terrible day—in front of her former apartment building, the Hillcrest apartments. She decided to try her luck with the landlord. He'd been eager enough for her body when she lived there; she hadn't paid even a small silver coin in rent, though threatening to tell his wife she was fucking him had helped with that. She briefly wondered if he was the one who called the coppers on her. She quickly rejected that thought; he'd have lost his lover. Besides, he had no clue what she did when she walked out the door.

As she walked up the steps, she looked at her reflection in the glass of the door. Since the last time she'd been here, she'd tied her hair in a ponytail as a precaution against being identified by the coppers. She was confident the landlord would not recognize her either, and she knew he'd be just as eager now as he'd been then.

She opened the door and walked inside. She looked at the desk in the foyer—the landlord was not there. Instead there was a younger man—somewhat overweight—behind the large oak countertop, and he was looking back at her. The dim gaslights in the lobby highlighted his long nose, and his rounding stomach. Oh well, she'd had worse when she was taking men one after another on the stage in that tavern. She hadn't gotten any of the money she'd made back then. It had gone to Larry Harper, her pimp.

She smiled at the young man, walking slowly toward him.

"You here all by yourself?"

"Right now I am," he responded, glancing at Adria's breasts, partly exposed in the opening of her half unbuttoned bodice.

"Well, I hate to think you would be lonely here so late at night. Is your wife about? Are you married?"

"My wife is asleep in our apartment on the second floor."

"Does she make you less lonely?"

He licked his lips nervously. "She is with child now; seven months. She is not interested in...physical relief of...loneliness right now."

"Poor baby," Adria crooned, leaning over the desk watching as the man's eyes traveled along with her breasts on down until she was pressing them against the desktop.

"I bet all that...loneliness of yours has been just building and building, hasn't it? Getting heavier and heavier? Getting harder and harder not to think about?"

The man stammered, "Is there some way you can think of that will make me less lonesome?"

Adria laughed, "Everything has a cost, you know, even companionship on a long dark night; and the taking away of loneliness has a fee as well."

She released two more buttons from her bodice, revealing even further the honey colored swell of her almost completely exposed breasts.

That was enough for him. They quickly agreed upon a price—a very high price. Adria knew well how to take advantage of a desperate man. She moved slowly around the desk, never losing eye contact as she approached him. She saw him swallow nervously, and winked at him. She took his right hand and slowly slid it inside her bodice, letting him get a good feel.

"Wanna touch me? Do you like that?"

She winked again, getting down on her knees. She knew men liked it this way, and it was a lot easier for her as well; she wouldn't even have to take off her clothing, and they usually finished a lot quicker, as well.

Receiving the money first, of course, she grinned up at the man and began opening the snaps on the front of his trousers slowly—one by one. She muffled a giggle when she heard the door open with the soft jingle of a hanging bell. She began in earnest on the desk clerk.

"Everything alright in here?"

The clerk looked nervously at the police officer. "Yes, sir," he responded, "quiet as a church it is."

Adria bit slightly, and the man gasped. She put her lips around him tightly.

"Are you sure you're okay? You look…distracted."

"No really, I'm fine. I'm just staying hard at work."

Adria snorted softly, enjoying the joke only they understood.

"Very well then, I'll leave you to your job."

Adria had to stop for a second at the unintended humor in the copper's statement. Then she was back to work.

The clerk gasped. "Thank you, Officer, for checking in on me like this at night."

"Well, you know this is one of the locations the Vampire Killer used."

Adria bit again, and the clerk jumped. "I do know."

The bell jangled once more and they were alone. It was fortunate, for just then the clerk realized he was quite suddenly well beyond the ability to speak as he was consumed with pleasure.

Adria rose, wiping her mouth with the clerk's kerchief she'd pilfered from his hip pocket. She smiled at him, handing it back to him.

"If you ever pass by here again," he said, "drop in. I find I get lonely a lot."

"That might be arranged," Adria said, appraising the young man as a potential sacrifice when the calling came. He had a wife with an unborn child—now that blood would be really special! Yes, he'd do just fine; he even had long hair. As she looked at the money in her hand, she realized that the night was yet young. Surely there were men waiting elsewhere who were just as eager to give their money to her for what she could give in return. She opened the door, stepping out into the cool darkness of very early morning. Before she'd gone three blocks, a policeman walking his beat stopped her.

"It's dangerous to be out this late, Miss," the officer warned in a friendly manner, tipping his hat.

Adria smiled at him, brushing back her brown hair. He was the policeman who'd just been in the apartment lobby. She recognized his voice. She saw a piece of paper in the police officer's pocket, and wondered casually what it might be, though she had her suspicions.

"This? This is a drawing of a person we're looking for, Miss." He withdrew the drawing from his pocket and showed it to the young woman. She looked at it with a critical eye. It did bear some fair resemblance, but of course in the drawing the woman showed all of her teeth.

"Looks a bit like me, doesn't it?"

The officer laughed, holding the drawing up next to Adria's face. He too could see a resemblance, but when Adria smiled he saw the opening left by the two missing teeth. That damn arms manufacturer's son had knocked out her teeth. He'd managed to strike her with his fist just as she was taking him with her knife. Now she was glad the teeth were gone. She smiled broadly at the policeman.

He lowered the drawing, placing it back in his jacket pocket. Adria was ecstatic; he was looking right at the person they were all hunting and it was like he couldn't even see her. This was a very good thing to know—she could now go out, at least after dark, with little or no chance of being recognized, even by the coppers! It changed everything. She smiled again at the officer, lowering her head and looking up at him through her lashes.

"I would bet it gets lonely out here on this patrol of yours, doesn't it? All lonely and cold?"

"Yes, it does," he responded, "but you get used to it, and generally the late night shift is the quiet one; by now most of the drunks are asleep."

"Would you like some…company as you walk? It would make me feel ever so much safer with a big strong policeman at my side."

"Glad to oblige, Miss."

"A…Aileen is my name, sir."

Silently Adria cursed; she'd almost given him her real name.

But she could see now that his eyes and his thoughts were elsewhere. She'd neglected to button her bodice after her encounter with the hotel desk clerk. She didn't mind—her breasts were always a good lead-in. She bent forward slightly, pretending to look at the ground. He was staring between her breasts; it was time for her to proposition the copper. Wouldn't that be funny? Imagine, having sex in an alley with an officer of law who had your picture right in his pocket, and he was just too stupid to realize it. It would be too good to not try.

"Do you like my breasts?"

The officer jumped, and Adria laughed. "It's all right if you do, you know. Would you like to touch them? I'll let you."

He put his hand inside her bodice, seeking her nipple. Now she knew she had him. She led him to the next alley, and after giving her two silver coins; she pushed him up against the grimy wall next to an overflowing garbage can. He was furiously working the snaps of his trousers while she lifted her skirt, exposing herself to him.

"You're not wearing any underwear," he said in awe.

"It just gets in the way, don't you agree?"

"My wife would never go out in public, or anywhere else without underwear."

"Does she wear underwear to bed? Oh, I'm sorry…I hope I didn't offend you. Sometimes men want me to leave my underwear on when we do it."

"Actually, with my work hours, we don't get much underwear time together."

"Then it's a good thing I'm not your wife. I rather like the idea of spending some time with you."

He grinned at her. He was finally ready. She pushed herself up against him, guiding him inside, and shoved him against the wall with each thrust. It didn't take long. She'd discovered that most men finished quickly when she took them outside. As she backed away from him, she lingered, kissing him lasciviously as she deliberately rubbed herself against him to stain his uniform trousers with their lust.

She wondered what his wife would think about that! She laughed softly as she walked away from the policeman, once again counting her money. She hadn't felt the urge to kill him either, but she knew it was coming. The money she'd made on these two had been more than what the so-called 'wild' girls had made in a week begging. Yes, she decided, she needed to introduce them to this business. She'd start with the oldest—ten was old enough. She knew the others would certainly follow her example, and her lead.

CHAPTER 4

Sunrise comes a little earlier at nine thousand feet than it does on the surface of the earth. The bright sunlight reflected mercilessly off the polished aluminum ceiling of the crew sleeping quarters, brightly illuminating the sleeping Bishop's face. Eventually, the intense light and the warmth finally awoke the Bishop. He opened his eyes and then quickly squeezed them closed once more with a small hiss of pain as the brightness assailed him.

Finally, with a sigh of defeat and a grunt, he sat up on the edge of his bunk. He yawned, stretching. Across from him, Harold's bunk was already vacant. The Bishop turned toward the small galley to see his servant putting the finishing touches on a freshly brewed pot of tea; there was even some toast.

Harold carried the tray carefully to the small table and set it down. By this time the Bishop had arisen and had slipped his black robe over his undergarments, catching hint of his armpits as he lifted his arms. He wrinkled his nose. He would be glad to be in his own chambers once again, with a nice, long bath and a change of clothing—and perhaps one of those delightful young maidens he'd heard so much about. He certainly wanted to try out the local girls, to make sure they'd be fit for export north.

For the great things that were about to happen, he could put up with a little annoyance, and body odor.

"Thank you, Harold," he said with a smile.

"You're welcome, Your Eminence."

Harold poured the tea, handing a cup and saucer to his master. He waited for the Bishop to taste it. The Bishop approved, motioning Harold to sit with him.

"You have been with me a very long time, have you not?"

"I have, Your Eminence."

"Do you know why we're here?"

"I know why I'm here, Your Eminence. I'm here because you're here."

The Bishop laughed. "I mean do you know what we're about to try?"

"I know only what you have told me."

"Very well." The Bishop leaned forward and, in a conspiratorial whisper, said, "We are going to accomplish the impossible, Harold. We're going to change the fate of our faithful in Los Angeles, and then we will take the entire world back for the Redeemed God."

The Bishop glanced nervously toward the bow of the airship, watching the crew performing their various tasks. No one seemed to be paying them any attention, but one could never be sure.

"It's best if we wait until we are again on the ground before we go into any detail."

Harold nodded knowingly. "You think this...resistance can spy on us even here?"

"That I do not know; but zeppelins always go two ways—an airship heading toward The Green on one day will head back north on another day carrying spies and their secrets. We can take no chances right now, not when we're so very close to success."

"I understand, Your Eminence."

The commander of the airship was asleep. He'd been up most of the night checking and rechecking the flight charts. Now, he could sleep. The pilot was at the wheel—it was a large wood and brass affair exactly like one would expect to find on a crystal ship. Out the forward ports, he could see nothing but clear blue sky, and far below, the clear blue water of the western sea. He was softly humming to himself as they moved through their private ocean—an ocean of air.

"Sir?"

The pilot turned to the engine master's assistant who was now monitoring the engines.

"Yes, Jones, what is it?"

"Number six engine is running a bit warm, sir. I think we should shut it down for a little while to let it cool a bit and then we can fire it back up and see how it is."

"Make it happen, Jones."

"Aye, sir."

The pilot made a slight adjustment of the rudder to compensate for the lessening power on the port side. He checked his wind speed and relative ground speed. He nodded. Everything was going by the book.

The engine master's assistant shut off the gas jet that fed the number six engine. Without the hydrogen flame to boil the water, the steam engine quickly came to a stop. He continued to monitor the heat of that engine. This was always a potential problem on a vessel filled with highly flammable hydrogen; if an engine got too hot and caught fire it could easily bring down the entire airship. It was always better to be safe than sorry—especially with a nine thousand foot fall to look forward to!

The Bishop sat back in his chair, sipping his tea. He was reading the last missive he'd received from the south. The city was progressing as planned. They already had a few thousand inhabitants, mostly civilians. The walls were almost completed as well. He smiled and turned the page. The city by the river was also progressing nicely, though at a slower pace. He'd take care of that problem once he was on the ground again. His greatness would inspire confidence and that would translate into faster, more dedicated work.

He lifted that sheet, scanning the final missive. The half-human occupants of this land had tried several times to resist his soldiers. They'd failed, but some soldiers had nevertheless died. He needed those machines he'd ordered a while back from a specialty manufacturer in Atlanta. A supporter and colleague there had notified him of the new invention, and he'd immediately placed an order for three, with more to come later.

Once he had them, those miserable half-humans would cease thinking of fighting, and think more of placating. He closed the report. Half-humans were only good for a couple of things. The men were good for labor, and the women and girl children were good for pleasure houses—both those being built in The Green, and those to the north as well.

He rose, walking to the large windows to peer out onto the sea. They were flying close to the coast, and far below he could see the blue water turning white where it met the sandy beaches. He walked forward into the pilothouse.

"By tomorrow at this time, we'll be in New Los Angeles, with our feet firmly on the earth, Your Eminence," the commander stated, slightly adjusting the large ship's wheel.

"I can hardly wait, truth be told."

"Are you airsick, Your Eminence?"

"No, just sick of wearing the same clothes for more than three days."

The commander laughed. "I am sorry about that, Your Eminence, but the airdrome in New Los Angeles will not yet take the very large, luxury class vessels. We would not be able to land."

"I understand, but I still eagerly await the end of this journey."

"It's almost time for lunch, Your Eminence. I find that eating a good meal always brightens my attitude for a while—at least while I'm eating."

"I'll try your remedy then," the Bishop responded with a laugh, "I assume your cook is preparing something now?"

The Bishop sniffed the air, and the commander laughed with him.

* * * *

It was just before dawn. Tom Leatham was still slumped at his desk. He picked up the telephone and dialed.

"Hello, this is Tom, Mister Jackson. Are you sure you will be up to this, this morning?"

"Yes, I certainly am," the voice answered, "I'm rather looking forward to meeting your new friends."

Tom laughed. "Well, I'll be interested to see their response when they hear your story and you tell them who you are…or rather, who you were."

"I can deal with that. By the way, I meant to tell you the accommodations you found for me on such short notice are more than adequate. Thank you so much."

"It was the least I could do, considering the assistance you've given me and the resistance this last year."

"I just want the killings to stop. Apparently the Bishop and Father Woods think differently."

"Well, you're safe now. I'm arranging transportation for you that will take you well away from Los Angeles and the Cathedral. I've already procured new identification documents for you as well. When you arrive at your new home, you'll be a completely different person.

I estimate that will be in a week—no more."

"And for that I thank you as well, Tom. You're a true friend. I don't think I could have continued there any longer and remained... real."

"I'll send a car to pick you up, Henry. Thanks again for doing this. The quest these people are attempting is the stuff of legends. But legends are only written about those who succeed, not those who simply walk into an unknown and never return."

* * * *

Mister Henry Jackson, formerly Father Jackson of the Cathedral, was an older man who'd been a priest for most of his life. Brought into the priesthood at a young age by his very devout parents, he'd never questioned anything about his religion, or his place within it.

He'd developed an interest early on in the study of the ancient sciences of psychiatry and psychology—the sciences of the great city builders of legend. The access granted to him as a priest permitted him to peruse the many books in the Cathedral's basements, which had, in turn, allowed this interest of his to bear fruit. Due to his understanding of the way the criminal mind works, he'd become a valuable asset to various police departments all along the western coast. He helped them track down elusive and sometimes clever criminals and the occasional psychopathic killer.

But his studies of the mind had had another effect—one he'd not expected. He'd begun questioning the most fundamental book of his faith, the Book of the Prophets. This book, written in the dim past by unidentified authors who were said to have been prophets, claimed their teaching was the one true teaching and that their religion was the one true religion—everyone else was wrong. It was as simple as that.

In his studies of the criminal mind, he'd repeatedly come face to face with individuals who were absolutely convinced they were right, and everyone else in the world was wrong. He realized that the religion of the Redeemed God and its accompanying mandatory doctrine—that absolute truth had been revealed only to them—was clearly an ego driven belief. If that were true, then both the book and the religion it described was simply the work of ego driven men; it was a religion with no hint of anything Divine or spiritual behind it. Then he'd made the mistake of speaking his doubts aloud.

Once the Bishop became aware of Father Jackson's view, he had immediately reduced his responsibilities in the Cathedral. He was no longer allowed to be a teacher of children. He had been relegated to the zeppelin barns to oversee the paperwork of the various repair and maintenance shops. Henry realized it could have been worse—if he wasn't still such a valuable ally for contacts with various police agencies, the Bishop would certainly have had him killed long ago and sent him to be fertilizer in the towering hydroponics gardens that fed most of the city's population—he'd seen it done before.

Then the so-called 'Vampire Killer' case erupted in the city. He'd worked with the priests and the police, of course, to try to identify how this killer might think and behave, and show them a way to capture or kill the woman.

That turned out to be part of the problem. Reports stated that all evidence seemed to indicate the killer was a woman. The Bishop knew with certainty the killer was a woman, for one of his own priests had brought her there! He refused, however, to allow the press or the police to know what he knew. He had a simple motive; according to doctrine, women were an inferior mis-creation by the equally inferior Divine Feminine. To admit a mere woman was eluding the police and the priesthood would be too damaging to the image of the church—an image already damaged enough.

In desperation, Father Jackson had begun leaking information to the press. It was said in the news stories that the information came from an undisclosed police informant. But finally, it was just too much. Father Jackson had seen firsthand the work of deranged repeat killers—the images still gave him nightmares. There was only one thing he could do, and so he did it. He left the Cathedral as a priest, and entered the Black City as a civilian. Henry Jackson was about to depart for points unknown.

He had but one more act to play in this drama, he was going to address the small band of brave souls traveling into the jungles to save their friends—and perhaps find some way to stop the Bishop's mad intention to rule the world. It was an obligation—one on which he would not—no, could not turn his back.

CHAPTER 5

In his darkened bedroom, Dan Hendricks had not slept. Lying with his hands behind his head, eyes open, he stared into the blackness. He was thinking about his friend and resistance partner, Lawrence Ford, who'd turned traitor to their cause, helping the Bishop in his attempt to kill Lyria and Kel. Though the attempt had failed, Dan remained sleepless trying to figure out why his friend had betrayed them. The only possible answer was Lawrence's gambling problem. What a shame. But Dan was still in the fight. He had things to do in spite of his sorrow, and he was determined to do them.

Dan had been born in the Black City, an unwanted accident—an illegitimate child given away at birth. He'd grown up on the streets; running with other neglected and ignored boys. He learned how to steal and became legendary among his friends for his talent in picking pockets. That talent grew, and soon he and his friends were burglarizing homes, businesses, and museums. They were on top of the world.

It was during that time Dan had met the magician—a meeting that had completely changed his life. Suddenly he found he was worthy of trust and a keeper of important secrets. He'd put his thieving talents to work for the resistance in earnest. Several times he had infiltrated the Cathedral disguised as a priest to conduct surveillance and to steal artifacts and books from the many basements and sub-basements of the vast stone edifice.

That was how he came to fully realize the greed and egocentricity of that religion. He'd seen it for himself—vast libraries of books predating the destruction of the city builders. Halls filled with artwork that could better fill museums where all could enjoy them. All of this was being kept secret from the rest of the world simply because they didn't want to share. Their behavior reminded Dan of the behavior of a greedy child. He knew—he'd been that child!

Then there was that ancient sword forged centuries before the coming of the ice—a sword that had crossed the great eastern seas aboard a dragon boat in the hand of a half-mythic warrior in search of land and plunder. With the sword were ancient documents describing the sword and the great magic that resided within the pattern welded steel. He'd taken the sword to sell; it was not something the resistance needed or had any use for, although he instinctively knew it was worth a lot of money.

The sword had been the most valuable and by far the most visible item he'd taken—and the priests were finally on to him. He carefully hid the sword and went to the magician and his compatriots. It was from them he'd learned that the priests were hunting him.

But it was not Dan the priests found when they came looking for him. They found Daniel's love and his light—they'd found Daisy. They'd taken his Daisy, mercilessly raped her and took her to the Cathedral where they burned her alive. Dan watched with torment and anger, as there had been nothing he could do. There were too many armed men and by the time he realized what was they were actually planning, his beautiful Daisy had become a living torch.

Daniel stole what was left of Daisy's body from the priests that night and buried her in an unmarked grave in the city cemetery. He then fled the city, convinced of his cowardice. He eventually ended up in a large tribal village in the mountains east of Los Angeles, where he stayed. It was there that the people accepted him and did not question his past. There he found a home—the first real home he'd ever known in his life. But fate often intervenes when one becomes complacent.

Working as a hired guide for what he thought were traders, Dan had inadvertently fallen in with bandits. He was part of the raid on Kel and Lyria's village—the raid Lyria ended in just seventeen seconds of blood and death. Dan fled back to the safety of his village, and again, fate…or maybe something else, intervened.

Lyria, Kel, and he found one another on the road. Dan and others from his adopted tribe were searching for missing members of their tribe and their wagons. They learned from Lyria and Kel that bandits had slaughtered those they sought. They told of the overturned wagon, the arrows…and the stripped bodies. From Dan, Kel and Lyria learned of the missing member of that family—a daughter. A girl named Noria.

Later, in a tense negotiation, Lyria learned of Dan's involvement in the raid on her village. Learning this, she allowed Dan to live—and in return, Dan gave Lyria the sword he'd stolen from the Cathedral.

The ancient sword was forged in ancient magic—a sword with a mind of its own. Lyria quickly learned to communicate with the spirit of the blade, and as they conversed and bonded, so did Dan with his new friends. He decided to accompany them to the Black City and introduce them to the magician and the resistance.

Without Dan, their mission to the Black City would have certainly failed. So whether fate or something more, friends who'd been recently united were now to be separated for Daniel was not going south—he had work to do in the Black City. He lit the lantern and looked at the clock on the wall. It was four in the morning—it would be daylight soon, and time for his friends to leave. He closed his eyes for the hundredth time that night—sleep continued to elude him.

* * * *

The sun was just painting the eastern sky with pale shades of blue and pink. Though Adria was tired, she'd decided to make one final score for the night. She was watching for just the right man. Traffic was picking up now as many made their way to work. Adria smiled, she was already at work—she was hunting in the man-made canyons of the city.

And there he was. She spotted the man coming toward her in the dimness of the dawn. She watched him carefully, seeing the flash of gold jewelry on a finger, a glint of some precious stone on a watch chain as he passed beneath a gaslight. Why this man was walking instead of being driven in one of the fancy and expensive steam-cars that were now occasionally moving up and down the road intrigued her. She approached him slowly, a smile on her face.

"Hello, sir, I notice you are walking."

The man looked at the girl suspiciously. Could she be dangerous? He quickly decided she could not; she was, after all, a mere woman. In his mind he heard his friend speaking to him, remembering the great joke he'd been told right after last Sunday's church services. As they left the Cathedral, his friend said that the Bishop was right—women should be obscene and not heard. How they'd laughed!

He laughed now as well. "My automobile would not start this morning; apparently the boiler has a leak."

"That is too bad. So you are walking to your work?"

"No, young lady, I'm walking to the bus stop on the next corner."

"When does the bus arrive?"

Adria watched with greedy interest as the man procured his pocket watch, she was sure that it was gold as well. He flipped the lid.

"The bus will be here in thirty minutes."

"Well...that is more than enough time."

"More than enough time for what?"

"More than enough time for you to fuck me."

The man was taken aback for a moment, but Adria watched, as he looked her up and down quickly. She had him.

"We can do it right here, kind sir."

"In an alley?"

"Why not? It will be exciting and dirty—you would like me to do dirty things to you, would you not?"

The man grinned. "Like what kind of dirty things?"

Adria leaned in, whispering in the man's ear as she ran her hand slowly up and down the front of his trousers. He nodded, and they stepped into the darkness of the alley. She watched as he opened his wallet, handing her a small gold coin. She knew she was well worth it. She quickly undid the snaps of his trousers, hiking up her skirt for the second time this morning.

Just like all the rest of them, it didn't take the man very long. His weakness was dirty talk, and Adria could be very imaginative when she put her mind and body into it. As he gasped in pleasure, leaning forward slightly, she put her hand against his face and abruptly slammed the back of his head against the brick wall—hard. He looked surprised. She did it a second time, hearing the satisfying thud, and then both surprise and consciousness fled from the man's face.

Adria looked up and down the alley, they were alone. She withdrew the knife from her handbag, turning it in the light. She placed the razor edge against the man's neck. She watched in fascination as the edge pushed the flesh. Just a little more pressure and ...and then she returned the knife to her bag.

This was not the right one; he didn't even have long hair. In fact, he hardly had hair at all! She giggled. But that didn't mean he didn't have some interesting attributes. She quickly relieved the man of his watch, rings, and wallet. When she'd taken all she wanted, she gave something to him. She squatted over his chest and urinated on him. She laughed, here was one wealthy man who was going to be late for work today. She dropped the jewelry and the wallet into her handbag, and casually walked out of the alley into a new dawn. She was smiling.

CHAPTER 6

The sun was just creeping over the horizon. Outside the office window, birds were chirping merrily. In the next room, Kel awoke. He looked over at Lyria, still sleeping beside him. Raven, a short distance away, was also still asleep. He sighed—how he longed to actually belong to Lyria—to become one with her. Until he completed the mysterious Shadow Walk, that part of his relationship with his betrothed would have to wait. He rose quietly, going into the bath.

He ran water in the sink and washed his face. While he was drying himself, he heard Lyria beginning to stir in the next room. He finished his morning ablutions and returned in time to see Lyria just standing up from the bed.

"Good morning, my love."

She grinned at him. "Good morning in return, my Kel."

"We will be fine."

She looked at Kel, and then snickered. "Are you trying to convince me or yourself?"

Kel snorted. "I guess a little of both. Remember, wherever we go and whatever happens, I will always love you."

"And I you, my dear. Now let me pass or we will never be on time for our meeting with Tom."

Kel sighed. "Yes. The meeting. I look forward to this adventure and I fear it as well. We have much to gain, but we also have much to lose."

"Well, my love, that is why I have my sword."

Kel laughed as he moved out of Lyria's way. She walked into the bathroom, closing the door. Kel sat on the bed and put on his shoes. He was still not completely used to the stiff leather shoes of the city; shoes with buckles or buttons or convoluted lacing. He wanted to wear his moccasins.

By the time Lyria returned, Kel was dressed. He sat with his back turned as Lyria put on her clothing. When she was dressed, she woke Raven, who quickly prepared herself. She was the only one, it seemed, eager to be gone—but then, her memories of the Bishop and this city probably had something to do with that.

When Raven returned from the bath, Lyria put her hand on Kel's shoulder and the three of them rose and walked out into Tom Leatham's office, and into the start of a new journey—a journey whose ending nobody could guess. Tom was still sitting silently at his desk where he'd been all night. He smiled at his guests when they entered.

Kel saw that the wine bottle was empty.

Tom looked up. "Are you ready?"

"Ready as we can be," Kel answered.

"Then let us go to the conference room and we will begin."

They followed the editor out of his office and down the hallway. Tom held open the door of the conference room and Lyria, Kel, and Raven entered quietly. Tom then entered and closed the door behind them.

CHAPTER 7

Tom quietly closed the door of the meeting room. Lyria, Kel, and Raven sat at the polished mahogany table. Raven was admiring the soft leather of the chairs, running her fingertips down the chair's armrest. Her village had had leather chairs, to be sure—but they were not as soft and padded. The door opened once again, just a moment later, and Dan Hendricks entered, looking sheepishly at Tom.

"I'm sorry I'm late, Tom."

"It does not matter; we were just beginning."

Dan nodded, taking a seat beside Raven. The girl smiled up at him, taking his hand in hers. She and Dan had a special relationship, for they'd known each other since Raven was five—from the time Dan had fled the Black City after Daisy's murder, for tribal life in his new home in Mountain Village.

She loved her Dandan, as she called him. He'd spent much time playing with the children of Mountain Village before the attack on the trading party that had killed her family and sent her into sexual slavery at the bidding of the priests of the Cathedral. But not everyone present was a friend—or even an acquaintance, for that matter. They all stared at the stranger sitting at the head of the table beside Tom.

The stranger was an older white-haired man, cleanly shaven, in a simply cut dark suit. He had a silver chain for his watch, which hung across his chest. He sat silently in the front of the room beside Tom, hands folded on the table before him. His demeanor was serious. Kel looked questioningly at Leatham.

The editor smiled reassuringly. "Before we head for the docks, there's someone I think you need to meet. May I present Mr. Henry Jackson?"

The old man nodded in the direction of the others.

"Mr. Jackson, if you please?"

The man rose and cleared his throat. "Until yesterday I was a priest of the Cathedral."

Kel and Dan both rose instinctively and defensively—fists clenched, ready for battle.

Tom raised both palms toward the two men. "Be calm. What he

has to tell you is very important for your mission."

The two men sat down, and Tom again gestured with a nod for the man to speak.

"For some time now," the old man began, "I've not been looked upon favorably by the Bishop and the other leaders of the church here in the West. You see, I began to question even the most basic teachings of the faith. Keep in mind that I was born into a family that devoutly followed this religion—it was all I heard about from infancy.

"As I matured, my parents literally drove me to be a priest. They even sent me to the Cathedral school—at a substantial cost. To please them, I studied very hard, and then finally I was a real priest just as they'd desired. I remember that they were so proud of me.

"Gradually, as I worked as a teacher myself, I became interested in the working of the human mind—a science that the city builders of old called psychology. At first, I wanted to use such knowledge to help me teach the children in our school.

"Because I was a priest, I had access to many old books held in the basements and sub-basements of the Cathedral—some were original copies printed long before the age of ice, the wars, and the killing plague that followed.

"Eventually, my knowledge in these areas of study came to be of use to the various police forces of this city and, in fact, all of the cities of the West. I had become a specialist, you see, in the workings of the criminal mind.

"But as time went by and I began talking with criminals and researching police files, I began to notice certain things. Though most of the policemen I came into contact with through the years were truly dedicated to protecting the citizens of their cities to the best of their ability, some members of the various police departments were of my religion. In some cases—not all, mind you, but in some cases—those policemen deliberately chose to ignore or twist the information I gave to them.

"Those officers saw to it that clearly innocent people were sometimes condemned to prison and even to the hangman's noose at the behest of the Bishop—some were even murdered in their cells before they could be brought before a judge. Suicide, they label it—all to protect another citizen who just happened to be a follower of the Redeemed God. I began to wonder what kind of Divinity would favor lying and murder, for hanging an innocent person is surely murder."

Kel nodded. "That is something I will agree on."

The others nodded, even Raven.

The old man held up a book for them all to see.

"This is the Book of the Prophets. It's the dogma and doctrine of our religion. I diligently searched and found that the teachings within actually condoned this kind of killing, if it protected the church or its members—guilty or not. It seems the prophets thought the Redeemed God should be the One to punish the faithful if they needed it—in the life after this one. How convenient was that? It literally gave the faithful the ability...not the right, mind you, but the ability to do pretty much what they pleased, and get away with it—even murder, robbery, and rape. It was then that I began to question the book itself, for what God would allow anyone, especially His followers, to literally get away with murder?"

"You were a priest and you had not read the book?"

Henry turned to Lyria and smiled. "I did not. You see, in the Cathedral school we were told what to know and what to read. We read books written about the Book of the Prophets, but we were not encouraged to read the actual book itself."

"But why?"

"The answer to that is simple. There are passages in the book they wish to keep somewhat to the higher echelons. To be sure, the book was readily available, but based on how we were trained, we just assumed the books we'd used in classes had the same information, and that it had simply been put into a more easy-to-read format."

"So that way, they really can't be accused of keeping something from you. It is not their fault if you do not take it upon yourself to read the original book," Kel said.

The former priest nodded in affirmation. "Everything was always open and aboveboard. The Bishop and his underlings were not keeping anything from us; they simply led us to believe we'd received it in our studies. In that way they were like stage magicians—they attract you with one hand, and deceive you with the other.

"But as I advanced my understanding of the way men think, and why they behave as they do, I gradually came to realize that a book—any book—is simply a creation of man, not God. That would, of course, also include this book. I began to wonder why it is that all the religions of this land are basically the same with regard to the equality between the God and Goddess, with the sole exception of the followers of the prophets who supposedly wrote this particular book."

"I have wondered that as well," Kel said thoughtfully. "All seem to teach the same Divine creation stories, stories of celestial dragons and the sacred dance of the Universe. All of them teach the harmony that exists between God and Goddess, except the religion of the Cathedral."

"How well I have come to realize that," the old man said with a firm nod.

Lyria asked, "How can they look at the vast harmony of things and think its creation was the result of an unbalanced Divinity, the other half bound and in chains?"

"There's a simple answer to that," the ex-priest said, smiling. "Power. The Book of the Prophets gives its followers—all of them—power. They cleverly invented a burning place for evil folk and named it Hell. They point toward volcanoes and suggest they are the vents of Hell, and if the vents are that hot, how much hotter must Hell be? They taught that all, save the followers of that one book, would burn eternally with the Goddess, for She is surely living evil.

"This kind of thinking gives power even to the most downtrodden members of the church. Even the poorest and most abused know that they'll dwell with the Redeemed God and that everyone else will burn eternally. Their rich landlord, their employer, even the heads of state, will all burn together if they are not followers of the faith. It makes the lowly miner digging into the darkness of the earth, or the poorest orphan gloat in the smugness of salvation.

"It did one more thing; it gave the church complete control over its followers. We were taught that all women are evil—creations of the mentally deficient Goddess to lure men away from worshipping the true, strong male God. Women had to be subservient to the will of man; they were like the Goddess on earth, in a way, evil at their worst, and merely corrupt at their best, or simply weak willed at the very least.

"To be redeemed, they had to enslave themselves—to be bound as they claim the Goddess is bound. This gave the men in charge even more power, for their women willingly and gratefully gave themselves over into this slavery.

"When the Bishop came to power, he declared that not only were women expected to serve their husbands at the table and in bed, they were also expected to serve, if required, as prostitutes for the Cathedral. For what better way could women learn humility than being forced to endure endless sexual assault? Even their girl children, regardless of age, were expected to fill this role—and the men of the church, primarily the priests, of course, became even more powerful, and even more sure of their ultimate salvation."

"How does a kidnapped child fit into this picture," Lyria spat angrily. "Did Raven willingly submit?"

The old man shook his head sadly. "Of course she didn't. In fact, the taking of children from the tribes in the zeppelin raids of the past disgusts me. I found out that even bandits were being paid to kidnap children of the free tribes for the perverted use of the priests and followers of this…religion."

Lyria hissed, "Then how could you just…go along with it?"

The former priest opened his hands. "I didn't, once I became fully aware of what was going on. Remember that I have many connections with the police forces of all the cities of the West so I am privy to much information not available to the press, or even the Bishop himself in some instances. I also heard things the Bishop and others didn't know I'd heard.

"For instance, I began hearing of certain bandits who'd been arrested for various crimes within the city, some of them on more than one occasion, and then mysteriously freed from jail with no explanation. In each of those instances, I came to find the hand of the Cathedral always present in some capacity."

Here he paused, looking around the room—would they accept his advice? He couldn't tell by looking at them, but he hoped they would at least listen and take note; their lives might just depend on it.

"It was I who talked the Bishop into ceasing the raids outside the city by warning him of the danger of a counter attack by the free tribes. When I told him that the tribes just might unite into one fighting force of perhaps millions, he decided to agree with me—but that didn't stop the bandit predations—the Bishop reasoned that bandits would never be tracked back to him, the city, or the Cathedral."

He paused again for a moment, allowing what he'd said to sink in. Once more he looked into the faces staring back at him.

"I discovered that the Cathedral was being paid great sums of money by men eager to abuse children—many of those men not even of this religion. You see, corruption is like mold on a loaf of bread; if it's not cut out, it spreads to the wholesome part, eventually corrupting everything. The abusers of women and children are not limited to the so-called true faith—believe me!

"They have prostitutes who serve them willingly, of course, selling themselves eagerly to help the church and redeem what they consider to be their evil and worthless spirits. Now, while these women are deceived, they are nonetheless willing participants in the sex trade. Those not willing to sell themselves, such as women and children who are not followers of the Bishop, or those taken from the free tribes, are quickly addicted to narcotic drugs and then raped repeatedly to destroy their will and any feeling of self-worth. They're made totally dependent on the Cathedral to supply them with the narcotics they now need to live."

The old man sighed. "My...questioning of the Bishop's motives and subsequently the book itself is why I was relegated to the zeppelin barn. Banished is probably a more appropriate word."

He laughed bitterly. "As I once said to Tom, do I look like someone who knows anything at all about airships? They couldn't kill me, you see; they still needed my expertise—my special connections with the various police departments in all the cities of the West. I'm like their book, in a way. I give them power and I give them inside information. But now that's at an end."

The others said nothing for a moment, shocked at the candidness of someone who should be a dire enemy. Imagine—a priest denouncing his religion as a construct of man! None of them had ever heard of such a thing. Kel heard the words of his old tribal blacksmith, Llo, echoing in his mind.

Not everything that is black is evil...

The ex-priest coughed quietly to get everyone's attention.

"Kelley Draco," he said with a crooked smile, "I want you to take this book with you. Tom has told me that you can read. If you plan to pass yourself off as any kind of high ranking official, military or civilian, in some relationship with the Cathedral, you would surely own a copy. This one is well worn and has the appearance of much use. Take it. Read it. Learn from it. Keep it visible. When your enemies come for you, and be certain they will," he held up the book tapping its cover with his index finger, "this is where the attack will come from. Know your enemy."

"What are you going to do now?" Lyria wanted to know. "Will the Bishop try to kill you?"

"Probably," he answered with a grin, "if he can find me; but from what Tom has told me, they're searching as we speak for a dead man. They think I came into the city and was waylaid. But I know the Bishop well; I know his mind probably better than he does. I doubt he will ever be able to find me. I think I can continue to be of service to the resistance, and perhaps I can help lawmakers in designing laws that will end forced religious prostitution and child rape—laws that have power at least within the borders of Los Angeles. This is work I can do from a distance, sending my thoughts and ideas to Tom by zeppelin. Later, perhaps the same can be accomplished in all of the other cities of the West. I believe all people who do not follow this book are tired of having their children kidnapped, their daughters addicted to narcotics and sold on the streets to anyone with sufficient money and sufficient selfishness."

"But now," Tom interrupted, "it's time to go."

Kel and Lyria looked at each other; they were ready.

Raven took Lyria's hand, whispering softly, "Birds and fireflies!"

Lyria hugged her closely for a moment. Tom opened the door and they filed out, then down the steps and into the newspaper's parking garage. There was a steam-car waiting in the cool darkness of the man-made cavern.

It was there that Dan said goodbye to his friends.

Lyria gave him a hug. "You have shown me that people can change; that everyone is not who they might seem at first look. I thank you for that insight, Dan."

Raven was crying. "Dandan, aren't you coming with us?"

Dan hugged the little girl. "No, honey, I have to stay here and help the magician and his friends."

"Will you be here when we come back?"

"Of course, sweetie," he said. "I have no immediate plans to go anywhere until my business here is finished."

"You better," the girl said, fists on her hips, "I'll be very mad if you aren't here to give me a hug when we return."

"I'll give you ten hugs—how about that?"

"You better; I can count that high, you know!"

"Of that I have no doubt," Dan said with a fond smile. "Besides, the magician and his friends need someone around here who can get things done the right way."

With that, he suddenly fumbled with his hat, almost but not quite dropping it. He winked at Raven. The child laughed at his jest, but her eyes were sad nevertheless. Dan wished at that moment that he was leaving with them—or better yet, that none of them had to leave at all. But he knew he had work to do here, and he trusted Lyria and Kel completely. He knew that they would take care of his precious Noria, now called Raven.

The magician held the door of the steam-car for them as they climbed into the back seat. He also held the door for Tom, who was driving. He walked to the passenger side and took his seat next to the editor. He nodded, and the car pulled from the parking space, rapidly picking up speed. Lyria looked out the windows at the great black buildings. She was glad they were leaving, yet she knew she'd miss Dan—a man she'd wanted to kill only a short time ago.

"The docks are only a short distance away," the magician said. "We'll be there in an hour, your ship is waiting for you."

Kel looked at Lyria nervously and she smiled at him. Raven sat quietly between them, watching the city pass by with interest.

"Are we not going the wrong direction?"

Tom grinned. "Very observant, Kel."

"If we are going to the docks, they would have to be to the west, yet we travel even now to the east."

"Your sense of direction is excellent."

Tom glanced once more into the side mirror of his automobile. That brown lorry had been behind them for a period of time now. Were they being followed? Better safe than sorry.

Tom glanced at the magician. "I do have a reason. There's a brown lorry behind us. I wish to see if we're being followed."

Tom turned right at the next intersection, carefully watching his mirror. Though traffic was not very heavy, he watched as the lorry behind them still took a risk to make the corner quickly, cutting off a fast-moving taxi. They all heard the steam whistle of the cab screeching angrily. At the next intersection, Tom turned left. The lorry followed.

"Well, I don't know for certain who it might be, though I can take an educated guess."

"The priests?"

Tom glanced at the magician. "No, more likely the police—maybe even our old friend Sergeant Jinks. I imagine that my newspaper is suspect in the minds of the Bishop and his followers by now. I have not proven to be a very kind observer of their behavior."

The magician laughed. "So, do you have a plan?"

"I always have a plan."

The magician turned to his friends in back. "He always has a plan."

"I also have a plan," Lyria commented. "Give me my sword, and then pull over and wait for them."

"They have firearms."

"I keep forgetting that," she responded with a laugh.

With that, Tom made another right turn, and then another, and drove slowly into a narrow alley. Halfway to the next street, there was a large trash container. It stood almost eight feet high and was at least six feet wide. Kel wondered how they could empty something so large.

The magician explained. "When the time comes to empty it, they simply use a steel cable to pull it up onto a flat trailer. They then take it away with a lorry to empty it."

"I imagine they must empty it every moon?"

The magician laughed. "No, much more often than that. I imagine it's hauled away every week and replaced with an empty one. Everyone in the building uses it, and the building has sixty stories."

The conversation ended when Tom suddenly pulled the auto to the other side of the trash container, pulling tightly up to a large corrugated metal gate. By the time he lowered the steam pressure, another vehicle had pulled into the alley coming the other direction. That auto drove slowly toward them, taking its time.

"All right," Tom said, "we get out here. Do not make any loud noises."

The magician and Kel opened their doors simultaneously, and as they did, the metal door they were next to began sliding up in its frame. It rattled a little, but the chains and gears were well oiled and maintained. It only lifted four feet, and then stopped.

"Everyone duck under and go inside, please."

As Lyria stooped and entered the dark warehouse, the auto that had been approaching had finally reached them. It stopped beside their vehicle. The driver rolled down his window and leaned out. Kel stood for a moment, mystified by the strange behavior of the driver. He was leaning way out, having an animated conversation…with no one. He was talking to an empty auto.

"Very clever."

Kel turned to the magician. "What is clever?"

The magician laughed quietly. "Our followers will think we stopped here simply for a rendezvous with that man. They will assume we are still in the vehicle."

"And we'd better get moving," Tom said. "We can only fool them for so long."

With that, they all entered the warehouse. As soon as they were all inside, the door slowly and quietly slid back to the cement floor. Although there were no windows, it was not dark inside. Gaslights lining the walls every twenty feet illuminated their surroundings, and the mule drawn wagon waiting patiently, facing another steel sliding door that faced the street behind the alley.

Tom grinned. "How about a hayride?"

Kel looked at Lyria with a bemused smile and shrugged. They both walked forward to the wagon, with Raven by their side. They were not going to have to climb into a pile of hay after all. Behind the seats of the wagon was a second, partitioned off section. The hay was mounded high behind that partition.

When Lyria and Kel climbed onto the wagon, they could see inside this narrow compartment. There were two rough cut wooden seats firmly anchored to the floor. Wordlessly they climbed in. One of the mules flicked his ears, turning to see what was happening to his cart. Raven settled herself on Lyria's lap while Tom and the magician quickly put large, dusty coats over their clothing. Upon their heads they placed wide straw hats with sagging brims. When they lowered their heads, nobody would be able to see their faces.

"Open it."

On Tom's order, a young man pulled on a chain and the metal door in front of them slid up smoothly. A mule wagon carrying nothing but hay rumbled slowly out into the roadway, its ironclad spoked wooden wheels creaking noisily. Once in the street, they turned back to the west, leaving the watching police car behind them. When the magician turned briefly to look, he could see whoever was driving the auto staring intently down the alley and turning occasionally to speak to his partner. They didn't even notice the mule cart!

He laughed. "I have to hand it to you, Tom, you know how to lose a pursuer!"

"Oh, I've picked up a thing or two in my life."

"Now what are we going to do?" queried the magician. "It'll take forever to reach the docks from this location in a mule cart."

As if in protest to his slight, the left mule brayed.

Raven giggled. "You should speak kindly of your mule—especially while he is saving your life."

The mule brayed again, in agreement, and that made all of them laugh.

"Fast or slow, we're not going all the way to the ship in this conveyance," Tom reassured the group. "We're only going about a quarter mile down this road, then we'll meet one of my associates, with a faster mode of transportation."

"You're better organized than the leader of the resistance," the magician said in awe. "Whoever he may be, I think he'd be impressed with this operation."

"That may be," the editor responded, "but we don't yet know if this is a successful operation."

The magician again glanced nervously to their rear. The only vehicle he could see was a white lorry, and it was heading the other direction.

CHAPTER 8

Back in the alley, the man in the sedan finally waved, as if to old friends, and pulled forward. He drove blithely past the waiting police car as though he had no idea it was there. He didn't even so much as glance at the men inside. He turned left, and was on his way. Once he was out of the alley, the policemen drove forward cautiously, not knowing if they faced an ambush.

The driver parked close to the wall, leaving enough room for his partner to exit. They left their doors slightly ajar, not wanting to make any sounds indicating their approach. Both men reached under their jackets and withdrew their revolvers. They sidled along the garbage container until they were right by the edge—their target vehicle was now just on the other side, a mere foot away. They moved quickly and simultaneously, raising their revolvers in front of them as they went.

The driver had time to shout, "Police! Don't move!"

But the car was empty. Their quarry had fled. They both holstered their side arms in disgust.

"Damn it," John Olsen said. "We missed them."

Just then the iron gate rattled and began rising. Once again the two officers drew their revolvers, and once again they holstered them. Standing before them was a young man of about eighteen years of age, with extremely red hair and bright green eyes. He looked quizzically at the officers.

"Can I do something for you, gentlemen?"

"Where is the owner of this auto?"

"Why, he left some time ago, officers. I believe it was probably fifteen minutes or so."

"Well, where did he go?"

"That I cannot tell you."

"You'd better tell us, young man, or you're off to jail!"

"What I mean, sir, is I don't know where he went after he left his automobile with me."

Hogan Williams, John's partner spoke. "You know who it is that owns this auto?"

The young man now looked truly baffled, and slightly fearful.

"Of course I do, sir. It belongs to Mister Thomas Leatham—he's the editor of the Los Angeles Journal, you know."

Hogan hissed, "I know who he is."

"Well then, why did you ask, sir?"

"What is the auto doing here?"

Again, the young man seemed mystified by all the attention. He shook his head in wonderment. "Why, he left it here for a checkup; he said there might be something wrong with the boiler and he wanted me to check it out."

John Olsen was about at the end of his patience. "Check his boiler—is that correct?"

"That's correct, sir," the young man responded, wiping his hands on a greasy rag. "Now if you're finished, I need to have this job done by seven this evening. I promised."

Detectives Olsen and Williams turned with no further comment and returned to their vehicle. The young man, a journeyman reporter new to the paper, grinned as he climbed into the automobile and drove it into the warehouse. That was where it would sit until the police were well away. At that point he'd take it out for a drive—and that would be well before seven this evening. He laughed.

"Jinks isn't going to be happy about this."

Olsen snorted. "Jinks is never happy about anything."

Hogan laughed. "You really pegged him, didn't you? You should be a detective!"

Olsen nodded with a grin. "And you, sir, are clearly a defective on the city's police farce!"

Hogan retorted, "I didn't farce; that must've been you!"

They both laughed as they drove away.

* * * *

A short time later, the mule wagon came to a halt.

"We can get out now," Tom said.

They all scrambled out of the wagon to find an automobile waiting for them—the same one they'd been in a short time ago. The driver's door opened, and a young man of about eighteen years stepped into the road with a big grin on his face.

"How did I do?"

"You did magnificently, son."

Tom turned to the others. "This fine gentlemen is Braeden O'Malley. He's a rather new employee of my newspaper, but I can see that he knows how to take care of himself."

The young man smiled self-consciously.

"Now, don't get all modest on us," Tom said kindly. "Shall we be off then? Feel like more driving, Braeden?"

"Yes, sir," the boy said eagerly and stepped back into the auto. "I told the policemen I had to test this vehicle, and I would certainly not want to disappoint them."

Everyone laughed.

In a moment, they were once more on their way, with nobody following them. They turned to the west, heading unerringly toward the sea and the waiting crystal ship that would carry Kel and Lyria into a land of legend.

As they traveled, Lyria, Kel, and Raven watched as the tall buildings of the central part of the city gave way to low warehouses and manufacturing businesses with massive skylights stretching across their roofs to illuminate their interiors. It seemed things here were even dirtier than farther in town. *Cities are messy, dirty, and dangerous places,* Kel thought to himself—he was glad to be leaving.

Eventually they passed into a very rundown neighborhood of small, seedy taverns, and even smaller restaurants. Kel saw an occasional prostitute hanging out in an alley or leaning against a wall on a corner. He wondered how many of them were dominated by the Bishop.

Lyria noticed where his attention was focused, and she elbowed him sharply in the ribs.

"Hey there," he said, rubbing his side, a slight smile on his face, "I was just looking at the city."

"If that were the case," she said sweetly, "I would not have done that."

Kel grinned at her, "Women are part of the city."

She smiled back, "This is true; but seeing them like that makes me sad—in the tribes they might have been mothers, healers, or warriors."

"I know," Kel responded, "and it is even worse if they have no choice in the matter."

Raven didn't notice the exchange—she was staring ahead into the open space in front of the automobile, eyes wide with wonder, mouth hanging open. Kel looked and gasped.

Water. That was all—water was everything and everywhere. He never thought there could be so much water—this must surely be the sea. The car drove over one last hill, descending toward some low gray painted wood and stone buildings squatting on the shore.

The magician, pointing off to the left, said, "You see that small ship there? That's your transportation."

Kel looked longingly at the much larger ships they were now passing.

Such a small ship, he thought, *and it seems such a very large ocean!*

Braeden stopped at the wharf. Everyone but he exited and then stood staring at the immensity of water before them. The magician and the editor, who'd seen this sight many times, led the way nonchalantly down the dock to where a man was waiting by the gangplank leading up into the ship. He was wearing a white uniform.

As they walked, they heard their footsteps thudding on the heavy wooden planking of the dock, and the sloshing sound of the water beneath their feet. Now, at last, they were standing in front of the man who'd been patiently waiting for them. The strange man nodded to the magician as they approached.

"Welcome," the man said, bowing.

Kel and Lyria stared at the man; they'd never seen anyone with skin that color! The man looked back in amusement—this wasn't the first time he'd encountered that wonder, especially in the Far West.

He bowed, saying, "Welcome to my ship. My name is Jian and I am your captain for this voyage."

Kel and Lyria bowed in return and introduced themselves, using their new names. The captain smiled kindly at Raven. She smiled back, seemingly not the least bit shy. Lyria was satisfied—if Raven had no objection, neither did she.

"Come aboard, please," Jian said, "we must leave right away."

They walked up the gangplank onto the deck of the ship. Kel

looked around the deck, and then at Jian.

"You are wondering as to the location of your belongings, are you not?"

"I am, sir."

"Mister Leatham and your magician had your baggage delivered earlier. You will find everything awaiting you in your cabin."

"You are very kind," Lyria commented.

Jian bowed and smiled. "Thank you, Miss—now, you all must go to your cabin."

As they walked to the deck hatch that gave access to the cabins below, Kel stared in wonder at the large quartz crystal mounted in the stern of the vessel. It must have been at least six feet across, its faceted and pointed top, highly polished, reaching another six feet above the deck. The captain led them to their stateroom on the port side of the vessel. He opened the door for them and they entered.

"It would be best if you stayed below until we sail," the captain said. "The docks have many eyes."

They didn't have to wait very long. Kel saw the magician give the captain a package, then return to the dock. He looked around at the workers and loiterers moving in the immediate vicinity. No one seemed to be particularly interested in the little ship from the Far East, or its passengers. The magician returned to the automobile, climbed into the back seat, and the small vehicle turned back the way it had come.

Behind them, the dockworkers were already unmooring the crystal ship. The Chinese men on the decks quickly and efficiently drew up the gangplank and then the forward lines, coiling them quickly into neat piles. By the time they'd finished at the bow, the men at the stern of the vessel had also released the stern lines, completing the process. The ship began drifting slowly away from the dock, being pushed now by the small tugs that swarmed the harbor. Soon they'd be facing the great wide ocean under their own power.

Jian watched the docks slip away. He was glad to be back on the ocean. He may have been born in China, but his home was the western sea. He returned to the pilothouse, and took command of the wheel, patiently waiting for the tugs to finish their part of the mission so he could once again be in control of his own fate.

CHAPTER 9

The travelers sat in their quarters, feeling the gentle rocking of the ship as it drifted out from the dock.

"I once read in a book that once a ship gets underway, its speed will help stop some of the rocking," Kel said, as much to calm himself as the others.

"I like it," Raven said. "It reminds me of a mother rocking her baby to sleep."

Kel smiled at the child. He marveled at the way she could see the good in almost every event despite the horrors she'd endured at the hands of the priests and other degenerates.

"Do you think we will be able to find our lost friends when we arrive?"

Kel looked at Lyria. "If we cannot, I am willing to say that Hawk will be able to."

During their time below deck before they left the city behind, they unpacked their clothing and weapons. The first thing Lyria did, before hanging her clothing in the closet, was to carefully clean and oil her ancient sword and the daggers Llo had made for her. These were her most cherished possessions—for what woman could truly feel like a woman without her protective blades nearby?

Once everything was put in order to their satisfaction, they moved to the round portholes in the side of the vessel. Because their room was on the port side of the ship, they could watch the great city slipping slowly past them like some bad dream. Kel held Raven so she could see out as well.

Soon, even the docks were out of sight, vanishing behind the ship. Kel noticed the vibrations of the ship's engines; they were finally under their own power. Lyria took his hand and smiled.

From his reading, Kel knew the giant, frosty white crystals, looking almost like a part of the great northern ice, could be found only in the high mountains of the Far East. The clearest of these, carefully polished, were used to ignite either wood or coal which was then burned in the great furnaces below deck to supply the steam power needed to run the ship.

In vessels much smaller than this one, Kel had read, the crystals actually condensed the sun sufficiently all by themselves to heat the water without any additional fire. Although this method would only work during the day, it nevertheless saved substantially on the fuel needed to get from one destination to another. It was a very efficient system. He could hardly wait to see the inner workings of what would be their home for the next two weeks.

An hour later, there was a soft knock on the door of their cabin. Kel walked across the room and opened the door. A man in a dark blue uniform stood there and bowed deeply; then he wordlessly gestured for them to follow him. The three travelers left their rooms, venturing out into the corridor. They followed the silent man along the narrow, wood-paneled passageway to the end where a steep stairway waited.

The man in the uniform gestured for them to go up to the main deck. He followed them through a hatchway into the open air. There, Jian was waiting for them. He bowed formally. Kel and Lyria bowed, and the captain and the silent man both smiled as Raven also bowed. *It seemed to please them,* Kel thought, *the Far East must be a very formal place!*

Kel turned astern, looking for the column of black smoke that should be billowing from the ship's engine room by now. Surprisingly, he saw no chimney at all, and no smoke. There was only the blue sky—an ocean itself through which white clouds sailed placidly.

He turned to Jian in confusion, and asked, "Where is your chimney? How do you vent the smoke from your fires?"

Jian laughed. "Small ships like mine do not need big furnaces— we use only the heat from the sun, magnified and focused by the crystal to boil the water that runs our engines. We have found that if properly polished, the crystals will focus the sun strongly enough without the need for any fire."

"I did not know a ship of this size could run like that, with just the crystals to heat the water."

Jian smiled at Kel. "It is the special way we polish the base of the crystal. Ship builders in the west do not polish the way we do and so they must burn more fuel."

"It is a very clean way to sail," Lyria said admiringly. "You do not blot the beautiful sky with black smoke."

"You have a poet's soul," Jian said. "What you say is very true. We do have a very small furnace aboard for night use; otherwise we would have to drop anchor every night and await the morning sun. No chimney is needed though. The smoke we produce vents out through several ducts in the sides of the vessel—many small streams of smoke are not as visible as one large one, even at night. And they disperse more quickly as well.

"It is also true that a small ship that leaves no trace of its passing may travel unseen where others would give their positions for miles around—one would simply have to follow the trail of black smoke. This can be convenient when one is bringing something into a country when one does not wish to pay the revenues."

Kel laughed, "Well, it looks like we sail with a pirate!"

Jian turned to him and said very seriously, "We never raid shipping or kill crews to take what is rightfully theirs as pirates would. Sometimes, though, men like your friend the magician may need things brought to them in secret—quietly and without undue attention."

"I apologize," Kel said, humiliated. "I did not mean to insult you or your crew."

"There has been no offense, young sir; you are not familiar with the ways of the ocean or of smugglers."

Jian motioned them into the forward cabin, which was the captain's dining room. The room was not large, but it was sumptuously outfitted with a red lacquered table and black lacquered chairs. On the walls hung silk scrolls, carefully embroidered with exotic animals and landscapes. The dragons fascinated Lyria—it was said that fierce warrior magicians aboard a dragon-headed boat originally carried her sword into this land.

Jian asked them to sit at his table as a servant brought in dishes of exotic foods such as rice and a variety of specially prepared meats and boiled vegetables that none of them had ever eaten before; many of the delicacies they'd never even heard of.

During the meal Jian explained what their course would be. "For this journey we will be never leaving sight of the shore. Land you will always be able to see from the port side of the ship, day or night."

Lyria looked at Kel with amusement as Jian said, "Your friend from the Black City has told me of your…uncertainty of this kind of travel. It is very understandable for I am certain you have never seen an ocean before. If you ever need to see land, just come on deck, or look out your portholes and there will be land."

"That is considerate of you," Lyria said.

"I like it either way," Raven added, "the water is clean. You may travel its paths and be forever unknown if that is your wish."

"This is true," Jian said with a nod to the girl, "many turn to the sea for just such a life."

"Is that why you sail, sir?"

"Your child has a penetrating mind." He turned to Raven. "In a way, child, that is my path. My parents were poor farmers; we lived a hard life, but a fair one. We ate what we harvested, sharing with our neighbors, and receiving from them also."

"So how did you end up on the water?" Raven looked at Jian with a quizzical expression.

"There was war in the land. An army came. We never knew whose army it was, and it did not matter. All armies have the same purpose and that is war. The land they pass is, to them, only forage. This army camped for five days on my parents' land. When they moved on, they took our animals and marched all over our fields, grinding into the earth what food remained for us. That winter was hard. A lung illness killed my parents and many others in our little community. By spring, there was no reason for me to stay, and so I fled to the ocean. Even the greatest armies of the Khans, with thousands of horses and millions of men could not trample the great oceans of the world."

"I'm sorry," Raven said quietly.

"It is the cycle," Jian said philosophically. "Besides, this event gave me a new life. I am truly a free man."

"Your crew is like your tribe, then," Raven said. "It must be a wonderful life; going everywhere and always having your friends with you."

"It is, child. But now, we should eat. The food is best eaten when it is yet warm."

After lunch, the captain took them on a tour of the small ship.

Below the deck on which they lived, there was only one other open space. That was the cargo hold, and it was massive.

"We have a small crew," Jian explained. "Therefore we have much room for carrying things that the peoples of the many lands believe they need to have."

Lyria laughed. "Believe they need? That is the truth, surely. What we have seen in the great city amazes us. People seem to need so very many different kinds of clothing, and jewelry and furnishings."

"This ship is my only possession. I do not feel the need for big homes and armies as some of my countrymen do. But I am glad, nevertheless, that others crave the things I carry."

"I believe that is true in all lands, Jian," Kel said. "Many people seem to crave more than they need or could ever use—it seems a greedy existence to me."

"As long as they pay for it," Jian said with a smile, "I am happy to make them happy."

Kel laughed.

Jian then took them to the engine room; this was what Kel was waiting for. Jian turned a massive iron wheel, tugging the equally massive iron door in the rear bulkhead open. One by one they stepped over the lower sill into the engine room. There were two crew members present, checking large brass mounted pressure gauges and monitoring engine speed.

"As I mentioned, we have found a way to grind and polish the bottom end of the crystal so the light is highly focused into a very small area. This creates a great deal of heat to make our steam. The pointed top of the crystal you saw in the stern has a number of flat surfaces called 'facets.' At almost any time of the day, regardless of our direction of travel, some of them face the sun. That sunlight then moves through the crystal where it is focused through the base, which is carved and polished into a lens like a magnifying glass. "

"That is amazing," Kel said. "I would not have thought of that!"

"It took my countrymen a few hundred years to figure it out. The crystal ships of the west do not use these specially polished crystals as yet; that is why they all, even the smallest, have furnaces to heat the water."

Raven asked timidly, "Can you tell us how it works?"

"Certainly," Jian said, "the engine in this, and most crystal ships, is called a 'multiple expansion engine' and was invented and perfected by a great engineer of the west named Richard E. Carter many centuries ago, well before the western war and the plague.

"As steam expands in a high-pressure engine such as this one, its temperature drops—this results in steam entering the cylinder at high temperature and leaving at a lower temperature. This causes heating and cooling of the cylinder with every stroke, which is inefficient.

"A way to lessen this heating and cooling was found by Mister Carter. In a compound engine such as this, high-pressure steam from the boiler expands in a high-pressure cylinder; then enters several lower pressure cylinders as it travels through the engine. To get the same work from lower pressure steam, as from the originally high-pressure steam, requires a larger cylinder as the steam occupies a greater volume.

"In the end, each cylinder moves a piston attached to a crankshaft that turns the screws that push the ship through the water. When the steam leaves the engine, it is now cooling rapidly and so is pumped back into the boiler to be used over again. This way we can use the same tank of water for the entire voyage."

Upon seeing the befuddled looks of his passengers, Jian apologized and, with sketches he made in a notebook, he diagramed the engine's operation as he explained it. In the end, even Raven had a basic idea of how the engine ran.

After the tour, they returned once more to their cabin. It had been an eventful day thus far and they were very tired. Though it was only mid-afternoon, Raven's eyes were closing even before the door was shut. Lyria helped the girl to her bed, and then sat with Kel on her bunk.

"Well," she said, "our journey is almost over."

"I truly hope that is so," Kel said. "Jian said the city in The Green is very large; not as large as Los Angeles, but growing all the time. There will be many places they might hide our kidnapped shamans."

"Well," Lyria said with confidence, "we will find them."

"I hope that is true, my love," Kel said. "Maybe this will be easy."

Lyria laughed. "If not, I have a spirit sword that will make it easy!"

Then they stopped talking. Kel put his arm around Lyria. She sighed, leaning into him, feeling the strength of his body against hers. He gently turned her face toward his, kissing her softly on her lips. She smiled, returning the kiss. Their lips parted and they shared the very breath of their lives as they kissed, tongues connecting.

Lyria moved to sit in Kel's lap, one arm around his waist, the other on the back of his head. She gently caressed him. Kel slid his arm around her, pulling her hard against him. He felt her firm breasts pressing against his chest. He kissed her again, longingly. Finally Lyria pulled herself away, leaning back from him. She giggled like a little girl. "That is enough of that! We must wait, and you know it!"

"Perhaps we need a new way," Kel said in jest.

Lyria playfully slapped him on his shoulder as she climbed off his lap to sit next to him once again, answering, "Even if we did, we must think of Raven."

They both looked guiltily over at the sleeping girl; then they laughed quietly. Lyria kissed Kel briefly, and then suddenly pushed him off her bed. He landed on his hands and rump, a very surprised look on his face. Lyria was looking at him and grinning. He got to his feet, rubbing his behind.

"Awww," she mocked, "did the big man hurt his backside?"

Kel stood straight, saying, "It will take more than that to hurt one such as I!"

With that they both burst into laughter. Kel climbed into the top bunk, and they all took a much-needed rest.

"Kel? Where is Raven?"

Kel awoke to being shaken by Lyria. He sat up, rubbing the sleep from his eyes. How late was it? It felt as though he'd just closed his eyes. He looked around inside the cabin, slowly reorienting his mind to his present location. The ship. The ocean. He looked around the small room. It could be no more than late afternoon by the light. The little girl wasn't there. He leaped down from his bunk, sitting on Lyria's bed to put on his shoes.

"When I awoke, she was gone," Lyria said in a worried voice.

"We need to look for her."

Kel hurriedly put on his clothes, tied his shoes, and headed for the door. Stepping into the narrow passage, he saw that several of the other cabins' doors were standing open. He walked to the first, inquiring of the occupants if they'd seen Raven. They looked blankly at Kel, and indicated that they hadn't seen the girl and didn't appreciate the intrusion. City dwellers, Kel surmised, interested only in their own concerns. He shrugged, moving on.

Now Lyria was behind him. They moved quickly down the passage, questioning any they saw. In the last cabin, occupied by two scruffy looking men, they inquired once more. One of the men, the one with a black patch over his left eye, said he saw the girl go up to the main deck about thirty minutes previously.

He smiled sympathetically. "Kids are harder to keep track of than soldiers under your command. If you wish, I'll help you search."

"Thank you, sir," Kel said with a smile. "The ship is not so large that she can have gotten far."

The man laughed again, the long white scar on his face turning up with his merriment. "Make sure you look in all the small dark places. There's nothing better than hiding from grown ups when you're young."

"You have children?"

"No, sir," the man answered, "but my sister's kids could offer excellent training for warriors in hit and run tactics."

Kel laughed and thanked the man again, and then they turned back into the hallway.

He and Lyria climbed the stairway—it was steep, almost like a ladder. Once up on the deck, squinting in the late afternoon sunlight, they moved quickly toward the bow of the ship, and that was where they found Raven. They couldn't see her right away, but they heard her childish laughter mingled with that of several men. Coming around the forward mast, they were now clear of both the pilothouse and captain's cabin. Near the bow, on the starboard side, they saw three men squatting down on their haunches. Raven was next to them, speaking their language.

Kel and Lyria stared a moment, not believing what they were

seeing and hearing. As they walked toward the small group, one of the men noticed them approaching, and quickly stood, bowing to Kel. The others stood as well. Kel bowed in return.

The sailors were surprised. It wasn't often that people of the west showed any respect for lowly sailors or deck hands, or for people who didn't look or dress as they did. Raven was sitting on the deck cross-legged, with a thick rope in her hands. She looked up at them with a big grin on her face.

"Look," she said enthusiastically, "they are teaching me to tie knots!"

She stood, holding the rope out for Kel to examine. There was indeed a rather complex knot in the center of it.

"Untie it," Raven said to him.

Kel pulled and tugged, but it was a knot after all, and wouldn't be undone.

Raven took it, pulled on one of the loops, then on the end, and the knot simply fell apart.

"That was amazing," Lyria said, clapping her hands.

She looked at the sailors and smiled. She bowed, saying, "Thank you for being kind to our daughter."

Raven laughed, translating what she said into Chinese. The men bowed again. Then as they turned and went back to their various duties, Kel and Lyria gave Raven an appraising look.

"When was it that you learned their language?" Kel was mystified.

Raven shrugged. "Right now."

"You just learned it right now? While you were here on deck with the sailors?"

Lyria didn't know what to say.

"It was easy," the little girl said, "I just listened to them speaking and then I was thinking their words and then I knew what they meant."

"A rare gift," Kel said in awe, "even for a natural seer, this is truly special."

Raven didn't seem to think it was special at all—not nearly as special as the disappearing knot trick. She wished Dan were here so she could show him what she'd learned.

They returned below to eat their evening meal. As they ate, Lyria looked at Raven; she was a beautiful and strange child. Perhaps, as Kel had seen her in his dream long ago, she really was a star come down to dwell on the earth.

"Raven, honey," she began, "we do not mind if you explore the ship but from now on let us know where you are going, okay? You had us frightened."

"I didn't think of that," Raven said contritely, "and I won't do it again."

Kel hugged her, kissing her on the top of her head, saying, "We just don't want anything bad to happen to you."

"I will not run off again without letting you know. You were asleep and I didn't want to wake you."

"That was thoughtful," Lyria said, "but next time, wake us up."

"All right," the girl said, "I will."

CHAPTER 10

"Welcome back," Dan said to the magician when he'd returned to the newspaper office.

The magician smiled at his friend. "We have work to do. Dan, I am truly sorry about your friend Mister Ford."

"I read the news article," Dan said, with a shake of his head. "Lawrence always was somewhat compulsive in his behavior, even as a child. I shouldn't really be surprised that he became a gambler. You know, he was always the real risk taker when we worked together in the old days and I was always the one holding back, wanting to plan longer."

The magician shook his head. "Done is done, I suppose. But now I think we need to get back to business. I have a show to put on tonight in the Green Hyena."

Dan laughed. "You've always been fascinated by magic, haven't you?"

"I have. But in this way, I can gather information in a place that is ripe with rumor without notice. The magic I use mostly in the Green Hyena is the magic of drink-loosened tongues!"

Dan snorted. "One day you'll have to tell me how you came to be involved in so unlikely a pursuit."

"One day, perhaps I shall."

They said their goodbyes to Tom Leatham and then they were back on the street, heading once again to the Bloomgarden Apartments.

"I was concerned," Dan said as he drove, "I heard about the police in your neighborhood, several times as a matter of fact. I worried that the Cathedral found out about you."

"Indeed. There was a killing in my building and I understand they raided an apartment right across the street. They thought the so-called Vampire Killer was living there. It seems they found a lot of evidence. They were loading things into a lorry when I saw them."

"It would seem they missed her though…it is a 'her,' is it not?"

The magician said, "I guess it probably depends on whom you ask. Henry is convinced based on direct information from the Cathedral; I don't know how we could get a more reliable opinion."

They drove on in silence. Traffic was heavy in the early afternoon, so they decided to stop for lunch—there was a restaurant just around the corner from the magician's apartment building.

After their food was placed on their table, the magician looked carefully through the newspaper that had been left on the chair. He searched it thoroughly, but there was no word of any further killing. Maybe the killer was gone, or had died in some kind of accident. The magician knew that was just wishful thinking.

"While the Cathedral and their police officers are searching for this woman, we may have the opportunity to harass them," Dan said with a snicker. "Our little trip to the print shop for Lyria and Kel's false identification papers gave me an idea."

"What idea is that?"

"We could print what we know about the killer, including that she was taken by a Cathedral zeppelin from her tribe, then corrupted with drugs, and finally turned loose on the city."

The magician snickered as well. "That's something I hadn't thought of. We could do that without making the newspaper a target."

"Once the flyers are out on the street," Dan said, "the flyers become the news! Tom's newspaper can then continue the onslaught as they investigate all those ugly rumors put forward in the flyers."

By the time they'd finished lunch, they'd worked out the content of the flyer—the magician's napkin was a mass of scribbles. He folded it carefully, placing it in his vest pocket. *Too bad the Bishop wasn't still in the city*, Dan thought, *this would probably make his head explode, just as the safe house had.*

They returned to their auto and fought the afternoon traffic back to the newspaper office; the apartment could wait for now. They had a lot of work to do.

* * * *

Father Woods hadn't known about the flyers until he saw the story in the newspapers in the morning and he was furious. He phoned all three papers in rapid succession, first calling Tom.

"This is outrageous," he fumed, "you're spreading slander against us and our religion."

Tom was calm. He'd been expecting the call; he was surprised it hadn't come sooner. He first published the story yesterday! With the Bishop gone, things clearly weren't running as smoothly for Father Woods as he was letting on.

"Nonsense," Tom answered, "we simply found out about the flyers from a concerned citizen. They're plastered all over the city, you know. We, too, are wondering who would post such heinous and libelous things about you and your Cathedral."

"What?"

"Well of course we're concerned, Your Grace, this kind of thing can ruin a person's reputation. We want to find out who's responsible as much as you do."

"That's not what I mean," the priest shouted.

"Your Grace," Tom said in mock respect, "there are thousands of those flyers out there. We just picked one up and began investigating who might've written such a terrible thing."

"But you published the content of those lying flyers in your paper!"

Tom smiled. He could tell the priest was gritting his teeth, trying to remain civil.

"Well," he said, "we had to. It's news, after all, is it not? We thought that if people read it, perhaps someone might call us with the name of the perpetrators. Maybe someone saw someone telling someone to ask someone to put them up all over the city."

"What you're doing is further spreading the lies!"

"I doubt I could spread those words farther than they've already spread. If you wish to stop it, I suggest you hire people quickly to go around and pull them down if you think they are lies."

Father Woods slammed the receiver into its cradle. He felt a blood vessel in his temple throbbing. Thirty minutes later, he was still sitting in the Bishop's chair. The other two newspapers in the city, though much smaller than the Journal, had also published the content of that hateful flyer, and their opinion on the matter was exactly the same as that of Tom Leatham's—it was almost like they had all agreed beforehand that they would do this.

They were merely investigating, the editors said. Trying to get to the bottom of it, they said. He slammed his fist hard on the desk blotter. Pencils jumped and papers moved. He took several deep, calming breaths and then he got back on the phone.

In a short time, he'd enlisted the help of the Bishop's private army—those still in the city, that is, staff accountants, servants, cooks, and zeppelin fitters. He instructed them not to wear their uniforms as they rode down the darkening streets of the city.

They worked for four days, working well into the night each day, before the flyers had been removed—most of them, anyway. In that time, all three newspapers had run the content of the flyers two more times, ostensibly asking for witnesses or leads, pleading for public support. Of course there were no witnesses, or public support.

* * * *

The magician slapped Dan on the back in congratulations for thinking up such a great way to further damage the reputation of the Cathedral.

"It's too bad you had to leave those years past," the magician chuckled. "By now, if you'd stayed, we'd have the Bishop on his knees, and not to pray to his Redeemed God!"

"The past is done," Dan said, "we've only the future to plan for."

"I agree, my boy, I wish I could've seen the priest's face when he read that. Tom said he had no idea until it was already well publicized."

"Still, we must be careful," warned Dan. "That priest the Bishop left in charge is the same man who orchestrated zeppelin raids years ago to kidnap children and young women from the tribes and to take the shamans Kel and Lyria seek."

The magician rubbed his chin thoughtfully. "I think you're correct, Dan. Between the Bishop and Father Woods, Woods is the risk taker, and therefore he's probably the more dangerous of the two of them. He's impetuous—less likely to think out his course of action before he makes a rash move."

"He could plan a raid to pick you up if he knows of you," Dan said worriedly.

The magician just smiled. "They would've taken me long ago if they suspected me. They'd figure they could torture me for the name of the leader of our organization."

"Is it safe for you to continue your magic acts in the Green

Hyena?"

"I hope so," he said with a grin, "they have the prettiest serving women of any tavern I've ever worked in!"

Dan laughed. "Maybe tonight I'll come and watch your show. The time I've spent with young Raven has reopened my eyes to wonder."

"Never lose the wonder, my friend," the magician said sincerely. "Wonder is the first manifestation of the Divine."

CHAPTER 11

"Lyria, wake up! Wake up!"

Lyria opened her sleep-clouded eyes. Raven stood beside her bed, grinning.

"What is it, honey?"

"She's under the ship!"

Lyria sat up, looked closely at the girl. "Under the ship?"

"Yes. Hurry. Wake Kel so he can see too."

Mystified, Lyria woke Kel with a shake. They dressed quickly as an anxious Raven danced from one foot to the other.

"I'm sorry," the girl said, "I promised to wake you if I was going on the deck."

"Up on the deck?"

Kel stared at the girl. "It's the middle of the night, Raven, what could be on the deck at this hour?"

"Not on the deck," the little girl said impatiently, "she's under the ship!"

Kel and Lyria looked at each other, and then they followed Raven out the door, down the corridor to the steps that led to the deck.

"Hurry," Raven said, "she's going to let us see her!"

"Who is going to let us see her?"

"She is," the girl answered impatiently.

Up on the deck, a cool wind was blowing from the north, the sky was clear and filled with stars, and the moon shone nearly full. The girl ran to the bow of the ship, leaning expectantly against the railing. Kel and Lyria hurried up behind her, holding the enthusiastic girl to keep her from falling right over the railing into the sea.

And then suddenly the seas parted in front of their eyes. An island rose up from the deep just off the starboard bow. The island glittered in the moonlight, looking unearthly—unreal. Whatever it was, it looked to be at least as long as their ship. Suddenly there was a mighty geyser spraying up into the air as the great whale exhaled her breath. The animal rolled slowly in the water, and then sank from sight for a moment. She rose again, this time in the company of two smaller whales.

"Those are her babies," Raven explained. "Aren't they beautiful?"

Moonlight and starlight glittered on the water rolling over the backs of the whales as they swam along with the ship, looking like flowing jewels.

Kel pointed in astonishment. Lyria followed his gaze, and gasped. There were at least a dozen more of the great mammals surfacing in front of and along both sides of the ship, rolling like the waves themselves. The white mist of their blowing filled the air, and in the moonlight they created sudden, tiny rainbows momentarily in the mist. A giant tail lifted high above the water, then slapped down with a loud, almost explosive sound.

The night watch, high in the crow's nest atop the main mast, shouted something and several crewmembers and the captain came on deck to watch the display. The whales danced as Raven clapped her hands in joy.

"I love animals," she said. "They do not lie. They do not hurt their own kind for fun."

One of the whales breached, rising high out of the water and crashed back. The waves off its back struck the bow in incandescent ripples. The captain laughed, saying, "This is indeed a good sign. For where danger lurks, these creatures will not venture."

Presently the whales departed. The two adults and the child stood on the deck for a while, looking to see if they'd show themselves again. They saw the faint glimmer of rising mist a half mile ahead, then that too was gone. Raven seemed transfixed by the sighting of the whales. Reluctantly, she finally agreed to go below and back to bed. The three of them moved down the corridor to their room. It had been quite a show!

The next day, Kel reckoned they were almost halfway to their destination. The days passed slowly, indolently. The farther south they traveled, the warmer the weather became. This far south, the aurora was not visible at all in the northern skies, not even at night. It was almost like the age of ice was just a bad dream. Kel was surprised to find he missed the unearthly lights in the sky.

They'd passed a long area of land, a peninsula, the captain called it, and now after several more days, they could again see the lights of human habitation very far away along the otherwise dark coast at night. The villages along the coast of this land called Mexico were small, and the passengers aboard the ship talked with disdain about the people of that land. There were some jokes, all demeaning and ridiculous, in Kel's mind. He knew these narrow-minded people would say the same of Lyria and him if they knew they were of tribal origin.

Most of the forty passengers on the ship were devoted followers of the Cathedral and considered anyone not living in one of their cities to be half-human. They were yet just another mistake of many on the part of the Divine Feminine before the Redeemed God realized her deceit and stupidity and subdued Her.

Kel had a hard time holding his tongue when in the presence of such ignorant people, but his mission required that he appear to be one of them. To that end, he listened carefully to what they said, and how they said it. The right way of saying something could help him pass among the people of New Los Angeles. If one appears as a snake, he may travel among snakes unrecognized. Lyria stayed at his side, quietly fuming about having to look subservient.

For Garn's sake, and that of the others held in captivity, she refrained from throwing a particularly obnoxious passenger over the railing into the sea. After that, they avoided that person—no point in pressing their luck. She grinned to herself, imagining the woman in the water…floundering in all that dress…with all those sharks…

Raven continued spending time with the crew, learning about ships, knots, and night navigation using the positions of the stars. The crewmen loved her—for her interest in what they knew and for her well-behaved politeness. But mostly they loved her because she could speak with them in their own language. Everywhere along the coast of the western lands, the crew found that they were expected to learn the local language while very few bothered to learn theirs.

Kel hoped they might stop at some of the villages along the way, but the captain kept a steady course and speed, running about ten miles from the coastline. As they traveled, they gradually got to know the other passengers—most they avoided as much as they could.

Some of them, like the two scruffy men in the last cabin who'd told Kel where Raven was, were mercenaries traveling to The Green for adventure and perhaps wealth. Kel thought they seemed nice enough.

"It is for the image," Lyria said one evening when they were eating in their cabin. "Hired fighters are supposed to look tough and ready for anything. I believe those two young men look the way they do for that image. Whether they are as tough as they try to appear, remains to be seen."

"They are nice folk," Kel said. "I hope for their sake they are as tough as they act. Where we go, they will need to be."

Raven giggled, adding, "It is city-looking!"

Lyria looked at her. "Like city-speaking, is it not?"

They all laughed, as Kel said, "And we are doing both! Our papers present us as something we are not, for the image."

"You are very good at it," Raven added. "Even I believe we're a Dragon family!"

They laughed again, and then settled down to finish their dinner.

CHAPTER 12

That night, as his friends sailed off toward unknown lands, Dan attended the magician's show at the Green Hyena tavern. It had been some years since he'd seen the old man's show and he wondered if it had changed much. He already knew about the mind altering herb and chemical concoction the old man paid the tavern barkeep to place in patrons' drinks—he'd been doing that for years, so when he arrived he bought two drinks, claiming one was for a friend. That way, when the magic show began, he knew his second drink would be a mug of ale and nothing more. For resistance members attending his shows, this had become standard procedure.

He wondered where the magician had learned that trick with the herbs—none of the other stage magicians he'd ever met knew about it and so they were limited to mere sleight of hand magic. It was impressive, to be sure, but nothing like what people could see at the Green Hyena. The magician was legendary!

The large steam organ and the guitar players in the house band finished their loud performance with a flourish. As they placed their alligator skull guitars on stands for a short break, Dan looked around the establishment. He smiled—it was just as he'd remembered it. It was ill lit, with coal oil lanterns on most of the tables, and candles on others. The place was filled with a murky light at best.

He knew the patrons preferred it this way. The patrons also looked pretty much as he'd remembered them from long ago. Some things never change. To his immediate right, there were five men sitting together drinking. They were joking with the serving girl who was proving to be amazingly adept at avoiding the groping hands of the drunken men—he had to give her credit for her maneuvers.

Almost to the wall opposite him sat a small band of what the city dwellers called 'Outlanders.' It was their term, derogatory at best, for any members of the free tribes who might have wandered into the city for adventure, drinking, women, or trade. This particular group of three men seemed to be a jovial lot; their leader had even removed his iron and leather armored jerkin and had laid it on the table beside him. On top of the jerkin, his long, heavy dagger rested—a warning to any who might think an Outlander could be tricked or robbed without consequence.

To the left of the tribesmen a group of six sat—four men and two women. Dan scrutinized them with his practiced thief's eye. He quickly determined that the women were the wives of two of the men. They were pretty—and yet two of the men, obviously not the ones married to them in Dan's opinion, were not flirting or groping them. It meant the women in question were already spoken for. All the men, and the women, were already extremely drunk. Dan smiled. This was the life he remembered—the life he'd lived before he'd met Daisy.

There was a moment of quiet as the heavy velour burgundy curtain concealing the stage began slowly rising. The magician walked out onto the stage. Immediately there was a tumult of shouts, hoots, and foot stomping. Bottles and heavy glass mugs thumped on oak tabletops. Dan smiled. There was no doubt about it; the old guy had a following!

The serving girls went from table to table, supplying fresh drinks for the revelers, compliments of the house. The patrons loved the free drinks they got for this show—and they liked the way the serving women, clad in short, filmy skirts and tops with plunging necklines, would bend very low as they served the drinks, offering a spectacular view no matter where one was sitting in the room.

When everyone's drinks were replaced, the real show began. The old man had changed his routine from the last time Dan had seen it. He sat up with interest, sipping his unaltered ale. The band had returned, and there was a brief musical introduction as the magician smiled and bowed to the audience. Then the music quieted once more.

"Ladies and gentlemen," the old man began, "we're now quickly approaching the Autumn Equinox. In days long past, this was a traditional celebration of the harvest in all villages and towns and cities. It was a celebration of the bounty of food they could set back for the coming winter months.

"Now, of course, here in the city we have hydroponics. If one were to travel away from the city, into the wild regions of the land…" here he bowed in recognition of the tribesmen at the far table. The men raised their mugs and shouted a toast to the magician.

"Thank you, kind sirs," he responded. There was general applause.

"In the lands of these men we have with us tonight, and all the peoples of the other free tribes, the harvest celebrations still go on to this very day. This is the time of balance—the time when the light equals the dark. It is a time of magic."

He watched his audience carefully. He wanted them all to have had time to drink deeply of the magic they'd soon be seeing. He continued with his speech a little longer, and as he spoke, his vocalization changed. It became more authoritative—more demanding.

Dan, of course, couldn't see the images suggested by the magician; he couldn't see the wooly mammoths that were now up on the stage with his friend helping in a harvest scene. He didn't see them swinging giant scythes with their trunks while giant cave bears sang and whistled and growled—and lifted the bundled grain stalks onto large wooden wagons drawn by equally happy wooly rhinoceroses.

The audience hooted and stomped. Dan almost regretted not having taken the infused drink. He was missing a marvel—of that, he was certain! As the band played, the magician again addressed the crowd.

"And when the harvest was finished, everyone celebrated."

Suddenly the music changed. The band began playing a rather risqué song that was well known among striptease dancers and the men who follow such shows. The audience was shouting approval.

The magician then described and explained what the patrons saw. The mammoths were now dancing on their hind legs, wearing delicate wisps of silky material that did very little to hide their fur and their bulk. They were doing a striptease for the bears and rhinos! The audience loved it. As the bears and rhinos hooted and shouted encouragement to the mammoths, the mammoths' clothing was slowly discarded with much gyration and spectacular undulations.

When the show finally came to an end with a strong flourish from the band, the images suddenly vanished just as they'd appeared and the audience howled. The magician stepped forward. He raised his hands in a placating gesture, bowing deeply.

He waited for a lull. "All right ladies and gentlemen, if you insist, they'll come back for a curtain call!"

The show ended one more time with the patrons seeing the mammoths once more on the stage facing the audience. They lifted their skirts, turned and began wiggling their shaggy behinds, encased in huge, tight-fitting polka dotted pantaloons. They then turned again, blowing kisses into the audience, and vanished. The magician got a standing ovation for that last little bit. The owner of the tavern was smiling. This man, whoever he might really be, surely could bring in the paying customers.

Dan watched the magician leave the stage and go out into the audience, accepting tips, handshakes, and pats on the back. He'd stop from time to time, sit a moment and accept an occasional drink from his audience.

Dan noticed the magician lingered longer at some tables than others. *The man always seemed to be working,* he thought. *Listening to little tidbits of rumor and hushed conversation coming from liquor-loosened tongues of Cathedral office workers, mercenaries, and especially the very vocal, brash, young priests in training.*

Dan grinned; this was just like the old days. He lifted his beer mug in a toast to his friend when he glanced in Dan's direction. The magician smiled back at him.

With the show ended, Dan decided to go out on the street to look for a hooker for the night. He hadn't seen the mammoths, so he knew it was not the show that put him in the mood. He laughed, feeling the effects of perhaps one too many beers—or had it been two too many? Printing flyers wasn't all he was good at—he could drink and whore with the best of them.

He stumbled slightly as he left the tavern, and turned to the left. He walked slowly past the now closed amphitheater. He looked up. It was fully dark by this time, and he knew the street women would be out, looking for business. Well, he had the money, and he was ready.

He walked two blocks further before he saw anyone. Some shadows moved a short distance ahead. There, beside a vacant warehouse, were two men and a woman. *She must be a whore,* Dan thought. The men were touching her and lifting her skirt. He saw her push one of the man's hands away. That was strange behavior for a hooker, unless perhaps she had not been paid yet. He chuckled.

Suddenly the young woman was looking directly at him, and in the darkness of the night, there could be no mistaking the terror in her eyes. She was young, perhaps twenty years. One of the men, young and very sure of himself, turned toward Dan threateningly, and spoke in a rough, gravelly voice, "Move on, mister! There's nothing for you here. Can't you see we're very busy at the moment?"

The other man laughed and slapped the woman hard across the face. Dan heard the smacking impact of his hand. The woman clutched at her face, crying. He saw her handbag, in the gutter by the curbing. The contents had been spilled out. Next to her purse, a notebook lay, cover open, pages rippling in the soft breeze. Dan realized now that this was no mere interlude with a hooker—this was a rape in progress.

The man standing in front of the woman exposed himself; he was going to take the woman right there against the wall. *It was none of his business*, Dan rationalized. This happened all the time; clearly no decent woman should be out on the streets alone at this hour anyway. He should just cross the street, find his own woman for the night, and be done with it. The man pushed the young woman against the building hard. Dan heard her head hit the bricks. He punched her in the stomach and she sank slowly to her knees with a whimper.

The man who'd struck her laughed harshly, dropped to his knees behind her, and again pushed up her skirt. Dan saw they'd already ripped off her underwear. In the glow of the gaslight on the corner, Dan saw bright blood dripping from her mouth. Her auburn hair flashed in the yellow glow of the gaslight, seeming to blaze. He was preparing to cross the street, and then he stopped.

Daisy.

He looked again at the woman. No! He couldn't just pass this by. Coward or not, this act could not be allowed.

Without speaking, Dan stepped quickly into the alley and picked up a trashcan. It was steel and quite heavy. The drunken man who'd threatened him never saw it coming; the heavy container struck him full in the face, instantly knocking him down and half burying him in garbage that tumbled from the can. The other man shoved the woman roughly to the ground, turning to face Dan with a snarl. He made an easy target for a strong kick— being he had already conveniently bared his most sensitive area.

Dan's kick landed squarely in the man's naked testicles. The man's feet lifted briefly from the ground. He passed out before his feet touched the sidewalk, and collapsed to the roadway with a very satisfying thud.

Dan ran to the woman's side, helping her to her feet. Dan noticed she only had one shoe. She was weak and very frightened; her left eye was swelling shut from the slap, turning an angry shade of red. He quickly scooped up the contents of her handbag and her notebook, stuffing them in the pockets of his coat. There was no time to retrieve her bag, and who knew where her other shoe had gone.

A taxi was passing by. Dan hailed the cab, helping the injured woman into the back seat. He glanced over his shoulder. Neither of the two men had moved. He grinned as he climbed in. As they pulled away from the curb, a police car pulled to the curb behind them. The officers got out, and as the cab negotiated the corner, Dan saw them shoving the men into the back of the police car for a rather uncomfortable ride to the hospital.

Dan looked at the woman slumped in the seat beside him. She'd passed out, he noticed with concern. He flashed some money, telling the driver to take them to a hospital.

"Here is a small silver coin for the trip to the hospital."

"On the way, sir," the driver said, snatching the coin from Dan's fingers.

"And that's not all, my fine man. If you get us there quicker than an ambulance might, I'll give you an additional silver coin—one of the large ones."

"Believe it or not, sir, we're already there!"

The driver pushed the accelerator to the floor, screeching his steam whistle at anyone foolish enough to pull in front of him or anyone even more foolish who would step in front of him.

Ten minutes later, the woman was in the care of nurses and doctors. Dan paced the floor of the emergency room; he just couldn't sit. He wondered why he was so concerned—this woman really was nothing to him. She was pretty enough, but there were lots of pretty women in the Black City. Why was he so concerned about this one in particular?

Then, within himself, he found the reason. Back in his city dwelling days, years before, he probably wouldn't have considered helping the woman. He would have just walked on by. But living in Noria's tribe had done something to him—it had changed him somehow. There, no one was truly anonymous. There, everyone had value, every life mattered—young and old, man or woman. He was shocked to realize he'd become a better person, a caring person. He smiled—it was a good way to feel.

He turned quickly from reverie when the door opened and the doctor walked up to him. He'd just glanced at his watch and realized that he had been waiting an hour. It didn't seem possible.

"She has a minor concussion," the examining doctor said. "But she hasn't been raped. You stopped those men just in time."

"Can I see her?"

"She'll sleep through the night," the doctor replied. "We gave her a sedative to calm her and relieve the pain. In the morning she'll be very sore, but otherwise we believe she should be in good health. She can leave in the morning. That's more than I can say for the two men who came in just after you arrived."

"Oh yeah?"

"Yeah. Very bad. In any event, your rescued lady will be fine."

"Thank you, Doctor," Dan said. "May I wait in the room?"

"Are you a relative?"

"Yes," Dan lied, "I'm her brother."

The doctor was skeptical, but opened the door anyway. This man had saved the woman at some risk to himself; brother or not, he deserved some consideration. He opened the door, allowing Dan to enter. Dan walked to the woman's bedside, sat in a chair by the head of the bed, and looked at the young woman.

What if I hadn't come along, he thought. What if I'd gone to the right instead when I left the Green Hyena? What if I'd not stepped in to save her—I almost didn't! This last was a marvel to Dan; had he been brave or just compulsive? It didn't matter; either way the woman was safe.

CHAPTER 13

Dan awoke, slumped in the chair. There was a hand resting softly on his arm. He glanced over to the bed. The young woman was awake and smiling at him in spite of her bruises and swollen eye.

"Were you here with me all night?"

"Yes, my name is Dan Hendricks," he said with a smile. "I had been in the Green Hyena and was on my way home."

A little white lie wouldn't hurt here he rationalized.

"You were very brave to come to my assistance. Both of those men carried knives, you know."

Dan was shocked; he hadn't considered the possibility that the men might've been armed—there hadn't been time to think about much of anything.

"They didn't have time to get to them," he laughed.

She laughed as well. "I heard that kick land, Mr. Hendricks. You must be an athlete."

He snickered, "I was once. I was an amateur cycle jouster some years ago."

"Well, you've not lost any of your bravery. You know, two other men came by before you did. They just crossed the street and left me all alone with those men." A tear ran down her cheek. Dan reached over and gently brushed it away. He also brushed her hair from her eyes, and she smiled.

"I thought about just crossing the street," Dan said, realizing that he actually meant it.

"I'm Sharrone Cushing," the young woman said with a dazzling smile, "and I cannot tell you how very happy I am to meet you."

Dan smiled back at her; she was like a flower someone had tried to crush but was now springing back, determined to survive and live. He knew he was smitten.

Dan needed to leave the hospital briefly to confer with the magician. The hospital staff assured him that they would allow nobody in her room. An especially helpful nurse said quite casually that if her file were to be misplaced, it would be difficult for anyone to find out in which room she was resting.

"You know," she said, fanning herself with Sharrone's medical file, "the letter C looks an awful lot like the letter O. It would be completely believable that someone could make a mistake like that, especially if they were being rushed by the rest of the staff."

"Are you being rushed?"

The woman laughed. "I'm always being rushed."

She was suddenly very serious. "I have a baby sister. I don't want to find out she's been brought here like your sister was."

Dan leaned in close, and whispered, "She's not really my sister, you know."

The nurse grinned. "Really? With all that…family resemblance?"

"Thank you so much for this. It truly is a matter of life and death."

"I strongly prefer life, Mister Hendricks—I see too much death here as it is."

Dan nodded, turned, and walked down the hall to the lift.

The taxi arrived at the Bloomgarden Apartments. Dan leapt from the vehicle and quickly paid the fare. He ran into the building. After telling the magician what had happened, he asked if he could borrow his auto.

By the time he was in the street, running to the auto, the magician was already on the phone with Tom Leatham. He returned to the hospital quickly with the magician's stream-car to assist Sharrone in finding her way back home. Back in her room, he found two nurses who insisted that Sharrone must ride out in a wheelchair. Dan didn't mind as the nurses agreed to let him push her. Once out of the hospital, Sharrone got to her feet. Dan motioned her to the magician's vehicle.

"You have your own auto," she said in awe.

Dan laughed. "No, this one belongs to a friend. I'm personally thinking about getting another steam-cycle."

"I've never been on one of those," the young woman said. "When you get it will you give me a ride?"

"It would be an honor," he said, opening the door, helping her climb into the automobile.

A hospital attendant retrieved the wheelchair, rolling it back into the hospital.

As Dan waited for the steam pressure to rise, he looked at his new friend. He thought she was beautiful. He smiled at her, and she smiled back. As he pulled from the curb, he asked her a question that had been on his mind since the night before when he'd first seen her.

"Sharrone, what on earth were you doing out on the street in that part of town at night?"

"I'm trying to become a reporter. I'm working on a story about the Cathedral and their prostitute business."

"That's a dangerous line of inquiry," Dan said, shocked.

"I knew it, I suppose, on some level, but it never truly hit home until last night."

"Well, there's nothing like an assault to wake you up."

"Because I'm a woman, I've been able to talk with some of the street women who work for the Bishop. They're cautious, but with proper and respectful questions, I'm getting the story I want."

Dan gave her an appraising look. This woman was full of surprises!

"Tell me some of what you've found," he requested. "I know some people who might be able to help you with the story, and perhaps even get it published."

Sharrone looked over at him, evaluating how much to tell him. She decided to tell him everything. He had, after all, come to her rescue when all others had just walked away.

"Those men who attacked me," she began, "are acolytes of the Cathedral."

Dan started at that. She really was playing a dangerous game—everything she said made him see her life in a precarious position.

"Those acolytes told me they'd help me with information for my story," she said with a rueful smile. "The information they gave me, though, was how they were going to rape me, kidnap me, and make me one of their street women. They laughed and said I could get all the firsthand information I wanted if I were living the life."

Dan didn't know how to respond to that. He now realized there'd been much more than a sexual assault at stake last night; those men were going to steal Sharrone's entire life.

"I should have killed them!"

"I think they may actually wish you had. They came into the hospital last night for treatment of their injuries shortly after I did. I could hear the doctors talking in the next room."

"Good," Dan said firmly, "I hope their pain was severe."

"Oh, it was," she responded. "The one you kicked will never be a man again. The doctor who treated me last night told me so. He said you completely crushed the man, and that he required amputation."

"Couldn't have happened to a nicer guy," Dan said. "But he wasn't all that much of a man to begin with, all things considered."

Sharrone laughed. "He wasn't all that much of a man as I saw it either, and I had a closer look!"

She laughed again. "The other man lost his right eye. It seems the handle of the can you struck him with cut his eyeball almost in half."

"Again, I'm very glad," Dan said in all sincerity.

"I don't feel much sympathy for either of them."

They both laughed, as Dan made one final turn onto Sharrone's street. The young woman directed Dan to her apartment building. He parked the auto just away from the entrance and walked quickly around the vehicle to open the door for her.

He also scanned the immediate area; you never knew when danger might strike—and now Sharrone was a prime candidate. He held the door as she stepped out.

"Polite and brave," she commented, "I'm liking you more and more."

Dan's heart skipped a beat. Did she really mean that, he wondered?

"Why don't you come up with me," she suggested. "I can at least make you some lunch for bringing me home."

Dan noticed she was limping slightly as she walked to the lift. He slid the brass gate open for her, and followed her in. She put the indicator on fifteen.

"Are you in much pain?"

She looked up at him. *He is such a nice man,* she thought, *so different from so many of the city's men.*

"I have a headache," she responded, "and my right knee hurts from when I hit the ground. The doctor gave me some pain medicine, but I don't want to take it if I don't have to. I like to keep my wits about me."

"A wise decision, considering what you're doing and who you're meeting with," he remarked.

The lift stopped, and they exited into the hallway. Her apartment was right across from the lift. Dan took her key and cautiously opened the door.

"Wait here," he whispered.

A moment later, he was back. He held the door for her and quickly closed it once they were both inside. He locked the door and put on the safety chain. He then walked to the windows and pulled the drapes closed.

"You didn't say your apartment was right by the lift."

"It makes it convenient for coming and going," she said with a shrug.

Dan glanced around the place. "Do you own this, or do you rent?"

"I rent by the month, why?"

"It's almost the end of the month," Dan commented. "I think you should move."

"Why?"

"Those men from last night have friends with a very long reach— and you live right by the lift. They could get to your rooms easily with hardly any exposure on their part."

Sharrone rattled her door, wanting to make sure herself it was locked. She was thinking about what Dan just said—she hadn't thought that someone might come after her. It was a disturbing thought.

"What do you think I should do?"

"I'm not trying to scare you, Sharrone, but I think you should move immediately, today. Right now."

"But all my things…" she began.

"Those friends of mine I mentioned to you? They'll come and move your things. I'm terribly afraid for you right now."

Sharrone nodded, he was right and she knew it. It was a good thing he came along with her. Dan again looked around her apartment, this time examining it as a living space—to learn more about this very fascinating woman. Her place was decorated in a feminine style, but without any of the stuffed bears and crystal animal figurines most women of the city seemed to favor as decoration.

Daisy.

The memory came unbidden; now he would no longer push it away. He firmly believed that Daisy would have approved of the way he saved the young woman now standing in the kitchen preparing food for them. He knew she'd be proud of him. He smiled at the thought, walking into the kitchen to watch Sharrone.

"I'm stepping into the hall to make some calls. I'll lock the door behind me, and I'll knock three times before unlocking it and coming back inside."

"Are you always this careful?"

"Only when I feel I'm protecting something important to me."

He left then, returning but a few minutes later. By then, their food was ready. They sat at Sharrone's table and shared their first meal together.

"My friend is sending over three men to help us move your things," Dan said. "He will be here shortly. He will also knock three times to let us know it's safe to unlock the door."

"Do you really think the Cathedral will come for me that quickly?"

"I do," he replied, and then told her the saga of the safe house and the subsequent explosion.

"I read that story! You were involved in all that?"

"I still am," Dan confessed, "I'm part of the group fighting against the Cathedral's control of the city and its government and its women."

There was a soft knock on the door: tap, tap, tap. Dan opened it cautiously, leaving the security chain attached. The magician smiled at him though the opening. Dan flung the door open, and the magician entered with two friends. All were quickly introduced. The two men with the magician began immediately packing Sharrone's things in the boxes they'd brought with them. They were speedy but careful.

"You're a very brave young woman," the magician said to Sharrone. "I believe I can be of assistance in what you're trying to do."

There was another knock on the door. The magician opened it without hesitation. Tom Leatham came quickly inside, shutting the door behind him. He'd also brought some boxes to help with the packing.

"So," he said after introductions, "this is the young lady investigating the Cathedral's prostitute ring. Do you know who I am?"

"Yes, sir," she answered, "I read your paper every day."

"Well then, how would you like a provisionary position as a special reporter?"

Sharrone looked at Dan, then back at the editor; she was speechless for a moment and then said, "I…I would love the opportunity. Let me show you what I have so far."

She went to the table, grabbing one of several notebooks resting there. She hurried back to Tom, handing him the book expectantly.

Tom held up his hand and smiled. "Later," he said, "right now you have to get out of here."

Thirty minutes later they were hustling the young woman and her things out the back door of the apartment building. She was wearing a long driving coat over trousers and a vest complete with a watch chain. Her hair was tied tightly atop her head and covered with a very fashionable top hat that made her appearance at casual inspection to be that of a young man.

When they drove from behind the building, the magician stopped at the corner.

"Look," he said, "see those two men talking to the people in that delivery lorry?"

The rest looked over. The men in question talked briefly. Four men got out of the lorry's rear compartment and one more stepped from the front. The driver stayed in the vehicle, steam kept at full pressure for a fast getaway. The seven men hurried up the steps, through the wide brass and glass doors into the lobby—sunlight glinted dully off the pistol one of the men carried at his side. The magician released the hand brake and the automobile began moving. He turned the corner and sped away.

CHAPTER 14

The Bishop stood in the pilothouse of the airship. How he was looking forward to getting out of this machine! In the distance, he could see a dark line on the horizon, cloudy and indistinct. But he knew what it was. That would be his new home, at least for a while. He stood silently, hands clasped behind his back, staring at the smudge on the horizon, willing it closer. The ship's commander glanced at him.

"We will be coming in for a landing very early tomorrow morning, Your Eminence."

The Bishop smiled. "Thank you."

"It is beautiful, is it not?"

"What might that be?"

"Why, the ocean of course, and the brilliant blue sky."

"Yes, it is."

"Have you ever been to The Green, Your Eminence?"

"No, I have not."

"It has a beauty all its own. I've been down here on this run about twenty times, and every time I see that vast greenness coming up under the ship, I'm awed."

"I suppose you are correct; but do not become too enamored with beauty. Remember it is a pitfall placed in the world by the Redeemed God's inferior and spiteful feminine counterpart."

The commander made a slight course correction, rotated the great wheel a quarter turn to port, and laughed. "Believe me, Your Eminence, I know all about the spiteful feminine half. I had a beautiful wife, but when she found I was seeing whores—she left me. Took all the money we had and disappeared."

The Bishop laughed. "It sounds to me like you got the better part of the deal; you got to keep the whores."

They both laughed. Presently, Harold came to the front to admire the view. He was worried about what it would be like in such a primitive and dangerous land. If he'd not been sworn to the Bishop, he would have never come on this strange and secret journey.

"There's a ship below us," the engine master said.

They all glanced down to the sea. Far below, a crystal ship of medium size was cruising in the same general direction as they were. The zeppelin was moving faster—they'd beat the crystal ship by a full day.

"If you'd like to look at her more closely, you can use the starboard telescope, Your Eminence," the commander said.

"I believe I shall. It might be an entertaining break in the monotony."

The engine master led the Bishop to the starboard side of the vessel and showed him how to manipulate the mounted brass telescope. The Bishop put his eye to the glass and made a small focusing adjustment. He was always amazed at how telescopes worked. He remembered reading about the giant telescopes the ancient city builders had constructed. He wanted one. Perhaps, once he was the master of the world, he'd commission one.

He peered through the eyepiece at the deck of the ship. Though it was about eight thousand feet below them, he could still make out the details of the ship. He examined the quartz crystal, and then watched the passengers and crew on the deck. Several of them were casually looking back at his zeppelin. One of the crewmen looked up, and the Bishop was startled. Though the distance was great, this man's face was not a normal human color—he must be one of those Far Easterners. They knew the seas and how to sail over them, but they were not trustworthy.

The Bishop snorted in disgust, turning away from the telescope. He was hungry, and he could smell something delightful being cooked up in the galley by his servant.

* * * *

There was another ship on the ocean, also traveling south, several days behind the Bishop's zeppelin, Kel was looking up into the clear blue skies of a hot and humid morning. He was watching a small black object far above him rapidly approaching from behind them from the north. He knew that it was a Cathedral zeppelin. He stared at the flying machine, watching as it slowly passed them. He put one hand to his brow to shield his eyes from the bright sunlight. He felt a hand take his, and looked down. Lyria stood at his side, and Raven was next to her.

"What is it you watch so intently, my love?"

Kel smiled at Lyria. "Look up there."

She followed his gesture, seeing nothing for a moment. Then she saw it. She stared in fascination. "I think if we could have flown in one of those, we'd be there already."

"Darkness and death ride in that thing."

Both Kel and Lyria looked down at Raven. She was huddled close to Lyria's side, half hiding behind the woman.

"Well, the one we would ride in would be painted bright blue, and it would have flowers painted all over it."

Raven giggled. "Would they have pies?"

"More kinds of pies than you could ever imagine. I bet they'd even have ice pie!"

"Ice pie? What is an ice pie?"

Lyria laughed. "I do not know, Raven—we'll just have to wait and find out for ourselves."

They laughed, and then descended below deck for the morning meal.

* * * *

The mercenary soldiers traveling from the Black City to The Green aboard the zeppelin didn't even notice the ship far below them. They were engrossed in gambling and the telling of their braggart stories. A small ship on the vast ocean would have been of no concern to them in any event.

* * * *

The Bishop was ravenous. He sat without speaking, shoving his fork, overflowing with eggs and potatoes into his mouth. Harold watched him eat without comment; his master's strange eating habits were not his to comment upon. He thought the Bishop ate like a pig. He turned away, feigning clean-up work in the galley. That was where he ate his breakfast that morning.

By the time of the midday meal that smudge on the horizon didn't look a bit closer than it had in the morning. Maybe it looked a little wider, though. The Bishop shook his head in disgust, turning back to eat yet another merely satisfactory meal aboard this…thing. He realized he was beginning to hate zeppelins, and that was not a good sign.

While Harold prepared the meal, the Bishop sat in the pilothouse, reading his very worn and dog-eared copy of the Book of the Prophets. With an interruption for lunch, and one more for dinner, he spent all of his time reading until the sun was so low in the western sky that he no longer had sufficient light. He sighed, closed his book, and prepared for sleep. He knew he'd have a lot to do in the morning.

The change in pitch and volume of the engines awoke the Bishop. He sat up with a start—he'd been dreaming of glaciers. He wasn't surprised, considering the warm, muggy air now circulating through the portholes of the gondola. He quickly rose, putting on his robe. Harold was not in his bunk, nor was he preparing breakfast. That was probably a good thing, the Bishop surmised. He was more excited than hungry this morning. He rose, moving into the pilothouse to stand next to his servant.

Both men stared at the vista before them. No wonder it was called Green Hell. The Bishop could barely comprehend this much green. They were coming down gradually, heading right into the jungle, it seemed.

"We'll be landing in about an hour, Your Eminence," the commander said.

"I can hardly wait."

"We're currently about eight hundred feet in the air, and descending according to plan. It will be a gentle landing."

The commander grinned; the Bishop was not his first passenger to develop what he liked to call 'confinement fever'—a condition that almost bordered on panic. He had to concede the Bishop handled it better than some.

At seven in the morning, the airship finally dropped its mooring lines to the men waiting below. They were quickly tied to the windlasses, and the great airship was brought to earth. The final process took almost thirty minutes and the Bishop paced the length of the sleeping quarters the whole time. Finally, much to his relief and to that of Harold who'd sat watching his master the entire time, the ship stopped moving. They were finally grounded.

The hatchway was opened, and the ladder was quickly rolled up to allow the men to climb down. The Bishop went first with Harold right behind him. The crew stayed aboard to unload all of the Bishop's belongings. His desk took the most time to unload.

By the time the desk was in the back of a small lorry with the rest of the luggage, the Bishop's auto had arrived at the new Cathedral. He surveyed the large building with some satisfaction. It wasn't as large as the one in the north, and it only had one basement, but it would do for the interim. To his surprise, there was a lift inside that quickly brought him to the second level and his rooms.

The rooms were not as big as the ones up north either—but the desk. In his office was the most magnificent desk he could ever have imagined. He walked over, slowly running his fingertips over the highly polished surface. He could almost see his reflection. This was a much finer desk than the one he'd brought with him. He'd have to find out what kind of wood it was made of. He was thinking about how much fine wood like this would bring in the north. He thought rich folk would pay plenty for this kind of exotic luxury.

He wondered if the ordinary people living here and moving down by the hundreds would have fine furniture such as this. Probably, he concluded, and why not? It wasn't like there was any shortage of resources here in The Green, and all of it free for the taking. His thoughts turned briefly to the ship they'd seen far below them the previous day—devout followers, no doubt, coming to live on a pure continent—a continent belonging to the Cathedral. He sat at his new fine desk, running his fingers over the reddish black swirling grain patterns in the wood. He knew he had a speech to put the finishing touches on, and how he loved giving speeches.

CHAPTER 15

That evening in Tom Leatham's office, Sharrone told them what she'd discovered so far regarding the Cathedral's sex trafficking. On the desk before them sat two boxes full of papers, notes, and even some photographs. Everyone was both surprised and amazed at the depth of the research and the amount of information, documentation, and quotes the young woman had gathered, which were meticulously footnoted as well.

She watched as Tom leafed through some of the documents, occasionally raising an eyebrow as he read, sometimes smiling.

"Well," she said, "what do you think?"

"I think we should consider immediate publication of some of this information," the editor said. "Your research and documentation is impeccable."

"Do you think it's wise to do that right now?"

Tom looked over at Dan. "Your friend will be much safer if this information is delivered into the public's hands. Don't you see that once this is out—if anything happens to Sharrone everyone will suspect and blame the Cathedral? With this information in the hands of the public, they wouldn't dare touch her. Hurting her would cause them far more harm than good."

Dan hadn't thought of that, and it made sense.

"The best they'll be able to do is request some time and print space to make their position on the subject known. That's fine with me. I've found that whenever Father Woods opens his mouth in public, the general population likes him less. He's constantly tripping over his ego and his ridiculous attitude regarding women—we have a fair number of female readers. He makes stupider statements than the Bishop—and he'll be easier to trip up. Despite what he might think, he doesn't have the Bishop's expertise, however little that may be!"

That brought a laugh from everyone.

Sharrone asked, "What information should be printed first, do you think?"

"I think we should start with a couple of your interviews with the prostitutes. That way, the issue will immediately have a 'face,' you might say. It then involves actual living, breathing human beings rather than just some abstract concept to be bandied about by philosophers. It will engage the readers immediately, and make them want to read more—and from what I've seen here, we can give them a lot more."

"We still need to find a safe place for Sharrone to stay," Dan said. "Here will be fine for a day or two, but she'll need real lodging."

Sharrone smiled at Dan, he was genuinely concerned about her wellbeing. It had been a while since anyone had treated her like a person.

"That we'll do," Tom answered. "I have several ideas in mind, but for tonight, I think she should stay here. Tomorrow I'll send someone to question the deskman at her old lodging to find out what happened there and what he may know. In the meantime, we should find a couple of good stories to run in tomorrow's morning edition. I think something tragic would be best to introduce this series of stories."

* * * *

Father Woods was livid. How could they dare to publish such inflammatory information about the Bishop and the Cathedral? Never mind that it was true. He decided right then to see if he could somehow find out which of the whores had talked to this evil journalist woman. He looked again at the newspaper lying in disarray in front of him on his desk. He read the article again, his anger mounting.

Hellien, is a fictitious name I have given to the woman in this article. Her name has been changed to protect her from possible murder. What follows is an interview with a woman working as a prostitute on the streets of Los Angeles under the thumb of the Cathedral and its Bishop.

Sharrone: "How old are you, and how did you come to be in this position?"

Hellien: "I'm fourteen now. I was kidnapped several years ago from my bed. I was eleven at the time. I knew something was going to happen because two men came to talk to my mother earlier that day. I saw them offer her money, although I didn't know what it was for. Mom became angry and told the men to leave and not come back."

Sharrone: "What happened then?"

Hellien: "I asked Mom what the men wanted. She was scared. She told me my teacher in school had called them—he thought they'd like me. I knew what that meant since the boys at school made it clear which girls they liked and sometimes the ways they liked them. I knew this was true since my teacher always talked about his church and how women needed to learn to serve men in all things rather than themselves. My mom said the men were priests from the Cathedral and that they had tried to buy me."

Sharrone: "What did she do?"

Hellien: "She said we would leave. We had relatives in San Diego and we were going there. But it never happened."

Sharrone: "Why is that?"

Hellien: "That night they came through my bedroom window and took me. I was asleep at the time, and when I awoke, I was already held with a hand over my mouth. He was pinching my nose—I couldn't breathe. I knew where we went, as the blindfold wasn't down all the way over my eyes. They took me to the Cathedral."

Sharrone: "What happened there?"

Hellien: "They started giving me instructions, telling me it was for my own good. First I was taught how to properly behave in front of men. I was beaten if I did something wrong like not looking down when a man entered the room. Then they gave me instructions on how to please men with sex.

"I was raped over and over again by many priests. Then they started giving me heroin, and I was theirs. I had to have the narcotic; they were the only ones I knew who could help me, so I gave them the money I got from men on the street and they gave me food, shelter, and heroin.

"I've been working on the street for three years. There are some men who really like what I do so I make a lot of money from my repeat customers. One is a police sergeant who investigates murders. He doesn't have to pay though—it's a rule. Sometimes the priests still use me. I don't get paid for that, either."

Father Woods hurled the newspaper across the office. He should've had that woman killed. He should have the whore killed. He should have the teacher killed. He took several deep breaths to calm down—ten minutes later he was in a more rational state of mind. He needed help dealing with this situation. He thought about the priests, wondering who might be the best one to confront the newspaper editor. He decided that he'd be the best man for the job. He sat forward in the chair, picked up the phone and dialed Tom Leatham's number.

CHAPTER 16

"Gentlemen, soldiers, and priests of the one faith," the Bishop shouted, standing on the second floor balcony of the new Cathedral, surveying his surroundings. He looked at the throng spread out below him—all faces turned up, expectant and smiling.

"Today is a glorious day. Today I am dedicating this continent to the followers of the one true faith—the faith of the Redeemed God!"

There was loud applause. He waited for silence.

"We will begin instituting new rules and regulations. Because we want a pure state, one undefiled by unbelievers, from this day onward no one shall come to live here that is not a dedicated follower of the faith. Now that may mean second generation faithful, or it could even mean new converts—should they appropriately prove their loyalty and their honor."

He looked at the crowd—nobody seemed upset so far.

"If you are newly converted, or less than second generation, you must do something that will prove your faith. You can give all your wealth to the church, having faith that we will sustain you and house you. We will ignore no one."

Now it would get interesting, he thought.

"Another way of showing support would be to give your young daughters and sisters for the mutual benefit and pleasure of our soldiers and priests who are so very far from home. Whatever your sacrifice, be assured it will be lovingly accepted.

"With the exception of our mercenary fighters, all who are not of our faith will be required to convert—with appropriate show of intent—or leave. There will be no exceptions. This land will be purged of non-believers. This land will shine as a perfect land, a land filled with perfect people, dedicated to a perfect cause—glorifying the Redeemed God!"

There was roaring applause—although not all shared in the merriment. There were several hundred folk who'd come here seeking a new start away from rules and regulations—including the Book of the Prophets. They now understood this land was not for them. They also realized they'd have to leave quickly, although some had used all their assets to book passage on the crystal ship to get here, with visions of gold panning and mining in their heads. They now realized their visions were just that—mere daydreams.

He remained on the balcony, allowing his followers to see him, to adore him. Once all the cheering stopped, he turned, and walked back inside.

"I'd like an escort, please."

"Yes, Your Eminence…to the same place?"

The Bishop looked at his servant. "That would be exactly where I want to go, Harold."

"I wish you wouldn't, Your Eminence. It's dangerous."

"Nonsense, Harold—it isn't dangerous anymore."

"If you say so, Your Eminence."

"I do say so, Harold, now call for my escort."

Harold placed the call, and soon there were two heavily armed soldiers and a young priest walking with the Bishop through the main hall of the building. He just had to see it again, though he couldn't exactly say why—maybe it was simply the power of having it, or maybe it was what it represented. He didn't really know, or care. He knew he had to see it.

"Do we have to get close?"

The Bishop looked at the young priest. "Are you afraid?"

"Yes, Your Eminence."

"That is good. For if you fear it even now, imagine the fear it will instill in the heathens in the north—and even the faithful."

The Bishop and his escorts walked past the security guard, and exited by the door at the back of the Cathedral. There was the stockade—it was big and strong and made by the hands of man. There was nothing in the natural world that did not bow before the faithful—not even that thing.

As the Bishop and his military escort advanced to the stockade, the young priest held back—nothing could make him get close to that thing again.

* * * *

Kel studied the map the captain had loaned him; he roughly knew where they were. Raven would ask the seamen periodically, and then tell him what they said. The next day they'd be nearing an area called Panama on the map. It looked to Kel as though there was no way for the ship to reach New Los Angeles from their position. He shook his head, realizing the map was old.

Jian explained that they were going to sail right through the land called Panama at the narrowest part. He'd told Kel of the massive earthquake the region had experienced a number of years previously. The earth had split, and great sections of it sank below the waves in a matter of hours.

Now the western sea and the waters of New Los Angeles mingled—a natural passageway existing where once only dry land had been. The map Jian carried aboard was made before the earthquake and didn't show the passage. Kel was rolling the map back up just as Lyria and Raven came into the cabin.

"So," Lyria said, "do we know where we are?"

"Certainly," Kel said with confidence, "we're right...here!"

He was pointing straight down at the deck. Raven snickered.

Lyria chose to ignore that comment. "Raven and I have decided to eat on deck. Would you like to join us?"

"It's real nice up there," Raven coaxed, "warm and sunny!"

"That sounds nice," Kel said, giving Lyria a kiss.

Raven tugged at his sleeve. He laughed softly, bending over to kiss her as well.

"I'm glad you are my new parents," Raven said. "You take me to the most interesting places."

"That is one way of saying it," Lyria laughed, "though I do not know if I would call dangerous, interesting."

"I would," was the girl's response.

They left the cabin, climbing to the deck where a crewman brought them their meal. Lyria noticed how nice everyone was being. *Raven really has a winning way with strangers,* she thought, *even strangers who speak even stranger languages.* As they ate, Raven explained to them how night navigation was done using the stars.

"Did you know," Raven said, "the stars down here are different from the stars we see at home?"

"I've noticed that," Kel said, "the sky encircles the earth and is filled with stars."

"You have to know different stars if you are going to sail the world," Raven said enthusiastically. "I think I might want to be a sailor when I'm grown."

"Perhaps a ship with an all women crew," Lyria speculated. "Everyone would know about you."

"I don't want everyone to know about me," the little girl said somberly. "Except for the people I love, I wish I was invisible."

Kel looked at the girl. "That would allow you to do all kinds of things, would it not? You could take a pie and nobody would see you."

"That would be stealing," Raven said, hands on her hips, "besides, I would be invisible but the pie would not. A pie floating in the air would bring more attention than if I were visible."

Kel hugged the girl again. She was so smart—the girl was quick as well as cute. After they finished their meal, they climbed to the roof of the pilothouse, where Jian joined them. This was certainly not the crow's nest, but it was higher than the deck. The captain was shielding his eyes from the bright sunlight, looking ahead of them as he talked. He pointed to the horizon and said, "See the sail?"

His three guests stared hard, and then they finally saw it—a sailing ship was cutting through the water heading south as well. Though the ship was making good time, it was obvious that Jian's steamboat was gaining.

"We will move closer toward the shore," Jian said, "this way we will not pass too closely by that vessel."

"Does it matter?"

The captain looked a Lyria. "We do not want to risk being boarded. I believe that vessel is a Cathedral ship."

"Does not the Bishop pay for this ship on this run as well?"

Jian looked at Kel with merriment in his eyes. "That is correct! Everyone on board is heading to New Los Angeles—that is what the contract calls for. Still, there is no reason to take a risk. The Bishop would not be happy if he knew you were aboard—it would be very bad for business."

"Well, I can see how that could be." Kel laughed, but he knew Jian was speaking the truth. He was a merchant first and foremost.

Then finally, they were turning to the east; ahead lay an open waterway that on Jian's map had shown only land. Kel was still nervous, what if there were rocks to tear the bottom of the ship? He stood in the bow with the captain's telescope, watching the sailing vessel as it glided closer and closer to land. The pilot of that ship wasn't even hesitating, Kel noticed. With all sails extended, the ship plowed into the water separating the two great masses of land.

They were getting closer now as well, and Raven was standing by the rail with Kel eagerly watching the land approach. Lyria was in their cabin, oiling her swords once more. The air was heavy with moisture, she'd pointed out, and swords needed more care in this kind of weather.

Kel and the girl stared to the south. The fast approaching land seemed to be either barren rock or lush green jungle.

"Is this The Green?"

Kel answered, "This is part of it, sweetheart, I'm sure. As I understand it, except for mountains and plains far to the east, everything is as green as we see it here."

Kel felt a hand go around his waist. Lyria had come up to join them.

"It is beautiful, is it not?"

"That it is," answered Kel, "but also dangerous."

"There are priests where we're going," Raven said flatly, "will they be looking for us?"

"No, honey," Lyria assured the girl, "they think we are dead, remember?"

Raven nodded, still looking at the jungle. "I think I'm the happiest dead person there could ever be."

Lyria laughed. "That may well be, though I have not asked many dead people how happy they were being dead."

Raven laughed, and they returned to their contemplation of the jungle and the grey cliffs that marked where land once had lived.

The crystal ship slowed its speed as it approached the channel between the landmasses. The sailing ship, being smaller, had maintained its speed and was now pulling away from them. The closer they got to the cliffs, the taller they looked. The freshly cloven rock faces shone whitely against the deep blues and greens of the water. By the time they were between the great cliffs, the sailing ship could no longer be seen.

"I wonder if it hit a rock and sank?"

Lyria looked at Kel with a frown. "You should look for the good side. Perhaps if the ship has sunk, it pushed the rock it hit out of our way."

Kel looked at her in disbelief and began laughing.

Jian walked up to the front of the ship. He had heard part of the conversation. He looked skeptically at Kel.

"Surely you do not believe I would risk my ship, my only possession, on a passage that might sink us."

"No," Lyria reassured, "we were jesting."

Kel changed the subject. "How long is this part of the journey?"

Jian turned to Kel. "The passage is fifty miles beginning to end. You may wonder about the earthquake that made this happen," the captain went on. "But keep in mind that there were deep incursions by water in this area already, so the quake might not have been as powerful as one might think it needed to be to collapse so much earth and rock into the sea."

"How long until we reach New Los Angeles," Lyria wanted to know.

"A few more days," Jian said, "the worst part of the journey is over and we did not hit any storms—that's a good omen."

"I'll take that as truth," Kel laughed, "you know more about these areas that I."

The captain bowed, turning back to the pilothouse and leaving the three of them alone once more.

That night they decided to sleep on deck. Raven wanted to impress them with her new knowledge of the stars. As the little girl lectured them, Kel and Lyria glanced at each other and smiled, and then turned their attention back to Raven. She would probably ask them questions when she finished. Once Raven was finished, Lyria told some of the stories she'd heard when she was a child in the tribes.

Raven wanted to know what shamanism was like—that was Kel's domain. He explained to her about the three worlds. The upper world where the shaman met and conversed with his or her teacher, the middle world was essentially this reality, and explored in the spirit realm, and finally, there was the lower world. This, Kel explained, was where one met one's animal totems.

"Do I have a totem?"

"You do," Kel answered, "it is Raven—given to you by the Splendid Lady Herself."

"But could a person have more than one?"

"Certainly," Kel answered, "some shamans have several and sometimes one leaves and another takes its place."

"Your totem is a hawk, isn't it," the little girl queried.

"Yes, it is," Kel said.

"What is it like to travel with a hawk high in the sky?"

Kel smiled and said, "I have a poem of the first time I flew with Hawk a number of years ago now."

"Tell me," the girl said eagerly.

"Very well," Kel answered, "here is how it goes. I have called this poem Aerial."

Stepping from the rocky shore
Into the aerial sea,
Freefalling for a second;
No fear could shiver me.
The shadow of those silent wings
Cooled me as I fell.
Suddenly I'm weightless,
Rising on the swell.
I feel the feathered power
As I'm lifted to the sky!
Through unguessed fathoms soaring,
To the sun... we'll maybe try!
A wondrous combination
Feathered soul and man,
United in one being
From past to future span.

"Oh Kel," Lyria said. "That is beautiful!"

"I could feel it," Raven said with glee, "maybe one day I can fly with my Raven."

"That would not surprise me," Kel said. "You are a gifted and blessed child, even if you are invisible."

Raven laughed. "Silly! I'm not invisible, the pie is!"

She then made overly dramatic gestures as though she was eating a pie only she could see. Kel and Lyria laughed.

"I could almost taste it," Kel said with a smile. "I bet that was a really good pie!"

Raven looked at him mischievously. "The thing is, invisible pies do not have any taste."

At that they all roared.

Raven said, very seriously, "Do you suppose they have pies in that city?"

Kel answered, "I am certain they do, and you can see them as well. Although you will have to be fast because I like pies too!"

Raven giggled. "I know you would give me your pie, if I asked."

"Well…part of it, anyway," he answered with a fond smile.

CHAPTER 17

Two days later, the crystal ship docked in New Los Angeles. Kel surveyed the city with dismay; it was much larger than he thought it'd be. As they walked down the gangplank to the dock, Jian bade them farewell.

"May your Gods bring you and your people together once more."

Kel bowed. "Thank you, Jian. You and your crew have been so nice to Raven. How can I ever thank you?"

"The girl is a marvel," the captain said. "Bring her back safely. That will be thanks enough."

Kel bowed again, and then turned and walked down the dock with Lyria and Raven into the city.

Everywhere they looked, there were people. It seemed this Los Angeles was every bit as populated at its more northern sister.

"Listen," Raven said.

Kel and Lyria paused; they heard a rending, crashing sound in the near distance.

Kel said, "That sounds like falling trees."

"They are killing The Green," Raven said. "They are going to chop it all up."

"They must be using the trees for making homes," Lyria said. "There are many wooden buildings here."

"Well," Kel said, looking worriedly at the sky, "we need to find shelter. It looks like it is going to rain very soon."

They all looked at the sky. It was leaden. Lightning flashed a short distance away to the south over the jungle.

"The Green does not like what they are doing," Raven said. "It will eat them."

"That may be," Lyria said, "but with luck, we'll be gone by the time it happens."

"Some of us will," the girl responded.

Lyria glanced at her. The young girl was watching the approaching storm with interest—apparently unaware of the comment she'd just made.

They found lodging in a long, single story roadhouse not unlike the one they stayed in at Mountain Village. They put their belongings in the room. Kel dressed in his military uniform, strapping Lyria's sword to his side. Lyria carried her daggers around her waist—she refused to leave them.

"Let's see if we can find something to eat," Kel said.

"Pies?"

They all laughed at Raven's comment as they walked out into the gusting wind.

"Look!"

The comment by the stranger caught their attention. They looked where the man was pointing. In the sky a short distance away, a zeppelin hung over the outer edges of the jungle—black against the thunderheads.

Lyria said, "It seems so small…"

"They make 'em like that down here," the stranger said. "Four engines instead of eight; two hundred feet instead of a thousand in length. They consider them warships. With the shortage of hydrogen hereabouts, it makes sense to need less of it."

The trees, towering over the partly constructed wall separating the city from the wild, seemed to reach out toward the foundering airship. It was having trouble maneuvering in the high, gusting winds. It turned slowly, trying to get away from the trees—it almost made it.

A sharp gust of wind caught the zeppelin, turning it into the trees at the edge of the jungle. The front of the ship struck the high canopy of the trees stripping the topmost branches from the trees. The nose of the airship dipped; the heavy fabric of its outer shell tore. A great gash opened in the black outer fabric. The wind then took hold, greedily ripping a large section from the nose of the zeppelin; but by now the airship was free of the trees and, with sections of fabric flapping around like absurd wings, the giant ship turned and slowly lumbered away from them.

"It's goin' to the Cathedral," the man said. "They'll get 'er fixed!"

Kel turned to look at the man. He bowed in front of Kel.

"Welcome to New Los Angeles," the man said. "We always need more soldiers."

"Why is that?" Kel asked.

"Some of the local half-humans from The Green don't like us cutting all the trees down around here. It seems they live nearby and are afraid we'll drive them out. We will, but we need an army to do that."

"I was under the impression we had an army here," Kel responded.

The man laughed and said sarcastically, "Where you from, the city of Atlanta?"

He laughed at his seeming joke.

"New Orleans," Kel said matter-of-factly.

The man gave him a surprised look. "The problem we have here is a few soldiers and a lot of mercenaries. Some of those men don't strike me as fighters at all, much less soldiers."

"Perhaps I should see them for myself," Kel said. "Could you take me to the military barracks?"

"It would be an honor," the man said. "By the way, my name is Carlaise. Wally Carlaise."

"Nice to meet you, Wally, my name is Kelley Draco."

Lyria had already led Raven away from Kel and his new acquaintance, as she knew Kel had found an opportunity to look for information. She decided to find a place where she and Raven could eat without Kel.

"We will see you at our room later, honey," she called to Kel.

Kel waved acknowledgment and turned back to his new friend.

"What is it you do," he asked, "do you work with the military?"

"I'm not a soldier, if that's what you mean, sir. I help maintain their weapons. I guess you'd call me an armorer."

They walked down the street, part of which was already paved with cobblestones. Kel noticed the street lamps.

"Gaslights?"

"All the comforts of home," the man laughed, "though the supply of natural gas is rather spotty right now. They've found deposits of natural gas and petroleum nearby, and the digging is well commenced. With these resources, we'll be able to produce the light we need and fuel for our steam engines, and we can make hydrogen. That still has to be brought down in ships, you see. That'll change in a couple of months, if we can get better control of the locals."

"Why not befriend the locals? They could help with the digging, the security, and many other things if we weren't enemies," Kel pointed out.

The man looked at Kel suspiciously—then burst into laughter. He thought Kel was joking. Kel decided it might be better to leave it that way. He laughed as well, pointing at Wally as though he'd almost deceived him. Ahead of them, a very long one-story structure loomed.

"That be military barracks, sir," Wally said. "If you would like an introduction…"

Kel shook his head. "That'll be fine, Wally. Thank you for bringing me here."

Wally nodded, walking off in the direction the zeppelin had gone. Kel looked up at the sign over the main entrance to the barracks. It read, Barracks 3. Kel thought, *there are probably two more; there are a lot of soldiers for a city of this size—even if they aren't real soldiers!* He climbed three wooden steps to the entrance—each step was hewn from a single, large log. The building was also made of wood. He pushed the door open and entered.

The inside was dark, though some gas jets were lit. This seemed to be a meeting room with hallways leading off in both directions. There were several large tables in the center. On the tables were rolls of what looked like maps. Kel walked forward to have a look. They were indeed maps; the one that lay open showed what appeared to be a river navigation chart. On both sides of the meandering river, were the ominous words, The Green. This was a map of a pathway into the jungle.

He wondered why they'd want to enter so deeply into such a dangerous and deadly place. The only hint on the map was at the extreme southern end. A short distance from the river on the west side, there appeared to be an illustrated clearing. In that clearing were the words, 'here be dragons.' What could that mean? Surely they didn't think they'd find a dragon. Kel figured it might be a code symbol.

"Hey, you, what you doin' there?"

A rough voice caused Kel to whirl, hand going the hilt of his sword. The owner of the voice backed up, saying, "I'm sorry. I didn't know you were military."

"You know now," Kel said curtly. "Who are you?"

The man came to attention and said, "Sergeant Hallifax, sir!"

"Well, Sergeant Hallifax, come forward and explain this chart to me. I am newly arrived from the city of New Orleans—a military observer and attaché."

The man walked over, glanced down, and said, "I don't know, sir. That's a map the priests left here by mistake, I think."

"And you have no idea what it represents?"

"I know the priests and their private bodyguards took a steamship up the river a few months or so ago. That's all I know. The priests were here to discuss something very important. They ran us all out into the street, sir, like they was too good for us."

"Watch your mouth, sergeant," Kel warned. "I suggest you take this back to the Cathedral right now."

"With all respect, sir, I would rather not while the Bishop is here."

"The Bishop? Here?"

"Yes, sir," the sergeant answered, "he arrived a little bit ago. All I know is that he's the one interested in this map. That man scares me, sir."

"He's a man of God," Kel said sternly. "You will take this to him immediately."

"Yes, sir," the man said reluctantly.

The sergeant rolled up the map, tucking it into a protective tube and left the barracks double time; Kel followed at a distance. He wanted to know where the Cathedral was located—where the Bishop was located. The sergeant wound his way through narrow streets, avoiding both horse-drawn carts and a few steam-cars.

Kel looked around at the environment. The city was large, mostly made of wood. There was a stockade being built around it. A lot of trees had been cut to build what was already here, and there was no sign the construction would be stopping soon. Kel shook his head, no wonder the locals were upset with the city builders. While passing an open area not yet completely built up with homes or shops, he was able to see to the tree line. From his vantage point he could see hundreds of stumps—stumps that had once been mighty trees.

Then he saw the Cathedral. The man he was following ran up the front steps, opened the massive door and was gone from sight. Kel noticed that this building was made of black stone just like its northern counterpart. He slowly walked around the great building, and found that it had no easy entrance. He rounded the far end of the building, and was stopped by a black clad soldier.

"Can't go any farther, sir," the man said, noticing Kel's rank.

"What do you mean, soldier?"

The man laid his Mauser rifle across his arms. "Nobody can go past this point, sir. Orders of the Bishop himself."

"Well, in that case, I bid you good day," Kel said with a smile. "I am glad to see you maintaining strict security—be advised I will tell the Bishop of your diligence. What is your name, soldier?"

The man puffed up. "Sir, I am Corporal Wainwright."

"Well, Corporal Wainwright, keep up the good work!"

"I will, sir, and thank you, sir."

The man saluted Kel. He responded in like and walked away. Behind the Cathedral he'd glimpsed another stockade. Its purpose, however, was not apparent—perhaps it was some type of prison. He turned, retracing his steps back to the center of town where Lyria and Raven would be waiting. He'd learned little. Whatever the mystery, it would take further digging to ferret out an answer.

CHAPTER 18

Adria looked up at the sky, sniffing the cool autumn air. Winter was coming—she could feel it. She must prepare. She counted up the money she and the children had gotten from her prostitution and their begging over the last week. It'd be enough, she hoped. She woke the three children. It was time at least one of them earned her keep. Adria was not about to support them all the time.

"Biancca? You are the oldest; you will come with me."

Lucy and Christy looked at each other.

Adria smiled. "We have some shopping to do, young ones. We will be back in time for lunch."

Satisfied, the two prepared for their day of begging in the streets near the park. They'd leave the park early in the morning, venturing into the nearby business district to solicit money from passers by. It was surprising how many people would leave a copper coin or even a small silver coin with a child who appeared to be starving—especially when that child could cry at will.

Adria led Biancca into the city. She was now in her familiar hunting ground near the apartment building that had once been her home. She thought about the new desk clerk, but no, that would not work. He was just one man, and besides, he wouldn't be on the desk until nightfall; there was no point in waiting that long. She was looking for the apothecary she knew was in the area. When she found it, she quickly led Biancca through the door. The bell jingled merrily as they entered.

"What can I get for you young ladies?" the jovial pharmacist asked, hurrying in from the back room.

Adria noticed the man did not recognize her even though she'd shopped here regularly. "I want five pounds of salt, an ounce of saltpeter, one of those barrels, and a cheap hand-cart to carry it all."

The man laughed. "Getting ready for winter, are you?"

Adria looked up at him. "Yes, sir. It's a school project for my little sister," she nodded at Biancca. "She's learning how the half-humans store meat for winter, and I thought it might be well for her to learn firsthand."

"Interesting," the man said, "nothing like doing something to learn about it. Give me a moment, please."

A short while later, Adria and Biancca were inside the local grocery where she usually shopped when she'd lived in the area—before those hated coppers raided her apartment. What right did they have to invade her home and steal what was her divine right to possess? She was still furious about it.

The people in the grocery, a family run business, didn't recognize her either, though she'd shopped there frequently. She looked at the shelves of goods, quickly finding the molasses and cayenne pepper she needed, paying for them with a silver coin. She also bought a hard candy for Biannca. The young girl was delighted as she popped the sweet into her mouth.

Once they were back on the street, Adria put all of the things she'd bought into the barrel and pressed on the top—it was easy to move the barrel using the cart. Adria had a plan, though it was something Biancca didn't know about—yet. It was another way to make money. She'd need it for food and narcotics for the winter. Why shouldn't the girl earn her keep? She led Biancca to a tavern near her former apartment.

"We're not supposed to go in taverns," the young girl said in protest, pulling back. "Our parents told us they were evil places."

"Evil can be used, if you pay the price" Adria replied knowingly. "Besides, your parents are gone. Now I am taking care of you and you will do as I say."

Without further comment, she rolled the cart through the doorway into the dark interior of the tavern, pulling the girl behind her, roughly by the arm.

Inside, Adria talked to the barkeep in a lowered voice. She gestured toward Biancca who was standing nervously by the cart, looking around the interior of the tavern. The bartender nodded. Adria walked through the tavern, talking to the men. Biannca watched Adria with interest, not comprehending what was coming. It almost seemed like Adria knew these men the way she was whispering to them and touching them.

Adria was looking for someone who'd pay for the use of Biancca's body. It didn't take long—there was always at least one man who could rationalize what he was about to do. After all, the girl probably wanted it—if not, why would she be with a pimp in the first place? And since she was offering, why not accept? Nobody would know. That one man nodded, handing Adria several coins. Adria mentioned the girl's age and her virginity. He hesitated and then handed over a gold coin as well. He approached the young girl, smiling oddly…

Biancca fled into the street crying. Adria, faced with an angry client and barkeep, dropped most of the money he'd given her onto the floor. There was a scramble for the coins—knives flashed and men bled. Adria ran into the street after Biancca, still clutching the gold coin and pushing her handcart. She caught the frightened girl almost at the edge of the park.

"It was just a joke," Adria said to the girl. "I know those men."

The girl, not mollified, shouted, "He tried to grab me! He smelled bad and his hands were rough. I'm telling the others. I don't want you in our tribe anymore."

Adria was angry now. Lorra and Abi would be home any minute—something had to be done! She looked hatefully at Palom—knowing the girl didn't look exactly like Palom, one of her young friends from her previous tribal life, but that was some kind of trick on the part of the girl—the little bitch! Trying to trick her like that! Adria struck out, hard…

* * * *

"Where's Biancca?"

Lucy and Christy were looking up at Adria, complete trust in their eyes. Adria knew this was all an act. She knew that Lorra and Abi were also trying to trick her—they were jealous of her magnificence just like everyone else. They probably wanted to steal her magic—her heroin and mescaline. There wasn't enough to share.

"She's right over here," Adria said calmly, "behind these bushes."

The girls followed Adria, and then they screamed. Adria was ready. That hateful woman in the apartment building had decided to change her mind and not sacrifice herself that time back in the city. She screamed as well. This time, Adria's knife was already out.

Now all was silence. Adria was glad. All that noise was so distracting. She had to get ready for winter, after all. Biancca was already gutted; her meat lay on a tarp rolled in salt. Soon the other girls would join her. The day after tomorrow, the meat would be ready for processing. The ingredients she bought at the apothecary and grocer would complete the process of preserving the meat in the barrel through the winter.

She saved a cup of blood from her last victim. The incandescent rainbow of the girl's divinity flashed in the dark liquid as she drank it. Afterward, she piled what remained, and the hides of the creatures onto a second tarp. She smiled. *Let's see them figure this out, she thought.*

That night, after the meat was salted and ready, Adria slung the tarpaulin over her shoulder and walked into the city—it was heavier than she'd thought. Near the park, the streets were empty this time of night. She was sweating by the time she reached her destination. She hid in the alleyway, watching the entrance to the Hillcrest Apartments. She grinned in the darkness—they'd taken her home from her. *Well,* she thought, *let's see how they like this.*

She crept out of the shadows and was briefly exposed in the street's gaslights. She didn't care. She was divine. She dumped the contents of the tarpaulin onto the front steps of the apartment, spreading things around nice and even. Nobody would leave by this exit in the morning without having to step in—something. She giggled.

Lots of people would probably move out and that would serve them right for letting the coppers take what was hers. She went back into the alley, and made her way back to the park. She sat in her tent and checked on her supply of heroin—she'd be in need of more soon.

HILLCREST HORROR!
Is this the work of the Cathedral Vampire?

Tom Leatham grinned as he read the headline—calling the killer the Cathedral Vampire was Sharrone's idea. He chuckled. That woman would make a great reporter! Under the heading was a description of what was found that morning by tenants of the Hillcrest Apartments who'd been preparing to leave for work. In a linked article, the paper ran another of Sharrone's interviews with a young prostitute. The story was heart rending. Tom smiled.

"Run it," he said to the young man waiting in his office. "I want it in this evening's edition."

"Yes, sir," the man answered.

The evening edition sold out quickly. Tom ordered a second run for the early morning. He knew he'd hear from Father Woods, but he didn't think it would be through his reporters. The evening edition spurred some in the city to begin organizing a demonstration against the Cathedral. By noon the next day, following the second publication of the stories, they were ready.

By that evening, the streets were filled with people marching on the Cathedral. Their arrival was a complete surprise to the priests. They'd read the article in the paper, but instead of calling the editor, they'd been preparing a written statement they hoped to have published. If the public liked flyers, they could play that game too. They'd already printed up a few thousand extolling the virtues and righteousness of their faith—only now there was another problem.

Father Woods looked out of the high windows of the Bishop's office with dismay. There were hundreds of people gathered below shouting hateful things. For the first time in his life he felt fear. He picked up the phone as he wiped the perspiration from his forehead, shouting, "Give me the police immediately!"

The demonstrators carried signs. Some read, "Send the Bishop to his Hell," "Stop Child Prostitution," and "Leave Our City!" The crowd was rowdy, shouting insults at the façade of the building. They taunted, trying to get someone from inside to respond. Father Woods decided not to respond. Instead, he had the doors bolted securely—he knew they'd be very hard to break down.

His soldiers, grim and determined, stood by in the Cathedral itself. They had two Maximum Rapid-fire guns, simply called Maxims by the soldiers who used them, set up on their small, two-wheeled carts. Two men hunkered down behind the steel armor of each gun, facing the doorway. One man was ready to fire the gun, and the other was there to assist in loading. His job would be feeding the belt of ammunition into the gun's receiver or exchanging an empty ammunition box with a full one, should it be necessary. The priest decided to ignore the protesters—let the police take care of them.

* * * *

Tom Leatham picked up his phone. He was about to leave his office when the call came—it was from one of his younger reporters. The man was breathless as he explained what was happening near the Cathedral.

"Can you stay there and get us some copy?"

"Yes, sir," the reporter answered enthusiastically. "I'm already on it. I've already interviewed several of the demonstrators. You might want to have photographers here in the morning."

"Why is that?"

"You should read what some of the people are painting on the front wall. Some of it's hilarious, some sinister, and all of it insulting to the priests."

"Stay far enough back that you won't get hurt when the police arrive," Tom warned.

"I will," the young reporter said, "so far everyone is being relatively orderly."

Tom hung up the phone, but decided to stay in his office for a while. You never knew what might come of something like this.

It was dusk by the time the police arrived in enough force to form a line between the Cathedral and the crowd. Some of the policemen snickered as they read portions of the graffiti scrawled over the black basalt in white paint. "Baby Eaters," one read. Another said, "Our children are not your playthings." A couple of them were more ominous. "Kill the Bishop!" "Burn the priests. Let them get to know their Hell."

Many of the comments consisted of single obscene words or short phrases—a few were full paragraphs. Some of them, the police noticed with amusement, were quite clever—if impossible to accomplish. Nobody could be THAT flexible—not even a priest or a Redeemed God.

By the time the crowd was dispersed by the police, it was totally dark. Five policemen stayed to patrol the area to make sure things stayed quiet, walking a beat around the large structure. The priests had yet to make an appearance. All in all, the demonstration had been well planned and carried out with no acts of violence on the part of the demonstrators.

One police officer, glancing at the scrawled comments on the front wall, chuckled and said jokingly to his companion, "I might even try that one myself. Where can I get two horses and an alligator?"

His companion laughed.

CHAPTER 19

The next morning at first light, Tom sent two photographers to the scene of the demonstration. They managed to get several photos of church workers furiously scrubbing the façade of the building to remove the paint. Although much of the graffiti had been removed before the photographers arrived, some of it still made the evening paper, along with a third installment of Sharrone's interviews. *The woman was very perceptive*, Tom thought, *she knew what would make the readers empathize with the street women she'd talked to—she made them real.* Sharrone had shown how these were women like any other in the city—they weren't just words: whore, or slut, or prostitute. They were women, many taken by force as children and forged into tools for the priests to use in the fires of abuse, rape, and narcotics addiction.

Tomorrow morning, they'd run a story about some banking issues that had recently been uncovered. It looked like the Bishop had a secret account that was listed as a medical supply business, yet known priests were the only ones who made deposits or withdrawals. The money was all in small denomination bills and coins. He felt certain this was prostitution money, but had no way of proving it.

None of the women Sharrone talked with knew where their money went after it was given to the priests. The article coming out in the morning would simply be asking, why? He knew people would draw their own conclusions considering one more series of interviews with other street women would be run on the same page. Tom knew the city elections were coming up soon. There were laws pending against child prostitution and abuse that might be pushed through now by men wanting to guarantee that they'd keep their seats in the governing body—whether they actually supported the laws or not.

* * * *

Dan awoke in Sharrone's new home in the outer regions of the city. It turned out that Tom Leatham owned a number of houses in various places. The house was not large, but it was located on six acres. It had a guesthouse at the front of the property that, from the street, appeared to be the main house. Tom's security force for Sharrone lived in that house.

There were six bodyguards patrolling the property constantly, with six more, all heavily armed, in the residence. It was a safe place for her to live. Soon this would no longer be necessary. As more and more of her stories reached the public, the value of stopping her decreased and the negative impact of killing her was rapidly becoming greater than any advantage.

Dan stretched and yawned, and sniffed a couple of times. Breakfast was being prepared! He leaped to his feet, quickly pulling on a bathrobe. He grinned into the mirror over the bureau. Last night had been wonderful! He was surprised that he could fall for someone so quickly—he'd thought he'd never find love again. He was very glad he'd been mistaken! The sexual intimacy that flowed from love was so much more pleasurable than the ugly sweating and pushing of sex with prostitutes—which in the end was only sex and nothing more.

"Mmmm, that smells good," he commented as he walked into the kitchen.

Sharrone smiled at him, her auburn hair flowing over her shoulders, not yet arranged for the day. She handed him a plate and said, "The flatware is already on the table, Dan. Would you pour the milk, please?"

As they ate breakfast, they discussed the day's work. Sharrone was going to the bank with the questionable account to try to charm the man who'd brought it to their attention in the first place. It was possible he knew more and was, perhaps, afraid to speak further. *If anyone can get the information, Sharrone can,* Dan thought with a smile.

* * * *

Adria decided that perhaps she should use her remaining money to buy more heroin and mescaline—no point in running out. She looked at the barrel sitting in the corner of her tent. She had meat in plenty now, and with some seeds she'd gathered or stolen, she planned to start a garden next spring. She poured out the money she had onto her makeshift table. She counted the coins. There was barely enough if she wanted to keep the gold coin. She decided to do some begging before she looked for her dealer; maybe she could continue to make money that way.

Three hours later, she realized she was too old to beg as the children had done—nobody had shown any sympathy for her at all. Clearly they were all jealous. Well then, she'd go back into the taverns and put on some shows. She'd made Larry Harper a lot of money doing that, and nothing was easier than convincing drunken men to fuck her. She sat down for lunch, and then began to prepare herself, remembering everything the priests taught her.

She went down to the river to wash. She knew her clothing was a bit bedraggled right now, but if she were naked the men wouldn't notice. She could shop for clothes once she had more money. She washed carefully, keeping in mind that the men she was going to lure may be drunk, but they still had a sense of smell! She combed out her hair using the mirror Biancca, or was it Palom, had given her when she went away. *It was nice of her to leave me such a gift,* Adria thought happily, *even if she was a conniving bitch!* Adria shook her head in confusion—lately her thoughts had been so jumbled. *I'll worry about that tomorrow,* she thought, and promptly forgot the whole thing.

She found a backstreet tavern very near the park and ventured inside. It was early afternoon and most of the patrons were male. There were a few women present as well, and Adria knew that, like her, they were whores. But she was willing to do something the other women wouldn't. She approached the bartender and smiled.

It'd been easier to get the barkeep to allow her on the stage than she'd thought—she gave over a large silver coin, agreeing to pay him a quarter of the money she made. The mescaline she took was now beginning to take effect, and the people around her were beginning to glow. She knew she'd have to watch her step and not kill any sacrifices here—later she might follow someone, if their minds connected in a positive way. The bartender went into the back room to tell the band it was time to play. They straggled into the tavern with their guitars and a banjo made from the round shell of a sea turtle. When they were tuned and ready, the barkeep got up on the stage and called everyone's attention. He then announced what was about to take place.

Adria got up on the stage to a raucous round of applause and foot stomping—they loved her already. The band began playing and Adria began dancing. She tantalized the men, slowly removing her clothing in time to the music. She smiled. They were coming closer to the stage to see her, and she decided she'd give them something to see. She moved near the edge of the platform, sitting in a chair she brought with her from backstage. She smiled at the men and opened her legs.

The bartender collected the money, and the men lined up. A couple of the women walked out—Adria knew they couldn't take the competition. One man also rose to leave. He may only like other men, she thought. Too bad, he'd never realize he was passing up on the opportunity to couple with a Goddess.

She smiled at the first man who mounted her. How he glowed! She really wanted to taste his blood, but she restrained herself. She rose to meet him, allowing him to ride her with enthusiasm, making the appropriate comments or gasps at the right times. When the man finished, he actually thought she'd climaxed with him. Men were such fools, she decided, predictable fools. Then she took the next man and the next and the next.

It was dark by the time she'd exhausted herself. Sweat covered her body, and inside of her she carried the divine essence of at least twenty-five men. The bartender was impressed. He willingly gave over her rightful share, offering to allow her to come back the next day. Then he asked if she might do him a personal favor. She dropped to her knees, and unbuttoned his trousers. Men were so easy.

Back in her tent, Adria counted her money. She'd made quite a lot today. She decided she'd go back the next day. She wanted more money and she had to make sure her divine essence was maintained to protect her against that vile Lyria's curse. She sat back, taking a deep breath—life was good! Too bad her young friends had left. They just seemed to be gone, leaving their things behind. *My friends were very thoughtful*, Adria said to herself. *They must have come to the city just to set up the tents for me!* She was happy to have such loyal friends.

Though she'd washed at the tavern, she returned again to the river. She had to maintain her cleanliness now that she was getting naked in public again. How the men loved her! They had no idea she was stealing their divinity. She bathed carefully, returning to her tent for the night. Tomorrow she'd get an earlier start. If she used twenty men in the morning, she could take a lunch break and be back on the stage in the evening to do another twenty. In a couple of days, she could go clothes shopping. She was looking forward to that.

* * * *

"I've read your interviews, Miss Cushing. There's no way I'm talking to you."

"But Mister Hancock," she said in a reasoning voice, "it might be better to tell me what you know. That way I can avoid using your name and I can make it look as though the information came from somewhere else—an overly talkative priest, for instance. You'll remain innocent of any wrongdoing. You'll continue to be the president of this bank."

"No."

"Mister Hancock, as it stands now, if the courts call you to testify—and after they read tomorrow's paper, they will—they'll take your books and question your employees. You may not be willing to talk to stay out of prison, but I'm certain some of your co-workers will not be so willing to protect the Cathedral."

She pulled a printer's copy of tomorrow's front page from her handbag, unfolded it and spread it out on the desk. The man read the first few lines and blanched.

"Where did you get this information?"

"It shouldn't matter where it came from, but where the information is going."

Richard Hancock looked again at the test sheet for the next day's front page. He sighed, looked into Sharrone's eyes, and said, "If I talk to you, you must promise to make it look like you got the information somewhere else—I have a wife and daughter."

"Really? How old is your daughter?"

The man smiled, taking a framed photograph from his desk and handing it to Sharrone. She looked at the family photo.

"My daughter is eleven, Miss Cushing."

She looked hard into his eyes. "What would you do if she were kidnapped tonight? Taken from her bed? What lengths would you go to, if you knew where she was—knew that she was going to be gang raped and forcefully addicted to drugs to serve out the rest of her short life as a girl for sale to any man who wished to have her?"

"Very well," Hancock sighed, "I'll help you."

* * * *

An hour later she was back in the steam-car that Dan had kept running at the curb. She flashed a sheaf of papers from her purse with a grin.

"We have them," she said. "Names of priests who deposited money, dates of transactions, amounts—everything."

He pulled from the curb, heading toward the newspaper office.

"But is there anything to link this money to the prostitution?"

"Not directly," she admitted, "but it'll look damn suspicious, considering that the Cathedral has a separate account of daily church transactions in the very same bank. If these transactions were not something they wished to hide, why not just put it in the regular account?"

Dan realized that innuendo could go a long way considering the circumstances.

"We have to find a way to make it look like this documentation came from a priest or someone in the finance department of the Cathedral to keep Mr. Hancock in the clear— that was the deal."

"I don't like it," Dan stated, "but I'll go along with it. Do you have a stool pigeon in mind?"

She grinned at him, reaching over suddenly to give him a kiss.

"As a matter of fact," she said, "I do. There's an accountant close to the Bishop whose name is listed several times in these documents. What we'll do is say he had a change of heart after reading our articles about the abuse of women and young girls and he gave this to us."

She patted her purse, smiling.

"Won't that make him a target for Cathedral assassins?"

Sharrone looked at Daniel very seriously. "Two of the women I interviewed named him as among their first rapes for pay. Apparently he doesn't like women, though he is married. He only likes to force himself on girls not yet grown to womanhood. But still, I wonder about his wife…"

"Ask Tom—he has connections, he should be able to find out," Daniel replied.

CATHEDRAL CONNECTION
TO CHILD PROSTITUTION!

Tom read the test page with a critical eye. There'd be no room for errors with a story as explosive as this one.

"Tell me again how you managed to get this Gilroy MacPhearson to give you these documents?"

"We went to the bank as you ordered, sir," Sharrone said. "Mister Hancock said he knew nothing of this matter and frankly, I believed him. So I was wondering, if he didn't know about it, who would?"

"We talked it over, sir," Daniel put in, "she asked Mister Hancock if he knew of anyone living in the city who might know."

"And you were there and heard this?"

"Well, no, sir," Daniel confessed. "It's what she told me when she got back into the steam-car."

"I have a question," Sharrone said. "The man is married—what about his wife? Does she live with him?"

"I'll check it out," Tom said, "if it turns out he's divorced or a widower, we'll just run with the story, otherwise we'll have to make other plans."

Sharrone nodded.

"Your story sounds a bit contrived to me," Tom said, "but we know what's going on, so your story's at least probable. I can live with that."

He reached for his phone and asked to be connected to the press-room. As Sharrone and Daniel were leaving the office, Tom was on the phone to one of his informants.

"Yes, that is correct, Gilroy MacPhearson. I see. Thank you very much."

Tom called Daniel and Sharrone back to his desk, and said, "My connections indicate that he's living alone now—his wife left him several months ago."

Sharrone and Dan smiled at each other—there'd be no innocents in the house should the Cathedral come calling. They walked out hand in hand, happy that they were able to make a difference. Either way, the man would get what he deserved. Tom called the pressroom and told them to run the edition. It'd hit the streets in the morning.

* * * *

"That traitorous bastard!" Father Woods was practically foaming at the mouth with rage. He looked at Father Anderson, spitting out his words.

"This man must be silenced immediately! If they call him to court, he cannot be alive to testify. At best, they'll then have documents of unsure origin, which the court will disallow. But we need to do it now."

"I can take care of that," the old priest said with a smile. "This is one of the things I do best. I'm thinking another note and suicide like the bus driver."

"However you do it, make it happen immediately."

"Consider him already dead," the priest said.

Father Anderson left the Bishop's office, returning to his own. From there he made several phone calls to his operatives. There were four new men he wished to initiate, and this operation would be perfect for them. The plan was already in motion ten minutes from inception. By the Redeemed God, he loved his work!

"What if he's not there? He might've seen the paper already."

The man driving the black steam-car glanced at his partner and just shrugged.

"Wouldn't the paper have put him in protective custody, all things considered?"

"Look," his companion said, "I don't know any more than you. All I know is that we're to kill one Mister Gilroy MacPhearson quietly and quickly."

His assistant nodded, checking his Mauser 96 one more time.

"You checked that damn thing three times now," the driver said with humor. "Put it away before you accidentally shoot yourself, or much worse, shoot me!"

The man laughed, watching the street signs carefully.

"There it is," he said, nodding to a small white clapboard home. They turned into the driveway just as the front door opened.

"That's him," the driver said, "he just picked up the paper—let's move!"

* * * *

Gilroy opened the newspaper and began reading as he reentered his home.

"Anything exciting in the paper, honey?"

"No...nothing important," he said.

He heard the car stop in the drive, turned to see two men exiting the auto. He hurried to his bedroom, opened the bureau drawer and retrieved his Mauser pistol. Turning to his wife he said, "Run, honey! Run out the back door now!"

"Why?"

She looked at him with a frightened expression.

"I think those two men are here to kill me, Molly! If you're here, they'll kill you as well. Run!"

The woman ran to the back door just as it was kicked in. The second team of assassins had come over the fence into the backyard. One of the men shoved Gilroy's wife roughly back into the living room. Gilroy was ready—he opened fire, killing one intruder instantly, slightly wounded the other. Hearing gunfire within, the first team threw caution to the wind, kicking in the front door. They raised their pistols, firing simultaneously. Gilroy slumped to the floor, dead before he reached his final destination. The assassins quickly closed the door.

Gilroy's wife was attractive and much younger than he'd been. They decided they might as well entertain themselves before they killed her. One of the men pushed her roughly to her knees, yanking up her skirts.

"This is how they do this in prison, Molly, my dear," the man laughed. "Your husband wouldn't have liked it, let's see if you do!"

She screamed, but one of the other assassins quickly gagged the struggling woman. They took her in every possible way before hanging her, bound, from the top railing of the banister in the living room. With the rope secured, they slowly lowered her until the rope was taut. Then they sat calmly in comfortable chairs, joking, drinking Gilroy's liquor, and making bets on how long it would take her to slowly strangle. Her feet were drumming against the wall below the steps—her toes just barely touching the floor. As long as strength remained, and she stayed up on her toes, she could breathe—a little. She was making gagging noises now. The men knew that was to be expected.

They were still sitting, waiting for that one last foot to stop twitching, betting cash lying on the table in front of them, when they heard the steam whistles. Someone must've called the police! They needed to leave immediately! One of the men reached out, yanking savagely on the strangling woman's legs. It took three tries to finally break her neck and end her suffering—actually, to end her possibility of identifying any of them. One of the men went to the body of their companion.

"There's no time," another said, "we need to leave now!"

As they walked past Gilroy's silent form, one of them shot him again through the head just for good measure. Their cars were already a block from the house by the time the police arrived.

CHAPTER 20

"What in the name of the Redeemed God were they thinking?"

Father Woods couldn't believe what he was being told by Father Anderson.

"Gunfire, torture, rape? Why didn't they just kill the neighbors as well? Your men even left one of their own dead on the floor!"

Father Anderson was just as concerned as Father Woods, more so in fact. The problem originated with his men! He shook his head.

"What are we to do? The story will be in the paper tomorrow, so will the murders of Gilroy and his wife," Father Woods said, now in a pleading tone.

Everything was falling apart. He'd thought himself a better man than the Bishop—he hoped to take charge one day. He could see his ambitions fluttering out the window like a sparrow released from its cage.

"We have one possible solution," Father Anderson said. "It's drastic, but I believe it'll work."

"For the sake of the Redeemed God, tell me!"

"From our studies of ancient texts, we learned of a process the city builders used ages ago to facilitate the healing of minds. We can use that same process to destroy minds."

"Continue," Father Woods urged.

"We can take two of the remaining assassins and hypnotize them. We know we can exert tremendous control using this process. We'll convince the men that they're deranged, that they broke into the home at random, committing the acts out of lust for the woman and fun for the rest."

"Fun?"

"Yes! Don't you see? They're insane! We see to it that the police find them and corner them—that part is easy. Next, we allow them to converse with the police, telling them what they did and why. They'll insist they won't be taken alive. When they begin shooting, the coppers will do our work for us."

Father Woods thought about this. It would make the best of a very bad situation. Still, this story would stretch credibility to the limit. He mentioned his doubts to Father Anderson.

"The facts will be right there," the priest said with confidence. "The police and the newspaper will have the guns, the bodies, and the shouted confessions of two very deranged men. Furthermore, he added with a grin, they'll find the woman's underwear, appropriately stained. Credible or not, the facts will be hard to argue."

"How did you manage to get her panties?"

"Very simply," the spy priest said. "The first officer at the scene was one Sergeant Jinks. He snagged the panties just before the other officers entered. He has a wily sense about him, I must say. He'd have made a good spy!"

"Very well," Father Woods said, "use the hypnosis. Make it happen."

CATHEDRAL CHILD PROSTITUTION CONFIRMED!

Tom read the headline. *Yes,* he thought, *it might be a little lacking in actual facts. Still, the court of public opinion would fill in the blanks.* He had three reporters standing by for quick deployment that evening, just in case.

The news delivery trucks were rolling when the report came into his office by telephone of a police standoff in a seedy part of town. What his reporter told him was that the men who tortured and killed Gilroy and his wife were cornered.

"You stay on that, young man," Tom said, "and I'll give you the exclusive byline. By the way, how did you come to find out about this?"

"Pure chance," the man said, "I was sitting in a café with a policeman who happens to be my cousin—he's on the police strike force. He gets called whenever there's an armed person hiding in a building or someone with hostages. We were having breakfast when the waiter came to our table and said there was a phone call. When my cousin retuned, he said we needed to roll," the man laughed. "I got a police escort right to the scene, steam whistle and all!"

Tom laughed. "I see! Keep me apprised of the situation."

"I shall, sir," the young man answered.

Just then in the background, Tom heard a volley of gunfire, followed by many more shots and his reporter hung up the phone. He waited anxiously for the next call. He'd told the pressroom to be prepared for a possible extra edition earlier in the afternoon. Then, ten minutes later, his phone rang again.

"Yes?"

"It's all over," the reporter said, "both of them are dead. They killed a police officer before they were gunned down."

"Is your cousin all right?"

The young reporter was impressed; the first question Mr. Leatham asked was about the welfare of his cousin rather than the 'scoop.' He was glad he had chosen this paper when he graduated from journalism school.

"He's fine, sir, and thanks for asking!"

"Did you hear anything regarding the criminals?"

"The police tried to talk them out of the house, telling them to come peacefully. The police knew they were the men who killed MacPhearson and his wife."

"Anything else?"

"Yes, sir. My cousin said they found what they believe to be the wife's…panties laying on the dining room table—right in the middle like it was some kind of centerpiece. He said there were some bloodstains on them, and quite a bit of what appeared to be semen, sir."

"Bring the story home, son," Tom said. "You did well. You write the story."

"Thank you, sir," the young man said with enthusiasm.

"Damn," Tom said to himself, "this means there can be no criminal investigation, but there can still be the news story."

What a coincidence, though, he thought. Who would think random mad killers would choose that exact home, the very day after he 'confessed' to the newspaper? Surely his readers would wonder the same thing.

At that moment, the door to his office crashed open. Sharrone stormed in, standing in front of his desk, fists on her hips.

"The wife was there!" she shouted angrily. "I saw the report—that poor woman was gang raped and hung! You said there was no wife in the picture!"

"My informant told me MacPhearson's wife had left him. I guess he was wrong."

"You guess he was wrong? And that's just the end of it then?"

"Look, Miss Cushing," Tom said, "all of our information cannot be right all the time. And remember, you're the one who picked him."

She looked at him startled.

"Oh come on, Miss Cushing," he said, "I've been a newsman for thirty years. I can spot a made up story! That means simply that if I am somehow to blame, you are more so—you're the one who directed the killers to his house! Now get out and let me get some work done. Come back when you have another story."

Sharrone turned and left Tom's office. He glanced up as she was leaving. She didn't slam the door. He sighed. Everyone knew that a paper ran on news—no news, no paper. She wrote up factual information and attributed it to someone she disliked. He got wrong information from his informant. They both got what they wanted, in a way. She got to know a child rapist was dead, and he got an even bigger story of multiple murders. That was just the way things worked.

* * * *

Adria awoke refreshed. Though she sorely missed her young friends, it was nice and quiet in the park in the early morning with no one else around. She arose, stretched and yawned. She'd bathe in the river and then go to the tavern to make more money. She wondered briefly why she'd not had her "monthly visitation," as the girls in the tribe called it, last month. She dismissed the thought; surely it was because the scorpion spirit was keeping it away so she could make more money more quickly. It was amazing, really, how everything seemed to go her way all the time.

Once she bathed, she returned to her tent to dress. After, giving herself her heroin and mescaline injections, and looking at her arms, she realized that the scars from the needle were becoming obvious. She should find another injection site. She heard that some inject between their toes. She'd try that in the morning. For now, she needed to get to the tavern. Depending on how much she made today, she might go clothes shopping tomorrow. She could find some nice costumes the men would like—ones that didn't cover very much and came off easily. She laughed at her joke.

She walked down the street toward the tavern. Occasionally, a man by himself would pause to look at her. She was pleased that men found her attractive. She wondered about her betrothed, Father Woods. Why had he not taken her when she was pretending to be under the control of the Cathedral? Did he not love her anymore? No, that couldn't be, he was an important and very rich man—probably his many duties kept him away. Someday she'd figure out a way to go back to him. She was confident that would happen sooner or later. She was daydreaming about Father Woods when she reached the tavern and she almost walked right past.

It was only about eight in the morning, so there were not many people inside. She found the bartender wiping the bar with a wet rag. He smiled at her. He'd made some money yesterday and was a happy man.

"Hello, Adria," he said, "going to put on a show for us today?"

"I am hoping to do just that," she said, again silently cursing herself for telling him her real name. "Tomorrow I want to go out and buy clothes. I know where I can buy some really cute costumes that will drive your customers crazy."

The bartender laughed. "Usually crazy customers are well paying customers. I had two men yesterday asking if you'd be back again. They liked what you gave them."

She smiled coyly at the man. "Did you like what I gave you yesterday as well?"

"Oh yes," he said enthusiastically, "I was wondering, since we're not real busy right now, if I might avail myself of your services."

Adria looked into his eyes, grinned, and touched herself.

"Would you like me to come behind the bar and do you right there?"

"I think the back room might be better," he said.

"Why?"

"Um…more privacy!"

"The men didn't need privacy yesterday as they fucked me on the stage."

"That was quite a spectacle, I must say. I never saw a show like you put on."

Adria walked slowly around the bar, closing in on the bartender.

"You know," she whispered in his ear, "the idea you might get caught might make it more fun for you."

He licked his lips—he wanted her.

"Very well," he said with a laugh, "do with me what you will."

She lowered herself to her knees, slowly opening his trousers one button at a time. She could tell he was almost ready to finish before she even began. That was good, she thought, since he wasn't paying her.

Afterward, Adria stood, letting the man see her licking her lips.

"I like to have all of it," she said with a sly wink.

"I believe that's what you got, too," he said with a smile.

The bartender went into the back room to see if his band was ready for the day's work. The drummer hadn't shown up today. That was two days in a row he was late. Still, it was early so he was inclined to forgive. While musicians were commonplace, musicians who could get along with each other were not.

The musicians slouched out of the back room to the area by the stage where their instruments lay. By the time they were tuned up, another dozen men had come in for morning drinks. *For some of them, the early morning drink was an all day drink—at least they spent money all day*, the barkeep thought.

Adria wandered through the bar, talking and laughing with the men. She felt a hand on her backside here, a touch on her leg there. She knew the men were working up the courage to proposition her. One man was very well dressed. Not a common occurrence in this part of town. She made her way over to where he was sitting. He looked up at her and smiled. She smiled back, and then sat in his lap facing him. She took his hand, placing it on her breast as she leaned forward, kissing him roughly. He was just about to get the bodice of her dress open, when she suddenly stood. She shook a finger at him in a disapproving manner.

"Ah ah! If you want me, you have to take me."

With that, she turned and ran toward the stage. She leaped the three feet to the raised platform, landing in a crouched position. She turned, looking over her shoulder into the room. Every man was watching her. As she stood, she saw several of the men rise, coming closer to the stage. She winked at the well-dressed man, turned, and walked to the bed that was on the stage. She was glad for the bed—the floor of the stage had hurt her back yesterday. By the time she'd undressed to her underwear, the first man had given the barkeep his money and he was on the stage with her.

"Would you leave those on?"

"I believe we've met before, sir," she said with a smile, pulling him down to her.

It was the start of another day.

CHAPTER 21

The young reporter returned quickly to the newspaper. A police car pulled to the curb, and he stepped out, thanking the driver—his cousin. He ran up the steps into the building. Tom met him just inside the front door, shouting, "Go! Get your story written, and bring it directly to me. Do it quickly."

The young man nodded, taking off for the pressroom at a run. Tom watched him go with a smile. He returned to his office where he sat at his desk, drumming a pencil against the blotter.

A half hour later, there was a knock on his door.

"Come."

The door opened and the young reporter came in, handing two typed pages to Tom. Tom nodded to a chair by the door. The young man sat, apprehensively awaiting the verdict on his writing. Tom was impressed—this fellow was good. He couldn't even find a misspelled word. He glanced at the byline.

"Well, Roger," he said with a smile, "I like it. Take it to the type room and get it run up immediately. We're running a special short edition this afternoon—your story will be the front page."

Roger Larsen ran to the linotype room, a grin on his face, he'd finally made it!

HIRED ASSASSINS OR MADMEN?

The special edition hit the streets at two in the afternoon, newsboys shouting the headline in shrill voices, and by five in the evening most of the editions had been sold. By six, the word was spreading quickly through the community. Tom asked Roger and two other reporters to be on standby this evening; he could feel the tension in the city and knew something was going to happen.

* * * *

Father Woods didn't know about the special edition of the paper. He and the rest of the priests were still holed up behind the massive stone walls of the Cathedral. The priest sat at his desk. *What a mess*, he thought. How could Father Anderson's killers bungle the job so badly? It should've been an easy hit—in and out, one man suddenly vanished. He shook his head, his anger building once again. *Maybe they should just burn down the newspaper office,* he thought, *that'd fix 'em!* But no, that would be a bad idea. He wouldn't bungle the confidence the Bishop had placed in him.

The Bishop...why did he have to get involved in this adventuring in the far south anyway? Things had been going smoothly here; the Cathedral was doing well on the donations of its members. Now, membership was dropping, and along with it, donations. If this stupid idea of building cities in Green Hell for the faithful to flee to hadn't happened, the Cathedral wouldn't have gotten involved in stealing children from the tribes or from unwilling church members, or even non-members. Enough of the faithful willingly handed over their young girls to the Cathedral to learn humility and respect. The priests never seemed to run out of young girls to 'educate' in the ways of men and to save their souls. But no! Now, with this crisis going on, the very leader of the church wasn't even present. Again, Father Woods shook his head in disgust.

* * * *

At seven that evening, two student priests left the Cathedral grounds. They were young, and they wanted women for the night. They'd not seen the new edition of the paper either. They rounded the corner, stepping into the corner tavern, which they considered to be their hangout. Many of the younger priests came here to "hunt ass" as they liked to put it. They carried the smugness of certain redemption, and the invincibility of youth. They sat at a table near the door, looking over the women as they came and went. One tugged at his tight collar, then froze. He nudged his companion, nodding toward the bar.

Three women were staring at them. They looked at each other. Sure, they wordlessly decided, they could do three women. One got up and approached the bar. He began talking to the women. He disliked the fact that they didn't lower their heads. Also, they seemed educated and knowledgeable. That was no way for women to behave. Perhaps he and his friend could teach them some humility as well as take pleasure from them.

The women looked at each other, nodded, and walked with the

student priest to the table. There were introductions, and then the five of them walked out together. They got as far as the alley adjacent to the next apartment building.

* * * *

The shrill whistling of police cars disrupted the evening calm. The cars passed the corner tavern, coming to a screeching halt less than half a block away. Patrons walked out into the street and down toward the confusion. By the time they got there, a small crowd was already gathered. Some of them pushed through the crowd to see—some of them wished they hadn't.

In the alley, two men lay writhing in agony. They were no longer gagged, but they could make only incoherent sounds. The cobblestones of the alley were bright with blood. The two men, obviously priests based upon their clothing, moaned and screamed. In the near distance, another emergency vehicle whistle could be heard approaching—an ambulance, no doubt. The crowd looked on as two policemen tried to comfort the men as they waited for the ambulance.

The bystanders saw that both men had been stripped naked. Their clothing was neatly folded and stacked by the wall. If one looked carefully, the white collar of a priest of the Cathedral could be seen peeking out from the middle of the folded black garments. They also saw that both men had been roughly castrated—well, that wasn't exactly what'd happened to them. In actuality, their entire sexual apparatus had been removed. The bloody organs lay atop their neatly folded clothing.

After they'd been mutilated sexually, their attacker hadn't been finished with them. They each bore knife wounds on their chests. Some of the spectators strained to read the words the cutting displayed. "No"...that was the first word..."No baby rape." That was it. The second man was also carved up..."Goddess"...yes, that was right—the bleeding made it hard to make out..."Goddess Revenge" was the second cryptic message.

Then the ambulance arrived and the two men were whisked away to the hospital. Their organs were transported as well, for sanitary disposal.

"All right, all right," a policeman shouted at the crowd, "there's nothing to see here, move along please."

The crowd slowly dispersed; the show was over, anyway. Many walked back to the tavern—there was no in point letting this interfere with their drinking!

Back in the tavern, three pretty young women were sitting together at the bar. They were toasting each other, laughing. A man walked up, thinking to proposition one of them. He stood casually at the bar, listening to their conversation. He walked away. These women weren't anyone he wanted to be near. They were discussing the cutting up of the priests almost as if they'd done it themselves. Where was the younger generation going, he wondered?

* * * *

Adria arrived home tired and sore. Some of her clients had been rough tonight. How she'd wanted to slaughter them. As she counted out her coins, she realized she made a fair amount of money today. A number of her clients had ridden her the day before as well. She was developing a following again. She thought about the arrangement.

Suddenly a realization struck her. Of course! How could she be so blind? Now she knew how it worked—the last man each evening was the last so she could follow him. The last man was offering himself. She'd been worried that the curse would get stronger without the necessary blood to keep it at bay. She thought about it with relish.

She left her tent, venturing back into the city. She needed more heroin. She needed to find her dealer. She wasn't worried; he'd be where he always was. She turned the corner, and she saw him, standing in his spot right by the alley. She approached him with a smile.

Something was wrong. That wasn't her supplier. It was that man...Kel was his name—the man who stole her life from her. She hissed in anger, pulling her knife from its sheath. When she looked up, Kel was gone and the familiar face of her friendly local drug dealer was looking at her once more. She relaxed, allowing the dagger to slip back into its sheath. She walked up to him quickly.

"Hey, girl," he greeted her, a bit nervously, "I haven't seen you for a while, where you been? I was thinking you might have started being unfaithful."

Adria laughed at his joke—as if anyone was faithful to anybody but themselves!

"I've been around," she answered, "I ran into some of the stuff I like in an old warehouse and have been using that."

"Wow, girl," he answered, "that could be mighty dangerous—who knows what might've been mixed in with it."

Adria hadn't thought of that.

"So you want the usual?"

"What else," she answered.

After she handed over the money and received the parcel of narcotics, the dealer put his hand on her arm to stop her from walking away.

"You know the coppers are looking for you?"

"Yeah, I guess," she answered unconcernedly.

"They talked to me, girl," he warned, "they know I sell you your stuff. They told me I should call them if you showed up again."

"And?"

"And they offered me a reward," he said looking calmly at the young woman.

Adria pulled the man into the alley behind the trash bin, and asked, "Can they give you this?" She quickly opened his trousers and began rubbing him. She looked up into his eyes, tauntingly. He smiled. Obviously the bitch had no clue he'd tried to give her over to the police.

"You like that, don't you," she said in a low, purring voice. "I can just feel it."

They laughed. Now she was kissing him, biting him. She shoved him against the wall roughly, and dropped to her knees...

They returned to the entryway of the alley. The dealer was still adjusting his clothing. While she'd done a very good job, she'd actually bitten him—right on his...he winced at the sudden stab of pain. He knew he'd be sore for a few days. He made up his mind not to do that again, she was just too dangerous. He didn't want to end up like those two priests in the alley about a mile from here. When one of his customers told him what happened, he laughed it off.

Now, he wondered if perhaps this strange woman, who everyone was looking for, had mutilated the two priests. It might be safer, he thought, to turn her in. Perhaps he could auction his information between the police and the priesthood. If she'd done that to the two priests, they'd pay handsomely to get their hands on her. He made up his mind to follow her the next time they connected—if he knew where she lived, he'd have some real bargaining power. But then another eager customer, cash in hand, needing to have all of his dreams fulfilled, interrupted his reverie.

* * * *

The story of the assault on the two priests made page one the next morning—there were some angry phone calls regarding an editorial Tom wrote suggesting the priests had it coming. He actually thought there would be more complaints than there were. Perhaps that was an indication the tide was finally turning against the priests and their destructive religion. Tom decided to stay late in his office in case any more news came in regarding the assault. So far it seemed the police had no hint as to who the attackers were. The priests had been under anesthetic for a time, but when they awoke, they said it was three women who attacked them. Tom snickered; somehow that seemed appropriate.

CHAPTER 22

Three priests were traveling into the city to collect money from some of the Cathedral's prostitutes. All three were armed; after last night's attack they'd be careful. It was late, but still daylight. If someone approached them, they'd at least have forewarning. Imagine—women attacking priests. It merely demonstrated how inferior women really were. They were approaching the entryway to the apartment building where eighteen of their hookers lived.

They looked around carefully before entering the building. There were some pedestrians on the street, but nobody was close to them or seemed to be paying any attention to them. The first man pushed open the heavy door and they entered. Once inside, they removed their hands from their pockets, allowing the pistols to fall from their hands. They moved quickly to the lift, riding to the eleventh level. Prostitutes occupied seven of the ten apartments on this floor. By making them live together, the expense was less.

They moved quickly from room to room, the money was waiting for them as it usually was. There were two types of women, the priests believed; the unredeemable women who refused to bow before the Redeemed God who would burn in Hell, and the women who would eventually, through servitude, save their inferior souls.

The prostitutes they also divided into two groups. There were the loyal servants of the Cathedral who'd never think of keeping any of the money they brought in, and the less sincere women who served at the beck and call of heroin. They'd not keep money either; they knew better. Their lives on earth would be a mere foretaste of Hell as they struggled through the days without the drug they so desperately needed. After days of withdrawal, the priests would again begin their injections—it was counterproductive to actually allow them to completely clear the narcotic from their systems.

In the last room, two women lived together. The money was in the church-provided box with an image of the Redeemed God on the lid. They counted it. The amount seemed right, so they only did a cursory search of the apartment. No hidden money was found in any of the rooms that night. The priests then stayed, rather than returning to the Cathedral immediately. They decided to do the younger of the hookers.

In an hour, they were finished. They'd all used her in different ways, so their bodily juices wouldn't mingle as it would if they'd all taken her in the common way. Satisfied, they turned, and left the apartment. They were feeling pretty good, all things considered. The woman was a willing servant; she serviced each of them eagerly, and the other one was made to watch.

They walked out of the lift, heading toward the door, discussing what they'd eat now that the business part of the evening had been accomplished. They weren't paying close attention as they left the building, so they didn't notice the three women walking toward them on the sidewalk.

The older priest was the first to see the women. By then there was a mere eight feet between them. He panicked, shrieked incoherently, and pulled his .32 caliber Mauser Model 1914 from his pocket, and opened fire. In two heartbeats, all eight rounds had found their marks.

Two of the women fell instantly dead, shot through the heart and lungs. The third was hit in the forehead with a round that didn't penetrate but rather coursed around the contour of the woman's head tearing a long ugly gash before expending itself on the stone face of the building behind her. Stunned, she dropped to her knees. Her shopping bag spilled open pouring out various fruits, which scattered along the sidewalk and rolled into the gutter. She collapsed next to her two dead friends.

The silence after the pistol's reports could almost be felt. The two younger priests stood in shocked immobility. The man who fired the gun stared in disbelief at the carnage he'd wrought. His mouth was dry; it felt as though he hadn't had a drink in days. He looked down at his hand, still holding the warm pistol—it was shaking.

People were running toward them from all directions. He slid the pistol back into his pocket and attempted to walk away. A bystander grabbed him by the shoulders. He reached into his pocket again in fear, not remembering his pistol was empty. The man swung on him, knocking him to the ground. In the distance but approaching quickly, the distinctive steam whistle of a police car could be heard.

PRIEST OF THE CATHEDRAL MURDERS TWO WOMEN
A third woman was shot but will recover. Priest arrested.

The headline summed it up. The story that followed explained how three priests with pockets full of cash were seen leaving an apartment building known as a residence for prostitutes. Once on the street, panicked by the mutilations committed the day before, one of the priests gunned down three innocent women who had been grocery shopping. The dead included a fifty-year-old woman and another who was almost sixty-five. The third woman, lucky to be alive, was twenty. She was to be married in a week. The bullet tore savagely through her forehead and scalp. It took thirty-two sutures to close the wound—she'd be scarred for life.

* * * *

Adria felt somehow heavy; it was difficult to get out of the chair in which she was sitting. The knocking at the front door was incessant—loud. She moved slowly. What was wrong with her? She turned the knob and the door swung open. A woman was facing her—a woman who was pointing with her left hand at Adria's stomach. She was laughing! Lyria! The witch who'd tormented her in her previous life!

She took a step back as the woman at the door opened her hand, showing Adria her palm. There was blood! She laughed again, passing her right hand over her left. When her hand had passed, the blood was gone. Then, still laughing, she made a tossing gesture in Adria's direction. Adria felt something strike her in the stomach. Looking down she was shocked to see her belly distended so far she couldn't even see her feet! She knew she was with child. Lyria just kept pointing and laughing...

* * * *

Adria awoke bathed in sweat. *So that's what's been happening,* she thought. The scorpion was buzzing furiously in her brain, helping her to see the truth at last—she'd been mistaken all this time! The killing, the blood, all of it was unnecessary. She'd mistaken the omens—that was obvious now. The dried blood in the witch's hand wasn't a sign that her blood was drying up and needed to be replaced—no, it really referred to her monthly flow.

The witch…what was her name? Oh, yes…Lyria. She made the blood dry up—she stopped her monthly visitation. That had to be why she missed it last month and was already late this month. Well, she thought, she could fix that little problem. In the tribes she'd heard of an herb used sometimes by women who no longer wished to be pregnant. What was it called…oh, yes, Pennyroyal. She breathed a sigh of relief. Tomorrow when the apothecary opened, she'd simply buy some and brew the tea—that'd solve the problem once and for all. She laughed. She was smarter than any witch!

Adria went to the river to bathe at dawn. The water was cold but she liked it that way—it was more like home. As she sat in the river, she struck her stomach several times in a vain attempt to hurt the parasite indwelling her body, draining her life force and her divinity. She scrubbed furiously; she wanted to be clean for her work at the tavern later.

She dressed in her ragged clothing. She really needed to buy some clothes one of these days. That could wait, however. She combed her hair with a comb that her thoughtful friends had left for her. She ate the last of the bread from the night before and turned toward the city.

As she made her way along the dark, early morning streets, she thought about her fate. She knew the police were hunting her, though even with a drawing, they hadn't identified her, so far. But that was at night, she reminded herself. To be on the safe side, she decided that when she bought the Pennyroyal, she'd also buy some of the liquid the city women used to change the color of their hair. She could no longer be a blonde, as she would more likely be identified. She needed to dye her hair dark. *Why stay the same all the time?*

The apothecary was just opening when she arrived. The proprietor retrieved the Pennyroyal from a high shelf, setting it on the counter.

"You must be careful with this," he cautioned, "too much can kill you."

"Nothing can kill me," Adria responded.

The druggist just shook his head as he walked away, returning in a moment with the hair coloring. Adria asked him how to use it, and he read the label to her. She nodded, paid, and walked out.

There was a clothing shop two doors down, and she tarried a moment looking in the windows at the nice, clean clothing. She decided that would have to wait. Right now there was an alien being eating at her from the inside and it had to die as quickly as possible. The druggist suggested three cups of tea a day for three days. He told her to brew the entire plant to make the tea. He warned about using it to terminate later pregnancies, but Adria didn't consider this pregnancy, or herself to be ordinary.

Back at her camp in the park, Adria began brewing her first tea. She drank it down quickly, and then sat back. She knew it wouldn't work right away, but she hoped for that anyway. In the early afternoon, she drank another cup and was preparing to leave for the tavern, when she felt a wave of nausea wash over her. She sat back down. The nausea passed, but she didn't feel well and decided to stay in her camp.

In the evening, she drank a third cup. The nausea returned more strongly an hour later. She fought to keep down the food that she'd just eaten. The nausea passed again and Adria slept. She'd been told of this effect. She didn't care though—she just wanted her own blood flow to return, and with it that killer lurking inside her would be flooded away.

The second day Adria again spent at home. She was desperate to make more money and she needed new clothing and a costume or two if she was to keep attracting the men in the taverns. The nausea was bad that day, so she opted to stay at home, taking care of herself. She checked repeatedly, but there was no indication of blood—the apothecary said it would take at least three days.

She mollified herself with the thought that the creature within her was feeling the effects of the liquid that was slowly killing it. She smiled, glad it was taking a long time—glad the monster would be feeling pain and terror as its life slowly came to an end. With this thought in her mind, she stayed home the third day as well, waiting to venture out until it was almost dark. She knew she could still pick up some money at the tavern tonight.

She bathed, dressed, and looked in the mirror, the dark brown of her hair still startled her, but she'd get used to it. Better that than having the police pick her up. A short time later, she was on her way to the tavern.

She danced on stage to the loud, fast music the band was playing. The patrons were already drunk, so her job would be easy. She slowly peeled off her clothing, revealing tantalizing hints of a breast here, a thigh there. She could see the men were ready for her. The bartender was already taking their money as they lined up to use her. She looked at the line—twenty already.

She beckoned to the first man. This was one of her regulars. The man had ridden her three times since she began working here. She knew what he liked. She pulled the ropes from his jacket pocket, tying his hands together. His feet were next. She straddled him, dancing over his face, lowering herself to almost contact distance—and then quickly pulling away. She sat in his lap, moving herself against the rising hardness. She opened his trousers, and touched him. She looked into his eyes, and said, "I'm going to fuck you now and you can't do a thing about it." She was on him. He didn't last very long; he never did. It was an easy number one.

She finished her third man and was preparing for the fourth when sudden cramps struck her. She gasped, doubling over. The spasms continued, each stronger than the last. She sank to her knees and felt wetness on her thigh.

"Blood! She's bleeding," the man on the stage shouted, recoiling in fear.

He turned back to the barkeep, demanding a refund of his money. Adria didn't hear him. She could only feel pain rocking through her body. Suddenly something let go inside of her, and she fell to the stage, rolling onto her back. She pushed herself up, screaming in pain as the miscarriage happened.

Her baby was ejected from her body and her blood flowed. She grasped the cord in both hands, pulling frantically to rid herself of the afterbirth. She crabbed sideways to distance herself quickly from the parasite—and then darkness overwhelmed her.

CHAPTER 23

Father Woods was beside himself. He'd announced that he would make a public statement on the steps of the Cathedral at noon. Father Anderson and he worked through the morning on the speech, and by eleven-thirty, he felt it was ready. With Father Anderson as an audience, he went through it twice. The rehearsals went smoothly. He had, after all, dealt with the tribes and survived. He rose, and headed down the steps to the front door of the Cathedral.

CATHEDRAL ISSUES STATEMENT
Priest involvement in prostitution and murder discussed.

Father Woods, acting head of the Cathedral in the Bishop's absence, issued a statement today regarding the recent shooting of three women by a priest connected with the Cathedral. In the statement Father Woods stated his surprise and disgust with both the shooting and with the suspected involvement of priests in a prostitution scandal. He disclaimed any knowledge of these issues, saying that he's actively involved with the police in an investigation of the issues.

Father Woods was quoted as saying, "Priests do not walk around armed, and that these three were armed presents a disturbing image of a criminal element involving some priests. Both the police and the Cathedral will investigate that possibility, and if any priests are found to be involved in such activities, the Cathedral will assist the police in bringing the criminals to justice."

At the present time, former Father Lifford, now simply Simon Lifford, the man who shot the three women, is in police custody undergoing questioning. The other two priests, as yet unidentified to us, have been questioned and released as having no involvement in the shooting. At this hour the police are questioning the tenants of the apartment building to see what, if anything, they know about the priests and their reason for being there.

In a related issue, the police as yet have no suspects in the mutilations of two priests four days ago, the only lead being a vague description of three women who carried knives. Police investigator Sergeant Jinks told us that it was possible the attackers were either outlanders or members of another religious faction jealous of the power and prestige of the Cathedral. This newspaper thinks it more likely the attack has something to do with the issues of suspected child rape by priests. The investigation is progressing, and when further information is available, you'll read about it first in the pages of the Los Angeles Journal.

Tom was pleased with the story—it gave a seemingly balanced account of the priest's comments. He imagined that, like the killers of Gilroy MacPhearson and his wife, the Cathedral would give up the priest with the gun and his friends. He hoped that wouldn't be the case, but he was a practical man, and that's what he would do in a similar situation.

The real question was if the women in the apartment building would talk to the police or if they'd help with the cover up. Either way, the bank account was compromised and the funds were no longer available to the priests—that part was at least a victory.

"The women told us nothing," Sergeant Jinks told the group of reporters gathered at the police station two days later.

"They didn't name any priests?"

Jinks shook his head, responding, "They knew no names, only that men dressed as priests would come to collect the money from them. When they were shown a lineup of the three priests picked up at the scene of the shooting, not all were sure that these were the men. Most said they were the pimps or said they thought they recognized them as probably being their pimps."

"So basically we have nothing," one reporter said with disgust.

"Not true," Jinks retorted, "these three priests are named in the bank account in question and two have already confessed that they established a secret group using prostitution to funnel money to the Cathedral. They noted however that all the women involved were over sixteen and therefore were consenting adults, admitting that while prostitution was still illegal, they did this with only the best intentions of the Cathedral at heart."

"And so nothing will be done?"

"Again, not true! The three priests have been barred from the Cathedral and are no longer priests. The man who fired the gun will be prosecuted for murder and assault. Furthermore, the Cathedral has issued a statement that all the money in that account is to be donated to the city orphan homes for their support. Though the money is legally theirs, the Cathedral wants no part of prostitution money."

* * * *

Father Woods was pleased with how the news conference and the investigations were going. Only one priest would be incarcerated, and he deserved it for his stupidity. As for the money in the bank, well, that was only one of their alternate accounts and not the biggest by far. That account would be closed once the city took possession of the money for the orphans. He snickered at that brilliant bit of drama he'd concocted for the press.

While the money would be missed, it was only about a fifth of what they had available at any one time in the bank. Most of the money was already on its way south to pay the construction teams and mercenary armies who were building the Bishop's refuge cities. Maybe he wasn't so far off after all, Father Woods thought—the tide was indeed turning against their righteous and true religion.

Though he hated the thought of running, down in The Green they'd have untouched land for their exclusive use and they could still bring captive girls down from the north to teach them humility and service and thereby save their souls from Hell. In the meantime, it would be a simple matter to turn the girls in the apartment building over to Larry Harper. He knew how to control women and had no obvious connection with the Cathedral.

* * * *

Sharrone was furious. She moved about the house throwing things and slamming doors. Finally Dan captured her in his arms, gently kissing her forehead.

"We've done what we could do," he reasoned. "Your articles will continue to be published. Public sentiment is going against the Bishop and his priests, whether or not what they do seems technically legal. We're winning the fight even if we lose a few battles."

Sharrone heaved a great sigh, slumping in his arms. She put her face to his shoulder and began crying. Then she looked up into Dan's face. She was suddenly determined as she said, "I'm going to find a way to interview the women who cut the priests—they might know something we don't."

"That might be dangerous," Dan said with dismay.

Sharrone laughed. "Life itself is dangerous, Dan. Is it more important to live long and do nothing or risk it all seeking the truth and perhaps justice for these women and young girls who are enslaved by that so-called religion?"

Dan was silent for a moment, and then said, "Perhaps if we run an advertisement in the personal columns, someone who knows someone might help us connect."

Sharrone reached up, put both hands on the back of Dan's head and drew him down to give him a long, searching kiss.

"You're a brilliant man, Dan," she said, pushing tightly up against him.

"Ooh! Not just brilliant but eager as well."

She rubbed herself against him briefly, and then took his hand, leading him to the bedroom. This time she didn't slam the door.

* * * *

Adria awoke. She felt very tired and disoriented. What happened? She opened her eyes slowly, cautiously. She knew she was in a bed—she felt the sheets and the pillow beneath her head. As her vision returned, she realized she was looking up at the ceiling, but this wasn't the tavern. She looked to her left and saw a large glass bottle hanging from a metal bar. The bottle was red.

Instinctively Adria knew this was blood; someone was trying to help her. Someone realized her divinity. She relaxed, closing her eyes. When she next opened her eyes, it was night. The room was dark but she could still see the glass bottle with the blood—it was over half empty. She followed the tube from the bottle to her arm. Now she had doubts. Were they putting blood into her...or taking it out? She felt panic rising. Suddenly there was someone at her side. A woman all in white was bending over her, smiling.

"Well," the woman said, "I'm glad to see you awake, you gave us a scare."

"A scare?"

"We were afraid you were going to die, my dear. You'd lost so much blood, but the transfusions have brought you back. Do you remember anything?"

Adria thought, and remembered. The stage. The cramps. The thing coming out of her body...

"Is it dead?"

The nurse, taken back by Adria's tone said, "Yes, your son is dead. He came much too early to survive."

Adria breathed a sigh of relief. The parasite was gone, dead. The curse that hideous creature Lyria had put on her was over. She smiled at the nurse, and again slipped into sleep.

She awoke refreshed. The bottle of blood was gone, so she must be better now, ready to leave. She recalled the glad news the nurse brought her of that thing's death—she was finally free. Now all she needed to do was get out of this place. It was either dusk or dawn again, so she waited, watching. The light faded—it was dusk. How many days had it been? She had no way of knowing. Voices in the hallway attracted her attention. Someone was talking about her.

"You'll have to wait until at least tomorrow to question her," a woman's voice said, "she's barely conscious."

"We need to question this woman as soon as possible, Miss."

"I'm not a Miss," she retorted, "I'm a nurse. You do your police things and I'll do my nurse things, sir," was her tart response.

"Very well," he answered in a resigned voice, "we'll put a policeman by the door, just in case."

"That's fine," the nurse answered, "come back in the morning and you'll be able to talk with her."

"You're certain she said her name was Adria?"

"For the third time, that's what I was told when she was brought in."

Adria heard footsteps fading down the hall. Then she heard the sound of a chair scraping along the floor—the policeman. She had to get out of here.

When the nurse left her room the next time, Adria arose quietly. She went to the closet, but there were no clothes. She looked down at herself—she couldn't walk around in this odd piece of clothing. *It would be nice on the stage,* she thought, and decided to keep it. She needed something else.

She slipped the cloth belt from around her waist, testing its strength, and then she waited. An hour later, she heard the nurse again outside her room. She was conversing with the policeman. Adria waited, tensely. The door opened. The nurse thought Adria was asleep. When the twisted cloth belt was pulled suddenly around her throat, she didn't even scream—there was no time.

Adria quickly put on the nurse's garments; the fit was almost right. She had no weapon, so she'd have to rely on the scorpion spirit to help her escape. She boldly walked to the door, opened it, and walked right past the drowsing policeman, down the hallway to the main entrance and out of the hospital—returning once again to the darkness of the city.

CHAPTER 24

It was early in the evening when the knock on the door sounded. It was an anxious, repetitive knocking. The Bishop looked up, annoyed. He hated to be disturbed in his study, especially when dusk was falling and his ability to read by natural light was falling with it. *A couple of years ago*, he thought sourly, *I could've read just as well by firelight. Now though, the flickering of the flame makes it hard to see the letters.* He hated thinking about getting old.

"Yes, yes…come in!"

The latch clicked open and the heavy wooden door swung in as two young priests entered. They bowed before the Bishop and then knelt. Both men were sweating—either from their exertion in coming up the flights of steps, or maybe from the heat. The heat was always oppressive this far south—even the Bishop was sweating. He was longing for the cool air that blew from the glacier to the north. How he wanted to go back to the northern Cathedral and leave this hot green land to the people who lived here and seemed to like it. Still, there was that other option…

"Well, speak up!"

The Bishop waited impatiently for a reply.

"It has laid," the first young priest said, looking up, hopeful of seeing interest in the eyes of the Bishop. He'd shown precious little interest in much of anything since his arrival and the priests were worried about him—he was their spiritual leader after all.

The Bishop rose quickly to his feet and shouted, "Have you taken it away from her?"

"Not yet," the second priest said, "we thought you'd want to know immediately."

"Go quickly and use the sleeping gas before that horror accidentally steps on it. When she's asleep, go in and get the thing. We must know if it's viable before…" He didn't need to finish the sentence.

"Yes, Your Eminence! We'll go at once."

Both men rose as though they were attached to one puppeteer's set of strings and hurried out. They forgot to close the Bishop's door.

The Bishop stalked across the room and slammed the door. "Excellent," he whispered to himself. "This means I can be leaving this God forsaken place soon; I've been here too long already."

He mopped his brow with his linen kerchief. "No wonder they named this place Green Hell," he muttered to himself.

He strode back to his chair, sat down, and resumed reading.

He tugged at the tight collar of his robe and muttered, "Whoever thought up these garments for the priesthood must've been sadists."

He grumbled a little, but then he became engrossed in the book he was reading and temporarily forgot the heat, where he was, and what all of this meant.

Both of the young priests, eager to please the Bishop ran down several flights of steps into the foyer of the Cathedral and hurried out the rear door of the building that was hidden behind the altar, a door reserved for the priesthood. No city folk and especially no locals were allowed to see what was on the other side. This was the Cathedral's most closely guarded secret. The doorway backed almost to the edge of the jungle and nobody would dare to venture there. The locals knew the priests had forbidden it, and the people who'd come from the north were scared of being that close to The Green.

It'd been brought into the city at night—so asleep that at first they thought it might have perished. But no, it awoke the next morning full of fight and anger. It was a good thing they made the wooden stockade as strong as they had. The thing battered the tree trunks repeatedly until they had to gas it again.

After a week they worked out how much of the sleeping formula would keep the thing docile, and as calm as something like this could ever be, and still live. The Bishop was concerned that too much of the gas might either kill the thing prematurely or interfere with the rest of the process. He made it very clear he wanted to spend as little time as possible here in the south. Mistakes regarding this…thing wouldn't be tolerated.

* * * *

Both of these young men were with the expedition that captured the thing. The trip was a nightmare expedition up the great river by boat. They'd traveled for hundreds of miles inland being virtually eaten alive by every kind of insect both large and small that infested the great jungle. Finally their native guide told them they were very near to where they wanted to go.

They stopped the ship and dropped its anchor into the murky water. Then they lowered the small rowboats that served both as transportation to shore and as lifeboats should the ship strike a hidden rock and sink. Both priests knew they wouldn't use the lifeboats if that were to happen. Drowning in the river quickly would be preferable to actually making it to the jungle, five hundred miles from civilization. They secured the small boats to one of the many huge trees that grew along the shore. At least docking in a jungle was easy.

About a mile through the trees was a great clearing. The clearing must have been five miles across and was mainly grassland with occasional scrub trees—few large trees grew here. In the center of the clearing was a lake that was about a mile wide and perhaps a bit more in length. No river or stream could be seen coming into the lake. The priests supposed it was fed by an underground water source—probably bubbling up from Hell itself.

Some of the creatures were in the water—others were on the shore or out farther into the grass. This is where the things always came to drink, the guide explained. The priests supposed some also came to relax in the sun, for many were slouched or recumbent—either asleep, or nearly so.

The fool of a guide had been led to believe that the men in the long black clothing just wanted to look at them, maybe even worship them. The deception had been necessary so they could trick the half-humans into leading them here.

The terror the priests had at first seeing them! The guide and a handful of local tribesmen who'd come along with the expedition didn't seem to fear them. Neither of the priests could understand how that could be—just looking at them was to know fear. Perhaps it was because they really thought them gods...

Finally they found one by itself, near the tree line and close to the river. It was the right kind too! They'd been lucky. Come to think of it, they'd been unnaturally lucky on this whole adventure. Either God really wanted them to do this, or He was going to give them a big surprise at the end of it all. Both priests sincerely hoped and wanted to believe it would be the former.

As it had turned out, the shamans, whom the Cathedral spent quite a sum in time, money, and preparation to kidnap, could do nothing—nothing at all. It was disappointing! Despite all their fantastic claims of magical power and supernatural "traveling" abilities, none of them could communicate with any of these things at all. They were able to point out which ones they thought were females, and which ones might be carrying eggs. But that was done by the coloring of the creatures and their gait—not by magic of any kind. Anyone could have done that. The shamans were simply frauds.

The priests were annoyed that the heathen, only half-human tribal shamans had even been brought along on this sacred mission. Imagine—they actually thought women should have equal say in religion and government! Thank the Redeemed God that many women in the Black City knew their place. And the Cathedral saw to it that they stayed in their place—well, the devout ones anyway. That would change too, and soon. Imagine believing that any almighty God would continue to allow the soft, inefficient, deceitful, feminine divinity to reign with Him over the newly created Universe. Ha!

"Well," they'd said smugly to each other after the killings and the subsequent capture, "at least the only ones killed were the half-humans!"

They'd gotten a laugh out of that. Two of the "tribal witch doctors," as the Bishop called them, had been eaten. They undoubtedly deserved it.

Once the thing was gassed, loading it on the boat had been a bit of a problem. The locals wouldn't go near the thing or help them in any way—they claimed it was sacred. Sacred? That thing? Sure, it was big. Sure, it was sort of serpent-like. Sure, it was feathered. But it was just an animal despite the local insistence in referring to it as "The Feathered Serpent," a local divinity that clearly had its origins in long past native sightings of these great beasts. It was merely a tool for the Bishop—a way to wrest permanent control of Los Angeles of the north and the other cities of the west from the hands of non-believers.

Finally, with the crane and counterweight system they'd brought for the purpose, the thing was moved aboard the crystal ship. Large canvas coverings were lashed down over it to hide it from any eyes that might attempt to see what the ship was bringing from the river.

When the ship unmoored with its cargo, two of the Cathedral soldiers gunned down the locals that had come along with them—no sense in having flapping mouths spreading rumors and anger among the locals who considered these things divine. They were only half-humans anyway, so it was a small thing.

Both priests remembered looking into the black waters of the great river when the bodies were cast overboard. The river boiled— like a cauldron of soup. Something in the river...no, many somethings in the river consumed the dead half-humans in less than a minute. The two young priests looked at each other in disbelief. Perhaps they WOULD get in the lifeboats if the large ship came to harm after all. The rest of the long river journey was uneventful, if being eaten by mosquitoes an inch long and other nameless giant insects was considered uneventful, that is.

From the river mouth it had been a short trip through tranquil nighttime waters along the coast to the wharf by the Cathedral. The city had its own wharf, but this was Cathedral business...not city business.

* * * *

Cautiously, the two men approached the enclosure—they knew better than to get too close. A guard made that mistake just yesterday. The soldier here had only been on the job one day—he was a replacement. One of the priests nodded to the young soldier standing guard. The soldier picked up a round copper container with one hand, putting the mask over his face with the other hand.

Scientists discovered ages ago that charcoal would filter out some dangerous chemicals that might be dispersed into the air. As it happened, it worked quite well with the sleeping gas. Another act of God? Coincidence? Neither of the priests knew the answer to that question and, truth be told, they didn't much care. They just wanted to be done with this. They donned the extra masks hanging on a peg near where the soldier was standing.

The canisters of charcoal projected annoyingly out in front of their faces like the snouts of beasts, partly blocking their view through the heavy glass lenses built into the mask. The masks fit tightly and uncomfortably, but it was the animal-like look the masks gave them that they hated most. Fortunately, they didn't have to wear the masks very often.

When the soldier approached the enclosure, they could see the thing move inside. It was huge—too huge to be a living creature in a sane world. But then, sanity was in very short supply in The Green.

There was a huff as it exhaled. It was tired after laying the egg—that was the prize! This creature could never be tamed. It was a mindless, soulless wild thing that had lived too long without the hands of men to guide it. But one straight from the egg could be controlled. It could be taught pain and obedience and fear. The three techniques that made humans easy to manipulate were the same ones that would allow the priests to control this soon to be born "Celestial Dragon." Those three processes—pain, fear, and obedience would allow them to use it for a purpose undreamed of even in the offices of the leaders of the Black City.

The soldier opened the brass valve atop the canister and the white sleeping gas clouded the air inside the enclosure. The thing inside huffed again, then slumped to the floor, closing its eyes. The guard looked nervously at the priests. They nodded and he reluctantly unlocked the gate. This was the small gate for humans, not the big gate they used and then permanently closed once the thing—the "divine celestial dragon"—was inside.

The two priests walked cautiously past the jaws of the sleeping Tyrannosaur. They felt its hot breath against their faces as it exhaled and they gagged—those jaws had eaten MEN! They glanced nervously at each other. Sweat was beginning to fog the lenses of their masks. The heat and fear made them sweat excessively. Once past the head of the creature they picked up the egg. It wasn't as big as they thought it would be—that was a good thing. It meant the beast inside would be small as well, and it would stay smaller longer so the priests could have plenty of time to teach it who was boss. They carefully laid the egg in a woven palm leaf basket, and pushed it out the door.

One of the Tyrannosaur's eyes was open. The golden eye, with a pupil black as night, followed the priests' progression out the door with her egg with malice. For some reason she couldn't understand, she couldn't move, and was unable to protect her egg. Inside, she raged.

The guard locked up the gate and the men took off their masks. The two priests slid the basket with the egg to a wheeled cart that was padded with straw, lifted it onto the cart, and rolled it out of sight. The mother watched as her offspring was taken away from her, around the corner, and gone.

My egg. My egg. My egg.

The cart was rolled back into the Cathedral and the egg was carefully taken down one short flight of steps to a waiting room. Inside there was a fireplace with a fire well stoked and burning brightly. It was hot, but the Bishop said the egg had to be incubated in a hot environment to make sure it'd hatch. Now all the two priests had to do was sit and wait. They sat on a bench along the wall and watched the egg. They sweated and they waited.

* * * *

Inside the enclosure, the Tyrannosaur awoke. She got shakily to her feet, shaking her head. The short, dark grey feathers that covered her body shivered with a slight rustling sound. The red feathers on the crest of her head and around her neck were beginning to rise. She sniffed the earth where her egg had lain just minutes before.

CHAPTER 25

Kel, Lyria, and Raven walked in the city square. They'd been in The Green six days now, and were more at ease among the city's residents. The sky was dark and cloudy—it was drizzling rain. Though smaller than the great city of Los Angeles far to the north, this was a fair miniature of that city and housed several thousand individuals, with many more arriving daily. It was a thriving metropolis and though Kel had successfully infiltrated the military barracks, he'd been unable to find out what was really going on here—even after a week of snooping.

He was disturbed by the dream he'd had. The odd cloth covering something huge on the deck of a ship—the odd little white puffs or clouds that emerged periodically from underneath the tarpaulins. He sighed. Sooner or later he'd find out what the Cathedral was doing here. It was obvious to him now that this whole operation must be Cathedral organized since nobody in the city had any real idea what was going on. The soldiers patrolled, the doctors and engineers and tradesmen all did their work just as they would have in the city to the north. The women shopped silently as was befitting their stature and children ran in the streets—boys allowed to run free, girls getting cuffed by any adult within reach. It all seemed so...ordinary.

During that afternoon and evening they wandered in and out of the various shops. There were clothing stores that interested both Lyria and Raven and there were shops that sold herbs and local native medicines. Kel talked with the men running the various apothecaries and bought some of the local plant remedies. Who knows—they could come in handy either here or at home. He doubted that any of the seeds would grow in the arid environment where their tribe lived, but it might be worth a try.

* * * *

The Bishop finally had to put down his book—it was too dark to read anyway. He sighed. Perhaps he'd take a stroll through the town square before he retired for the night.

* * * *

The egg moved. One of the young priests was still awake and saw it. Then it moved again. He shook his companion.

"It moved! It moved! We have to tell the Bishop!"

Both men leaped to their feet and hurried out of the room to begin the long run up the flights of stone stairs to the Bishop's study. They knocked on the door just as the Bishop was getting ready to open it to go for his evening walk.

"I saw it move, Your Eminence. It's alive!"

"Excellent! Tell the soldiers to kill that thing. We have the only dragon we'll need—the mother is unnecessary."

He smiled. Finally. Things were beginning to go his way. He was whistling as he walked down the stairs to the street. It was a short walk from the Cathedral into the city. This was one walk he'd enjoy, even in the heat.

* * * *

The Tyrannosaur was completely awake now. She looked through the stakes of the enclosure—golden eyes glittering in the firelight. The man-thing was asleep by the wall near the fire. She could see very well with the fire lighting everything so clearly. She saw where the heavy stakes that made up the enclosure had moved, and how the earth where she'd rammed them when she first came to be here was loose around the base of the stakes. She saw that several of the heavy poles were cracked near the bottom. She quietly moved to the farthest end of the enclosure, lowering her head. The red feathers that crested her mighty head and stood on her shoulders suddenly rose to their full height.

Raven came running up to Kel. She and Lyria had been buying things. Raven held a floppy hat with a wide brim. It was purple in color and had bright red flowers on the top.

Kel laughed. "Well, try it on! Let us see how you look."

Raven smiled as she plopped the hat on her head. Lyria helped her adjust it. Then they both stood back and admired the young girl. She was beaming.

She asked eagerly, "Do you think it suits me?"

Kel and Lyria both laughed. The girl was so cute in the hat, they couldn't tell her how horribly garish the colors were!

"You look magnificent," Kel said, and meant it. To see this horribly used child smiling was precious beyond words.

"I don't know," Lyria, teased, "I think you should have gotten the bright red outfit to go with it."

"Oh, Lyria," the girl said, sounding exasperated, "the red was just so outrageous!"

Lyria and Kel looked at each other, then burst into spontaneous laughter together. They stooped down and hugged Raven. She hugged them back with a giggle, her hat sliding back on her white-blonde head.

* * * *

The Bishop had just walked out of the Cathedral when he heard the rending crash. He didn't comprehend what had just happened. He paused, and then went on his way. He was in too good a mood to let an odd noise ruin things for him. He was whistling a happy tune.

* * * *

The guard noticed too late that the Tyrannosaur was coming. She hit the logs hard with her head lowered and the tree trunks that were once a stockade sagged, then splintered and collapsed. One struck the guard on the head—so mercifully, he was unconscious when her jaws descended on him. The creature looked around. She was outside! Her first instinct was to run back into the jungle—it was very close. She knew she'd be able to find her way home easily.

My egg. My egg. My egg...

* * * *

Kel and his companions heard a sound; it was an animal sound. It was ancient and alien, and it was terrifying. Kel froze—he'd heard that sound on several occasions in his dreams. He knew something was about to happen, something very bad.

* * * *

The soldiers who were sent by the priests to administer the lethal dose of sleeping gas to the Tyrannosaur found her enclosure empty and the guard nowhere to be found. One stayed at the ruined stockade while the other ran to the bell tower to signal the alert. The thing was out—people had to be warned.

* * * *

The Bishop heard the roar of the great beast and moments later the sound of the alarm bell. He collared a guard who was running past. "Go to the cells—bring those half-humans to the square and tie them to the display poles."

The guard ran to his mission and the Bishop quickly found an open shop in which he could hide until the soldiers came back with the alleged shamans or magicians or whatever they called themselves. They'd get one more chance to contact the beast, just one more.

* * * *

At the airfield, the small damaged zeppelin was being readied for flight—it was the only one still gassed, and there'd be no time to fill the others. The hydrogen was quickly topped off while the crew, some still pulling on their uniforms, assembled in the gondola. The ground crew was busy loading six small aerial bombs. Each was strapped carefully in place near the bomb bay doors in the center of the gondola floor. It was the only way they might kill the animal they'd been told to hunt. The bombs would be hand lifted to the guide rail from where they could be safely dropped from the airship, sliding along the rail until they were outside the craft.

The captain decided the bombs would be his last resort. His airship had been recently outfitted with the newly built Mauser M 1916 Zeppelin Rifle. The design of this semiautomatic weapon was recently unearthed in the Cathedral archives of all places and it was quickly put into production. It had been designed as a carbine for ground troops during the Great War of long ago according to old documents. Because the individual rounds had to be greased to make the weapon function, it was no good on the ground.

It was discovered, to the dismay of the infantry soldiers of the united tribes of the Black Cross, that the greased rounds were a dirt attractor—and the gun had to be meticulously clean to function. Because of this problem, the rifle was relegated to the airship fleets as defensive armament and for assisting in strafing unarmed civilians from low altitude. The rifle was light compared to the heavy bolt-action arms of the ground troops. A twenty-round detachable magazine jutted down in front of the trigger, and could be rapidly replaced with a full one. The gun was not as fast as the Maxims, but it was light and handy.

The crew was dismayed that they'd be taking up a damaged craft. The ground crew assured them that the outer fabric was now secured and no more would be ripped off in the wind—the craft could fly. Wind resistance would be a problem in maneuvering due to the large hole in the outer covering, but the flight would be short and low. Aside from sluggish maneuvering, the craft was now airworthy.

Something came out of the jungle the priests said over the phone line; some kind of dangerous animal was loose in the city. The captain wasn't sure why explosive bombs were needed. What kind of animal couldn't be put down quickly with arrows or ballistic weapons? If the M 1916s didn't do the job, people would surely die from the explosions of the bombs.

If that became necessary, he had to make sure the drop was done with pinpoint accuracy so that only those citizens close to the animal would die—those close by were probably going to die anyway if the animal was half as dangerous as the priests hinted. The engines on the black airship rumbled to life—the thing was now straining at its guide ropes. It was eager to be free. The lines were cast off and the zeppelin rose slowly into the air.

* * * *

At first it was only one or two people who ran past Kel and his companions. They didn't say a word—they just ran. Kel watched them run and decided to take action as well. He hustled Lyria and Raven into one of the shops. Through the large front window he saw a shadow approaching—a living shadow. He moved closer to the window. In the yellow firelight glow of the gaslights that illuminated the dark street, he saw the Tyrannosaur. He stopped breathing for an instant—then moved back further into the store. His heart was racing.

* * * *

The Tyrannosaur stopped where she was, looking at the gas street light. The yellow flame flickered in her golden eyes. She blinked. Then she turned and her mighty tail hit the post and the lamp fell. It broke through the large glass window of a shop across the street from where Kel and his companions were hiding and the merchandise inside quickly ignited.

A billow of hot flame burst the windows out into the street and a black cloud of heated air climbed into the night, mushrooming and carrying sparks and bits of flaming fabric and other debris with it. The wood of the building's sides and front porch was already smoking—it too would ignite in a moment.

The smoldering and, in many instances, still-burning bits of fabric drifted in the hot current of uplifting air, and as the air cooled around them, they fluttered and settled on the awnings of the open air markets like the bright butterflies of spring. Wherever they landed they immediately began smoking and burst into flame—the process of sparks and conflagration continued down the street. Before the dinosaur turned again to face the city square, a whole block of buildings was burning across the street.

* * * *

The airship was now fifty feet in the air and climbing. The crew was moving the new rifles to the open windows in preparation. If the bombs were needed, the small round hatch would be opened and the bomb rail quickly slid into position. They knew they were ready for any contingency. The engines roared more loudly and the zeppelin began moving toward the city.

* * * *

The Bishop saw the soldiers bringing the three remaining shamans into the square. They were binding them to the poles that were for the punishment of any criminals who might have disturbed the peace and tranquility of the city. From the sounds coming from only a block away, the Bishop knew there was no peace or tranquility in the city at all this night.

He hurried across the street into the town square. He ran to the bound shamans. Dignity be damned! His life was in danger for Heaven's sake!

"When that thing comes around the corner," he hissed into a shaman's face, "you better reach it and tell it to go away."

Garn coolly looked at the sweating Bishop. "You already know we cannot see into the mind of this creature—it is too old."

The Bishop shouted angrily, "How old can it be? Ten years? Twenty?"

"You don't understand," Garn patiently explained, "the creature itself isn't old—but its mind is ancient. Its kind was here long ago, ages before any man walked the Earth."

"Bah," the Bishop scoffed, "your excuses won't save your life—your actions will, if you decide to do what you claim you can do."

"Then we will die here on these poles," Garn said calmly.

"Then you will die," the Bishop spat. How could this half-human be calmer than he, a man of God? It was ridiculous. Why, he could even run. The Bishop thought that this might be a very good idea. From the sound of things, that beast was almost on top of them.

* * * *

With the street in flames behind it, the Tyrannosaur strode into the square. Her head turned to the right, then the left; the growing fire behind her glinted off her feathers. The red cluster on the back of her head was fully raised in a display of rage.

My egg.

CHAPTER 26

Raven snuck quietly into the back of the shop through an un-locked door to see if there was a back window or door through which she might see into the town square that lay directly behind the shop. She didn't notice the soft thud as two bolts of cloth slid down on the other side of the wall coming to rest against the door she'd just come through. She looked out the small window and saw the three men bound to the stakes.

She couldn't see the great beast yet but somehow she knew it was there—somehow she just knew. She looked back toward the front of the shop and shouted for Kel and Lyria to come look, but just then the gaslights in front of the shop exploded and the noise and the closed door drowned out her voice.

She looked back again through the window. There was no other option. There was no more time. She had to try at least—there was nobody else. She carefully laid her new purple and red hat on a desk near the window, unlatched the back door and stepped into the town square.

My egg. My egg. My egg...

Raven ran past the dinosaur at a diagonal and now she was be-tween the giant creature and the captive men. She walked forward, putting up the palms of both hands toward the beast. "Stop!"

The dinosaur paused. None of the man-things ever acted like this. This girl-thing didn't seem afraid. That was something to consider.

"You stop this minute," Raven shouted, "these men have done you no harm. Better food awaits you in the Cathedral."

The Tyrannosaur turned her head to look back the way she'd come—back toward the Cathedral. Then she rocked forward on her great taloned feet, bending her neck low enough to look into this strange little creature's eyes. She studied the odd little thing that could somehow talk to her.

* * * *

The airship was past the Cathedral grounds and coming in quick-ly over the city. The pilot and crew saw the burning street—they saw fires spreading rapidly from one row of shops and homes to the next.

People were running, but they didn't know where they should run—some ran directly back into the flames. The zeppelin made a slight course correction and headed for the town square.

"Where's Raven?"

"I thought she was with you," shouted Kel over the sound of the fire.

They both began frantically searching the front of the store for the little girl, looking behind shelving and under tables. Finally they saw the door to the back room. It'd been partly hidden when two bolts of cloth fell against it. Kel reached for one bolt while Lyria reached for the other.

* * * *

Then Raven knew. She looked into the huge beast's eyes and saw within their wild depths the Eternal Mother. Goddess to the girl, she couldn't understand the concept coming from the dinosaur. The thought, the image was too old to be conceptualized into words a human brain could understand or a human tongue could speak.

But the idea of motherhood could be understood. Suddenly Raven knew where the egg was located—and she grasped what the great creature was asking of her.

Tears streaming down her cheeks, she simply said, "I know," and ran off down the street toward the Cathedral.

* * * *

Kel and Lyria reached the window in the back of the shop and looked out. Lyria unconsciously placed her hand on Raven's wonderful hat. They saw a shadow flit in the direction of the Cathedral, but it was dark and the flaming city made havoc of logic and vision. The Tyrannosaur did not seem logical at all, yet there it stood. Lyria tugged on Kel's sleeve. Three men were tied to stakes right in front of the beast!

"Let us see if we can reach the thing," Kel whispered, "like we tried with the rhinoceros."

"We can at least try," Lyria responded.

* * * *

The captain of the airship could now see the town square. He gasped in horror. What was that...that THING! He called to the crew

and they came forward to stare in disbelief at the great creature coming into view inside the burning city. They knew they were after a dangerous animal, but this? They saw the monster looking up at them.

"We'll make a pass with the M 1916s—if that fails we'll have to bomb. Prepare the bombs for dropping."

The bombardier shouted, "They're ready—just make sure you're directly over the creature so we can get a good hit."

The captain wheeled on the man, hissing, "I have been flying Cathedral airships since before you were even in the service, watch your tongue."

"Yes sir," the chastised crewman said, "I...I'm sorry. I've never been in a situation like this before."

The captain glanced over at the crewman and gave him a mirthless grin. "You think any of us have? You better man your rifle."

He turned back to the business at hand—turned the large brass and wood wheel controlling the vessel and the airship began dropping, circling in an arc that would bring it directly over the great beast. Why was it just standing there like that?

* * * *

Raven reached the Cathedral and pushed against the great bronze door. Somehow she knew where the egg was located—a link always exists between mother and offspring. Between the feathered dinosaur and her egg, it seemed an invisible cord stretched that Raven could somehow feel and follow. She could hardly move the large door, but she shoved with her shoulder and it finally swung open.

Inside, many people were gathered. Some came in to pray, others to be inside a stone structure considering the great fires raging around them. A couple of people had seen the Tyrannosaur. They were babbling off in a corner. No one was paying any attention to them, and no one was paying any attention to Raven either. She hurried through the main foyer into the back of the Cathedral. She saw two priests approaching, but she hid in the shadows and they passed without seeing her. She went down a short flight of stairs. At the bottom, a young priest stood with his back to the door. Raven walked over to him and said, "I'm lost." She pitched her voice low so she sounded scared. The priest lowered his head.

"What did you say, little one?"

He put his hand on her shoulder and squeezed. Those were the last words he spoke. He clutched his throat with a look of sudden surprise as he saw his blood spewing from his throat to splash noisily onto the tile floor. It sounded to him like a spilled pitcher of water. He took one glance at Raven and saw the bone fragment in her hand. Just as he died, he knew what had happened. Raven stepped over the body, knocking on the door. In a moment it opened.

"You should help your friend," the cute little girl whispered, "he fell."

The second young priest squatted to see what was wrong with his friend. Wordlessly, Raven leaped upon his back and he collapsed on top of the corpse of his friend, driven down by Raven's added weight. He could feel an odd tugging and sharp pressure on his back over and over and over...

* * * *

The airship came in for a pass at the dinosaur. She saw it coming and quickly hopped to the edge of the town square. The M 1916s rattled short bursts of fire in her direction. One pass with the guns would be sufficient—the captain could see that the beast's feathers were absorbing the eight millimeter rounds and that the creature paid them no mind—the rounds weren't penetrating.

The airship couldn't drop its bombs now—the dinosaur was no longer under the craft. They'd have to try again. As the zeppelin began to come about, the Tyrannosaur roared a challenge. She lowered her body and head close to the ground. The feathers on her neck and head flared out in a deep crimson fan. A great bellow burst from the giant lungs of the animal. The airship was turning slowly as the wind caught inside its exposed interior, holding it back. The dinosaur charged.

When the giant animal was suddenly distracted by the airship, Kel and Lyria ran though the back door of the shop. They hurried over to the three poles where the helpless men were tied. Kel froze.

"Grandfather!"

"It is good to see you, Kel...would you be kind enough to cut these ropes?"

Kel was astonished at his calm, and quickly used his dagger to cut the ropes that bound his grandfather. By the time he was done, Lyria had freed the other two men. They turned to look at the dinosaur as it approached the turning airship. Then they fled into the night to get away from the danger and the fire.

* * * *

Raven walked into the small room. The fireplace was hot, though the logs had recently smoldered and gone out. She saw the egg in the basket of straw. She walked slowly toward it, tears streaming down her soot-grimed face—her tears carving clean, white lines through the sooty blackness.

* * * *

Once more the Tyrannosaur lowered her head, roaring her defiance at the flying thing that dared challenge her. The storm of her breath moved over the fires burning under the airship and lifted them. The gale of her breath caused bits of burning canvas awning from the open air shops to take flight along with fragments of burning tar paper from flaming roofs.

For just an instant she was the celestial fire-breathing dragon out of legend. The fire billowed up. The captain of the airship saw the fragments of canvas and tar drift through the great rent in the outer skin, striking the front hydrogen bag of the zeppelin. The tar! It clung. Then it burned through.

Suddenly there was a blinding explosion. The front gasbag of the airship was rent and a great flame engulfed it. The second explosion quickly followed the first as the next hydrogen bag detonated. The aluminum ribs that kept the airship rigid softened, sagged, and then were gone. The airship folded in the middle and fell into the conflagration. The crewmen probably screamed as the flames overtook them, but there was nobody to hear except a mother mourning her offspring.

* * * *

Raven knelt silently in front of the egg—she touched the shell and it moved. It was warm. She whimpered and once again raised the bone fragment that had become her sword. She drove it into the shell, hard. It penetrated the soft shell. She struck again and the shell split, spilling the Tyrannosaur fetus to the tile floor. It took only one breath before it died. As the invisible cord that connected it with its mother separated, Raven sent a message. *It's a boy.*

As Raven knelt in the fractured yolk and albumin of the lifeless egg, a thought passed through her mind.

"I have become Death," she whispered, "destroyer of worlds." And then she wept.

* * * *

There was no longer anything to keep the Tyrannosaur there. She wheeled suddenly and began to run. She crushed homes and scattered abandoned carts. She reached the edge of the city and ran into the jungle. As she hit the tree line, she uttered a low, long, keening wail. Raven lifted her head, listening. The cry was a call to all of the empty, dark spaces of the world. *I am coming,* it seemed to say, *now we are one.* She ran back toward her home—a place that men in their flaming city dared to call Hell.

* * * *

Raven rose silently. Her tears were finally at an end. She walked up the stairs and out of the Cathedral. She wandered down a street of shops not quite yet engulfed in flame. She found a shop and entered. There was nobody else there. She looked at her burned and sodden clothing. She was wet with the blood of priests and something much more profound. She found a table with clothing her size. She chose carefully—she chose black.

"I have become Death," she whispered to herself.

She chose black, finely tanned leather pants and a black shirt with long sleeves. Over this she put on a black linen skirt that hung just below her knees. She took her bone dagger and shredded the skirt from the hem almost to her waist. She found a black belt that she wrapped around her slender body and through this she thrust the bone dagger.

She wandered to the back of the shop—this was where the upper class women had their hair done, and their faces. She'd seen such women when she was enslaved in the north from time to time—they'd watch while their men would...

She looked at the hair coloring and chose the blackest one. She put her head over the sink, covering her hair with the dye. Her long white-blonde hair was now glossy black. She parted it in the middle, tying it into two long ponytails. They looked like the wings of a raven.

Destroyer of worlds.

She took the red lip paint—a lot of it and more of the black hair dye. She stood in front of the mirror gazing at her face—at the soot and the lines of clean skin her tears had made. She put red lip paint where the tears had run. Then she put together a second outfit a little larger size than the one she wore—she'd grow into it. She walked out of the shop.

She slunk through the streets. The dancing flames celebrated the shadows through which she moved unseen. She passed close by the back door of a store not yet burned. Through the glass in the back window she might have seen a funny purple hat with a wide brim and red flowers lying on a desk. She didn't look. She reached the edge of town and headed east. She knew where she was going. She was going away.

CHAPTER 27

Kel and his small band ran two blocks and turned into an alley. There they paused for a moment to catch their breath. From the narrow passage they saw the great Tyrannosaur run past without looking left or right. They could hear it crashing into the trees beyond. They all relaxed a bit—the animal had been too much for anyone to deal with. Fortunately it was gone now.

Kel grasped his grandfather, giving him a long hug. Then it was Lyria's turn. They smiled at each other and then they laughed uproariously, the agonizing tension dissipating with the laughter.

"That was close," Garn said between bursts of laughter.

"Too close." Lyria said, and then she was laughing again as well. "Raven."

Lyria's worried comment made Kel pause. He turned toward his grandfather.

"There was a girl with us—young, about nine or ten with white hair. Have you seen her?"

"Yes, we have," Garn answered. "She stopped the beast as it was coming for us and then ran off toward the Cathedral."

"Then that is where we must go," Lyria said.

Kel nodded.

As they hurried down the shadowed street, Garn introduced Kel and Lyria to the other two men they'd saved from the dinosaur.

"This is Galv—I think you already know him. Galv is the shaman of the tribe to the north of us."

Galv grinned at Kel. "This is a journey I did not think I would come out of!"

Lyria smiled at Galv and said, "I have heard your name—you are respected and revered among the people of our tribe."

"I hope I live long enough to deserve that respect," he said. "I have heard of you as well...Lady of the Ice Tiger."

Lyria blushed. Fortunately it was too dark for the men to see.

"And this fellow is called Drog. He is the shaman of one of the mountain tribes farther north than our trading circle."

Drog laughed, "We might have to do something about that."

"So we shall," answered Garn.

"I think we should keep moving."

Kel's suggestion was met with immediate support. They moved quickly but cautiously back out into the city square. The poles the men had been bound to were knocked flat by the dinosaur. Good! The priests would assume they'd been eaten. They were ghosts now. Kel smiled at the thought.

They crossed the square, mingling with a small crowd of survivors. Everyone was frightened. They thought the beast might return at any minute to eat them.

"We should leave the city immediately," suggested one of the women.

"I think it would be better to stay," said one of the men. "We've been here two years now. This is my home."

"Some home," the woman said. "Everything is burned."

"We can rebuild."

"Some of the buildings are stone. You'll notice they haven't burned!"

An older man said, "We made the mistake of building quickly of wood instead of more slowly using stone."

"That is true," another said in a matter-of-fact way, "the beast didn't knock down a single stone structure. With stone homes, and a stone wall, we'll be safe even if another of these beasts returns."

"It's unlikely they will," opined another, "I've been here for three years and I've never even heard mention of those animals!"

"They're either very rare, or somehow this one got here by mistake," said an older woman in the crowd.

"Or both," suggested the first man.

Kel and his party moved through the crowd and found a small abandoned stone building which they entered unseen by the crowd in the street. They would have to make plans, and make decisions.

"The Cathedral is now but a small distance," Kel offered.

Garn nodded. "But we must move carefully—there are many soldiers in the streets."

Drog spoke next. "It seems the girl succeeded where all of us failed—she talked to the beast!"

Kel spoke in surprise. "What? Explain that, please?"

Galv spoke. "She came out of nowhere. She told the great beast to stop and it stopped."

"It then bent down to stare at her and it seemed to be listening to her," Drog added. "I have never seen anything like it."

Lyria said in a worried tone, "She was under our protection."

"When she ran off toward the Cathedral," said Drog, "she didn't look like she needed any protection."

Kel looked at Lyria. "We have to go that direction immediately to see if we can find her."

The three older men looked at each other and nodded. They'd come along. This many shamans in a group could be a formidable force to reckon with if someone stood in their way.

As it turned out, no one stood in their way. Everything was in a state of confusion, and one small crowd of sooty refugees looked much like the rest. Even the military personnel were more concerned with putting out the fires than with stopping people on the street. They made it to the Cathedral unmolested.

Kel pushed open the heavy bronze door and they entered. Candles now lighted the inside—the gas to the copper piping that fed the gas-lights had been turned off as a safety precaution—no point in having any more explosions. Nobody seemed to be in charge at the moment, and everyone inside seemed to be concerned only with themselves and a few close people, probably friends or relatives. Again, a ragtag group of refugees caused no raised eyebrows—no notice of any kind.

They walked along one wall of the large room, staying out of the light and the crowds. They reached a doorway behind the large altar that seemed to lead outside. Kel pushed it open a crack and looked out. He saw the very heavy wooden stockade that had been made of tree trunks he'd seen earlier. Five of the heavy posts lay on the ground—snapped off by a titanic impact. Kel figured this is where the beast had come from. Why would the Cathedral want such a creature?

Beyond the fallen logs, Kel saw a group of armed soldiers. They were carrying ballistic weapons—heavy ones. Two of them, probably officers, were in an animated conversation with a priest. The priest seemed very annoyed and he was gesticulating and shouting. Kel didn't much care what they were discussing as long as they discussed it out there. He gently let the door close and stepped back where his companions were waiting.

At the same time, Lyria found a short stairwell leading down a level. At the bottom she saw two dead priests, one on top of the other. There was a lot of blood. Lyria cautiously descended the stairs and examined the bodies. She pulled down the back of the robe of the top man and inspected his wounds. Then she rolled him off the other man, turning the body over—his throat had been slashed ear to ear. He probably died of blood loss even before he hit the floor.

The second man hadn't died so quickly—he'd been stabbed six or eight times. The wounds were odd. Each wound was round with a center of flesh still inside; as though he'd been stabbed with something hollow. Lyria knew what kind of weapon would cause such wounds—Raven's bone dagger. She'd been here.

Lyria pushed open the door cautiously, quietly. Inside she could see two priests. What lay on the floor at their feet was more significant. Lyria was staring at a tiny version of the great beast she'd seen in the streets only an hour earlier. Next to the tiny monster was its shell. It was smashed, and the small animal had apparently spilled out onto the floor. Drying yolk and albumin lay in a congealed pool around the small creature.

Lyria's attention was drawn to one of the egg fragments. In the center of the piece she spotted the same circular stab mark—Raven had broken the egg and killed the tiny creature within. How did she even know about the egg? If she did know about it, how on earth did she find it? The mystery didn't explain itself so Lyria softly let the door close. No one in the room had seen her. She turned the one corpse back on top of the first and readjusted his robe so no one would know she'd been there. Then she crept back up the short stairway, rejoining her group.

Kel was just finishing his description of what he he'd seen outside. Then it was Lyria's turn to tell her story. Everyone was mystified.

Then Drog said, "The girl spoke with the great beast—of that we are certain. It also spoke to her. I believe the mother somehow told her where the egg could be found. I imagine the mother could never take the egg back into The Green with her—how could she transport it?"

"So…" Lyria speculated, "the beast asked Raven to destroy the egg?"

"That would be my guess," said Drog. "I do not know of any other way she could have known about the egg."

Lyria thought about that and decided it must be true. The great beast didn't want her offspring...her child…to live knowing what was in store for it at the hands of the priests. What a terrible burden for a ten-year-old child—what a terrible burden for a mother.

"Let us leave this place of darkness," said Garn. "The child is not here and right now we have no way of finding her."

"Perhaps later we can try a journey to seek her," Galv suggested, "but this is neither the place nor the time."

Lyria knew he spoke the truth—the girl was nowhere to be found. Whether alive or dead, they'd have to bide their time until the shamans could journey for the knowledge they so desperately sought. She thought about the hat that had made the little girl smile so. Quiet tears ran down her cheeks.

* * * *

Raven continued eastward. She couldn't have said why, except that it was away from the city, the priests…and something else. She traveled that night at the edge of The Green. She no longer held any fear of what may lurk in the jungle. She was Death—what could possibly harm her? She walked for two more hours and then exhaustion got the better of her. Even Death must rest at times. She turned into the jungle a short distance. Here there was a sort of natural hedgerow of dense vegetation. Though it was dark, she saw the great branches of a giant tree spreading over her head. She looked back in the direction she'd come. At four miles away, the flames were still visible, but the heat and the sounds could no longer be felt or heard. She sighed, curling up just under the hedge. The earth was soft and warm, and it was only a short time before the exhausted girl was fast asleep.

* * * *

Birds. Lots of birds. Raven lay under the shrubbery of the jungle with her eyes closed. She heard a profusion of bird songs. She listened, delighted. She'd always liked birds—she was fascinated with their ability to fly. She remembered her one attempt to fly. She must have been only four summers old when she decided she could be a bird. She'd been watching them fly all through that summer. By the time winter settled in the land, she felt sure she knew how they did it.

She climbed a tree near her home. Large trees were not common in the lower reaches of the mountains east of the Black City, which turned out to be fortunate. When she leaped from the tree, she was only about six feet above the ground. She recalled how she'd flapped her arms—she didn't think she'd ever moved her arms that quickly before. And then suddenly she was flying. But as it turned out, she was flying straight for the earth. She struck the ground before she had time to feel fear so she was still relaxed, which helped. As it was, she broke an arm.

She lay there stunned for a moment and then she looked up at the tree. A bird was looking down at her from the branch she'd been standing upon. The bird twittered, seeming to laugh at the impetuous, featherless creature sprawled on the ground. In spite of her pain, she laughed. It was okay, after all—she HAD flown!

She walked back to the village and her mother was furious. They hustled her into the home of the tribal healer. He examined her arm and then bound it tightly with a wooden slat on each side. Putting the wood and bindings on her arm had hurt more than the fall. She'd fully recovered, but by the time the splints were removed from her arm, she decided, with the firm advice of her parents, that flying was for the birds.

* * * *

Raven opened her eyes. The sunlight dazzled her momentarily. She squinted, looking up again into the trees. She was stunned—never in her life had she thought that birds could be that many colors. Red. Blue. Green. Yellow. Every color she could think of was displayed in the trees, and every bird sound she could think of was heard as well. Some of the birds had fantastically long tail feathers of blue that shifted sometimes to green.

"I wonder if I have died," she said softly. "I must surely be in another world." But then she was brought back to reality. When she looked to the west, she beheld a black shape in the sky. It was very far away, but Raven knew what it was. It was an airship hovering over the smoldering wreckage of the city. She saw the smoke rising black into the sky—the stain of man on the world.

Raven rose and looked about her, getting her bearings for the next leg of her journey. She was hungry, but she'd brought no food in her flight from the city. She looked up at the birds, watching as they ate the many kinds of fruits and nuts the trees bore. She figured if the birds could safely eat them, so could she.

When she returned to the edge of The Green, she began hunting around for fallen fruit and nuts. There was food in plenty for her. She ate hungrily, and then she sat for an hour and a half, weaving a basket from the grasses and leaves of some oddly shaped trees that put all their branches out at the very top instead of all along the trunk. The leaves, when taken from the ground where they fell, made excellent weaving material. When she was finished she picked up a variety of fruit and nuts to take with her.

She continued on her way east, stopping once to stare in surprise at the strange, small man-like animals that leaped and shrieked in the treetops. They could hang and actually swing on their tails. The creatures looked down at her curiously. She was no threat to them so they followed her at a distance, and watched. Eventually they grew bored and moved back into The Green. Raven continued on her way, simply putting one foot in front of the other. Seven days later, she knew a river lay ahead—she could smell the dampness in the air.

* * * *

Kel, Lyria, and their companions walked through the still smoldering rubble that had been the city. They knew they should be away from the region. Where would they go? Where was Raven? They were in a strange, dangerous land very far from home. They needed to be careful.

"You know what I think?" Kel looked at his companions, "I think we should stay in the city. Anyone who has anything to fear will run. There's a zeppelin in the skies over us right now. If we leave the city, they may notice us wandering away."

"I think that is wise council," Galv commented. "Those who have nothing to fear would not run."

Lyria snickered, "We should go over where they are helping the injured and homeless. Since they failed to kill us, should they not at least keep feeding us while we remain here?"

Everyone in the company laughed. Nearby, a few refugees looked over at them—what could be funny amid all this desolation? Kel's group noticed the attention they'd drawn and walked away, making a mental note not to make jokes until they were safely away from there.

A short distance up the road they came to an area where the buildings were not burned. There were fires burning, but they were under cauldrons that held steaming broth and soup. Lyria and Kel looked at each other.

"Shall we?"

"I believe we should," Lyria replied.

They walked to the back of the slowly moving line. Kel's stomach grumbled.

"Where have I heard that before," whispered Garn.

"I was thinking the same thing," said Lyria with a sly grin.

Eventually they reached the front of the line and each of them was served a bowl of soup, a bowl of stew with boar's meat, and bread. At least they wouldn't starve. They walked over to a group who appeared to be citizens of the city, sitting on the ground with them. They spoke little and listened much.

The rumor circulating was that the city would be rebuilt. Crystal ships would bring in supplies from the other city being built farther to the east. Kel and his companions looked at each other. Another city? Kel couldn't restrain himself and said, "I didn't know there was another city—are the people of Los Angeles moving here?"

The man sitting next to him laughed. "Nobody tells us exactly what's going on," he said, "the rumor is that they're preparing a line of smaller cities along the coast in the event Los Angeles, the black city, has to be evacuated because of the ice."

"I thought the ice was hundreds of years from the city," said another of the refugees sitting with Kel and his companions.

"It is," the first man replied, "but the city is nothing if not careful. I've heard that there's even a third city being constructed at the edge of the vast grasslands far to the east of The Green."

"Still," said the second man, "there are many opportunities here that aren't available in Los Angeles for those who follow the Redeemed God."

The first man quipped, "Like being eaten by a giant lizard with feathers? I for one have had my fill—I'm going back to the north. I figure I'll be long dead of natural causes before the ice can move against me."

They all laughed.

"I'm staying," said the second man, "we can have all the free land we can take and there's plenty of lumber for building. The cities will be strong enough to protect us if the half-human tribes rebel."

Lyria bristled. Kel took her hand and she looked at him but remained silent.

There was much to think about—they needed time to sort this all out. Kel and his companions wandered to where large tents had been pitched for survivors of the fire. The officials never gave Kel or the people with him so much as a glance or a comment.

CHAPTER 28

When Raven arrived at the river, she stopped. How could a river be so big? From her vantage point, it might as well have been an ocean. She couldn't see the far shore, though she believed there must be one. How could she get across? She thought about trying to swim. She thought back to her attempt to fly. She was neither bird nor fish—besides, there was something in the water. She moved back a distance from the shore.

Something very big and very small with many bulging eyes and sharp triangular teeth lurked just under the water. No, swimming was out of the question. She stood, looking upstream. A short distance away, maybe a mile, there was construction going on. She didn't see it immediately because foliage obscured most of the vista south of where she stood. She saw a partly erected palisade of heavy logs facing the jungle and many small buildings being constructed. She'd go there and find a way across the great river.

As she got closer to the construction, she realized this was a city—it was small, but a city nonetheless—she knew what cities were, and what happened to girls and women who lived in them. Most of the buildings going up were made of wood, though stone was being used to reinforce the base of the palisade. She looked past the buildings to the riverbank. There it was. There was her way across the river.

Moored to an impromptu dock jutting out into the slow moving river was a boat. This was no crystal ship—she saw the red rust of the boiler at the stern. It was steam powered, but with the abundance of wood, it was simpler to use it as fuel in the small boat.

She stared at the boat for a while trying to determine where it would be easiest to hide once she got aboard. She decided she'd move to the stern of the vessel—the ropes that moored the thing to the dock were attached at the front, and the wheel the pilot used to steer it was also near the front.

There was a large pile of wood on the deck in front of the rusted iron boiler—that must be the fuel supply. The wood would go into the burner at the front of the boiler. That meant that if her luck held out, no one would see a small girl hiding in the stern. With her decision made, she moved again, drawing ever closer to the shore and the boat that waited for her there.

* * * *

Three days after the fire, Kel, Lyria, and the rest of the small band gathered near The Green so that they might converse in private.

"Garn, what do you suggest?" Kel asked.

"A very good question, Kel." Garn thought a moment. "I think we should continue our masquerade as refugees and see if we can get the chiefs here to take us back to the north with anyone else who would wish to go."

"That sounds like a good plan." Kel then looked at Galv and asked, "What do you think?"

"They will try to talk people out of leaving, but I believe they will simply send others down in their place—newcomers will not know what has happened until they get here, and by then it will be too late."

Lyria said, "This will have happened a long time ago by the time new people can arrive. We also need to stay and find Raven."

"That we do. I believe that with as many things as the city people think they need, it will take them a long time to pack," Kel said, laughing.

Garn chuckled. "Anyone from the tribes would be ready in a day."

They all laughed at that.

Kel wandered away to seek information. He listened carefully to conversations as he passed. It seemed there were but two opinions—stay and reap the benefits of a new land, or flee back home to the comfort and familiarity of the old life. Had he been one of the city dwellers, he wasn't sure which of those two paths he'd take.

Kel headed toward the Cathedral—that would be where information would be found. As he walked, he noticed a small group of soldiers across the road. They were posting some kind of handbills to scorched timbers, still standing walls, and street signs. Curious, Kel crossed and approached them. He removed his counterfeit military identification from his pocket—he was glad now that he'd kept it.

"You there, sergeant. What are you posting?"

The sergeant paused, taking a quick look at Kel's papers—then saluted. "We're hanging these wanted posters, sir." As Kel looked at the poster he was dismayed to see photographs of the three shamans—along with a reward of two large gold coins for their capture! This would dramatically change their plans.

"Give me a handful, sergeant. I will have my men help distribute them."

"Thank you, sir," the sergeant answered, "that would be most helpful." With that, he handed a thick stack of the posters to Kel. With a curt nod, Kel turned back—the others needed to see this as quickly as possible. When he could no longer see the soldiers, he discarded all but one of the posters in a roadside trash bin. He tucked the remaining poster into his pocket, and increased his pace.

* * * *

Raven made it to the docks unseen. She heard the pilot of the small craft talking with another man. They were planning to go across the river. Raven decided she'd made a wise decision. She carefully crept aboard the craft, crawling along the left side until she was behind the boiler. There she waited.

A number of men approached the vessel from the dock, so Raven slid along to the side of the boiler where she knew they'd be unable to see her. They were putting things onto the boat—bundles wrapped in linen and tied with sturdy cords. She had no idea what they were carrying and she didn't care. They were going to take her where she wanted to go.

Raven saw a reflection of sunlight. She glanced farther to the stern. Something was glinting there. One of the men on the boat might notice it and go investigate. She cautiously reached out, snatching the item off the deck.

She held a small square of polished copper in her hand. It was about three inches square and was so highly polished she could see her reflection. She studied her face, and then reached into the bag she carried that contained her clothing and face paint. She took out one of the tubes of bright red coloring the city women used on their lips and redrew the red marks on her face that had faded since she began this trek. *A girl should look her best,* she thought, *even if she is the destroyer of worlds.*

The men who were loading the small boat moved back onto the

dock and suddenly the engine started. The cough and the chugging of the steam engine startled Raven. At the back of the engine she saw a large cast-iron pulley—it was turning. Around the pulley was a thick, flat leather belt. The moving belt passed through an opening in the deck. Fascinated, Raven crawled farther to the stern so she could look down into the opening.

The pathway of the belt narrowed as it went below. Raven saw why—another pulley was attached to a heavy shaft that looked as though it went right out the back of the boat. The lower pulley was turning much faster than the top one. Raven didn't understand why, but she watched it spinning for a couple minutes before caution again made her crawl back to her hiding place.

For the first hour she saw nobody. The engine and boiler that shielded her from their eyes also hid them from hers. She didn't care—all that mattered was getting to the other side and putting all that water between her and the burned city. She lay her head down, and without realizing it she fell asleep. The rhythmic pulsing of the engine and the ticking of the leather belt whenever the seam passed over the pulley lulled her.

"What in the name of the Redeemed God do we have here?"

Someone was shouting. Raven awoke suddenly to face three men with looks of consternation on their faces. Raven sat up and the three men jumped back hastily. They were afraid of her! She remembered how she looked. She stood boldly, putting her hand on the hilt of her bone dagger, looking into each man's eyes, trying to imagine what they must be thinking. She glanced to the left and saw that they were well over halfway to the farther bank.

"I am Death," she announced. "I have business on the far shore—take me and you will live."

They looked at her a moment and the pilot, who'd left the wheel momentarily to see what the commotion was, said, "Whatever you are, if you stay where you stand, I'll deliver you to the far shore."

"It is well that you have decided." Raven smiled inwardly. She had…power!

In two hours the boat pulled up to the shore. There was no wharf here. A small band of local tribesmen stood ready to unload the boat.

When Raven showed herself, the workers took one look and faded rapidly into the jungle. She smiled. She picked up the bag that held her possessions and stepped off the boat. She turned to the crew and said, "Thank you."

"I'm not sure if you're welcome or not," said the pilot, "but we're glad nonetheless that you're traveling on without us."

As she walked off toward the forest, she heard the crew cursing and shouting, trying to coax the workers to return to unload the craft. By the time she reached the tree line, she glanced back. About half the workers had returned. Apparently the other half decided that whatever they were being paid wasn't enough. Raven looked to the east and began walking again. When would she be far enough from the city people to once again feel safe?

* * * *

Kel returned to his companions and told them what he'd found out.

"A crystal ship is going to be here tomorrow with soldiers and engineers to help rebuild the city—though they think they're merely aiding with further construction and know nothing of this disaster. There are going to be more people coming down here to live as well."

"That is truly amazing," said Lyria. "What is so special about this location?"

Garn looked at her. "You do not think that the Cathedral will give up on the idea of capturing one of the feathered serpents, do you?"

Lyria sighed. "I suppose not. They are persistent. What could they possibly want with one of those huge animals?"

Garn answered, "I think they plan to use it to scare people. Maybe they are planning on hatching a number of them and using them as weapons—who can tell?"

"Well," said Kel, "we have another problem." He showed them one of the wanted posters. "We are now being hunted. Anyone who finds us will be very eager for the reward. We cannot stay here."

"Though we cannot journey, perhaps we can dream this night for Raven." Galv suggested.

Kel nodded, answering, "We can board the ship tomorrow headed back north.

-187-

"The city is big. It will be easy for us to disappear there." Galv remarked.

"I know someone who might be able to help us," Kel said.

Lyria asked, "The magician?"

Kel nodded. They were ready for their departure. There was no way any of the shamans could make a mystical journey there—they'd neither drum nor rattle and the area was so crowded with people, there wouldn't nearly be enough seclusion for such a working.

They'd have to wait until they were back in the north to try to find out what happened to Raven. What would they tell Raven's relatives when they met again on the side of the mountain? Kel wondered, as did Lyria. Neither was happy with the situation, but there was nothing they could do about it now.

The next morning, true to the city official's word, a large crystal ship came into view in front of the wharf. A crowd had already gathered waiting with their few possessions to board the ship and depart these lands. Kel and his companions were among them—anonymous people within a large group of anonymous people. They had to wait of course for the ship to unload its stores and passengers. As they waited, slightly apart from the crowd, the shamans told Lyria and Kel that though they'd dreamed, they were not certain as to Raven's location.

"I saw much green," Galv offered. "It seems she is far from here somewhere in the jungle."

"I witnessed a wide river—but from the far bank," Garn said with a sad shake of his head. "I know not what that may mean unless she is somehow across the nameless river that flows east of here."

Drog had nothing further to add. Even Lyria could see that Raven was beyond their reach now, and with men actively hunting them, they needed to flee. They watched as a detachment of soldiers marched off the ship—they carried ballistic weapons as well as heavy spears. Kel wondered how much good they'd do against creatures like the feathered serpent.

Next, the regular passengers disembarked. There were adventurers—people with families looking for the advantage of a new start and virtually unlimited new land. Here they wouldn't need the tall buildings of growing tanks to produce enough food for the city—the land was incredibly fertile and the forest itself abounded in food.

Kel looked at the people walking down the gangplank. All these people are coming to take advantage of the natural resources in the area. *They will be too greedy,* he thought. *They will take too much.* He knew The Green would defend itself, and then the men of the north would again depart from the Green Hell with more stories of horror and death. It would take a while, Kel discerned, but Nature has Her own ways of dealing with greed.

By afternoon, the people who were leaving were aboard the ship. A surprising number had been convinced to stay at the last moment. They'd been promised protection and they'd seen the soldiers. Those who chose to stay hadn't seen the great beast that initiated the fire with a tail almost twice as long as the great mammoths of the northern cold regions. Kel shook his head, going below to find his companions. It would be a long trip home. Still, they were all glad to be alive and safe that day.

* * * *

Raven walked on, day after day, simply moving east. Finally the forest began to thin. The trees gradually became smaller, more openly spaced. In place of the dense jungle, a more plains-like terrain greeted her. Here the small trees bore little fruit—she better gather enough while she could.

She spent that afternoon collecting what fruit and nuts she could. Her impromptu basket was only half full when she was finished. The abundance of The Green was behind her. She slept that night under what seemed to be the last large tree she could find, as she looked eastward. Again, she slept dreamlessly. As she drifted off, she wondered if perhaps she really was dead. It didn't seem to matter. She closed her eyes and slept.

Early the next morning she set out again. The few scrub trees were spaced very far apart now and the terrain was turning to grassland. She walked unseen in an ocean of golden grass higher than her head. She was invisible finally, and that was fitting for Death, was it not?

About noon, she sat and ate some of the fruit. She noticed that a few pieces she'd brought were partly rotten, and she carefully ate the better parts, throwing the bad pieces to the ground. After she finished eating she became concerned that she wasn't going in the right direction, as the sun was almost directly overhead. When she could determine the direction the sun was traveling, she'd find the east again.

To her dismay, she discovered she'd been walking north instead of east. She shrugged and began again in a roughly easterly direction—she guessed it really didn't matter anyway. She now knew what she was doing. She was walking until she was out of food and water and then she would walk until she died. It was fitting atonement for slaying the baby in the egg.

She remembered the sorrow the mother felt, and she knew why. These great animals were fading from the land. Once they'd ruled the Earth, but no more. The world had changed. The climate had changed, and it pushed them until there was nowhere else to go.

The Green was their last stand. Eggs came infrequently now, and they were often infertile. Chances are, the mother she'd seen would never bear another living descendent. The once masters of the earth were fading slowly into legend. Raven's eyes teared up as she thought about that noble animal's run for home. Would she even make it? Raven hoped so.

* * * *

The great ship set sail that evening. All of Kel's party was crammed into one room below decks. He'd hoped to have some time alone with Lyria, but that was not to be. The captain had been very certain—no passengers were allowed above. The cabins topside were reserved for the crew, officers, and the ever present priests of the Cathedral. Kel no longer wished to be known as an officer of the army.

They talked quietly about their experiences as they spent their first night aboard the vessel. After being brought food from the galley, more soup and stew, they got ready for bed. Fortunately, the ship was fitted with special rooms where bodily wastes could be discreetly dropped into the ocean. Kel thought it was a clever arrangement. Periodically along the side of the ship facing the ocean were small closet-like rooms. Inside, there was something like a chair but the seat was open to the sea, and the ocean could be seen below you if you looked through the seat. Kel wondered what would happen in a storm.

* * * *

Raven was now out of food. The last of the rotten fruit had to be thrown away. There were bugs crawling inside it and Raven didn't think they looked like the grubs her people, her former people, sometimes ate when normal sustenance was scarce. She discarded her basket, trudging on, no longer caring in what direction. She also discarded her package of clothing and belongings along the way as well. Now all she had to do was put one foot in front of the other until she finally passed into the Otherworld to greet her totem. Her protector. Her Goddess.

Raven stumbled on for a while longer and then collapsed severely dehydrated. She hadn't eaten for days, and hadn't found water in two days. She was so tired—she was finally ready. She rose, stumbled a final time and fell into unconsciousness. Her last thought was gratitude that the Goddess had granted her the boon of oblivion.

* * * *

Raven vaguely felt something nudge her—she was annoyed. Why would she not be allowed to die in peace? She was nudged again. She briefly opened her eyes. Standing over her, looking down into her face was a bird. The bird's great hooked beak was almost three feet long. She looked down the length of its body. The feathers were as black as a raven's.

So this must really be the Otherworld—this surely must be a messenger from the Goddess... she thought, and then she drifted back into oblivion.

A short time later she felt small hands touching her. She heard voices. Though she was too tired to open her eyes, she understood what was being said and that surprised her. Did they speak her language in the Otherworld?

A curious voice asked, "Is she the One?"

"Look at her," another said, "she has been taken by the sky."

Near her side, Raven heard a surprisingly musical laugh. "If so, then the sky has returned her to us."

Another voice. "Look at her clothes...and her weapon!"

"I see she bears no iron."

"Is she one of us?"

"She is of the race of men," said the woman's voice next to her. The woman was touching her.

"Look at her face—she is a wild child. We should leave her here."

The woman's voice spoke again, this time with the authority of a leader. "She is no longer her mother's or her father's child—she is our child. We shall not leave her."

Raven's eyes opened momentarily. Children—children surrounded her. But no, that wasn't right either. They were the size of children, but they were not. The sun was in Raven's eyes and all she saw was vague silhouettes haloed in light. Behind the children, or whatever they were, stood seven gargantuan black birds over which large, luminous fireflies flitted to and fro. Raven was fading again, slipping between the worlds.

She smiled, whispering, "Birds and fireflies…"

The woman said with concern, "We must get her to our village and to our healers."

The first voice asked, "What do we call her?"

Sleepily, Raven mumbled, "I am Death."

That musical laughter, "No child—you are Life!"

CHAPTER 29

Dan awoke early—dawn was breaking and the sun was shining through their bedroom window. He heard birds in the trees outside the window—it was a peaceful sound. He looked at Sharrone, asleep beside him, and smiled. He was far luckier than he had any right to be. He tried to make himself believe that he'd worn her out the night before, but he knew it had actually been the other way around. Her auburn hair picked up the light from the window and it glistened like red gold. He gently brushed a fallen lock of hair from her eyes. She smiled faintly, still asleep. Dan allowed himself to settle back onto his pillow. He was worried about the idea of trying to contact the women who had assaulted the priests. There was no telling who they might be, or what their real agenda was—too bad there wasn't another way.

Dan drifted back toward sleep, as they had no early appointments today. He knew Sharrone would awaken shortly, so he closed his eyes and relaxed. He must've fallen asleep—after all he was dreaming. Suddenly sitting upright in bed a moment later, he would swear he'd been awake the whole time. He thought back to the dream...

His dream was really only an image—an image of an old photograph in the Los Angeles Journal. He'd seen the image of the Bishop on the front page, and in the dream the photo was changing—shifting. It seemed the Bishop's face was moving—his wrinkles disappeared and his hair grew longer. What could it mean? *Of course,* he suddenly thought, *how could I have been so stupid?* He reached over and nudged Sharrone's shoulder. She grumbled and rolled over, showing him her back. He kissed her at the nape of her neck then slowly began kissing down her spine. She shivered.

"Dan?"

"I would certainly hope so," he said, laughing.

Sharrone laughed as well, and then turned toward him. The blankets and sheets were at her waist and the early sunlight shone on her naked body. She propped herself up on her elbow and stared at him. She looked down at herself, and smiled.

"If you want what I think you want, you'd better tell me the other reason you woke me up!"

Sharrone leaned over slowly, allowing her lips to brush Dan's. They kissed briefly, and then more passionately. Just when she felt Dan's tongue, she pulled back suddenly, a smirk on her face. "Oh, no you don't!"

"Life with you is...complicated," Dan said.

"Not really," she responded, "tell me why you woke me...the first reason."

Dan looked into her eyes. "I just had a dream, a very interesting dream."

"If you find it interesting, I probably would as well—spill it!"

Dan chuckled. "You sound more like a reporter every day! Very well, here it is."

He briefly explained what he'd seen; he then paused to see what Sharrone's reaction might be. She looked baffled.

"I think," Dan began, "if we really want to do some damage, instead of finding the women who attacked the priests, we should investigate the head priest—the Bishop!"

"That's an excellent idea!"

"Here's the question," Dan said. "Before the Bishop took over the Cathedral, the Church of the Redeemed God existed in relative harmony within the city and with the other faiths—sure, they had their domination thing going on internally, but there were no zeppelin raids, and no kidnappings." Dan paused for effect, and then went on. "Suddenly all that changed, the religion became confrontational. They began dealing in drugs, women, and children. Why? What motivated the Bishop?"

Sharrone sat up. Dan could see he'd captured her attention.

"We must begin right away! There's no time to lose!"

She began to rise, but Dan had other ideas, and pulled her back to the bed. He kissed her, allowing his hands to gently run over her breasts. She pushed herself up into his hands, feeling herself stiffening.

Five minutes later, they were both back in bed, all thoughts of the Bishop temporarily forgotten.

* * * *

When Father Woods awoke that morning, he had an idea. He was excited—it might even work. He got out of bed and hurriedly dressed.

He was humming to himself as he came down the steps on his way to breakfast, and was met in the hallway by Larry Harper. Father Woods grinned at his friend, and then he asked, "So, how do you like your... advancement?"

Larry laughed. "I can handle a few more women, Your Grace."

"Good," the priest answered, "I was hoping it wouldn't be too big a strain on you."

"Not at all, Your Grace," Larry said, "but that's not why I came to see you."

"Come," the priest said, "have breakfast with me and we can talk."

In the dining hall they sat in a corner, far away from the others present. Some of the priests, especially the younger ones, stared for a moment. Nobody would dare to disturb Father Woods when he was in what he called his 'conference room.' The server came to their table and took their orders. When he was out of earshot, the priest turned to his friend and said, "So, tell me what brings you here this early in the morning."

"I've good news," Larry said with a smile. "I've discovered the identities of two of the whores that talked to that female reporter."

"Really?" Father Woods couldn't believe what he was hearing.

"Yes, Your Grace," Larry continued. "I have two of them in custody right now. I believe with some persuasion, we might see if they know who the other two talkative whores might be."

"What are you planning?"

The priest was eager to hear the details as he stuffed toast and bacon into his mouth. Butter ran down the corner of his lip and he wiped it absent-mindedly on his sleeve.

"I'm going to drown them—one at a time," Larry said with a smirk.

"Drown them? How will that give us the information we need?"

"Pardon me, Your Grace," Larry said with a giggle, "I meant almost drown them. Father Anderson and Sergeant Jinks are going to help with this. Father Anderson claims he's an expert."

"He is that," Father Woods conceded. "Is he doing this himself, or will it be done by more of his...pupils?"

"He'll be seeing to it personally, Your Grace."

"One further question, Mister Harper," the priest said, pausing long enough to push a forkful of eggs and cheese into his mouth, "what if they don't know the others?"

"Oh, that won't matter," Larry said, giggling again, "the other whores, and I mean all of them, will never speak to a reporter again."

"Why is that?"

"Because these two, once they've told us everything they know, will be used as an example of what happens to whores who use their mouths for talking instead of what all women should reserve their mouths for."

The priest was grinning now, yolk smeared in a yellow film on his lips. "Go on, Mister Harper, don't keep me in suspense."

"Since these two whores have used their tongues for something inappropriate, we'll take them away. That solves the talking problem for them, and since neither of them can read or write, we're safe there as well. It'll be a warning to the rest of our prostitutes. Plus, we'll still have them to make money off of!"

"That's an excellent idea!"

"Well," Larry said, "that's the news. If you have no further need of me right now, I have some whores to chastise!"

"By all means," the priest said with a grin, "by all means!"

Larry rose to go, but the priest put a hand on his sleeve. Larry glanced down at Father Woods. "What do you think it will feel like inside their mouths once they're healed? I mean, I've never been in a woman's mouth that had no tongue. It sounds…boring."

They both laughed uproariously as Larry turned to go. A few of the priests in the dining hall glanced up at the laughter, and then turned back to their food.

After breakfast, Father Woods returned to his office—he had a phone call to make.

"Sergeant Jinks, please."

"This is Jinks, what can I do for you?"

"Well, sergeant, I was wondering if we might meet at some point today. I have an idea I would like to discuss with you."

"I was just on my way to the bar where the two priests were drinking just before they were assaulted—I can come by the Cathedral first, if that's all right, Your Grace. After that I have an appointment with two women."

"That'll be good, sergeant, I'll be awaiting you."

* * * *

Since Harold had traveled south with the Bishop, Father Woods answered the door himself when he heard the knock. He opened it, and invited the policeman inside. Jinks sat in a padded leather chair across the desk from Father Woods.

"So, Your Grace, what can I do for you?"

"I would like your opinion on an idea I have."

"Okay, what's your idea?"

"I'm thinking that since those two priests frequented the bar you mentioned, perhaps we should set an ambush."

"We've had a stakeout in the bar for several days now," said Jinks.

"I don't mean observers—I mean actual priests, who drink and talk to patrons, then leave and walk down the street. If the attackers go to that bar to hunt priests, let's give them some priests to hunt."

Jinks smiled. "Did you have anyone in mind, Your Grace?"

"As a matter of fact, I do—former Father Lifford's two friends."

"But they're no longer priests," the policeman objected.

"Yes, I know," Father Woods patiently explained. "But they were priests and their photographs have been in the papers as well as a discussion of their involvement in that prostitution scandal."

"I think I see where you're going with this," the policeman said. "You're figuring they'll make ideal bait in the trap—but will they do it?"

"Of course they will," the priest said with confidence. "I've told them that after this is over, they'll be reinstated in the Church and sent to New Fresno with new names and identities."

"Excellent idea," the policeman said with a smile, "we get the women, the priests leave the area, and we all win."

"All except the priests," Father Woods said with a smile. "If they're taken by the women, you must have trusted men following them. The attack must be finished before you make your arrest. Whichever police officers are there when the women are taken into custody must be trustworthy enough to then kill the former priests with the women's knives."

"I see," said Sergeant Jinks, "this way we execute the women for premeditated murder and the two former priests won't be able to talk."

"We should set this up now," Father Woods said, "no point in wasting time."

CHAPTER 30

Dan left the house early, riding his new steamcycle. It was a powerful machine, shiny and black. As he turned into the street from the driveway, he accelerated rapidly, putting up a white cloud of smoke from the wide rear tire. He leaned sharply as he negotiated the next turn, shifting gears smoothly. He smiled. He could still do this! He concentrated on the roadway, avoiding both autos and the many ever-present potholes. He was heading to the Cathedral on a dangerous mission—he was going to go down into the first basement library. From his forays there years before, he knew the great journals of priestly lineage were kept there. He'd see if there was any information on the Bishop. He tugged at his black collar—it was tight around his throat in proper priestly fashion.

Sharrone, still under protection, left a short time later with two bodyguards. She sat in the back seat of the auto planning how to begin her research in the Library of Los Angeles. She wondered if there would be any information at all. Well, she'd know soon enough.

An hour later the car was parked and Sharrone and her two escorts were in the main reference room of the library. She paused before the card catalog, unsure of where to begin.

"If I may make a suggestion," one of her bodyguards whispered, "look for general information regarding the Cathedral around the time the Bishop first showed up."

"That's a good idea," Sharrone said, smiling at the burly but well dressed man.

"I was a policeman before becoming a bodyguard," he explained. "The best way to begin any investigation is a general search in broad terms—once more information is at hand, the search can be narrowed."

She smiled again, thanking the man, and turned to the files.

Thirty minutes later, she was sitting at a table with three books in front of her. Two were modern histories of the Cathedral, and one discussed the roles of priests and the personal histories of some of the more famous ones. She opened the first history tome and began reading. While she read, her two guards sat attentively on either side of her table watching the comings and goings of everyone.

One or the other of her guardians would frequently rise to patrol the area, watching for anyone who seemed nervous or too focused on Sharrone. The first man smiled to himself on his initial perimeter check. Sharrone was beautiful, so every man who passed looked at her appreciatively.

In shoulder holsters beneath their jackets, both men carried the newest concealment pistol available—it was referred to as the 'FN,' but nobody seemed to know why. The manufacturer's actual name was lost in the dim, pre-ice-age past of barely recorded and half mythic history.

The recently resurrected design, being built in small numbers by the Heinreich Reichhardt Armory, was in a new .380 caliber. The bullet was both larger and heavier than that used in the more common .25 and .32 caliber pistols currently being sold as defensive arms in the city—it also produced a higher velocity. Though the pistol had a safety lever on the left side, neither man had it engaged. The new pistols had a unique grip safety that wouldn't allow the pistol to fire unless the grip was squeezed in the hand. This made the pistol safe to carry and instantly available for action without having to fumble with the tiny but necessary safety found on the side of the Mauser design.

Sharrone didn't even notice that her bodyguards were armed— she vaguely assumed that was the case, but she was engrossed in what she was reading. An hour later, she closed the third volume in disgust. The Bishop was mentioned in the third book. His parents' names were, Mary and Thomas Armstrong—but all the information was general in nature with nothing she could really use. However, she took copious notes, making sure she had the names of the Bishop's parents clearly noted. It was a beginning, if nothing else. She wondered how Dan was doing—she was worried about him.

* * * *

It was surprisingly easy to enter the Cathedral. Dan smiled as he descended the steps in a slow walk, imitating the way the priests around him moved. Nobody even gave him a second look. The steps to the basement were where he remembered, and in a very short time he was inside the library. This early in the morning, he was alone. He knew it wouldn't be this way throughout the day, so he hurried to the genealogies shelf. He looked over the titles. He smiled as he withdrew one of the heavy books—it was dated the time the Bishop had arrived.

He carried it to a bench, sitting to study it. It didn't take long. The Bishop had a name after all—it was Jesse Armstrong. He jotted the name on his forearm under his sleeve, that way he wouldn't be seen taking anything from the library should there be passers-by when he left. He sighed. It seemed there was surprisingly little actual information on the Bishop. That was odd, Dan thought—here was the Church leader for the entire western coast, and it almost seemed as though he'd just suddenly dropped down from the sky with no past at all.

He closed the large book and returned it carefully to the shelf. He then went to the door, listened for a moment, opened it, and walked out. When he reached the top of the stairwell another priest accosted him.

"I don't recognize you," the priest said with a smile, "are you newly assigned?"

Dan thought fast—he'd hoped to come in and leave unnoticed. Now he could see that wouldn't happen. "Actually," Dan improvised, "I'm just visiting from New Fresno."

"Beautiful city, I'm told," the priest said with a smile. "My name is Father Jones." The young priest held out his hand. Dan shook it, smiling.

"I'm Father Wagner."

"Have you had breakfast yet, Father?"

"I haven't," Dan said with a smile, allowing his new friend to lead him to the dining room.

After they'd been served, Dan began questioning his new friend.

"I came here to see the Bishop," he began, "but I'm told he's not in the Cathedral, nor even in the city."

Father Jones shook his head. "He's been gone for many weeks now. All we have heard is that he went south on important business."

"I've been told that by others as well," Dan responded. "I was hoping to get some information from him for our new library."

"What information are you looking for?"

"I'd hoped to discuss his ancestry and life as a child. It'd make interesting reading, do you not agree?"

"I do," the priest responded, "but unless he were willing to tell you more, there's virtually no information regarding his past history other than that he was trained as a priest in far away Atlanta. He was sent here a number of years ago—but as I understand it, he was just a priest at the time."

"So when did he become the Bishop?"

"Why, almost immediately upon his arrival is my understanding. I've heard from the older priests that there was controversy at the time. The Bishop couldn't show his Documents of Elevation to his station. He said he misplaced them."

"Is that so?"

"Yes, yes" the priest said with a dismissive wave of his hand, "it was nothing, it seems. The documents were found and the suspicion and trouble became past history."

They'd finished eating, so Dan bid farewell to Father Jones, saying he was going to walk the city for an hour to help walk off his breakfast.

"I would join you," Father Jones said, chuckling, "but I have some business in the zeppelin barn this morning."

Once outside the Cathedral, Dan breathed a sigh of relief—that was nerve wracking for sure. He was glad it was over. Still, he'd gathered some interesting information regarding the Bishop Jesse Armstrong. He found his cycle where he'd parked it, handsomely tipping the two young street thugs he'd hired to guard it, and rode off making a U-turn in the intersection. The two young men stared in wonder as the 'priest' roared away on the cycle. Who would ever believe this story...priests on steamcycles?

Dan was on his way to meet Sharrone at the house—it would be interesting to see what she'd found. He thought about what he himself had learned. What wasn't said was probably more important than what had been said. It would seem the Bishop Jesse Armstrong had a secret—one he guarded jealously. To undo that secret would undo the Bishop—of this Dan was certain.

He squeezed the clutch and downshifted the powerful bike at the intersection. There was no cross traffic. He twisted the right handgrip, hard. The engine roared deafeningly as the front wheel of the bike lifted from the street. Pedestrians and other drivers on the road stopped to stare at the young priest with a big grin, as he cut the intersection in half on one smoking tire, his robes flapping like bat wings around his legs.

* * * *

"Who are you and why have you brought me here?"

"Shhhh, Marielle," said the old priest who was not dressed as priest, "I just want to ask you some questions."

"What kind of questions?" Her voice quavered a little.

The priest smiled—she was already scared.

"I want you to tell me why you gave information to the reporter connecting the whores with the Cathedral. You were told in the beginning to keep your mouth full of men and empty of words."

"I've said nothing to anyone—I swear!"

There was a knock at the door, and the priest smiled. He walked to the door and opened it. Marielle gasped when she saw Sergeant Jinks enter with another bound, gagged, and blindfolded woman. The sergeant grinned at her mirthlessly.

"So, my Marielle," he said, "your stories of not being connected with anyone were all lies. I mean…linking up with a journalist?"

He shook his head sadly, and then walked quickly to her, and slapped her viciously across the face. He noticed there were tears in Marielle's eyes—good! There was a lot more than fear in store for her and the other ungrateful whore!

"You want to hear a bad copper story? Do you? You're looking at one very bad copper right now, my dear—I'm going to do very bad things to you, I'm afraid."

Marielle heard a scraping sound. She twisted in her chair to see the other man pulling a large copper basin into the room. He grinned at her as he made a number of trips into the other room, returning with large pitchers of water, which he emptied repeatedly into the basin. It was difficult to see over her shoulder with her arms bound so tightly— all the feeling was gone from her hands. Father Anderson smiled at her as he walked over, slipping a gag firmly into her mouth. He turned her chair so she was facing the basin. He then turned to the policeman and asked, "Shall we begin?"

"I thought you'd never ask," Jinks said with a snicker.

Marielle's eyes widened when she saw the old man lay out the pliers and curved bladed knife on the bed.

Jinks shoved the blindfolded woman he'd dragged into the room roughly to her knees. He grabbed the back of her head and pushed her face into the basin. The woman, unable to see, panicked—but Jinks held her tightly. Marielle saw the bubbles of the woman's exhaled breath break the surface of the water in the basin. When they ceased to rise, the policeman lifted her from the water. She gagged and choked, hardly able to breath.

"Tell us the names of the other two whores who talked with that bitch reporter!"

"I don't know! I don't know! How would I know?"

Four more times the woman's head was submerged in the basin. Four more times she was held until no bubbles broke the surface. The last time Jinks pulled her up, she vomited onto the floor, coughing water from her lungs. She was sobbing and gasping—her breathing was ragged, bubbly sounding. Tears streamed down Marielle's face as she watched in horror and fear.

Jinks looked up at the priest, shook his head, and said, "I believe she'd tell us after all that. She knows nothing—I think we should show dear Marielle what awaits her if she doesn't speak."

"I do not know," Marielle mumbled through the gag.

Then she was silent. Her eyes grew big as she watched in horror as Jinks deftly grabbed the other woman's tongue with the pliers, jerking it beyond the woman's lips. She fainted when the priest used the knife.

CHAPTER 31

Sharrone ran into Dan's arms when he opened the front door. She leaped up on him, wrapped her legs around his waist, burying her head in his shoulder.

"I've been so frightened," she cried, "what if I lost you?"

"You can't lose me," he said, "you just found me!"

She laughed, and allowed him to help her put her feet back on the ground.

"So, my love," he said with a grin, "what have you discovered?"

It didn't take Sharrone long to tell Dan that she'd found only the names of the Bishop's parents.

He smiled at her, and she asked, "What did you find?"

"I didn't find much either. I did find that the Bishop's name is Jesse Armstrong."

"Then why the big grin?"

He briefly explained to her about his chance meeting with Father Jones and what he'd learned.

"So you know as little as I, then," Sharrone said in a disappointed voice.

"Ah, but what we don't know shows us the way!"

"What're you talking about, Dan? Have you been into the champagne when I haven't been looking?"

"You spend *that* much time looking at the champagne?"

Sharrone playfully slapped Dan's shoulder, and then said, "You must explain your thinking, my dear."

"The answer is in plain view," he said with a shrug. "We seek the Bishop's big secret, and then publish it in the newspaper. Whatever it is, I'm certain it will finish him. Why else would he hide his past so carefully?"

"I know someone who may be able to help us with this," Sharrone said.

"Who?"

"Brett Holiday."

"Who the heck is Brett Holiday?"

"One of my bodyguards," she answered with a grin, "he was a

police detective before he began working for Mister Leatham. He was wounded in a gunfight and had to leave the force due to his injuries. He still has friends in the police department. We should see if he can find more information for us."

A half hour later, the burly bodyguard came into their house. Sharrone took his jacket, seeing for the first time the black and dangerous-looking pistol hanging beneath his left arm.

After Dan explained what they were looking for, Brett Holiday said, "I'll see what I can do. There are no promises—remember, I've been off the force for five years now. I'll call one of my former partners this afternoon when he's at home—I don't want to call the station for obvious reasons."

"I understand," Dan said.

Holiday looked at Dan with steel gray eyes. "You're a smart man, Dan Hendricks—you would've made an excellent detective."

"That's a true compliment coming from you, sir," he replied with a smile.

The phone rang later that afternoon. Dan answered.

"This is Holiday, sir," the former detective said. "My man says he'll look into the files tomorrow. Also, you should call Tom Leatham."

"Why?"

"There was an assault committed on two known prostitutes. Both of them were tortured, almost drowned, and repeatedly raped. Both had their tongues cut out—it looks like they died from a combination of exsanguination and drowning. The coroner thinks the rapes occurred post mortem."

Dan hung up the phone. He felt numb—just how depraved could city 'civilization' get? He turned to Sharrone, telling her what he'd heard. She wasted no time in calling the editor—the conversation was short and ended with Sharrone in tears.

"They're killing the women who talked with me," she sobbed. "They're sending a message to other street women—talk to me and you die a slow, horrifyingly painful death."

As Sharrone cried into his shoulder, Dan's clenched his hands into fists. Now he knew that revenge would once again play a part in his life—not entirely for himself this time, but for all the lost women in all the dark places who screamed silently as the priests of the Cathedral devoured their bodies and their souls. One way or another, this would end—this had to end!

* * * *

"They died?" Father Woods was incredulous. Every time they planned something, it turned out badly.

"It's no problem," Larry said with a grin, "the message is out—loud and clear."

"I suppose you're right," the priest conceded, "at least now there's no chance of them communicating with the press or the police."

"We still win," the pimp said.

"Tell me what went wrong. You were watching from the other room were you not?" the priest asked.

"Yes, I was. With the first one, the woman lunged back as the cut was made. It was probably an involuntary movement—she was blindfolded at the time. Father Anderson leaned into the cut, trying to finish severing the whore's tongue, and the knife went deeply into her throat. I believe he cut her carotid artery—you should have seen the blood!"

"Yes. Well, I'm glad I didn't. I don't need to know what happened to the other one."

"I understand, Your Grace," Larry said with a grin.

Father Woods sighed. He was now having doubts about his own plan to find the women who'd attacked his priests. Well, it was too late to stop that operation—things were already in motion. *It'd be nice if the Redeemed God would supply a little assistance,* he thought.

Larry left the priest's rooms and Father Woods descended to the dining hall. He sat with the rest of the priests. After he ordered his dinner, another priest walked up and sat next to him. When Father Woods asked him why he wasn't eating, he explained that he'd already eaten and was waiting to speak to him.

"Well," Father Woods said with a smile, "tell me what's so important, Father Jones."

Once again, Father Woods received an unpleasant surprise. Father Jones asked him about the visiting priest from New Fresno—there was no visiting priest from New Fresno! A quick description as supplied by Father Jones didn't sound like anyone Father Woods had met. Who could he be and why was he inquiring about the Bishop? At least, based on what Father Jones told him, the imposter learned nothing that was not already common knowledge. Father Woods hadn't been in Los Angeles back then—he'd been a new priest just starting his service in San Diego. Still, it was another bit of disturbing news.

* * * *

It was early evening and the Gaslight Tavern and Grill was booming. The two former priests, Kenneth Lee and Albert Turner, were now wearing the ordinary dress of the city. They were sitting at a table near the back of the room drinking and talking. They ordered beer rather than their usual liquor. They didn't want to get too drunk—not if some crazy females were going to try to hurt them! It was hard to believe that any woman could plan and actually carry out an assault of this kind. Both of them secretly believed the attackers had to have been helped by at least one man.

The evening wore on. Dozens of people came through the front door and left again a few hours later. It was almost nine in the evening when the attractive young woman with red hair came through the door and sauntered to the bar. She ordered a drink, and as she sipped it, she rebuffed the approaches of two male patrons. Two more young women came in and joined the woman at the bar. The three of them sat and looked out into the room.

"Probably trying to figure out which men might be willing to sleep with them," Ken stated.

Albert laughed and nodded his head, although he was wary—at one time or another, each woman had looked directly at him. Could these be the three bitches that assaulted the priests? He was starting to sweat. He waved the serving woman over and ordered another beer. The woman walked away to fill his order.

He sighed in relief when the three women rose from their bar stools and headed toward the door. They were leaving—they couldn't be the ones. Albert smiled as his new glass of beer arrived. He was distracted by the arrival of his drink and didn't notice the close scrutiny he and Kenneth were placed under by the three women as they passed close to their table and out into the night.

Thirty minutes later, they decided to leave—nothing was going to happen tonight. It was probable the attack was a lone event and would never be solved. In any event, it was a police matter. They'd do this a few more days, then report to Father Woods to be reinstated and sent to New Fresno. All in all, they felt pretty lucky to be getting a second chance—too bad Father Lifford had been so trigger-happy.

They left the bar, turned to the right and around the corner, heading east. They would do the walking part of the stakeout anyway—it was part of the deal. They were two blocks away, passing a dark alley in the shadow between two gaslights when two of the three women who'd been following them closed in, striking them across the back of the head with hammers. They never awoke.

PRIEST MUTILATORS SHOT DEAD IN POLICE AMBUSH

The headline the next morning told the story. Dan and Sharrone read the article in disbelief. Two police officers walking their beat had accidentally come across the assault as it was concluding. The women killed the two men this time—but before they cut their throats, they mutilated the two men, leaving similar inscriptions carved into the flesh of their chests as before. The policemen shot the women when they tried to stab them in an attempt to get away. The article guardedly suggested that if anyone had further information, or had seen anything, they should call the police—however, the phone number Tom listed was that of the newspaper office.

Tom called Sharrone, telling her what he'd done—accidentally, of course. He told her if anyone called, she'd be the first to know. She thanked him. Tom returned the receiver to its cradle wondering if any other witnesses to the crime existed.

He sat in his office, and reread his notes. It seemed incredible that all this had transpired as it had been reported—that the assault was conveniently completed when the policemen just happened to arrive at the scene. Why, he wondered, would the women choose to fight with knives against firearms when they could've simply run the other way down the alley? Sure, they might've been shot, but the bullets would've been in their backs—which wasn't the case. A little further digging informed him that the two patrol officers involved were weeks from retirement, devoted to the Redeemed God, and both were dramatically overweight. Those young, fit women could have easily outrun them.

According to his connection in the coroner's office, all three were shot at very close range in the chest. One had been shot one more time, in the face just below her nose. This was a convenient location for the shot, his connection said, as it allowed the bullet to travel virtually unimpeded though the mouth cavity before striking the brain base, which controls all life functions.

More significantly, though the bullet attempted to exit the back of the woman's skull, it remained lodged in the skin. The wound had clearly been shored, the man had told him. This meant the exit wound had been supported by something—in this case the stone of the building her head was resting against. The bullet couldn't completely exit, and the flesh of the exit wound clearly showed abraded edges where it'd been pushed forcefully against the supporting structure by the bullet and literally rubbed raw.

Furthermore, that last wound was delivered from near-contact distance, the coroner's assistant said. The edges of the entrance wound showed dark searing from the hot gasses expelled from the muzzle of the pistol and bits of unburned gunpowder were buried in the upper layers of flesh all around the wound. The pistol was almost touching the woman's face when the shot was fired.

This, the man said with certainty, was an execution—this woman had been on her back with her head resting against the stone wall when the final shot was delivered from a pistol held maybe an inch or two from her mouth. Tom called the newsroom. This information would be published in the paper the day after tomorrow—he wanted time to verify facts and see if any witnesses called. He wondered what the impact of this part of the story would be.

* * * *

The next morning, before they'd even had a chance to begin breakfast, the phone rang. Dan answered.

"This is Brett. We need to talk."

"You can come over now, if you wish, and have breakfast with us."

"Thank you. I'll be there in ten minutes."

True to his word, he arrived on time, having only to walk the distance from the guardhouse to Dan and Sharrone's. Dan opened the front door, inviting the man into the living room. Holiday removed his jacket, hanging it on the tall brass coat rack by the front door. He could smell eggs and bacon cooking in the kitchen. He followed Dan into the dining room. They sat at the table, which Dan had already set. In just a few minutes Sharrone brought breakfast in and joined them at the table.

After a couple minutes of small talk, Brett turned to Dan and Sharrone with a serious look on his face. "My former partner called me last evening. He brought over some information you might be interested in hearing—but first I have further info on the murders of the three women two days ago."

That aroused Sharrone's interest immediately. Brett gave a brief explanation of the murders of the three young priest mutilators. Sharrone was pale when he'd finished—it seemed the Cathedral and certain members of the police force would be willing to do anything to further their interests.

"Now for the good news...well, interesting news might be a better way to put it," Brett said.

Dan and Sharrone looked at Brett expectantly. They'd stopped eating during the explanation of the assassinations. Dan commenced eating again, but Sharrone had lost her appetite.

"My friend found some interesting information regarding our mysterious Bishop."

Dan stopped eating again and Sharrone just looked at him, waiting.

"A background check on the name Armstrong gave us some interesting results," the former detective said, "it seems that around fifty years ago, there were two individuals named Mary and Thomas Bhear. They arrived in the city with their son, a priest of the Cathedral. He was about twenty years of age at the time, and called Jesse Bhear. We searched further, and couldn't find any further mention of that family name—either before or after this occurrence."

"Well," Dan ventured, "it's a rather odd name, is it not?"

"That it is. Even odder though," Brett said, "is that virtually upon arriving in Los Angeles, they had their names legally changed to Armstrong."

"Interesting," Sharrone said. "Do we know where they came from?"

"Not the slightest clue."

Dan and Sharrone looked at each other. This was clearly significant information, but what did it mean? They looked back to Brett, hoping for an explanation.

"Usually," Brett explained, "people change their names for one of two reasons. One reason is that the name is so peculiar they'd rather not live with it. The other is that they're running from a past they hope will not find them if they have a different name."

"Is there any indication they came from Atlanta as the Cathedral claims?"

Brett looked at Dan and smiled. "That's a perceptive question, Dan. The answer is no. We don't know how they arrived in the city, but they came neither by railroad or airship."

"So that's all we have?"

Brett looked at Sharrone with a serious expression and said, "Do you remember what I said to you in the library regarding searching for information?"

"You told me to start with the most general information, then narrow the search based upon what you found out in the general search."

Brett smiled at her again. "So why are you not thinking in those terms?"

She looked at him, and then an idea occurred to her.

"I have it," she exclaimed, "we need to go back to the library!"

Brett chuckled, responding, "I see you're as smart as your man, young lady!"

"So we go to the library, do a search on the name Bhear to see what comes up?"

"Exactly," Brett exclaimed, putting the last of his toast into his mouth.

Dan and Sharrone cleared the breakfast dishes, stacking them in the sink—they just might wash themselves, but if not, they could be washed tonight.

Brett rose, going into the hallway, and said, "I'm calling the guard house, we need more people if we're going out in public to a place as obvious as the library."

Twenty minutes later, the steam-car was brought to the front of the house. They moved quickly into the vehicle. Dan and Sharrone sat in the back seat, and the two men with Brett sat in front. In less than a minute, they were on their way.

CHAPTER 32

"By the Redeemed God!"

Father Woods held the morning newspaper in his hand. The paper was rustling as his hands shook. Sergeant Jinks was in the office with him; it'd been he who brought the paper.

"How can they know this?" The priest was shouting now, and the policeman cringed.

"There's a leak somewhere," he said with certainty, "but I'll be damned if I can figure out where. Either someone on the ambush party talked or there was a witness we didn't see."

"Well, either way," the priest shouted again, "how do we handle this? You're supposed to be the law enforcement specialist, how do we handle this?"

"I still think it isn't a problem," the policeman said. "We've two older coppers, just short of retirement, and three crazed women with knives—if one last shot was fired, so what? The man was close to examine the woman, and she made an aggressive move, and the officer shot her. End of story."

"Do you really think that'll be the end of it?"

"I do," the policeman answered. "What the paper didn't print, but will come out tomorrow morning at the press conference, is that the woman in question also had a firearm on her body. It's likely she was reaching for it when Officer Moore shot her in the face."

"A firearm?"

"Why, yes," Jinks answered with a grin, "at least it was on her when the medics took the bodies to the morgue—why, I confiscated it myself at the scene!"

"I see," Father Woods said with a smile, "surely if she had a gun, the shooting would clearly be justified."

"Of course it was," Sergeant Jinks said, "they were insane and they were women! How could it have been any worse? How could it have been any more dangerous to the officers in question?"

The sergeant rose, heading toward the door—he needed to prepare for the press conference early the next morning. He chuckled to himself, hoping the newspaper would publish another inflammatory story in the morning edition—more rope with which to hang themselves.

Father Woods left the Cathedral a short time later. A zeppelin was coming in today from far to the south. He was curious what information the Bishop might send him. He was glad the man didn't know what was going on up here! As he hurried toward the landing field, he heard the drone of the engines somewhere in the sky. *The sound is loud,* he thought, *they must be coming in at full power.* Whatever news they bore must be important. He picked up his pace—he should've called a car, he thought as he ran. Running was undignified, but with how everything was going these days, that was the least of his worries.

By the time he reached the airfield, the zeppelin had feathered all but two of its engines. He could see the mooring ropes being dropped to the ground crew. He turned, and walked to the large, barn-like structure at the north end of the field. When the crew had disembarked, the pilot would come first, bearing his news—whatever it might be. The priest sat, waiting impatiently.

About thirty minutes later, there was a knock on the door.

"Come," he shouted.

The door opened and the pilot quickly entered the room and shut the door behind him. He was carrying a large leather case. He walked to where the priest sat, and laid the case upon the table. He then took one step back, and waited respectfully for permission to sit.

"You may sit," the priest said with a smile. "Tell me of the south."

"The news isn't good," the man said, shaking his head. "I have some bitter news for you. The Bishop is missing."

"Missing? What do you mean...missing?"

"There was an...accident," the man said, searching for the right words. "The details are in the pouch—I don't know them. What I do know, from having been there a very short time ago, is that some kind of large animal devastated New Los Angeles and buildings were knocked flat. The search for the Bishop was ongoing when I left, but the prospects for him aren't good."

"Don't keep me in suspense," the priest said calmly, "say the rest of it."

"As I mentioned, the details are there," the pilot said, gesturing to the leather case.

"What happened to the Bishop?"

"Well, when I left, the stories were either that he was…eaten by this creature, or that he's buried in the rubble of some of the shops, homes, or other buildings this monster destroyed. The problem is nobody knows with certainty where to begin looking."

"They have no idea even where he might be?"

"Vaguely," the other man said, "but even so, there were at least a dozen buildings knocked flat, and he could be under any of them. And then of course, there was the fire."

"Excuse me? The…fire?"

"The gas streetlamps ignited an inferno—there was also a zeppelin brought down. That burning hydrogen didn't help matters much at all."

"Very well," the priest said, "you may go, but stay close."

"Yes, Your Grace," the man said, rising to leave.

Father Woods sat stunned. Then he had a thought; if the Bishop were dead, why could he not assume the mantle of command? He needed to see the Bishop's will immediately! He was just as good as the Bishop was at leading people and taking care of his flock, wasn't he? Of course he was!

"Bishop Woods," he said softly, trying the words on for size, they felt very large indeed.

After a moment, he shook his head, reaching for the leather case. Inside were a number of documents, some in the Bishop's hand, some in the hand of others. Several detailed the attempt to use the baby dinosaur as an icon of the Divine Dragons to take political control of Los Angeles, and later the other cities of the west, and the final disaster that was the result.

The priest was astounded—they found monsters such as this in The Green? It was no wonder no humans wanted to go there. Except they were going there, he realized. He read in astonishment the accounts of crystal ships and zeppelins making repeated round trips, bringing vast numbers of the faithful not just from Los Angeles—but also from Atlanta, New Orleans, and Jacksonville. It looked like the Church of the Redeemed God was indeed relocating, and he'd be the ultimate ruler of that empire!

Reading further, he saw how the military was screening new arrivals and even those who'd come a year or more before, looking for anyone who wasn't a true believer. The Bishop apparently wanted a pure nation. Father Woods thought that might not be a bad idea—with the way things had been working out in Los Angeles, he'd probably have to travel south soon himself.

There was one final document. It was a missive from the Bishop in his own hand requesting the zeppelin that delivered the message be dispatched immediately to Atlanta. The Bishop wanted something from an equipment manufacturing plant located there. He read further. Whatever this equipment was, it had been ordered months earlier. The letter from the Bishop seemed confident that the three machines were now ready for shipping. The airship was to relay the message to the factory, ordering the machines to be shipped by rail to Los Angeles where they were to be loaded onto a crystal ship, and then sent south. The Bishop seemed very eager to have these machines—whatever they were. He called them simply 'trimotives'—as though that was any kind of an explanation.

Even though it seemed the Bishop might be dead, he'd continue with the request. If the Bishop thought he needed them, then Father Woods would probably need them as well. He sighed. Perhaps, monsters or not, the faithful having their own land with unlimited resources and only token half-human barbarians to resist them, might be the answer after all.

Father Woods closed the case, keeping the letter from the Bishop in his hand as he walked to the barracks where the crewmen of the recently arrived airship were resting. On his way, he stopped to talk to the ground crew who were moving the zeppelin to the barn. The men were surprised when the priest told them to do a quick safety check on the craft, refuel the hydrogen cell that fed the engines, and prepare the airship for departure at first light. He then walked to the barracks. Inside, he found the officer he'd been talking with only an hour previously. He gave the letter to the ship's captain with an additional note to speed delivery—that was his idea. He smiled. Whatever this was, obviously it was considered important to the Cathedral citizens in The Green. He knew in his heart that soon he'd be one of them.

The captain took the news well; he was a dedicated believer and a good soldier. After a short discussion, it was decided the zeppelin could make it to Atlanta in approximately two days. With luck, if the machinery was in fact finished and ready to ship, it would be back in Los Angeles in another three or four days. The whole operation should take less than a week. Perhaps, the priest reasoned, he'd take personal command then—leaving this accursed place once and for all for a new, pure beginning far to the south.

He walked back to the Cathedral. It was now late in the afternoon. Shadows lay heavy in the passageways between the buildings and high walls. He was thinking about what they might be able to take with them from the great libraries and storage facilities in the basements of the Cathedral.

He decided in the end that very little could be taken—though he'd been granted the oversight of the removal of the most critical documents, books, and artifacts for over a month now, there was just too much to take. What they didn't move south when the final evacuation came would be destroyed with fire and explosion. This trove of ancient history and marvelous artifacts couldn't be left for unbelievers and half-humans to find and use. History and knowledge was the province of the true church—the Church of the Redeemed God.

As he climbed the steps to the side door, he was preoccupied with his thoughts. He didn't see the bright, almost feral eyes watching him from the darkness between a wall and a trash container. Those eyes watched him carefully as he opened the door, disappearing into the Cathedral.

He went immediately to the Bishop's office—he knew there'd be a safe in here somewhere. He hadn't needed to know its whereabouts until now. He searched frantically, finally finding the safe behind a painting of the Redeemed God. He smiled to himself, went to the telephone, and called the zeppelin barn—they'd have the tools to open that safe. It took less than twenty minutes for an engineer and his assistants to arrive with a cutting torch. Opening the safe took another ten minutes. When the door opened, Father Woods dismissed the men. They left the priest by himself.

Father Woods licked his lips as he opened the door of the safe. He found a number of things inside. On top was a series of photographs of a young girl with amazingly white hair tied to a bed. He smiled as he looked through the series of photos. He set those aside for future viewing. He found the Bishop's will under everything else. Eagerly he opened it, and read the contents. He laughed out loud. It was done. There in black and white, in the Bishop's own hand, was his name listed as successor to the throne of power. The Bishop's official documents making him a Bishop were also in the safe. He laughed again. This would bring interesting responses at the press conference he intended to hold the next morning.

* * * *

Adria was crying, tears staining her grimy cheeks. It'd taken her days to find the location of the park again after sneaking out of the hospital, but she had found it. She was glad she had the foresight to buy some salted meat—after removing some from the barrel, she soaked it to remove the excess salt and tenderized it in the fashion of her former tribe. The meat was quite good, once it was cooked, though the taste was unfamiliar. Her strength somewhat returned, she next sought out the priest who was her betrothed. Tonight, after a two-day vigil, she'd seen him at last!

There must be some way to win him back, she reasoned. All she needed to do was accomplish something really important, something that would attract his attention. She knew in her heart he still loved her—they'd been separated by circumstances and if she could discover another set of just right circumstances, they could once again be united. The scorpion would help her, as it had helped her rid her body of that terrible parasite with which that Lyria bitch had impregnated her. She was certain. Now there was a smile on her face as she turned back toward her secret home in the park. A cold wind was blowing from the north. Adria shivered—winter was coming.

CHAPTER 33

The steam-car came to a halt in front of the library. Dan, Sharrone, Brett and one of the other guards exited the vehicle, walking quickly to the front door. The other guard stayed with the car. The steam pressure was lowered, but the engine was hot and ready to roll with no more than a moment's delay. He kept a watchful eye on the people walking to and fro along the sidewalk. He smiled as a young couple walked by with two young hyenas at leash. The animals were curiously sniffing at anything in nose-range, tugging at their leashes and wagging their tails furiously, obviously having the time of their lives.

In the card catalogue room, the two sentries took up inconspicuous posts around Dan and Sharrone. Sharrone was concentrating on the letters on the face of the card drawers, where should she start? Ancestry registers! She moved quickly to a separate stand of files. She found the file she needed, and turned into the stacks to hunt it down. Dan and Brett moved with her, ever watchful. She smiled as she pulled down the file labeled 'B.' Her happiness was short lived however—there was only one mention of the surname Bhear, the record of its change to Armstrong some fifty years earlier. She exhaled in disgust, closed the volume, and returned it to the shelf.

They walked back to the card files—Sharrone wasn't sure where to look next. It was Dan who came up with a novel approach.

"You know," he said, "sometimes individuals change their names to hide. They'll change it to something similar to what it was originally to avoid an identification error. Recall Kel's new first name? Kelley? Perhaps we're looking for the right word, but with the wrong spelling."

Brett clapped Dan on the back, saying with a smile, "You're a genius, my boy! Let's search out the most common spelling of that word, Bear."

The search didn't take a great deal of time—there were numerous references beyond the expected ones referring to various animals of differing size and dangerousness who all bore that name. Brett found the first important point. "Look here," he whispered to Sharrone, "read this!"

Sharrone took the book and read. Dan was standing behind her, reading over her shoulder. The citation in the book related to a tribal group that resided (or used to reside) north of New Fresno near the ice face. The people of the tribe referred to themselves as 'Bear People,' believing, the book said, that a primitive, half-human animal totem of a 'Great Bear' guided and protected them.

"Do you suppose this has something to do with our question?"

Brett laughed quietly. He pointed at the book once more. "You need to read a bit further," he said, "then tell me what you think."

Sharrone returned to the book, reading another paragraph. Then she gasped.

"See what I mean?"

She looked at Brett and quietly said, "Does this mean what I think it means?"

He shrugged, "Perhaps. It's a further reference point to research."

Sharrone read the two paragraphs once more. There'd once been a large tribal clan living north of New Fresno. At one point in time, the village did quite a bit of trading with both New Fresno and Los Angeles. Then there'd been some kind of internal trouble among its citizens. The article was vague, but it sounded as though there was an attempt by some members of the tribe to usurp the local religion for personal power. The family responsible had fled, seemingly for their lives. Twenty years later, a black zeppelin descended upon the sleeping village in the night. Something was expelled from the airship—a white cloud that killed almost everyone.

The population was so devastated that the remaining few individuals migrated to various other tribes where they became, in time, adopted members. The Bear Clan was no more. She closed the book. That happened about thirty years ago; the airship obviously came from the Cathedral, though the history book didn't say that. Could what she was thinking really be true?

Dan and Brett returned with yet another volume. Both of the men had broad smiles on their faces. Dan plopped the large book down in front of Sharrone. Dust welled up when the book struck the desk. She saw a slip of paper marking a page. She looked up at both men, and then opened the book.

"We found this in a restricted section," Dan said with a smirk, "Brett distracted the guard while I...opened the lock. Only priests and people with their permission are allowed to see the dozen or so books in this section."

The book was an historical account of the use of airships in warfare. She flipped through the first half of the book. This part discussed the early use of these craft during the Great War, but that was a very long time ago. She moved on into the second half, quickly turning to the marked section. She read for almost ten minutes, turning progressively paler as she read.

The Cathedral war against the tribal peoples was not limited to the Bear Clan alone—several of the northern tribes were attacked repeatedly. Apparently the men of the Cathedral had modified their killing agent into a sort of sleeping gas that only occasionally killed. The raids that Kel and Lyra had told Dan about weren't recent developments. The kidnappings of children and young women for the pleasure of the priesthood and the faithful had been going on for decades. They simply hadn't heard of them due to the isolation of the tribes and the mantle of secrecy surrounding the Cathedral.

Though the book didn't cover the most recent events, from what Dan had told her, she knew another chapter needed to be written regarding the disappearances of shamans from various tribes. It further discussed, in a peripheral way, the mysterious circumstances around Father Jesse Armstrong's rise to the position of Bishop. The suggestion, as posed in the book, was that the Bishop was a fraud who'd manufactured his own Documents of Elevation. Now what needed to be determined was exactly who this man really was.

After taking copious notes, they left the library. Once safely in the steam-car, they sped back to their home. It didn't appear as though they'd been followed, but caution was never a wasted effort. The guard stationed inside the house opened the door. They all entered quickly. Once inside, the guard told them Tom Leatham had called. He insisted that Sharrone phone him immediately upon her return. She looked worriedly at Dan who simply shrugged. Sharrone dialed the newsman's number.

"You wanted me to call?"

"Yes, I did," the newsman said, "we've heard rumors coming peripherally from the Cathedral that the Bishop may be dead!"

"What? Really?"

"That's the rumor," Tom responded. "He may have been killed recently by some kind of large animal in The Green."

"I'm not sure what to say…" Sharrone said.

She felt shock. On one hand, she was glad—on the other, she thought bringing him to some kind of justice in the city would have been a better outcome. She listened to Tom's story.

"A zeppelin from New Los Angeles landed at the Cathedral yesterday. This rumor came to me last night. Several very drunken priests, celebrating the deaths of the young priest-mutilating women, were spouting off in the tavern. One of my young reporters overheard them and engaged them in conversation. That's all the information I have right now," he said. "If I hear anything else, I'll let you know. Oh, by the way," he added, "there's one more thing—if the Bishop is truly dead, his replacement will probably be Father Woods. You remember him—he's the jackass who's been giving all the press interviews."

Sharrone hung up the phone.

"What did he say?"

She turned to Dan and gave him the news. Dan smiled, but Sharrone just shook her head, saying, "That'll leave Father Woods in charge, Dan. He's just as bad or maybe even worse than the Bishop."

Dan's face fell. He knew that what Sharrone was saying was the truth.

"So," he said, "anything we learn about the Bishop may no longer be of use. Damn!"

"We'll continue looking into that," Sharrone said with conviction. "I'm assuming for now that the rumor is false."

Dan thought about this a moment, then said, "Well, if the Bishop is a fraud, his 'will,' if there is such a thing, leaving control to Father Woods is also fraudulent."

"I'm thinking the same thing," Sharrone said.

She was grinning when she picked up the phone one more time, and dialed the newsroom. The phone rang four times before the editor answered.

"You caught me just in time—I was already out the door."

"I'm sorry, sir, but I have an idea I wanted to run by you immediately."

"Spill it," Tom said.

Sharrone spoke briefly to the editor and then hung up, a wide grin still spread over her face.

"The jackass is giving another press conference late tomorrow morning. Apparently reporters will now be there to question Father Woods regarding the legitimacy of the Bishop's rule—and his will."

Dan laughed. "That should ruin his personality parade, I'd say!"

"Father Woods will ask for proof, but for now, innuendo is all we have—and I think we should use it just as he does."

"I couldn't agree more," Dan responded.

* * * *

Father Woods went to bed early, a happy man. He had proof of his ascension to the position of Bishop in the dead man's own hand. He knew he could write his speech in the morning—there'd be plenty of time. Though he realized he'd be leaving soon to take command of the southern continent, maybe things weren't working out so badly here in Los Angeles. Those horrible, insane women were dead, and the whores who talked to the reporter were also dead. He was confident that none of the rest of their prostitutes would ever talk with a journalist again—they'd surely learned their lesson. He drifted off to a peaceful, dreamless sleep. His last thought was that the Redeemed God works in mysterious ways. He was asleep when the news regarding the three dead women reached the police station, the coroner, and oddly, the Los Angeles Journal in rapid succession.

* * * *

Ringing. Something was ringing near his ear. Ringing....

"Mmmm?"

The editor sat up in bed rubbing the sleep from his eyes. He glanced at his watch—it was three in the morning! He looked at his wife. She was still sound asleep. Tom sat on the edge of the bed with his back to his wife, and spoke quietly into the phone so as not to wake her.

"What is it? You know what time it is?"

"Yes, yes, I know," the assistant coroner said impatiently, "this you'll want to hear."

"Spill it then," the editor said, now fully awake.

"Those three women who were killed by the police? It looks like they may have all been related!"

"What?"

"Yes. The police and my office were just notified, that's why I called you."

Tom was dumbfounded. The three priest mutilators were all related? How could that be? From the descriptions of them, nothing matched between them—hair color, complexion, or even eye color. They were all young, probably twenty-five or thirty at the most. They were all approximately the same age, so how could they be related? Could they somehow be triplets? Cousins?

"You better make yourself clearer," he whispered to his spy from the coroner's office.

"The blood types of the three women are all different—they cannot have had the same parents. But get this—they all have the same last name!"

"What?"

Tom glanced at his wife. She stirred in her sleep, disturbed by his loud exclamation of surprise.

"They have the same last name?"

"Yes, they do—Bear."

"What?"

This time his shout did awaken his wife.

CHAPTER 34

Sharrone was dumbfounded as she hung up the phone the next morning and looked at Dan. He was waiting expectantly. The magician was also there—he'd come for a visit to see how his friends were faring. He also waited expectantly. Sharrone explained briefly what the editor of the Los Angeles Journal had told her—the three women who'd been killed by the police all had the same last name, but were unrelated.

"You know what this means," she said, looking from one man to the other. "It's circumstantial evidence to be sure, but in my mind it verifies our suspicions—the Bishop isn't only a mass murderer, he himself is one of what he refers to as 'half-humans!' His parents were tribal members—not city stock."

"I believe you're right," the magician said. "All the various things you've told me could've predicted this event—those women came here to exact vengeance on the priesthood for the destruction of the Bear Clan all those years ago."

"But why wait this long?"

The magician turned to answer Dan. "We can only surmise an answer, but it's quite obvious that those three women would've been mere babies at the time of the trouble in the tribe—they may even have still been in their mother's wombs which could explain why they survived the attack that killed every child in the tribe."

"So you're saying they were raised from childhood to come here to hunt priests?" Sharrone was incredulous, but there could be no other explanation.

"They took the name Bear in honor of their defunct tribe when they came to the city," the magician answered.

Dan said, "It's ironic, is it not?"

"Yes," answered the magician, "the Bishop's family came to the city, and changed their names to hide. These three women came to the city and changed their names to find them; to hunt down the Bishop and his family."

"But they were attacking random priests, not stalking the Bishop," Dan said.

"Yes," the magician retorted, "but remember, the Bishop is currently out of reach. I'm guessing this was the fallback plan—if they couldn't kill Jesse Armstrong or his parents, they would hunt down his priests. Or, even if they'd killed the Bishop, they intended to hunt and mutilate priests anyway."

"From the standpoint of vengeance, it makes sense," Sharrone said. "From what I've read and surmised it seems the Bishop's family converted to the Cathedral religion while still in the Bear Clan. They tried to force everyone to convert with them. Who can say what they might've done to some of the tribal women or even the children to prove their point."

"And," the magician said, finishing her thought, "they were probably driven out and hunted for whatever they did. We can be certain it was more than just a change of metaphysical belief. They must have committed serious crimes or they wouldn't have left."

Dan then added, "The women believed that all priests are guilty—not perhaps of that particular crime, but of others."

Sharrone then asked the magician, "How do you know so much about how tribal vengeance might work?"

The magician looked at Sharrone for a long moment. He was deciding what to say. Finally he decided, as is usually the case, the truth is best. He said, "Because I came from a tribe myself when I was a young teenager. I was one of those trader's sons you hear mention of who ran away to make his fortune in the big city. I am a so-called half-human!"

Dan looked at his longtime friend in surprise and smiled. This was the first he'd ever heard that story. Suddenly he realized the answer to a question he'd asked the magician long ago. "You learned magic in your tribe, didn't you? All those herbal mixtures you use to make people see things—you were being trained to be a shaman!"

The magician laughed, "That's exactly right, my friend, and now that we're making confessions, I suppose I should also tell you my real name—it is Mahrden."

Dan smiled, extending his hand, "I'm very glad to meet you Mahrden!"

"Well, then. We should confront the jackass with this information at his press conference in a couple hours," Sharrone said.

"No," Dan said, "we should not!"

Mahrden looked at Dan approvingly—he'd figured it out too!

"Because," Mahrden said, "they may not be the only ones. If we give out that information we might be jeopardizing the lives of others who've taken the sacred oath of vengeance."

Sharrone hadn't thought of that. She nodded her head in comprehension.

"We should let the newsmen challenge Father Wood's right to rule based upon the fraudulent nature of the Bishop's title and nothing more."

"I think," Dan, said, "we should also give that press conference a wide berth."

"I agree," Mahrden said. "Besides, we need to prepare for Kel and Lyria's return."

"How do you know they're coming back?"

Mahrden looked at Dan, winked, and then turned to Sharrone. "I'm a shaman remember? Well, almost one—I know how to journey. I've seen it. They're aboard a crystal ship sailing for Los Angeles as we speak. It seems as though it should take them well over a week to get back, but somehow I felt they'd be here in days rather than weeks."

"How could they get here so quickly?"

"Mahrden looked at Dan, and shrugged. "This I cannot say—all I can speak to is the feeling they are close, and traveling quickly."

Dan asked, "Could they be flying? In your vision, could you have mistaken the cabin of a zeppelin for a cabin on a crystal ship?"

Again Mahrden shrugged. "That is a possibility—I have had little experience with either."

"Then we must meet them!"

"We shall," Mahrden said calmly. "Remember, I'm a magician. I'll have one of my men waiting at the city airfield, just in case."

The rest of the morning was spent catching up—Mahrden had much to tell Dan and Sharrone. He'd also heard that the Bishop might be dead, though like Sharrone, he was assuming that wasn't the case. The rumors he'd heard were only slightly more detailed than the ones Tom had heard.

One disturbing rumor suggested that the entire Church of the Redeemed God was migrating south—everyone. Also, those now in the south that weren't of the 'pure faith' were being told to leave—only the faithful would be allowed on the southern continent.

"They're going to pillage the land, aren't they?" Sharrone spoke quietly, and then added, "Are there many local inhabitants?"

"There are some," Mahrden answered. "They plan to enslave them, I fear, using their women and children for their perverted enjoyment."

"And," Sharrone said, anger in her voice, "with them having complete control, nobody can do anything about it. They can even block ships from landing and do anything they wish."

Mahrden shook his head, "Of that I'm not so sure—something is happening in The Green. I cannot say what, but something. The Bishop's hoards will meet with stiff challenges, I feel."

"Let's hope they meet with spear and sword," Sharrone said.

"That," Mahrden said, "is a very distinct possibility."

* * * *

The news reached Father Woods of course, through his own channels within the police department. He'd heard that all three women had come from the same family. Well, that didn't matter—they were all dead and no longer a threat. Who exactly they were and why they'd done what they'd done was a matter for the police to unravel. He and the other priests were safe again—the bear's den had been cleared out. He laughed at the cleverness of his comparison. He was whistling to himself when he walked into the reception room of the Los Angeles Journal. He was the master of the world now. Reporters from three cities had come to hear his speech. He knew it was a good one.

Father Woods gave a short, smug speech at the start of the press conference. He announced the death of the Bishop, the finding of the will, and his impending promotion to Bishop of the Cathedral. When the first reporter raised his hand to ask a question, he smiled benevolently at the man.

"Yes, what is your question, my son?"

"Actually, I have two questions. What proof do you have that the Bishop is dead, and what proof can you offer to show that he is, or ever was, really a Bishop?"

Father Woods scowled.

"There is evidence," the reporter continued, "that the Bishop is a fraud—evidence that his title is counterfeit. There is evidence that he may very likely be a half-human himself."

Father Woods paled. Where had this come from? The uproar in the room drowned out his initial angry response. Now more reporters were shouting.

"Do you think the will would stand up to court scrutiny?"

"What if the court decides to investigate the Bishop's documents? Will you turn them over for an investigation?"

"If the stories regarding the Bishop's origins are true, shouldn't he be tried as a mass murderer?"

The uproar in the room went on unabated. Father Woods was beginning to panic—what if they just suddenly…went for him? He tried once or twice to answer other questions, but the Bishop's true identity had become the focus of the conference, not his personal rise to glory. He felt the sweat—it started under his stiff, tight collar, running down his chest and back in distracting, tickling tracks. What should he do? Run?

He decided fleeing would be the best decision right now. He held up his hands for quiet—he'd decided to flee with dignity. The shouting abated, the questioning stopped. Everyone was waiting expectantly. He took a moment to gather his thoughts—he couldn't afford to stutter or have a quavering voice. He looked around the room.

"The internal workings of the Cathedral are not open for civil interpretation," he shouted angrily, "neither you nor any 'court' has the right to challenge our faith, our beliefs, or the way we do things!"

He paused for effect. "What we do is beyond the courts, beyond your merely mortal laws. We follow the words of the prophets—and those words are not open to interpretation, change, or challenge. Also not open to interpretation, change, or challenge is my coming position as Bishop of the Cathedral. Get used to it!"

"Does that also include your 'right' to murder our people? Does that also include your 'right' to kidnap and defile our children? Our daughters? Our sisters?" The young woman's voice cut through the general shouting.

Suddenly there was silence. Father Woods looked into the audience, seeking the origin of that voice. He saw the woman then—she was about fourteen years of age and she was standing about twelve feet in front of him. She was the one standing behind the raised pistol.

One of the reporters lunged at the girl, knocking the pistol from her hand. It clattered to the floor, skidding under the chairs in front of her. By the time it stopped moving, four men were on top of the woman, pinning her to the floor amid a clutter of fallen chairs. She was dragged to her feet, hands held firmly behind her back. The reporter who'd knocked the pistol from her hand looked into her eyes. He could see the anger and the pain behind those blue eyes.

"What's your name? I'll write your story, if you'd be willing."

She stopped struggling now, resigned to captivity.

"My name is Helen Bear," she said in a clear, proud voice, "and I come from a very large family."

Turning a steady, almost glacial gaze on the pale priest standing a short distance from her, she said, "Did you ever wonder how it would feel? Cold, grinding cave bear jaws forever hot on your heels?"

Suddenly Father Woods heard snickering—then a few laughs quickly became guffaws. Why was everyone laughing at him? He was the new Bishop—he should be respected, not laughed at! Then he looked at the young woman who had tried to shoot him. She was laughing too, and suddenly he knew why. He looked down at his feet. He was standing in a spreading pool of urine and though his trousers were black, the wet stain spreading across the front and down his legs was quite obvious. He turned, running from the room, followed by gales of laughter.

CHAPTER 35

It was dark by the time Kel climbed to the top of the path through the mountains. He stood atop the ridge, gazing down into the valley below him. It was hard to see in the nearly moonless night and even harder to understand what it was he was looking at. Then he remembered this was the city nation of Los Angeles—the Black City of the West.

It was late; somehow Kel knew the sun would be rising behind him very soon. He also knew this is not where he was supposed to be. He looked toward the south. Surprisingly, he heard the shrill call of the hawk. He knew hawks didn't fly at night, but then one did.

Kel felt himself rising from the ground—the pull of the earth suddenly meant nothing—the real world was this vast, free sea of air through which he was swimming with long, powerful strokes. He heard the call of the hawk once more, glancing left, then right, searching. He was alone in the sky, soaring hundreds of feet upward on invisible currents of rising air. He realized with delight that the shrill call came from within him.

Kel banked sharply toward the south, diving now to gather speed. Speed was a thrill in this multi-dimensional ocean of air. He pulled the air into his lungs—it was cold. He knew he was at a very high altitude. He banked, turned, rose, and descended in the simple ecstasy of being. Ever southward he flew. The earth, that great ball of rock and trees that spun slowly by below him was almost meaningless now in this eternal moment of absolute freedom.

He lifted his head, and the far-seeing eyes of Hawk showed his destination. He was returning to The Green. Ahead, in the wan moonlight, he could just make out the vast blanket of verdure that covered the southern continent. All was dark—except at the edges of The Green near the water. There, lights shone brightly. The gaslights of the southern city had been restored. Even from this distance he smelled the pungent odor of burned wood, and charred meat. The men of the north were not wasting any time rebuilding this beachhead—the first, it seemed, heralding a full-scale invasion.

But this is not where he is supposed to be either. He looks to the east, his eyes search far beyond the lights that are now below him. There's something there—he can just barely see the wavering, golden curtain.

The river passes suddenly below. Though it's vast, Kel knows his speed will soon take him far beyond its black currents. The trees are thinner now, and soon there'll be only open plains. He looks ahead once more. There are small lights in the sky that flit about, soaring and diving. They're fireflies, he suddenly realizes, for what other small creature could give off so much light from the energy of its own body? They seemed to be at the edge of that mysterious golden curtain, dancing and weaving just over the top of it.

Kel suddenly found himself confused. He soared over the wavering gold, realizing it was a vast plain of grass. Now, however, no matter how high he soared, he couldn't reach the top. He lost all sense of direction—but then suddenly he was again facing the great forest far away. He'd turned inadvertently, returning to where he'd begun. He banked hard, turning back into the grass. It seemed from his vantage point that the prairie was far below. He climbed sharply, sure that he would pass high over the grass.

Again he found himself lost in the confusing, golden curtain. It was soft, yielding, yet somehow impenetrable. How could this be? He heard the laughter then, coming from far away. Was it ahead of him? Behind him? He couldn't tell. He plunged onward.

He was outside once more, facing the blackness of the forest. He pushed hard against the air, climbing...climbing. Once more he wheeled eastward. Beyond the perimeter of the strange golden barrier of grass, Kel saw a light. It was the merest pinprick, but it seemed to him that, in the midst of this sea of gold that almost gave off its own radiance, a star had come to earth and was dwelling in harmony and delight with other star-born entities.

* * * *

Kel awoke, looking to his right. Lyria was sleeping calmly, her breast rising and falling rhythmically. He reached over, gently nudging her. She stirred and he nudged her once more. Her eyes opened.

"Kel?"

"I have some news, my love," he said with a grin.

"News?"

Lyria was still in the fog of sleep, he realized. Kel reached over, gently kissing her on her forehead. She saw a tear running down his cheek.

"I dreamed," he continued. "Raven is all right. She is somewhere I could not go, but I know now that she is well and happy—guarded by a strange power I do not understand. It is a power that laughs with the sound of a stream in the springtime. It is a gentle power, but also fierce. Raven will come to no further harm while she is under the protection of this power."

Lyria threw herself into Kel's arms—she was weeping in gladness. Raven was safe! She looked into Kel's eyes and felt a weight lift from her. Suddenly it seemed she could breathe again. She kissed him fiercely, overcome with joy and love.

In the morning, after eating breakfast, Garn and Galv found Lyria and Kel in their room. The shamans seemed worried.

"We overheard the cook talking," Garn began, "there is some kind of trouble with the engine of this craft."

"Oh, no!" Lyria exclaimed. "What will happen now?"

"The word is that we are putting into Acapulco for repairs. The cook said he heard it would take three days."

"Three more days?" Kel was worried; they needed to get back to the city with word of what was going on in The Green.

"There is some good news as well," Galv said. "There is a zeppelin port in Acapulco. We can fly home!"

"Fly in a zeppelin?" Lyria was awed. "Kel, we may never get this opportunity again! We should take it!"

"Also," Garn added, "the zeppelin will get us to the Black City in less than three days instead of ten."

"Then that settles it," Kel said. "We are going flying!"

By nightfall, the crystal ship was moored in the harbor of Acapulco. The city was no Los Angeles, but the people looked and acted the same. There was a distinct disdain for anyone not born in the city. Kel wore his armor and Lyria's sword. He carried his forged documents with him as well. It turned out that Hannessy, master of the airfield, was a devout follower of the Redeemed God, and he was awed by

Kel's presence. Imagine—a high commander all the way from the city-state of New Orleans wanting passage on one of his zeppelins.

"By all means, sir," the man enthused, "you, your wife, and three friends will indeed ride in luxury. You'll have the commander's stateroom in the very front of the ship. Your view will be directly to the front."

Lyria looked at Kel—he could see the eagerness in her eyes. He smiled. It seemed as though Lyria would start bouncing in anticipation at any moment.

"The airship will leave at daybreak," the man said. "You can stay here as my guests, if you like. We've excellent accommodations for exalted personages such as yourselves!"

When the door to their rooms was finally closed, Lyria started giggling. "I never knew I was an exalted personage."

"I have always looked upon you that way," Kel said, taking her into his arms.

They kissed briefly, separating when there was a knock on the door. Kel opened the door to find Galv standing before him.

"Come in, friend," Kel said with a smile. Galv entered, and Kel closed the door.

"I have been meaning to ask you about Raven," the shaman said.

Both of the men sat and Kel began the tale. Lyria joined them a few minutes later, bringing water glasses and a pitcher. She poured them each a glass of water, and sat. When Kel and Lyria had finished their story, Galv shook his head.

"She can communicate with animals most shamans have difficulty with, such as the great shaggy rhinoceros of the northern regions… and those other things we met in the south. She is unique, indeed!" Kel said.

Kel then told Galv of his dream that morning. Galv's conclusions were the same as Kel's—at least for the time being, the girl was protected. Galv, however, had no explanation as to what that mysterious protective power might be.

Lyria said, "First things first. Mister Hannessy has invited us to dine with him and I think we should."

"I agree," Galv said, "we need to pretend at least until we are airborne."

"And even then," Lyria said with a smile, looking at Kel. "Shamans may fly with Hawk in journey, but they won't do so well if tossed from a zeppelin over the ocean!"

They all laughed at that, rising to meet Garn and Drog and head to the dining room.

The food was excellent. Most of what was served was new to all of them. There were several varieties of fish, and even mammoth meat. Kel and Lyria had heard of mammoths, of course, but had never seen one. The meat was well prepared and very tender. There was also a salad with a strange, small pepper that set their mouths on fire!

The conversation centered mostly on what was happening in the south. Hannessy had, it seemed, an insatiable appetite for news from that region. Upon questioning, they understood why; people were on the move, he told them. At the moment, and to their good fortune, only one airship remained at the field at this time. All the rest were making repeated trips from the north filled with travelers moving into The Green, and returning with trade items. They carried things such as brightly colored bird feathers and cages with odd, almost human-looking, shaggy creatures with long tails that chattered and swung from trees to the amusement of people visiting the various zoos both in the northern region and in Mexico City.

They were also told that crystal ships were heading south bringing the loyal followers of the Redeemed God to their new home. Those ships, on their return trips, were bringing exotic lumber and felled trees to San Diego and Los Angeles. The wealthy, Mister Hannessy explained, were using the new kinds of hardwoods to decorate their homes and offices. Each was competing with the other for the more exotic, larger, and expensive woods being brought from The Green.

Lyria asked, "Why do they not bring seeds and saplings?"

Mister Hannessy looked at Lyria with some disdain—a woman had addressed him at his dining table! He glanced at Kel who was scowling at Lyria—she lowered her head appropriately. Hannessy smiled—here was a man who knew how to control a woman. He didn't deign to answer the question until Garn posed it a second time.

"Why, the answer is quite simple, really," he said with a shrug.

"Why should they waste their time planting trees? They'd then have to wait for them to grow, which might take years. Now they can just cut down as much as they want and ship it north. The Green is, well, full of trees."

He laughed at his joke. Kel forced himself to laugh as well while Garn, Galv, and Drog only smiled.

Lyria bit her tongue, determined not to call Hannessy an idiot and a pillager. She remembered her role for the rest of the time they were together, and kept her head lowered and her mouth shut. The entire time, she was caressing the hilt of one of the daggers Llo made for her, which was hidden under her dress at her waist. It would be harder to get to it in an emergency than if it were properly on her belt where any sensible woman would wear it. But better hidden and at hand than left in their room and completely unreachable.

"I really wanted to hit that stupid man with that mammoth bone," she raged once they were back in their room again.

"I know," Kel answered, "I wonder what will become of The Green in time..."

"I know what will happen," Lyria said bitterly. "The Church of the Redeemed God will turn it into 'The Brown'—there will be nothing left but a desert."

"A desert still lives," Kel soothed, "and remember, we know something that man does not. We know something none of the priests and their minions know. The Green is awakening—I can feel it. Raven felt it. I do not believe they understand what is coming."

"I do not understand either," Lyria said in despair. "Will it come in time? Will it come in time to keep Raven safe?"

"She is safe for now," Kel said. "That will have to be enough for us. She is beyond our reach, and we have business north of here."

Lyria nodded her understanding. They sat for a few more minutes, then they went to bed—dawn would come early and they both needed their sleep.

In the morning, they gathered once more in their room where they spent the night at the airfield.

Garn was smiling. "I talked with Hannessy after you and Lyria left."

He chuckled. "I told him that Galv, Drog, Lyria, and I were being trained as spies—that we would infiltrate tribal rebellions, passing ourselves off as half-humans to gather intelligence for our army."

Kel smiled.

"So," Garn continued, "I am still Garn, Galv is still Galv, Lyria is still Lyria, and Drog is still Drog. Those are our tribal names and we must live with them now to be believable when we go into...the 'Wild.'"

Drog then spoke. "He now knows that Lyria is being trained to be forward—this way she will be just like all the other female barbarians."

Lyria laughed. "I would love to show him just how much of a barbarian I could be!"

At that they all had a good laugh as they headed off to breakfast. Upon arrival, Hannessy approached Kel in a subservient manner. "I must apologize for yesterday, sir," he began. "I had no idea these people were being specially trained by you for such an important mission."

Kel clapped the man on the shoulder, and with a big smile answered, "There is nothing you must apologize for, my friend. You did not know the circumstances, and your response was quick and proper—exemplary if I may say so."

The man was beaming.

"And when I next see the Bishop, I will tell him of your fine service and dedication. Perhaps he will think it best to rely more heavily on your business in the future."

"You are too kind," he said. "Is the Bishop in Los Angeles?"

"By now he should be," Kel said, "he left in his own zeppelin some time ago."

"I see," was Hannessy's response.

There was little conversation at the breakfast table and soon it was time to be off. The five travelers climbed the short stairway leading to the passenger section of the giant airship. Kel noticed that passengers were berthed in the upper part while the gondola was reserved for the crew. He wondered how comfortable they'd be. He didn't worry about that for too long, however, when he heard Lyria gasp as she opened the door to their stateroom. Kel couldn't help but be impressed as well. Their quarters were huge—three bedrooms and a bathroom with a shower. A sign over the door advised travelers to only run the shower for two minutes each, every three days—water was heavy, the sign said and the airship could only carry so much.

In the gondola, Mister Hannessy handed the commander a sealed letter with instructions to see that it got to the Cathedral immediately upon landing—it was to be his first chore once the ship was grounded. Everything else was secondary to the rapid delivery of the letter. The commander nodded, placing it in his jacket pocket.

Hannessy left the gondola, and a short time later, the giant airship was moving upward. He watched it climbing slowly into the sky. He hoped his letter would reach whoever was in charge in Los Angeles. Anyone attached to the Cathedral, especially anyone as seemingly important as this Kelley Draco, would know the Bishop was reported as missing in some kind of disaster that occurred in New Los Angeles days earlier. He didn't know what was going on, but he knew Kelley and his friends were not who they claimed to be. When the zeppelin was a mere dot in the sky, he returned to his office, regretting again the fallen telegraph lines. He was temporarily out of communication with the Black City—and there was nothing he could do about it.

As the zeppelin drifted over the western seas, the travelers stayed in their rooms most of the time. The view was breathtaking and the living conditions sumptuous. They spent hours in front of the large windows watching the land mass slide by to the starboard, talking quietly and telling their tales. Five hundred feet below them, the ocean didn't seem to move at all—eternally shifting yet somehow immovable. That night they slept well, knowing the morrow would bring their return to the city.

The moon was heading for its full phase. Lyria had risen to use the bathroom, pausing at the windows to gaze down at the sea. Far below, the tips of the waves glistened in the moonlight. She sighed, remembering how excited Raven had been when she knew the whales were beneath their ship. A tear slid down her cheek. "Be safe, my Raven," she whispered.

It was late in the afternoon when the zeppelin came in over the landing field on the outskirts of Los Angeles. The mooring lines were dropped and the ship was pulled slowly earthward. Lyria was again staring out the window, so she was the first to see. She tugged at Kel's sleeve. He turned his attention to the window. Thirty feet below them, he watched a man climb quickly into the back seat of a black steam-car. Lyria looked up at him.

"The man climbing into that machine is the captain of this airship, Kel."

"What?"

"Somehow we have been found out—I can feel it. Why would the man in charge of this machine risk sliding down a rope or climbing down a ladder when he could wait mere minutes and exit safely with everyone else? We must get away from here the instant the ship reaches the ground."

They all began quickly gathering their belongings together—they had little to take. Kel left his armor—it was heavy and he no longer needed it. Lyria strapped the ancient sword to her back, and they were ready. They left their stateroom even before the craft ceased moving. When the door opened, they were first in line to exit. They quickly climbed down the stairway to the hard-packed earth. No one was paying attention to them as they hurried away.

They hastily hired a waiting taxi to take them to the offices of the Los Angeles Journal, as they didn't know what else to do. Hopefully they'd arrive before any of the Cathedral's soldiers were dispatched to find them. They breathed a sigh of relief when they finally arrived. They didn't notice the other cab that had been following them. Kel paid the driver with what turned out to be almost the last of the money he'd brought with him. He thought briefly of Pela, his grandmother, who had thoughtfully given him the money—how he longed for their tribe, their people...their life.

Once inside, they quickly found their way to the editor's office. It was locked—the man was out somewhere.

"Excuse me," a voice said from behind them.

They whirled to face the man who'd spoken.

"If you're Lyria and Kel, the magician bids you welcome. You were quicker to disembark than I'd expected. Come with me—I'll take all of you to your friends." He glanced at the three shamans, unsure of who they might be.

Kel asked suspiciously, "Can you name any of our friends?"

The man grinned, and answered, "Well, let's see...there's Dan Hendricks...Sharrone Cushing...Thomas Leatham. I'm afraid those are the only ones I know."

Kel laughed. "That is good enough for me, lead on!"

They walked out the front door of the news office. The cab was parked a half block away in an area designated for their use. As they walked past a dark alleyway, none of them turned.

CHAPTER 36

None of them saw the disheveled young woman who happened to be slouched against the wall. She was returning to the street after having relieved herself in the alley. Her bright and almost feral eyes followed the procession passing before her. Was it a hallucination? No, she decided, hallucinations don't cast shadows. She recognized some of them—and then she saw her hated enemy. There was the bitch-witch—Lyria! Adria snarled, moved cautiously to the entrance, and watched them get into the cab.

As soon as the cab pulled from the curb, Adria was running toward the second one at the cab stop. A woman with a child opened the door of the cab, but Adria shoved her ruthlessly to the pavement. Her young son began crying.

"You get out of here," the driver said angrily.

He ceased resisting when Adria pressed the dagger against his throat.

"Drive," she hissed, "catch that other cab or you will die!"

"Yes, ma'am," the driver said, putting the car in motion. It took almost two blocks for them to catch the other taxicab.

"Not so close, stupid," Adria hissed. "I need to know where they are going—not alert them to our presence."

"Yes ma'am," the driver said a second time, backing off a little. He sniffed cautiously—the woman in the back seat had a decidedly unpleasant odor about her. He rolled down his window.

* * * *

When the cab pulled into the drive, Garn noticed the other cab speed past. He said nothing—the other vehicle hadn't even slowed down. The driver pulled to the front door, and Kel and Lyria exited the front of the cab as the shamans exited the back. As they reached the front door, the cabbie pulled away, his job finished.

Dan opened the front door upon hearing the knock. His eyes widened as he beheld his friends before him. They embraced as Kel introduced Dan to the three shamans.

"Mahrden told us you were coming in sooner than expected!"

"Mahrden?"

Dan just laughed as he ushered them all into the house. Sharrone was the first to run up to Lyria and hug her. Then she hugged Kel. "Daniel has told me so much about you both, I feel I already know you! I'm Sharrone Cushing—I'm a friend of Dan's."

After their introductions, they sat and listened to each person's tale. Kel and the shamans had been surprised to learn of the magician's true heritage—surprised and delighted. The three older men immediately gathered around Mahrden and began a long discussion regarding shamanic traditions, techniques, and such things. Tom smiled as he handed a copy of the afternoon's paper to Kel.

FATHER WOODS' AUTHORITY CHALLENGED; PRIEST WETS HIS PANTS

Kel couldn't help but laugh. He read the headline to the others and they all responded with laughter—the image of the priest in those circumstances was hilarious.

Kel and Lyria looked at each other when Tom explained the rumor that the Bishop was dead.

"That is what gave us away," Kel said.

"What do you mean?"

Kel turned to Sharrone and answered, "The man at the airfield in Acapulco. He asked about the Bishop and I told him I thought he was here in Los Angeles."

Tom rubbed his chin; this wasn't good news. Still, all they had was a suspicion, and nobody to follow up on.

Mahrden asked, "Did you get away from the airfield quickly?"

"We did," Kel answered, we took a cab to Tom's newspaper, and it was there we met your driver. He followed us because we got into another cab before he could reach us. I guess you could say we left in a hurry."

Tom laughed. "How did you like my…taxi, eh? I think it's pretty convincing, myself. Let the Cathedral try to find it!" He laughed again. "There're many suspicious characters in the city, and I doubt they could find us among the millions residing here."

After much talk and reuniting, they retired to the dining room for an early evening meal. The travelers were tired—it'd been another long day.

* * * *

Adria was again in the alleyway next to the Cathedral. She was waiting—sooner or later her betrothed would walk through that door. She smiled, and then coughed. She'd discovered the circumstances that would finally unite them in love. She longed to be married to such a wealthy and powerful man. She'd waited this long, another day or two wouldn't matter. In a short time she was falling asleep, her head resting on a rolled up rag she found lying on the ground next to the trash container. She shivered. Winter was coming.

* * * *

Sergeant Jinks decided to spend some quality time with this 'Helen Bear.' She was pretty and young, two perfect qualifications. He snickered. Believing her to be of tribal origin, he assumed she'd be a virgin. He thought he could solve that little problem for her very easily.

As it turned out, his friend and willing conspirator was sick tonight—the man on the desk at the end of the hallway wasn't an officer he even knew. That problem could be easily solved as well. He brought the man a hot, steaming cup of coffee. He placed it on his vacant desk. The man was in the bathroom—he'd soon be back. Jinks hid in a cell. It was unoccupied, standing open. He didn't have to wait long and he was glad; he was already aroused. Three minutes later, the desk officer was sleeping soundly, unaware he'd been drugged.

Jinks sauntered down the hall, heading toward the last cell. He'd picked that location for the young girl—it offered privacy. He touched himself.

"Well, Helen Bear," he said sarcastically, "tell me, pretty thing, what's your real name?"

The girl rose to her feet. "You know my name," she said defiantly, "let me out so I can kill priests."

He laughed, walking slowly to the cell, swinging the ring of keys in his hand.

"Stand away from the bars, bitch," he snarled.

Helen moved meekly back until her legs struck the bunk at the back of the cell. There she stopped. Sergeant Jinks opened the cell door. He walked up to the young girl and suddenly grabbed the collar of her blouse. He ripped it quickly to her waist. The girl gasped, clutching her breasts in her hands.

He forcefully moved one of her hands out of the away, pushing it behind her back. As he was looking at her body, his grip lessened.

"How old are you really, Helen? Thirteen? Twelve?"

He pushed himself against her, rubbing against her body. Both of his hands were now on her shoulders—naked shoulders he thought to himself.

Jinks moved one hand down to his fly, exposing himself. He opened his mouth to speak, but instead he merely gasped. He could now see he'd made a mistake. He'd assumed the girl had been thoroughly searched—but apparently the bumbling officers at the scene thought the pistol had been her only weapon. He watched with a numb, detached fascination as the dagger slid up his belly. It seemed to be traveling in slow motion, rising from his still erect manhood all the way to his rib cage. Suddenly he realized that the entire dagger was being shoved inside his body, hilt and all. Suddenly it was very hard to breath.

Helen struck hard, shoving the dagger deep with both hands. She jerked it up forcefully. She felt muscles resist, then part. She felt the heat of his blood wash over her hands. When the dagger struck his ribcage it stopped moving. She quickly tipped it up, hammering the entire thing into his body with the heel of her hand. He was bending forward now, his forehead on her shoulder. His pain must have become overwhelming.

"So tell me," Helen calmly whispered into the dying policeman's ear, "how do YOU like being penetrated? Your precious priests did that over and over again to my little sister, you pig! They made me watch. They took her in her own bed! Then they did it to me, but I managed to get away. I ran. There was nothing else I could do—my parents allowed it...they were members of your vile Cathedral—'doing God's will' they called it; 'saving her worthless soul, they called it.' Afterward, the priests took Lucy away with them."

Jinks slowly slid to the floor, his vision was turning grey. The girl's words were far away now, fading…fading. He struck the floor with his head, but he didn't feel it. The girl looked down at him, still speaking.

"You don't remember me. I came to you—to YOU three years ago. Remember now? You told me there was nothing you could do. You told me my sister must have done something or worn something that provoked the men, aroused them. You said I was mistaken about them being priests. You smiled at me. She was eight, you pig! Others like myself eventually found me—sisters in blood. We followed you. We knew you. We saw you with the Bishop—with the priest. Well, now you can rejoice—you're with your Redeemed God!"

Helen was crying now, the memory of her younger sister and her abandonment of her was overwhelming. She'd been ten at the time. She stared down at the silent form on the floor. He hadn't been a priest, but he was one with them, nevertheless. She had known him—been told about his activities on several occasions by other members of the Bear family. She had watched him going to and from the police station. He'd been a target just as the priests of the Cathedral were. She and her sisters in blood watched. They watched and waited, gathering intelligence—gathering weapons.

She bent down to the floor, kneeling in the still warm blood. She rolled Jinks onto his back. She took his badge and his pistol. She cautiously walked down the hall. She could see the policeman at the desk—he was sound asleep. She nudged him with the muzzle of her pistol. He didn't move. She removed his pistol from its holster as well as his badge; you never know when something like that might come in handy. Then she calmly walked to the front door of the station. The desk officer was shuffling paperwork, with his back to her. She strolled out into the night, and walked toward her home where her sisters in blood waited.

CHAPTER 37

An insistent knocking on their door awakened Lyria and Kel. Kel quickly rose, throwing on some clothes. He stumbled barefooted to the front door, swinging it open. Mahrden was standing there, newspaper in hand. He held out the paper for Kel.

TWO PEOPLE KILLED IN STREET GUNBATTLE
ONE WOMAN WOUNDED

Kel quickly read the lead story. Helen Bear, the girl who tried to shoot Father Woods at his press conference and had escaped jail that same evening after killing a police officer, was back in custody. She'd been wounded severely in a gunfight with unknown individuals. Helen was found lying in a pool of her own blood, with a Mauser pistol in each hand.

Two men were slain; they were wearing uniforms that vaguely resembled police uniforms, but the men weren't members of the city force. There was speculation on the street, the article said, that these men were mercenaries of the Cathedral. No comment had yet been issued by Father Woods, acting head of the Church while the Bishop was away. No word as to how, if this were true, the Cathedral was notified of the escape before the rest of the police force. The Los Angeles Journal called for an investigation.

Lyria was standing next to Kel, waiting to find out what the article said. After hearing the story, she asked, "How could these city women know about the Bear Clan?"

"I can't say," Kel answered with a slow shake of his head, "but they clearly do."

They ate breakfast in silence. Suddenly Lyria looked up at Kel— she had an idea!

"We need to speak to Sharrone."

"Speak then," the woman answered from the doorway. "All this fuss has awakened us anyway."

Lyria looked at the other woman and smiled; Dan was standing next to her. Kel handed the newspaper to them.

After they read the article, Lyria said "You need to interview this Helen Bear, say you're writing an article for your paper. This article says she will be tried quickly and if found guilty, she will be hung. The trial is set for one week."

"There is no question of her guilt, I am afraid," Mahrden said.

"We must know what she knows," Lyria said.

* * * *

"Completely out of the question!"

Sharrone was talking to the police liaison officer and the chief surgeon at the hospital receiving desk. "But the public has a right to know," she shouted.

"She's been shot," the doctor said firmly, "she's in no condition to talk to anyone."

"But she's in good enough condition to execute. You know, that sounds like a really good headline, don't you think?"

"Write whatever you want to, you will NOT talk to this vicious murderer! Sergeant Jinks was a valuable member of the police force and a personal friend of mine," the officer spat.

"Well," Sharrone said sarcastically, "now we know who called the Cathedral killers down on her, don't we?"

"Get out of here," the surgeon shouted.

Sharrone walked out the front door with Dan. Once outside, he whispered into her ear. While Sharrone was engaged with the officer and doctor, he'd been examining the register. Helen Bear was in room 315.

They met Kel and Lyria at the waiting auto. Tom had the blueprint of the hospital spread out on the back seat. They gathered their ropes and grapnels and disappeared into the shadows along the west side of the hospital, seeking the correct window.

Kel threw the line—the hook locked into the wooden window frame and Lyria immediately began the climb. Crouching on the window ledge, she saw the young woman asleep in the bed, her left shoulder heavily bandaged. This high up, the police hadn't locked the window—Lyria opened it silently. As she climbed into the room, Sharrone began her ascent. Kel and Dan stayed below—they had to guard the line should a quick escape become necessary.

"Helen?"

The girl stirred, and then opened her eyes.

"Do you know who I am?"

"Yes," the girl whispered with a smile, "you're the reporter who's been trying to help the street women—you're a sister in blood."

"I want you to tell me what that means. I need to write this story. The Cathedral is falling, but unless we give it a push, it's possible it'll come back even stronger than before."

"I know," the girl said quietly, "I've read how the legislation against child rape and forced prostitution is being held up in the Forum."

"Speak to me then," Sharrone urged. "I'll reveal nothing that may put other women in jeopardy."

"I believe you," the girl whispered.

Sharrone took out a pad of paper and her fountain pen—a gift from Tom upon the publishing of her first article. The girl paused, and then began her story.

Helen told the story again of her little sister, and the story of Sergeant Jinks. Sharrone was shocked that the girl's parents allowed this to happen. How could anyone follow a teaching that was so cruel? Helen Bear was once Helen Caruthers—a schoolgirl who made good grades in the girl's school, and was good at sewing and cooking.

Then came that night, and her flight into darkness. She lived on the streets for almost a year before she was befriended by a group of women who found her in an alley in the center of town. Helen paused, whispering how she'd stolen food and clothing...how she'd sold herself to keep alive.

The three women took her to a large house near the downtown region. There she met over a dozen more women and girls. Some had been prostitutes. Some had sisters and daughters taken away by the priests as Helen had. They called themselves the Bear Clan, she was told. She was fed, clothed, and allowed to sleep in safety for the first time in over a year.

The next morning she was introduced to the matriarch of the group. The woman was old and wrinkled—eighty-seven summers by her own admission. She once lived as a proud member of a tribe she called the Bear Clan. She'd been happy. She'd been a mother with four children and eleven grandchildren.

Then the black thing came out of the sky and her family was gone. The survivors knew who'd been inside the death machine. He and his family had been driven out for vicious attacks on the children of their tribe and the surrounding. 'Serving the Redeemed God,' they called it. 'Keeping women in their proper place,' they called it. It'd been years before, but they knew.

The black machine came from time to time to the tribes of the north to trade with them, and the priests would attempt to evangelize their people. They even left a priest who lived with the banned family—the only family in the tribe to 'go over.' After the attack, the survivors swore vengeance in the name of the Goddess: the Warbird—the Great Raven.

Now they were inside the Black City and their vengeance was coming to pass. Helen explained how they were going to continue to mercilessly hunt down the priests of the Cathedral and all who helped them—police, pimps, and drug dealers who made the women dependent on the priests. This included men and women who perhaps weren't even members of the church, but who went after the young girls using such excuses as, "She wanted it." "She willingly took money for it." "She was nine, sure—but she really knew what she was doing!" The Bear Clan was out for blood, and Helen said that when they'd finished, even the sun would be a fantastic, bloody red over L.A.

Sharrone and Lyria were numb—the venom coming from such a pretty young girl was a horror. They both realized that if something was not done quickly, the killing would spread. This kind of thing always spins out of control. They were killing priests and their accomplices now, but soon they'd be killing others—individuals who spoke out against the violence—people who'd work to stop it. A reign of terror was beginning in the city, and something had to be done.

They left the way they came, out the window and down to the street. On the way to the newspaper office, the women told the story. The implications were dangerous indeed.

"Maybe we can make contact with the Bear Clan and reason with them." Sharrone said.

"That's unlikely," Tom said. "After all these years of hatred and festering anger, it'd be like trying to reason with the Cathedral."

Kel suddenly sat up straight. He looked first at Tom, then at Sharrone.

"That might be the answer!"

"What might be the answer?"

Kel laughed, answering Sharrone's question. "We should invite priests who are not in favor of what the Bishop and Father Woods are doing to some sort of parlay on neutral ground. The Cathedral, the Bear Clan, and us—surely not every priest or member of the faith favors child rape and forced prostitution, even if they believe women should be subservient to their men. Perhaps we can overthrow the Bishop's reign of horrors from the inside out, before any more murders can occur."

The next day several thousand handbills were posted all around the downtown area asking any woman of the Clan to call the newspaper office. More were posted around the Cathedral, invoking the participation of priests who thought a counterfeit Bishop had usurped their religion for personal power and gain. To coincide with these handbills, the paper published both missives and extended a request for a meeting. Now all they could do was wait and hope.

By afternoon calls were coming in from families who'd hidden their daughters from the priests, former followers who broke away when the Bishop took over, older priests who remembered the old days of peace and harmony, and even young priests who just 'knew' somehow that what was going on was wrong.

The following day they received a call from a woman requesting Sharrone's presence at a meeting with the matriarch of the Bear Clan. She immediately accepted the invitation. That afternoon, as instructed, she got into the car that pulled up in front of the newspaper offices and was whisked away. Dan was beside himself—what if they'd taken her for some unknown ulterior motive? Kel and Lyria tried to calm him. Helen, they reminded him, knew who she was and considered her to be one of them. Nonetheless, Dan paced the floor the whole time she was gone. Lyria didn't think she would've handled this any better had it been Kel who'd gone.

The telephone rang—it startled all of them. Tom grabbed the receiver. "Yes?" He listened for a long moment; then hung up. "We have some good news. The medical reports have come in from the coroner and the hospital. You'll never guess what they showed!"

"Well, since we cannot guess, tell us," Kel urged.

Tom laughed. "Helen will not be put on trial for murder! The coroner's report from both the detective's body and Helen's clothing—from pieces still at the scene of Jinks's killing and still on her body when she was gunned down, indicate he was attempting to rape the girl at the time he was stabbed—the death has already been ruled self-defense by a judge."

"That's amazing!" Lyria exclaimed.

"There's more. A bottle was found in the detective's pocket. In the bottle were sleeping tablets. Residue from the pills was found in the desk officer's coffee cup. He's not going to be charged with dereliction of duty as was originally suggested. The detective drugged him to keep him out of the way—that makes the attempted rape clearly premeditated. All that currently faces Helen is a charge of pointing the pistol at the priest. The most she can get for that'll be sixty days, and I have it on reliable information that all of the reporters who were around her said she had the pistol, sure—but it must've simply fallen from her bag or something. Nobody seems to remember her pointing it at anyone. The night judge who'll hear the case tomorrow has let it be known that he'll likely throw that charge out as well upon testimony by the witnesses."

Kel laughed. "Wouldn't you like to see the look on Father Woods' face right now?"

Everyone laughed. Tom produced a bottle of bourbon from his desk drawer. They all took turns toasting Helen, the coroner, Kel and Lyria, Dan, and especially Sharrone, Tom, the reporters, and, of course, justice. Lyria drank but little—she disliked the disorientation that came with alcohol, and she needed to clean and oil her sword tonight.

CHAPTER 38

"I know where they a—are...I know where they a—are!"

Father Woods stopped in his tracks. He'd gone out the side door of the Cathedral for some fresh air—the reports coming into his office were deeply disturbing. Even his fellow priests were abandoning him—the most powerful man in the city! He looked around nervously, trying to ascertain where the odd, reedy, singsong voice was coming from.

Adria stepped out of the shadows. She was grinning. "I saw them. I know where they live."

The priest stared at the dirty and unkempt young woman. It took him a moment to recognize her. "Adria?"

The woman laughed. "I have come back, my love, with information you will want."

"What information is that?"

"I know where the outlanders who want to kill you and the Bishop are living. I followed them."

The priest paused. This would be good news if it was real, but with this one, who could tell. Still, it wouldn't hurt to find out. Though he now knew he'd probably lost the fight to take the city, he could still exact revenge before he left to take over operations in The Green.

"Come inside, Adria, my dear," he coaxed, "and you can tell me all about it."

Adria told him about the taxi ride—she even had a slip of paper with an address scrawled on it. The cab driver had written it down for her at the urging of the point of her dagger. She explained she was so happy that she had decided to let the cab driver live! Father Woods listened without comment. Her description of events seemed very real— not at all the raving of someone on narcotics.

"Adria, are you on heroin?"

"No," she answered, "I don't need that any more."

He felt she was telling the truth.

"How long have you been off the drug?"

"Oh, a long time now," she answered with a grin, "I've been living in the park, eating meat."

"I see," he responded. "Well, Adria, I have to say I didn't think I'd see you again."

"I will never leave you again."

The priest shuddered, but responded, "I certainly hope not! Listen, I'm going to have my people take care of you. You need a bath, new clothing, and such—do you think you'd like that?"

Adria sniffed her armpits, and then nodded.

The priest called for assistance and Adria was led away to be remade—he needed her to make sure his vengeance was completed.

* * * *

Sharrone returned with good news. The Bear Clan would participate in a meeting—all that remained to do was set a time. Tom began calling the priests, policemen, and families who'd contacted the paper in response to Tom's invitation and the meeting was set for the day after tomorrow. Sharrone called her contact in the Bear Clan. They agreed to the meeting date and time. Sharrone also informed them that Helen would probably be released from custody the night before the meeting—she could probably even attend. Everyone would meet at the Journal building at six in the evening.

* * * *

When the two couples returned home, they informed the waiting shamans of what had transpired—how the women of Bear House had agreed to the meeting Kel had suggested. Garn gave Kel an appraising glance, but said nothing. That night they all slept soundly. At two in the morning, a lone auto cruised past on the street. It didn't stop or slow down so the roving guards made no note of its presence—cars, after all, occasionally came down the street. After passing, the car turned the next corner and started back in the direction of the Cathedral.

* * * *

Early in the morning the telephone rang. Dan was up, beginning breakfast for the others so he took the call. It was a short conversation. He put the phone back in the cradle and walked into his bedroom. Sharrone had just risen and was dressing. Dan watched her as she slipped into her clothing, bathed in the aura of dawn filtering through the window. She turned and smiled at him, indicating her desire to have him help her close the back of the dress she was wearing. He walked up and as he was fastening the snaps, he kissed the nape of her neck. She shivered, turned into his arms and kissed him.

"Did you hear the phone, Sharrone?"

"Yes," she answered, "who was it?"

"It was Tom. His connection in the police department told him the judge has dismissed the gun charge against Helen this morning instead of waiting for his usual night shift. She's free to go."

"That is good news," she responded.

"Yes," he answered, "apparently she wishes to be picked up at the hospital by us—well, by you personally."

By the time they finished breakfast, Tom had arrived and it was agreed that Kel and Lyria would accompany them as well. Lyria put her sword in the trunk of Tom's car, just in case. She didn't like being separated from it. Brett Holiday would also accompany them in the auto. Dan and Sharrone would follow on Dan's new steamcycle.

Dan checked his pocket watch—it was time to go. The two-vehicle caravan wound its way downtown toward the hospital. They'd left with enough time to spare and traveled slowly. They didn't notice the small van shadowing them about three car lengths back.

When they arrived at the hospital, they were able to park directly in front of the building. The administration and staff knew what was happening and had reserved a spot for them. They knew reporters and even the editor of the paper would be on hand, and they wanted to put on a good face for the hospital and perhaps for themselves as well.

Dan parked his big bike in front of Tom's sedan. He and Sharrone climbed off. By then Kel, Lyria, Tom, and Brett Holiday had exited the auto and were standing on the sidewalk. There were several hospital representatives there as well. Everyone was smiling.

The small gray van pulled quietly into the parking lot. It stopped by the curb about fifty yards away. Doors opened and five men stepped out. They looked in all directions, cautiously scanning the area, and then turned toward the hospital entrance and began their approach. They walked at a slow, strolling pace. They were talking casually among themselves and, to anyone watching, appeared to be employees or perhaps visitors to the hospital.

Sharrone and Lyria entered the hospital escorted by a doctor and two nurses. Sharrone noticed, ironically, that the doctor was the same man who'd denied her entry to interview the girl. She thought it best to say nothing of that episode. She smiled thinking how quickly people could change opinions if they thought it was to their benefit.

They walked quickly to the lift as several other doctors and nurses looked on. It seemed everyone knew that something unusual was happening. The doctor closed the lift door and they rode to the third floor. A police officer was waiting at Helen's room. He opened the door for Sharrone and her entourage. Helen saw them enter and smiled.

"Hello," Sharrone said, quickly introducing everyone, "we're here to take you home."

"She'll need to come back in a couple days for us to change the bandage," the doctor said, "but she's healthy and the wound didn't infect."

"What of the bullet?"

"The bullet was fired from a pistol that had a longer barrel and a more powerful cartridge than we usually encounter—but she was lucky. The bullet didn't hit any bone, and passed all the way through her. It sounds bad, but it meant we didn't have to dig around inside of her searching for it."

Lyria and Sharrone both nodded in understanding.

"She was critical for the first day due to blood loss," the doctor explained, "but we gave her a pint of blood and that perked her right up."

A nurse appeared with a wheelchair. Helen started to object, but Sharrone insisted and the doctor, with a grateful glance her way, helped the young girl into the chair.

"I'll be leaving you here," the doctor said. "I have other patients to attend to."

"Thank you for all your consideration," Sharrone said with a smile.

The doctor paused for an instant and Sharrone knew she'd scored her point.

* * * *

An off-duty nurse in street clothing walked up and stood next to Kel, looking him over in an appraising way. She had a few minutes to kill before she had to go inside to work. She was asking him questions about Helen and what was going on—who he was and what his name might be. Kel could see what her real agenda was and he smiled inwardly. His love for Lyria, and her absolute blinding trust in him, left no room for indiscretions or doubts—even if he'd been tempted. He found he was not. Still, he politely talked with her, willing to risk an elbow-poke if Lyria should exit the building right now and see them together.

* * * *

As the five men from the van approached, they changed their pace and were now moving rapidly as the two men inside the van watched. The first man in the group nodded toward Kel and the nurse. Three of the men returned the nod, veering off from the other two. They were the ones who would grab the targeted individuals and get them into the van. The other two were to hold the others at gunpoint—or kill them, if necessary.

Though they'd been told to avoid gunfire, one man was already drawing his 96 Mauser from the shoulder holster beneath his jacket. The ten round magazine located in front of the trigger was fully loaded. He quickly pulled the cocking piece rearward, and released it to chamber a round, making the pistol operational.

The driver of the van put the vehicle in motion. He kept it close to the curb—no other cars were parked along that section. He inched forward slowly, watching what was transpiring before him.

* * * *

Brett was the first to notice that something was happening. He caught an odd motion from the corner of his eye, and turned to see what had attracted his attention. He saw the approaching men—and the creeping van. He then saw the man with the big Mauser step from behind the vehicle. What had caught his eye was the man pulling the large pistol from beneath his coat. Brett saw the man quickly pull the charger back on the 96 driving a round into the chamber and cocking the hammer.

Brett began to shout a warning and started to move toward Kel and the others. He opened his coat to pull out his own weapon when he heard a shot ring out and saw the three men grab Kel and the nurse from behind—they hadn't seen it coming. Brett saw the second man in the group pull something from his jacket pocket and watched the leather sap rise and fall. He heard the sharp slap as it struck Kel on the temple. Kel slumped into the man's arms. One of the other men gave Dan a sharp shove from behind. Dan tumbled face down on the sidewalk where he struck his head and lay stunned for a moment.

By this time the van had come to a stop almost side by side with Tom's auto. The man in the passenger seat rose, scuttled through the back of the van, and opened the rear door from inside. He stepped out, holding the door wide.

The three men dragged a semi-conscious Kel and the struggling nurse to the back of the van. The two captives were thrown into the rear like bales of hay. Two of Kel's assailants and the man who'd been holding the door leapt in behind them, quickly slamming the door. As the third kidnapper turned to get into the front of the van, he stumbled and fell. The driver, thinking the man had been shot, pulled away from the curb on squealing tires. The sudden movement of the van swung the passenger side door closed. The fallen man rose quickly to his feet and ran across the street and up an alley to escape the gunfight happening behind him.

CHAPTER 39

Gunfire. The 96 Mauser was spitting a steady stream of bullets into the side of Tom's sedan. Spent shell casings leaping from the top of the pistol caught the early morning light as they twinkled, tumbling through the air. The shooter half wondered what was wrong with his pistol—the reports were muffled and weak sounding. It also seemed to him that the spent casings were drifting up from his weapon—everything was happening so slowly. It was almost like time was coming to a stop.

* * * *

Tom felt a bullet strike his shoulder. He turned reflexively away from the pain, tripping on his own feet and falling heavily to the sidewalk.

Tom was struggling to regain his feet as his attacker pointed the pistol at him, preparing to kill him. *It was about time this vermin died,* the shooter was thinking. Regardless of any orders not to shoot unless necessary, killing this particular man was necessary. As the killer's vision dwindled to a tunnel, and time seemed to stand still, he pointed the heavy pistol at the fallen editor—noticing his eye color…that his hair was mussed…that his shirt had a red spot on one shoulder.

* * * *

The man with the Mauser might actually have heard the shotgun, but he never had time to comprehend what the sound meant. A microsecond later, his head exploded in an expanding mass of skull splinters, brain fragments, and blood. The heavy 12-gauge load of buckshot and the accompanying massive muzzle blast had been delivered at almost contact distance—the power of the rapidly expanding gasses quickly exceeded the pressure threshold of the killer's skull. He was instantly dead. His still smoking 96 clattered to the sidewalk, sliding beneath Tom's steam-car.

* * * *

Brett lowered the short double-barreled shotgun out of recoil, squeezing the left trigger—firing it a second time. Another of the assailants who'd just pulled his .32 Mauser from his coat pocket fell, his belly ripped by the buckshot load. In the intense silence that followed that brief exchange of thunder, the dead man's pistol struck the side-walk with a sharp 'clack!'

Now Brett swung the loading lever of the shotgun to one side allowing the barrels to be lowered. He quickly extracted the empty brass shell casings and smoothly slid new ones into the waiting chambers. Brett pushed the foot long barrels up, snapping them into place. He thumbed back both hammers simultaneously—but the third man was nowhere to be seen.

* * * *

Suddenly the door to the hospital was flung open. Lyria was down the stairs in an instant, eyes frantically searching in every direction.

"Where is Kel?"

She looked quickly at Dan who was still in the process of pushing himself up from the ground—then she looked at Brett and at Tom, who was now standing, leaning against his auto, holding his shoulder. Blood was bright on his fingers.

Sharrone came out of the hospital next with Helen. They saw the carnage on the street and shrank back.

"Where is Kel?"

Lyria's frantic question brought Brett Holiday's answer. "They took him, Lyria. I'm sorry."

"Who in the name of the Goddess and God are 'they'?"

"I believe," Dan said, "they were from the Cathedral—sent by Father Woods."

Lyria sank to her knees—she felt lightheaded. How could her beloved Kel be gone? Why would they kidnap him when Tom and Sharrone were the ones they would've recognized from the news articles? Why Kel?

"Oddly," Dan said, "I saw them grab a woman and take her as well."

"What woman?"

Lyria was having difficulty thinking. She felt dizzy.

"I believe she was a nurse coming on duty—she stopped for a moment to ask Kel what was going on."

"Why would they kidnap a nurse?"

None of it made any sense. Lyria was beginning to think she was in some horrible nightmare, and that she'd awaken any moment.

She took a deep breath and rose to her feet. "If they were from the Cathedral," she said with a new determination, "then that is where they would take him."

She looked at the editor, staring him right in the eyes. "Tom," she said, "open the trunk of the car—there is something in there I need."

The editor turned, stepped off the sidewalk behind the vehicle, quickly unlocked the trunk and swung the lid all the way open. The look in Lyria's eyes had frightened him.

"They wanted him for some reason other than murder, Lyria," Brett said. "They could've easily killed him outright if that were their intent. We need to have an organized plan of attack before we go in there—we have a little time."

Lyria stood in the street, her ancient sword in her hand.

"I have a plan," she said calmly, "I will open the front door, go in and kill all of them, and then bring my Kel home."

"There could be many men waiting," Tom warned.

"That is well," she said, "it means there will be even more of them for me to kill!"

Sharrone and Helen looked at each other. Helen knew that Lyria was feeling what she'd felt that night years earlier when the Cathedral came for her and her sister. Sharrone knew how Lyria was feeling as well. She was thinking of that night of horror on the street when she thought she was going to be raped and carried off to be a sex slave for the priests. Neither of the two women argued with Lyria to wait.

"And I am tired of this," Lyria said in disgust.

She pulled at the lacing of her blouse. She ripped it off of her body and without hesitation also removed her skirt and petticoats. Her friends stood staring—Lyria was dressed in leather beneath her city clothing! She stood amid a pile of satin and lace, her legs mostly bare. Her finely tanned buckskin trousers were cut off well above the knees. She also wore a strip of buckskin over her breasts. The leather wrapped around her and was secured behind with leather thongs. Another thong went around her neck holding the top in place. Her midriff was bare. Also around her neck was another leather thong attached to a long, curved piece of ivory—it was the tooth of her totem, the Ice

Tiger, that Llo had given her when he presented her with the daggers.

She strapped the fur and leather belt and sheaths containing her ivory hilted daggers around her waist and hung the great sword from her shoulder. Finally, taking some red lip paint from her bag, dipping her left fingers into the jar, she stroked her left cheek—imparting four crimson lines diagonally from her temple to her jaw—the stripes of the Ice Tiger. She was a warrior once more.

"There is one more thing I need," Lyria said, looking at Dan.

"A way to the Cathedral." he responded.

"No!" Sharrone was scared—not for herself, but for Dan. She didn't want to lose Dan any more than Lyria wanted to lose Kel.

"It'll be easy," he said with a smile. "I'm not going inside—I'll just ride near the place and let Lyria off."

"That is all I ask," the warrior woman said. "I would have you do no more."

Sharrone argued that she wanted to go as well and Dan countered with the practical answer that the bike wouldn't handily support a third rider.

"Then we can take the car," Sharrone said in desperation, "we can all go!"

"No, Sharrone," Dan said finally, "the traffic will be heavy this time of the morning and the bike is the quickest and most sensible way to go."

"We'll follow in the auto, to be sure," Brett said, "but we'll have to travel at a slower pace, due to the traffic."

"Who will take Helen back to her home?"

Lyria's question caught them all by surprise. They had a promise to keep to the Bear Clan. If their parlay were to have any chance of working, they needed to be seen as good for their word.

The nurse who'd accompanied Helen down the steps volunteered to lead the entourage, saying, "We'll take Helen home and then you folks can head to the Cathedral together."

"I want to be there quickly," Sharrone protested.

"And you will be," the nurse said with a grin, "I'll to take an ambulance. After we leave Helen with her people, we'll have the steam-whistle of our emergency vehicle to clear traffic."

"And we'll follow in the car," Tom said. "This is clearly our first duty. It would also be wise for the rest of us not to get separated now."

"That's true," Brett agreed, "we need to keep the rest of our forces together."

Sharrone couldn't argue with that. Clearly they needed to get Helen out of the way of any further danger—she had a sacred duty to protect the girl now that she was involved with all of this.

"Then it is settled?" Dan looked from Sharrone to Lyria to Tom. Everyone nodded. He grinned—the bike would get them to the Cathedral in record time.

"You know how to ride on one of these?"

"No," Lyria said, "but I'm a fast learner!"

Dan began by giving Lyria the rudiments of bike riding—leaning into turns and all the rest of it. She nodded in understanding, eager to be on their way. Kel was waiting—who knows what might be happening to him right now.

* * * *

Kel was disoriented. His head hurt terribly and he felt dizzy—the blow on his head had been heavy. He lay still, waiting for the real world to filter in once more. Slowly he came to his senses. He vaguely remembered being hustled into a vehicle of some type.

He opened his eyes—it was dark where he was, but from the feeling of movement, he knew he was still in the back of the van. That was a good thing. He'd not been unconscious very long, and knew he probably wasn't severely injured, regardless of how he felt. He became aware of a noise near him. Someone was crying softly. He remembered the nurse who'd been standing beside him. They must've taken her as well, but why?

Kel felt the vehicle slow and on several occasions come to a stop. Though he couldn't see out, he figured they were heading to the Cathedral. He was worried about his friends and Lyria—fortunately, his love had been in the hospital when the attack occurred. That at least was some consolation.

He tried to move, and found himself securely bound. In the dim light filtering in from the street through the drape that blocked his view of the cab, he saw that the woman taken with him was also bound and tightly gagged. Looking around as best he could, he saw one man in the rear of the van. Though he couldn't see into the cab, he heard the conversation of two men. He heard movement, so he shifted his attention to the guard sitting with them.

The guard was kneeling on the floor by the woman. He asked her if she was comfortable, then offered to loosen her clothing. Kel knew what was happening. He struggled with his bonds, but he was firmly tied. The man had his hands on the woman's breasts, caressing her through her clothing. Tears were in her eyes as she struggled valiantly.

Just as he began unlacing her dress, a voice from the front seat caused him to stop where he was. "You touch her and you'll have to answer to Bishop Woods," the driver said in a commanding voice.

"I was just gonna touch her a little," the man whined. "I was just gonna see if she would be subservient."

"That isn't your domain," the driver replied.

The two men in the cab had a short conversation that Kel couldn't quite hear. Grumbling, the guard was replaced in the back by the man from the front seat of the truck. The new guard simply sat on the metal bench along one wall of the van, doing nothing save watching his prisoners. Kel relaxed—at least the woman was safe for the time being.

* * * *

With a roar, the big bike was back on the street, rapidly picking up speed. Dan hunched low over the handlebars while Lyria sat against him, her arms around his waist. Occasionally, people on the sidewalk would stop and stare at the strange sight of a steambike being ridden way too fast by some madman and an almost naked woman with a very large sword strapped across her shoulders. Dan twisted the throttle and the machine jumped.

Behind Dan and Lyria, the rest of their party was climbing into Tom's shot up steam-car. Fortunately the engine and boiler hadn't been struck by gunfire. Helen Bear sat in the middle of the back seat with Sharrone on one side of her and Brett on the other—his short shotgun resting butt first on the seat between his legs. He'd lowered the hammers, but his thumb was hooked over them, ready to draw them back at a second's notice. He wouldn't be taken unaware again. In front of them, the nurse started the ambulance, and with her emergency whistle, she led the way.

Ahead was an intersection. Dan slowed a bit, looking both ways. He accelerated rapidly into the intersection after he determined there were no autos approaching. A pedestrian, apparently self absorbed, stepped out into the street. Dan heeled the bike over, cutting an arc around the pedestrian. Now the man could finally see what was happening—he shrieked, flinging the bag he'd been carrying high into the air. It tumbled, throwing fruit in all directions. Lyria reached out, and caught an apple before it struck the street. She bit into it, enjoying the sudden treat.

A short distance in front of them, Dan could see traffic slowing. There were too many autos for the width of the street and each one was determined to be first. Dan leaned the bike to the right without slowing and jumped the curb. He raced down the sidewalk, and people jumped out of the way in all directions. Dan then jumped the curb again, returning to the street.

There was a policeman standing in the center of the roadway directing traffic. He put his hand up toward Dan, whistle blowing furiously. Dan twisted the accelerator. As the bike flashed past him, the policeman suddenly found himself standing with an apple in his fist. He stared after the bike, then at the apple with one bite missing. Had the passenger of the bike actually given him an apple? He tasted it, and found it was good. He grinned—nobody at the station would believe THIS story.

CHAPTER 40

The van stopped. The men in the front seats were getting out. Suddenly the back door was flung open. Four men dragged Kel and the nurse out into the courtyard of the Cathedral. Without a word, they were both helped to their feet, and then taken under guard into the vast building. Kel watched closely where they were going—the information might come in handy if he had the opportunity to escape.

They moved through the aisle of the main part of the church. A few dozen people were inside, sitting in the pews or kneeling near the altar. They were praying and paid no attention to the newcomers who moved quietly and quickly through another door into a small room where they stopped.

One of the men knocked on the ironclad door at the back of the room, then used a large skeleton key to open the lock. He pushed on the door—it slowly began moving. Hands on the other side were pulling as well. Soon there was enough room for the hostages and their captors to move through. The man with the key stayed at his station, closing the door behind the descending party.

The space on this side of the door led only to a small landing above a stone stairway leading below ground level. Kel counted the steps, estimating their depth. By the time they reached the last step, Kel figured they'd come twenty feet below ground. Here there was another iron door.

It was opened in the same manner as the first and Kel and the nurse were pushed into the room. Again, the man with the key stayed where he was. Kel looked around. The room was lit by gaslight, making it much brighter than either of the above rooms or the stairway had been. They were shoved ahead. Kel stumbled, but one of the guards hastily caught him, preventing him from falling.

Finally they were taken to two stone pillars rising from the floor on either side of a low stone platform. It looked like an altar, but it was bare of any artifacts. He looked up at the ceiling high over his head. There, on the ceiling, was a large painting of the Redeemed God with his foot on the bound Goddess. In this depiction, the Goddess lay naked beneath the foot of God. Kel was tied to one pillar, the nurse to the other. Both of them were left gagged as the guards filed out of the room through another door. Now there was only silence. Kel looked at the woman—she was looking back at him, terror in her eyes. Never had he felt so helpless, and so terribly responsible.

* * * *

Dan shifted gears once again and the bike roared through the next intersection. A truck slammed on its brakes, the driver making an obscene gesture from his open window. Dan raced on obliviously. He was on a mission. Ahead they could finally see the black outline of the Cathedral. He zigzagged his way through traffic, cutting between two cars traveling side by side. He was in the open. There was no more traffic ahead. The only thing in front of them now was the blackness of the Cathedral, glowering down on them like a fragment of midnight that had refused to leave with the coming of the dawn. Dan slowed the steamcycle and looked for a place to park. He heard Lyria behind him—her face close to his ear as she hugged him tightly.

He listened. Could a human voice actually make a sound like that? He listened again. From next to his ear he heard a deep, slow, rhythmic rumbling breathing as though some large animal rode behind him. He looked down at his waist—the arms around him were decidedly human.

He pulled to the curb, swinging the bike into an alley near the Cathedral. He felt the bike rise slightly as Lyria stepped off. He looked at her—she was just Lyria and nothing else. He breathed slowly, calming himself as Lyria stepped up next to him.

"I'll be waiting right here," he told her.

"If it comes to pass that you are our only transport, you'll carry Kel and I'll stay."

Dan saw no use in arguing—they'd cross that bridge when they came to it.

"The blessing of the divine be with you, Lyria," he said with all sincerity.

"Thank you, Dan," she said smiling. "You're a good friend and a brave companion. Sharrone could not ask for more as she travels the adventure of her life."

"Nor I," Dan answered. "I thought love had fled from me—but it was just hiding!"

Lyria laughed, bending down to give Dan a kiss on his cheek. Then she turned, sprinting toward the black shadow that was the Cathedral.

* * * *

Only occasionally using the siren-whistle, nurse Margaret Sorrenson made good time as she raced the ambulance down the side streets of the city following Helen Bear's directions written hastily on a piece of paper.

"We are here," she said to herself as she pulled up in front of a very neat looking white painted three-story home. There were three women sitting alertly on the porch. As Margaret parked the ambulance, Tom pulled in behind her. Helen, Sharrone, and Brett all got out, and slowly crossed the street. One of the women on the porch rose, staring intently at the approaching group of people. Brett returned his shotgun to its holster inside the heavy leather overcoat he wore. Tom remained in the auto, keeping the steam pressure up for a quick departure.

A woman from the house was hustling across the street toward them. She was laughing as she gently hugged Helen, mindful of her bandaged shoulder. She looked at Helen's new friends and smiled. "I cannot tell you how much we appreciate what you've done for Helen these last few days."

"She pretty much did it herself," Sharrone said with a laugh. "She's a very brave young woman."

Now they were across the street and up the stairs to the porch. They moved into the family room, leaving two of the women sitting attentively on the front porch. The inside was bright and cheerful, with sunlight streaming in the windows and brightly upholstered furniture and large paintings decorating the walls. Near the fireplace, sitting in a straight-backed chair, Ma'hal awaited them.

After the introductions, they sat for a short period of time discussing the upcoming meeting…and the reason for their haste this day. As they rose to leave, Ma'hal thanked them for saving Helen and promised that she would be at the coming peace council.

Helen kissed Sharrone and Brett as they left, thanking them for showing her that not all city dwellers were monsters. They then turned and walked back across the street—they had an appointment at the Cathedral and they suspected that the festivities were already in full swing.

* * * *

The door opened, and then closed. Kel couldn't see who'd come into the room. He turned his head as far as he could and finally two people came into view. One he recognized from pictures in the newspaper—it was Father Woods. The other person was a woman with very attractive light brown hair. She had two teeth missing from her smile. Then he remembered where he'd seen her before. Adria! What was Adria doing here? His mind raced, but he could come up with no answers—he'd have to wait and learn. Adria was snickering as she slowly approached the bound captives.

"Kel," she laughed, "I never thought I would see you again."

Bishop Woods pulled the gag from his mouth so he could speak. He was enjoying this repartee between two half-humans.

"Adria…what are you doing here?"

"I am with my betrothed, Kel," she said.

A look of sudden confusion passed over her features. *Betrothed? But was she not betrothed to Kel? No, wait…that was before the bitch-witch!* She shook her head as though to clear it of some mental clutter.

"Now we have you both," she said with a grin.

"Both? Why did you kidnap this woman?"

"Don't play with us," Bishop Woods snapped, "we know you're traveling with a female companion."

Adria wandered in a circle around Kel, brushing her fingers over his cheek, neck, and crotch. He flinched away from her. She laughed, and then turned her attention to the nurse.

Adria hissed. "This is not the woman!"

"What?"

"I am telling you, your men got the wrong woman. I have never seen this…'thing' before."

Bishop Woods didn't know what to say. He called one of the guards into the room and quietly interrogated him. He nodded, returning to the middle of the room as the guard again left by the iron door.

"Who is she?"

"I do not even know her name," Kel said in anger. "She is a nurse—she works in the hospital. We were talking when your people attacked us."

Bishop Woods walked around the other side so he could look at the woman. He removed her gag.

"Is what this half-human says the truth? Speak up woman, you're being addressed by your superior!"

The nurse spat in his face and the priest recoiled in disgust—a woman had spit on him. With a snarl, he slapped her across the face—then he slapped her again. Adria laughed. Kel strained at his bindings.

* * * *

The front door of the Cathedral swung open. A lone woman strode in with her head held high. A number of the faithful looked in her direction, open disgust on their faces, but did nothing. Lyria looked ahead of her—two men were rapidly approaching, holding their hands out in front of them.

"Women are not allowed in here with their heads up—and certainly not dressed in THAT manner!"

"What about men?"

The two men looked at each other—they knew women were stupid, but even so, what could she mean?

Lyria answered the question for them. "I mean are men allowed in here with their heads still attached?"

Before they could respond, Lyria drew the great sword from her back. The reflections of the gaslights in the pattern welding of the metal made the blade look like a thing alive—almost like a flame itself. She raised the sword above her head, and then the voice of the sword spoke gently in her mind.

"Do not dishonor me."

She lowered the sword and the two unarmed men scurried away. Lyria walked back into the darker regions of the church—she was headed to the location where the priests held their orgies of sexual submission for the women and children they brought here. She had a rough idea where that was from talking to Sharrone. She strode on.

Suddenly three mercenary soldiers blocked her way. One carried a ballistic weapon—a rifle. The remaining two carried short spears. The spears were lowered across each other, blocking her way. The man with the rifle stood behind them at port arms. He said, "You don't belong here woman, flee now or die!"

The guard on the left was distracted by Lyria's strange eyes—though they were clearly blue, they were now seemingly green—how could that be? Lyria advanced toward them, head lowered. The guards were appraising her body.

"I am begging your forgiveness, master," she whined. "I have been misplaced by my husband and I am frightened—would you please help me?"

"Why are you dressed like that," the man with the rifle asked.

"It is a game, kind sir. My husband likes games."

The two men with the spears looked at each other in confusion. What was going on here? Then the Ice Tiger sprang.

With a ferocious snarl, Lyria was on them. With a two-handed downward stroke of the sword she cleaved the heads from both spears. The two men were left staring at the splinters remaining in their hands. The man with the rifle was not so lucky. Lyria crouched and sprang, pulling the pommel of her sword against her breast then suddenly thrusting the blade out in front of her. The point rode in just over the steel of the gun, striking the man's breastplate. The sword continued onward with no hesitation—the point entering the man's chest, almost cutting his right lung in half. He spat blood and collapsed to the floor.

Lyria wheeled on the two remaining soldiers, but they threw the cloven hafts of their spears to the floor and ran. Lyria watched them go for a moment, waiting to be sure they wouldn't return behind her. She then turned back toward the dark hallway down which she knew she must walk.

CHAPTER 41

"Well," Bishop Woods said, "I suppose since she's the wrong woman, and quite attractive, she can be used by my guards later tonight after I finish with you."

The Bishop slapped Kel across the face as he'd done the nurse.

"Tell me what you're doing here. Why have you come to the Black City?"

"We came to find the shamans you kidnapped."

Bishop Woods laughed loudly, and Adria flinched. "You will not find them here, beastling," he shouted.

"I know," Kel answered calmly, "you sent them into The Green where we rescued them from your 'Bishop' and your 'Feathered Serpent'!"

The priest struck Kel again.

Adria flinched. *Why is he hitting my betrothed? No, wait...*

"We have known of the Bishop's plan for a long time," Kel said. "Using magic we have divined his purpose."

The priest flinched this time.

"Why do you think the great animal would not obey, because the shamans could not talk to it? Or could it simply be that they wished it to eat your Bishop?"

Bishop Woods struck Kel again, this time with his fist. Adria whimpered.

"Be still," the Bishop shouted at her. "You'll be told when to speak."

He continued, "It no longer matters about the Bishop. I am the Bishop now!"

"Oh yes," Kel mocked, "I have heard of you—you are the Bishop with the wet trousers!"

With a snarl, Bishop Woods struck Kel in the stomach. Adria took a quick step forward, but thought the better of it—she was having trouble figuring out which of these men was actually her betrothed.

* * * *

At the end of the short corridor, gaslights bloomed. From the shadow of the pillar she was hiding behind, Lyria looked ahead into the light. There was a man standing by the iron door and on his belt hung a key. Lyria strode boldly toward the man, head down, her sword hidden behind her body and leg as she moved toward him. He looked at her suspiciously and she halted two paces away.

"I was told to report to Father Woods to do some cleaning up."

"I've heard no such thing," the man said in a surly tone.

"Then, kind sir," Lyria said in a whisper, "you may have to call His Grace. He will be very angry."

The man thought for a moment, and then unlocked the door. This was just a woman, after all—probably a whore by her attire, he rationalized, and she was no threat. When the door was swung open, Lyria struck the man a savage blow to his chin with the pommel of her sword. His teeth clashed together and he fell without a whimper. Lyria grabbed the key ring and ran down the stairs.

At the bottom there were five more men at arms. These men were very large and armed with lances and swords. The lack of firearms marked them as second-rate soldiers by city standards. As soon as she came into the light, they all had their lances pointed in her direction. They took a step toward her in unison, their spears forming a steel barrier between the door and the woman. Lyria took a deep breath—then the sword spoke to her.

"A true warrior leads the battle—she does not follow."

The men advanced another step.

"Spirit pulls the sword—it does not push it—the cut is accomplished before it has begun. Your foe is dead before you strike him."

This time Lyria took a step forward—warily. The voice of the sword spoke loudly in her mind, but calmly.

"Blade follows Spirit. Spirit has passed the foe before the blade strikes. Spirit cuts the will of the enemy before the blade cuts his body. A strong spirit can blind a weak one with its Light..."

Suddenly Lyria leaped toward the five men. They weren't expecting this mere woman to attack them. She snarled as the Ice Tiger once again took her. Her sword came up from the lower left, cleaving the lance of the man she faced. He dropped it, quickly starting to withdraw his sword from its sheath.

Lyria's sword descended from the apex of the last cut to the lower right, then just as quickly horizontally back to the starting point of the triangle she'd cut in the air. One of the man's legs was severed, the other cut to the bone. He looked for just an instant into Lyria's flashing green eyes and then he collapsed in a heap at her feet.

She moved quickly to her left, bringing the remaining four men into alignment. Now she had to fight only one of them at a time. She raised her sword and quickly swung it horizontally from left to right. The blade struck her opponent's helm, cleaving the ear protector in two and putting a severe cut across his forehead. Without hesitation, her blade came downward from high right in a descending angle that struck the man's left arm, cleaning separating it from his body. He shrieked in pain, dropping his sword. Lyria shoved him away with her left hand, stepped in quickly to thrust the point of her sword through the third man's throat. He fell, gurgling out the wet remains of his life.

The fourth man jumped forward with his lance and Lyria danced to the left at the last second, allowing the razor steel of the spear to move harmlessly over her right shoulder. She struck the man in his chest with her right shoulder, knocking him off balance. She struck upward with the pommel of her sword, breaking out the man's teeth and fracturing his jaw. He uttered a thin wail and collapsed atop his companions.

The last man looked at his four dead or severely injured companions and the spreading pool of blood on the floor. He was pale. Lyria advanced quickly, knocking his sword from his shaking hand. The man collapsed, whimpering in fear. The Ice Tiger sneered at him, glaring with supernaturally green eyes.

She pushed the tip of her sword against his breast—the tip punched through the iron plate as though it were no more than thin leather. The man began shrieking and Lyria withdrew her blade, stepped back and spoke to the man at her feet.

"I will allow you to run—or you can stand and fight like a girl!"

The guard rose shakily to his feet, turned, and ran down the hallway leaving tokens of his masculinity as he ran—his fallen helm, his hastily unbuckled iron and leather armor, his dagger.

* * * *

"Did you hear that?"

Bishop Woods was gleeful. He figured by now that the cursed woman Adria mentioned couldn't be far from this abomination now bound before him. He punched Kel again in the stomach, and then cut the rope binding him to the pillar.

"Your whore is dead, beastling," he laughed. "Did you not hear her last shriek of pain just then?"

Kel looked up from the floor into the Bishop's eyes. "How many men did you have outside this door?"

"There are five men guarding us right now," the Bishop announced triumphantly.

Kel laughed. "Only five?"

The Bishop spat on him, and said, "Lick my feet, half-human— I'm leaving tonight for The Green. Yes, don't look so surprised, half-wit! I'm taking over where the former Bishop left off. That land will be mine—the girls of that land will be mine. The wealth and the power will be mine! I will rule the world!"

He kicked Kel in the side of his head. Kel momentarily lost consciousness.

Adria rushed forward, at first out of concern for her betrothed, then with loathing for her enemy.

"Let me kill him," she commanded, "I want his life before we leave!"

The Bishop gave Adria a vicious kick that sent her sprawling.

"Half-human beastling whore! You think I'd take such a vile creature as you with me? The Green is filled with vile beasts should I want one!"

Adria was crying—she couldn't understand why her beloved suddenly hated her.

Then the door burst open. Adria, the Bishop, and the still-bound nurse turned to stare. Bishop Woods turned pale—how could this be? Adria hissed, drawing back from the others, crawling into a corner.

Lyria advanced, her bloodstained sword flashing red in the gaslight glow—the blood-red stripes of her totem slashed across her face, her eyes shifting blue, then green, then back. The priest was doing something. Lyria looked at him—he was pulling a gun from his clothing! She leaped at him, trying to strike him with her sword. He dodged at the last instant and the blade passed him, but the large hand-guard struck him in the face. He fell senselessly to the floor. Lyria looked quickly at Adria, recognizing her finally. "Adria?"

She was as shocked as Kel had been. Adria whimpered, began crying, and hid her face behind her hands. Whatever her problem was, it wasn't Lyria's problem. She'd come to get Kel. She knelt on the floor next to her unconscious love, laying her sword on the floor beside her.

"Kel? Kel, my love? Awaken…"

Love? Is that what the witch-bitch said? She loved Kel? No, that would not be allowed! Kel belonged to Adria, of that there could be no doubt. On her hands and knees, Adria silently crept toward the hateful woman bent over the man she'd not surrender. Now she was close enough. She snatched the sword, scuttling back, quickly rising to her feet. Lyria turned, knowing someone had gotten her sword. Kel awakened—he pushed himself up on his elbows.

"Adria…" both Kel and Lyria said simultaneously.

"I hate you, witch! You will not have my man."

Adria raised the sword over her head with both hands. She took a step toward Lyria and the sword spoke.

"I am the Guardian of Light!! Dishonor me and you will die on my steel!"

Adria hissed—how could that alien voice be louder than the scorpion? It didn't matter; Lyria was going to die! Lyria shied back against Kel as Adria took another step forward. Then something happened. The hem of one of Adria's petticoats was torn—the toe of her shoe snagged in the little dangle of lace, causing her to stumble. She tried to regain her balance, but the lace tugged again at her foot. She dropped the heavy sword. The sword fell, pommel first, striking the stone floor with a ringing sound. For an instant it stood there balanced. It began to fall, but Adria was already falling as well. The point of the sword entered her body just below her sternum. The blade pushed its way through her back. She gave out a groan, and turned slowly to her right side on the floor, curled up—knees close to her chest.

Lyria and Kel were next to her in a heartbeat. Lyria cradled Adria's head in her lap and whispered, "Adria, what has happened to you?"

Adria opened her eyes, looking up at Lyria with fading vision—her eyes ceasing to see as she became unconscious. Lyria could tell she was already between the worlds.

Adria looked into the approaching Light. She was crying—tears streamed down her cheeks. She looked into the Light and sobbed, "I don't know who I am..." Then she passed into the Light and was forever more beyond mortal judgment.

Lyria gently lowered the young woman's head to the floor. She stood, and as gently as she could, she withdrew the blade from the woman's body. A sound behind her made her whirl. It was the priest. He was standing up—he had the Mauser 96 in his hand. He was fumbling with the cocking piece.

He screamed hysterically. "You've stood in my way long enough!"

Lyria advanced on the priest, snarling.

"By the Redeemed God," the priest shrieked. "Go unto Hell!"

He raised the pistol, but Lyria's sword arm was quicker.

The room spun past him dizzily, tumbling irrationally. He couldn't understand why he was so disoriented. Then he saw the body, still standing erect—a geyser of blood spraying up from the severed neck. When the priest's eyes finally closed, there was only darkness waiting for him.

Suddenly the room was filling with people. Lyria saw Dan and Brett helping Kel to his feet. Sharrone had cut the bonds that held the nurse to the pillar. Lyria saw that Sharrone also had a 96 Mauser stuck in her belt. Dan had two smaller pistols, one in each hip pocket. Brett stood like a stone monument by the door with a large, two-barreled, pug-nosed ballistic weapon ready. The nightmare was over—everyone was safe. Lyria looked at Adria's silent form.

"We better be gone from here before they bring in organized reinforcements," Brett cautioned.

Lyria again looked at the still form lying in a bright pool of crimson.

"We need to take her with us," she said, "she was one of ours."

Wordlessly, Brett picked up Adria's body, slung it over his shoulder and said, "We need to move. Now!"

That got them all moving.

The soldiers walked down the steps slowly, cautiously. The muzzle of a rifle struck the stone wall with a 'thunk.' The three men froze.

'Thunk!'

Brett, about to step into the stairwell froze—he held a finger to his lips and quietly laid Adria's body back down. He thumbed back both hammers on his shotgun, holding it waist high with his left hand pushing down hard on the top of the barrels. He stepped into the opening.

"By the Redeemed God," the first man shouted, bringing his rifle up to his shoulder. He took too long. He heard what sounded like an explosion in the confines of the stone stairwell the same time he felt the buckshot strike his chest. One pellet ricocheted off the bolt of his rifle and struck him under the chin. It passed through the soft flesh, then through the roof of his mouth. Though he'd heard the start of an explosion, he didn't hear its conclusion.

Brett saw his first shot strike two of the soldiers solidly, and then fired the second barrel. The gun rose hard against the palm of his left hand, but its deadly load was already on its way.

Next to him, Sharrone brought her pistol into play, holding the heavy pistol in two hands—but there was nobody left to shoot. Brett and Sharrone shared a glance, and then he turned to Lyria.

"I'm sorry, but we cannot bring the body of this woman. We may have more fighting to do and we cannot take the chance. She's dead, we're alive."

Lyria nodded silently. Perhaps this was the way it was supposed to end. They continued up the stairway unopposed. Upon reaching the Cathedral proper, they encountered a crowd of several dozen people, but they weren't interested in fighting. They were fleeing the gunfire.

In minutes they were back on the street. Seconds later, the bullet-riddled steam-car and black cycle were heading back to the newspaper office and safety.

"I'm sorry about the woman," Brett said apologetically, "but we had no choice."

"I know," Lyria sadly said, "I know."

* * * *

In the Bishop's former office, a letter lay on his desk. It had been delivered by zeppelin from The Green and had only arrived that morning. It lay unopened until that evening when Father Jones found it. The letter was short.

Greetings, Father Woods:

A miracle has occurred; the Redeemed God truly works in mysterious ways. Our spiritual leader, our Bishop, has been found injured but alive. His doctors say that with time he will make a complete recovery!

Yours in the name of the Redeemed God,

Father McDonald

Father Jones quickly pocketed the letter, went to his room and began packing. It was time to leave this accursed city.

CHAPTER 42

As the appointed time for the meeting drew closer, word spread rapidly throughout the city that there had been some kind of trouble at the Cathedral. The stories were many and inconsistent, but one item was consistent—Father Woods had somehow died. People gathered around the newsstands early in the morning, hoping to be among the first to be able to read about the mysterious death of the priest and the ramifications it might have on their lives. Many people were worried—they didn't know what this might mean, especially in light of the meeting happening in just a few hours. Would the meeting go on as scheduled? Would it be cancelled?

When the delivery trucks carrying that morning's edition approached each newsstand, crowds surged against the cabs of the vehicles like a human tide, slowing the vehicles to a crawl up to a block away as they attempted to deliver the papers. The men and boys manning the newspaper stands were grinning—they'd almost certainly sell out immediately. There was quick money to be made, and there'd even be time to spend some of it! Once the papers were gone, they had nothing else to do until the afternoon edition hit the streets.

The Cathedral seemed quiet—no official statements had been issued, and even those not of that religion were wondering what had happened, if indeed anything had. Some people were already spreading rumors that the whole story was a fabrication, though what the motivation might be for starting such a rumor seemed lacking. Still, there was nothing like a good rumor to get people excited—reason became secondary when a really good story was involved.

One long-standing rumor was obviously true—members of the faith of the Redeemed God were fleeing the city. Homes were suddenly empty. Families left abruptly with no mention to their neighbors—some who'd been casual friends for many years. Positions in stores, factories, and warehouses were quickly vacant. For some it was a boon—jobs in their parts of town were available and employers needed them filled immediately.

Many couldn't believe the stories that all these people were moving to the southern continent to live in a jungle; it just didn't seem…

civilized. Still, what else was there for them to believe? The crystal ships were being filled—a thousand men, women, and children were leaving Los Angeles monthly.

Amid all the confusion that morning, a young priest walked into the newspaper offices at nine, asking to speak to Tom Leatham. He was wearing an overcoat that hid his black clothing and characteristic collar. Though the early spring morning was cool, the priest wore the coat to conceal his identity. He was hurriedly admitted.

"Mister Leatham, I'm Father Norville. I was one of the priests who called you yesterday."

"Yes Father, what can I do for you?"

"I have a request to make, considering the upcoming meeting."

"I'm listening, Father."

"Can you print an early edition of your paper?"

"It's been known to happen," the editor said. "What's this all about?"

The priest pulled a sheet of paper from his pocket, handing it to Tom. As the editor unfolded it, the priest continued, "In that document you'll find sworn statements from me and several other priests. What I'd like you to print is that Father Woods committed suicide last night."

"What? Why would I want to do that?"

"It's simple. You see, most of the Bishop's staunchest supporters have fled already to The Green, and more are leaving every day. A crystal ship is in the harbor right now being loaded with some kind of machinery heading south in the morning—it's something the Bishop ordered before his seeming death.

The rest of the Bishop's priests and the most dedicated of his entourage will be on that ship, and two zeppelins took off this morning carrying a large contingent of his mercenary army. More soldiers will be on the crystal ship as well."

"I'm beginning to see," Tom said thoughtfully, "you want what happened yesterday to have not happened. The only priests left in the Cathedral are those who didn't support the Bishop, and you don't want any mention of the kidnapping and subsequent rescue of my friends to further enflame the people of the city."

"That's correct," the priest said. "Are the people of the city not enflamed enough? I don't believe any of us would benefit from a breakdown of law and order. You know, priests have already been mutilated and killed and we would prefer it didn't happen to any more of our number. You can also announce that Father Woods planned to dynamite the Cathedral's basements and storage facilities. He'd have destroyed all of the stored documents and artifacts."

"What? Is that true?"

"Yes, it certainly is," Father Norville said with a firm nod. "I myself have seen some of the bombs his mercenaries constructed and planted before they left."

"So if the Bishop couldn't have the artifacts and histories held by the Cathedral, nobody could have them—is that about right?"

The priest nodded. Tom Leatham couldn't believe what he was hearing—the art, history, and ancient artifacts stored below the Cathedral were to have been destroyed. What kind of man could see himself as so important that he could dictate to the rest of humanity what they could read and study and what they couldn't?

Most people in the city didn't even know those basements and sub-basements existed. The priests who'd originally come to the Black City, fleeing both the war and persecution on the east coast, constructed the great building well over a thousand years ago. They brought with them the gathered knowledge and wisdom of previous ages they'd looted from museums and libraries in bombed out cities. Those in the know often speculated that all this information had been concealed so completely because much of it didn't match the teachings of the Cathedral—and since the 'prophets' were always right, anything else was dangerous and heresy.

"We found the bombs," the priest continued, "with the help of certain individuals who had second thoughts about the planned destruction. They even helped us defuse the explosives, and it's a good thing too. The explosions would've been great enough to collapse the basements in on themselves, causing the entire building to fall."

Tom looked up, surprised.

"It's true," Father Norville insisted. "Those of us who remain, to show our good faith, have decided to open the basements to experts from the libraries and museums. What the Bishop would've kept secret, in fact what our religious leaders for many hundreds of years have kept secret, we will reveal without reservation. As we speak, representatives from two of the city's museums are already at the Cathedral, deciding how the work is to be accomplished.

In only a few days they'll begin the long job of organizing and cataloging all of the collections—it's a job that will take years. We'll use those extra days to make sure we've safely removed all of the explosive charges. Those of us remaining are hoping that perhaps the basements of the Cathedral can be converted into auxiliary museums run by the civil government and overseen by the staffs of the city's libraries and museums."

The editor didn't have to think long—this was exceedingly good news that would be welcomed this evening when the peace treaty meeting was held.

"I'll call in my best reporter to write this story immediately," he said. "Would you mind talking to a woman?"

The priest laughed, shaking his head. "Though my religion requires me to believe women should be subservient to their husbands, and respectful to all men, it doesn't mean we believe women have no worth. I'll speak with your reporter."

Tom smiled, got on the phone, and placed a call to Sharrone, who was in the next room working on an early edition extolling the virtues of the upcoming meeting with several other reporters. This would be good news to her as well. It wouldn't be difficult to add Father Norville's story to that edition.

Tom escorted the priest to the next room where several reporters sat huddled in discussion. They looked up in surprise when Tom opened the door and walked in with the priest. Introductions were quickly made, and the editor then left them to their own devices. He headed off to check the paper storage facility to be sure there was enough blank paper for the next several days. With the way things were going, it was likely extra editions would be published in the ensuing days.

FATHER WOODS GONE: PRIEST COMMITS SUICIDE
AMID CATHEDRAL EVACUATIONS

Recovering at home, Helen Bear saw the article when the new edition of the Journal was brought breathlessly into the house by one of the younger women who'd run all the way from the newsstand carrying five copies of the special edition. Helen could hear celebrating going on in the family room. From her bed, Helen heard the loud laughing and talking downstairs. She looked again at her copy—it was hard to believe. Were all the vicious priests really gone, or was this just another trick of the Cathedral? They'd soon find out. She looked at the clock on the wall. The Bear Clan would be leaving for the meeting in an hour. She'd insisted on going with Ma'hal and the others.

* * * *

There were many people waiting to hear what would come of the meeting—far more than could fit in the building. Also, tight security required that only individuals with pre-approved passes would be allowed entry. Would there be peace? The crowds in the street in front of the Journal building were reasonably orderly, if a little bit noisy, as the participants of the summit gathered inside the main meeting room of the newspaper's building. Street performers moved through the crowds, entertaining those gathered and adding a festive air to the day's serious event.

A street band played on the sidewalk near the door of the Journal. Three men played guitars fashioned from alligator skulls. A fourth man was playing a long, curved flute made from a mastodon rib. A fifth member of the band worked his drums made of alternating sections of mammoth bone and ebony—the heads tightly stretched bison hide. The sixth member of the band was a woman. Her only instrument was her voice—but it was enough. Some of the people closer to the band tossed money into their open instrument cases.

Over a dozen policemen lined the street in front of the office, their backs to the wall. The officers had been carefully screened to determine their religious affiliations, if any. If anyone wanted to sabotage the meeting, the most dangerous threat would be from the armed police who might still be loyal to the Bishop and his cause. During the screening process, it had become clear that most of the force, even those who followed the religion of the Redeemed God, wanted nothing to do with the Bishop's brand of religion—many of them had wives and daughters to protect.

* * * *

Inside, the meeting was coming to order. It was decided the priests would speak first. Father Norville would represent them today. Next, a delegation from the city Forum would speak. There were three members present including the chief representative. After the presentations, questions would be allowed from those present. Everyone in the room and out on the streets was holding their breath—would this truly work? Would everyone involved be truthful? Could several generations of hate and mistrust really be set aside just like that? Only time would tell.

Father Norville was the first to speak—he was about thirty years old and it was already rumored that his cool head had saved many lives during the incident of the day before, whatever version of the incident the listener wished to believe. It was further rumored that he was next in line to govern the Cathedral when this meeting was concluded. Tom Leatham introduced the priest—it was now or never. He crossed his fingers.

"Ladies and Gentlemen," the young priest began, "the time of the Bishop is over. His reign of horrors is at an end. Now, we who remain here in the city ask your forgiveness. I know it'll be hard and I know it'll not happen overnight. All we ask is time to prove ourselves to you."

He paused, expecting to be interrupted, but he wasn't. There were skeptical looks on faces, sure, and there were mutterings here and there, as well as some shifting in chairs, but he was encouraged nonetheless. He smiled as he continued, holding his arms out in front of him, palms open and out in a supplicating gesture.

"We cannot undo what has been done. We cannot change the past. But we can help to build a future in which the shadow of the Bishop and his rule is dispelled by the light of truthfulness and openness."

He paused once more to take a sip of water from the glass on the podium. He listened to the audience. Did they believe him? He thought so, as mostly they were quiet. He took that as a good sign.

Kel, Lyria, and their companions, including the old shamans, sat to the back of the room. They listened and watched intently, scanning the audience as were the security guards, hoping there'd be no violence.

"Our basement vaults have been turned over to the city libraries and museums. There is a great amount of material there and, in time, it will be made available for all to see. Our books will be loaned for people to read. Any historical or artistic artifacts found will be turned over to the museums for conservation and eventual display. Secrecy is a thing of the past."

"What of all the torture and its aftermath? What of the heroin addictions and child abductions? How do we forgive that? How do we pretend that it never happened?"

The priest turned his gaze to Ma'hal. He was surprised—could she truly be as old as she appeared to be?

"As I said, we can't undo the past. What we will do is donate funds. In fact, we're donating all the funds remaining in all the Cathedral's bank accounts in the city. The funds will be used to help support the women and children the Bishop and his people have maimed, both physically and spiritually. We don't know which monies were gathered from the acts you mention and which were not; therefore, we're giving all of it. I know gold and silver cannot undo what's been done. If I could go back to the beginning of all this and end it before it began, I certainly would do so. But I can't, so this is what my fellow priests and I can do."

"Talk is cheap," Helen shouted, her young voice cutting through the low rumble of mass conversations taking place. She stared steadily at the priest, and then shouted, "What token can you offer that would make us believe you to be any different than the Bishop? Why should we trust you?"

The priest turned to Helen—he was holding a long scroll. He opened the seal, letting it unroll in front of him for all to see, turning slowly right and left before his audience.

"What I hold here in my hand is a pledge signed by every priest remaining in the Cathedral at this time and all of those residing in the rest of the city presiding over our smaller churches. The document has also been signed by several dozen of the most prominent citizens in the city who are followers of the Redeemed God: business leaders, teachers, government officials. This pledge you see before you is being presented right now, this minute, to the Forum."

The young priest left the podium to dramatically hand the scroll to the chief representative of the Forum who was sitting to the right of the podium. The man stood, taking the scroll with a smile and a nod of his head. He stood, walked to the podium and cleared his throat. He then addressed the gathering.

"I am Representative James Davis, for those of you who don't recognize me. The document just handed to me by Father Norville is the pledge of the priests and the most influential followers of their faith to support, and in fact demand, that the Forum immediately pass the languishing laws relating to child prostitution and forced prostitution—whether religiously or financially motivated.

The Forum will be meeting in the morning a short distance from here. My pledge, added to that of the Cathedral, and publicly stated here, is that those laws shall be immediately passed and implemented! There'll be no more dancing around this issue—there will be no more games. Consider these laws as already passed."

CHAPTER 43

Outside, gathered together in a small group, Larry Harper and others of his profession awaited the outcome of the meeting. They could tell that things were turning against them.

In discussion the night before, some suggested they leave Los Angeles and travel with their girls to San Diego or even New Fresno to start again in a city with more lenient laws. Larry convinced most of them to stay, explaining that if these laws were passed in Los Angeles, it'd only be a matter of time until they were passed in the other cities of the west as well.

No, if they were going to make their stand, it would have to be here. Larry was confident his cause still carried enough clout in the Forum to block the legislation. He knew at least three men on the governing body who were frequent clients of his very young whores. If nothing else, he figured, he could resort to blackmail.

And, he'd reasoned with the others, if the laws did pass, it would not mean the end of their businesses. In fact, one stipulation of the law would legalize prostitution for those who chose it as a profession. He explained to the others his thoughts on establishing open brothels. The pimps could run a legal business office right out in the open instead of on some dark street corner. The women would all be of legal age, though not necessarily employed of their own free will, and would do the customers right there in the brothels.

"Most of the women would be off the streets," he told them, "and under our direct control. The whores would steal less money if they were more closely watched, and searching them at the end of the day would be fun. They'd also be less likely to be injured or killed this way, thereby protecting our investment."

They could operate right out in the open. The police, he reasoned, couldn't tell if the women were there because they desired to be or not. He was confident that he and the other pimps could cause sufficient fear in the minds of the more reluctant women so that they'd simply agree they were willing partners in the business should the police interrogate them—after all, some of them had children and most had brothers, sisters, or parents. It would be a real shame if something bad were to happen to those parents, siblings, or children—a real shame indeed.

Nothing would change, he told the others. As far as the young whores, they'd have to be more careful with them in the future, saving them for the rich and influential. If Forum representatives and the big business leaders of the city were involved with them, prosecutions would be difficult. After all, all those men were married. They'd never talk—they'd simply have too much to lose. And who'd believe the word of a young girl using heroin? Even if one of them ran away and went to the police, everyone knew a girl like that would say anything if she thought it would benefit her financially or enhance her supply of drugs. So the pimps decided to stay on in the Black City.

* * * *

Now it was the editor's turn to speak. Tom rose, looking at the people gathered before him. This might be the most important speech of his life. He held up the scroll the priest had presented to the Forum.

"Let this notice be a warning to everyone within the city. Yes, prostitution will be made legal for women over the age of seventeen who wish to enter the profession. But, for those who seek out the innocent, for those who'd crush young souls—beware. We at the paper—along with the police—will be watching you. We have contacts and sources in places you can't guess—we have eyes and ears everywhere. If you violate these laws, we'll know about it. We'll make certain the police will know as well, and they will hunt you down."

Tom's speech brought applause from most of the audience. He noticed that most of the members of the 'Bear Clan' abstained, and that worried him. One of his primary goals had been to win them over. Perhaps once the bills were finally passed into actual law, they'd believe the sincerity of those who'd spoken today. He realized it might take time to build this trust.

The meeting concluded with questions posed by reporters and the audience that were answered as best as possible by those being questioned. In general, most present seemed satisfied. Ma'hal rose to leave with her entourage. She looked at Sharrone as she passed.

She leaned in close saying, "Bring your friends to our house this evening. I would have them see something—something these candy words and promised priest gold cannot cure. I'll show them something that can only be avenged—something only sharpened steel and warm blood can make right. I hope you'll come."

Then she turned and was gone. Sharrone looked at Lyria and Kel. Tom, though he'd been standing a short distance away, also heard the exchange between the women.

"Well," Tom said, "that sounded like an invitation to me—shall we go?"

Kel replied, "I feel we should all go. I don't exactly know why, but there is something we need to do—something important that is not yet visible to us. I can feel it, somehow, but I cannot say what it is."

Garn gave his grandson an appraising glance, and said nothing.

They left by the back door of the office, descending into the large garage one level below ground. It was here the delivery lorries were stored and maintained. With Brett driving Tom's auto, Lyria sat in the back with the three shamans. Kel and Tom sat in the front of the automobile with Brett. Dan and Sharrone chose to ride the steamcycle—they'd follow the automobile.

They traveled up the ramp from the garage, then through an alley. This avoided most of the congestion caused by the crowds gathered in front of the Journal building. As they crossed the intersection to the next block, they saw the priest and the three Forum representatives standing on the front steps of the news building, answering questions and making statements under the watchful protection of police officers and Tom's own private security guards. They picked up speed as they made their way through the darkening streets heading back into the center of the city.

Garn was the first to speak as they traveled. "Tell me further of this feeling of yours, Kel."

Kel shrugged his shoulders. "I do not know what it is I feel, but I somehow know that it is something very important. I feel we must do something or change something, and in so doing we'll change many things—though to what end, I cannot say. I am sorry I cannot be more specific."

Brett said, "Do you think we might be in any danger?"

Kel shook his head. "I do not believe so. We, especially Sharrone, have done much for these women who call themselves sisters in blood. They know it was Lyria who slew Father Woods. I don't think they mean to harm us, they simply want us to see something."

"Grandson? I want you to know I have placed your drum in the back of this vehicle—I thought we might need it. Lyria showed me where you'd left it sitting."

Kel laughed. "I thought about bringing it myself, Grandfather, but I forgot."

"That is why your grandfather is the shaman and you are the apprentice," Lyria teased.

They all laughed as the auto made the final turn into the street where the sisters lived. They saw the house ahead, brightly lit as though the building itself knew visitors were approaching—or as though it might be afraid of the dark. They slowed, approaching from the south, and parked at the road's edge in front of the house. Dan and Sharrone arrived a moment later and parked directly behind the editor's car. When they were all finally standing together in the street, they turned toward the house.

* * * *

A block away, a darkened auto sat on the other side of the street. A man was slouched behind the wheel and another sat in the front passenger seat. Both men were training telescopes on the big house. They watched a group of people gather, talk for a moment, and then move toward the house.

These men had been friends of Sergeant Jinks—fellow officers of the law. His death simply couldn't go unanswered. Everyone knew that seeking sexual release was a natural, divinely inspired, and frequently required masculine phenomenon and no mere woman, or even worse, young girl, had the right to interfere with that process. It didn't matter if she happened to be the outlet of that release or not—it was simply none of her business. As the Redeemed God had spoken through His prophets, so it should be.

And now, to make matters even worse, one of the child whores dwelling in that house had been a police prisoner—a criminal! Yet all charges had been dropped. The city was in a downward spiral—that was certain. Murderers were simply let go. Something would have to be done. They carefully checked their firearms one more time. Then they raised their telescopes again.

* * * *

The little group of friends climbed the three slate steps to the porch of the house. It was Helen who met them at the front door. She smiled first at Sharrone, and then the others. The young girl opened the door, holding it until everyone had entered, and then quietly closed it.

The living room of the house was as Sharrone remembered— brightly lit with both gaslights and lamps. Beautiful paintings hung on every wall. There were about a dozen women waiting for them. In the center of the room, in her straight-backed chair, sat their matriarch— Ma'hal of the Bear Clan.

As city politeness demanded, jackets were taken from the visitors and drinks were offered. Brett declined to remove his long leather coat, wishing to keep his shotgun close, should it be needed. He moved close to the front door and stood watchfully at the window as the women introduced themselves one at a time.

Sharrone looked at Ma'hal. "What is it that you'd like to show us?"

"Not what," the old woman said, "who."

She got unsteadily to her feet and motioned for them to follow her. Two women walked beside Ma'hal—they were clearly afraid she might fall. The old woman turned toward her guests at the bottom of the staircase and said, "You'll have to follow me up here. Forgive me for taking so long in the climb. I'm not as quick as I once was."

"Don't apologize," Sharrone said, "we're here as your guests."

The old woman smiled, turned, and started the long, painfully slow ascent.

Sharrone and the others watched her climb the stairs. When she was halfway to the top, Sharrone began climbing slowly after her. Helen came up to Sharrone, whispering, "It was thoughtful of you to wait like that—Grandmother Bear is very old and she cannot move quickly. Your consideration of our matron again shows me that you're indeed one of us."

Sharrone gave the young girl an uncomfortable smile—she wasn't sure if she wanted to be considered a member of a group of women who called themselves 'sisters in blood'!

When they reached the second floor landing behind Ma'hal, she turned and looked each of them in the eye. Seemingly satisfied by what she saw, she pointed toward a closed door a short distance down the hall to her right. She walked to that door, and with her hand resting lightly on the knob, she said, "This is why I'm not interested in what the priests and the others say. Even if their message is true, and I am not at all certain that that is the case, there's been far too much damage done for far too many years. The fight, the vengeance we've sought, must continue."

Kel and Dan looked at each other uncomfortably—it seemed as though the woman was completely unfazed by their attempts to help. Dan shrugged, and they turned once more toward Ma'hal.

"You're not convinced." she said. "Come in and then explain to me how we can have peace."

CHAPTER 44

The room they entered was a bedroom. Like the rest of the house, it too was brightly lit. The bed was neatly made, waiting for its occupant. The little girl with short blonde hair was sitting passively in a chair beside the bed. She sat with her hands folded in her lap. The girl didn't look up when the door to her room opened and then closed. Ma'hal walked over to the girl, putting her hand gently on the child's head. She turned to face her visitors.

"She cannot see you," the old woman said, "she eats when we tell her to, and she knows to relieve herself when it's necessary. Beyond that, she's gone somewhere. The priests—just like the one at the meeting this afternoon, stole her body for their use and at the same time they stole her soul. Tell me—how can peace bring her soul back? Can gold or silver restore her soul? "

Sharrone walked over to look more closely at the girl. She seemed about eight years old. Sharrone crouched down on her haunches directly in front of the girl, moving her hand slowly before the child's eyes. The unseeing stare didn't waver—the bright blue eyes didn't blink. Sharrone looked up at Ma'hal with tears in her eyes.

She asked the old woman, "What's the child's name?"

"We call her Sunny," Ma'hal responded, "in the hope that she'll rise one day into a new morning. Of course, we know she will not. Her real name we know not for she cannot tell us—she was as you see her when we found and rescued her."

"You said the priests stole her soul," Kel said. "Could you explain that, please?"

Ma'hal sat on the girl's neatly made bed and looked at Kel. She was radiating malice—Kel could feel it in the air like the pressure in the atmosphere when a storm is about to break.

"There's little to explain," the old woman said, "we found her in an apartment building not far from the tavern where we first attacked the priests—it's part of the reason we did our first attack there."

"So you know nothing about her?"

"There are some things we know," the woman said bitterly, "she was owned by someone called Larry who works for the Bishop. He's been elusive; so far we've met a few women who know of him. Some have even seen and been trained by him, but where he lives and where he travels remain a mystery. But it will not always be so. When we do find him, and we will, I'll have him brought here alive. I'll slowly kill him in front of the child so she can see her revenge enacted in blood and pain—I'm hoping that perhaps that will restore her soul and bring her back to the land of the living."

"You are saying this child was one of those used by the Bishop for prostitution?"

"That's what I am saying," the woman said. "We found out about her from a woman named Marissa. Marissa was a prostitute belonging to the Bishop. Since almost all here were once in that occupation, we knew how to talk to others like Marissa, gaining their confidence and gathering information."

Sharrone shook her head in disgust—maybe the woman was right. Who could do such an evil thing to such a beautiful child, to so many beautiful children? She'd seen the report of the mutilation and murder of Marissa—just another prostitute to die at the convenience of the Bishop.

"One of our saved girls knew Marissa. They lived together for a short time," Ma'hal continued, "and as she talked with Marissa, she learned of a child recently brought over from the black church to the apartment building. The girl had been well educated by the priests, Marissa told us—she'd been taught humility and submission."

Weeping, Ma'hal continued, "That's what the priests of the Redeemed God call it, you know. Marissa said the priests were proud of the fact the girl was as you see her here—mute and unfeeling. They bragged how men would hunger for a completely submissive child—a child one of them could take any way they desired without complaint. This child was worth a fortune, they said."

Kel looked at Lyria—he could see her temper rising. She also walked over to where the little girl sat, and crouched down in front of her next to Sharrone.

Kel said, "So you rescued her then?"

"Yes. She was apparently a very special one to this Larry. As I have said, she was worth a lot of money. She was being saved for only the very highest paying customers because of her youth and beauty—and because of her mental condition. The monsters with the most money are usually the ones who do the most damage, you know."

Kel nodded, thinking of Raven and what she'd endured in the hands of such monsters.

"I'd like to try something, if you will allow me," Kel said to the old woman.

"Tell me what you wish to do, and maybe I'll allow it," she responded, suspicion in her voice.

"Some of us here in this room are not of the city," Kel said, gesturing to Lyria and the three shamans. "We—Lyria and I—came to the Black City seeking these men. The Bishop kidnapped them as well. They were taken into The Green far south of here and from The Green we rescued them."

"You have been...there?"

The old woman was as awed as Kel had hoped she'd be. Not many people could say they'd been into The Green and come back to talk about it.

"Yes, we have. These men you see before you—and Lyria and I—are from tribal villages far to the east of here, over the western mountains and far beyond. We are part of a loose grouping of tribes who call themselves the Mastodon Clan."

"I once knew that life," the woman said wistfully. "I've heard of the Mastodon Clan—far south of where we lived. What is it you would ask of me?"

Kel took a deep breath, wondering if the woman would remember enough of her past, and whether it would even make a difference to her now.

"I want to take a journey with this girl," Kel said.

"Where would you take her?" Ma'hal was clearly suspicious.

"I will take her on a journey without leaving this room," Kel answered. "I wish to take her with me between the worlds to seek her totem—perhaps to even find her soul that you say is gone."

"You...are a shaman?" Ma'hal had seen much in her life and wasn't easily impressed, but this young man standing before her impressed her.

"He is," Garn responded to her question. "You should listen to him—he knows what he is talking about."

Kel glanced quickly at his grandfather, but the man simply nodded to him, then stood passively once more. Kel turned back to the old woman, searching her eyes for the answer to his question.

Helen then spoke, "Let him try, Grandmother. If any can help Sunny, these people are the ones. What harm can come to this child who is already living in darkness?"

Helen looked down and smiled at Sharrone, still crouching before the little girl, complete confidence in her young eyes.

"Very well," Ma'hal said. "What will you require?"

"I will require some incense and my drum."

"Incense we have," Ma'hal said.

"My drum is in the back of our auto—I must fetch it."

Tom interrupted, saying, "Stay here and let me go—I have the key."

Dan laughed in spite of himself, shook his head and thought, *They brought a drum? Who would've thought to bring a drum?* He looked at Kel, then at Garn, and knew the answer to that question.

Tom returned shortly carrying the drum and the drumstick. The drum was round, about two feet in diameter and perhaps four inches deep. The head was elk hide, stretched tightly and tied securely with rawhide thongs threaded through a series of holes that had been punched in the edge of the hide cover. Soaking the hide and the thongs before tying left the head of the drum stretched taut when it dried.

The back of the drum was open. The face was painted with a stylized hawk—wings spread in flight—in white paint. Over the hawk was a stylized sun painted yellow with a white crescent moon next to it symbolizing the twin aspects of the Divine—the God and Goddess.

The drumstick was a foot-long, thin tree limb, left in its natural state with a padded end covered with supple white leather. Several small hawk feathers hung suspended and dangling from the stick. Tom handed them to Kel. He smiled and handed them in turn to Lyria. The woman accepted the drum without comment—she'd done this on other occasions and was well versed in the process. Garn and the other two shamans simply stood, watching carefully. Kel could feel their eyes on him—he needed to relax.

He lit the incense Helen had provided. It was not a scent he recognized, though it was something that reminded him of wild spring flowers. He decided to use it even though it wasn't the usual sage—the spring flower scent made him think of the renewal and rebirth that comes with that season. It was a good association considering the work he was about to undertake. Using the flame of a lamp to light the incense, it now smoldered in a ceramic bowl on a bed of fine white sand, Kel began slowly walking around the room, allowing the air currents to spread the scent as he moved.

Lyria turned down lamps while Sharrone, unasked but attentive, turned the valve for the gas jets on the wall to their lowest setting—the jets were now barely giving off a dusky orange glow. The room darkened and everyone found a place to sit. The shamans sat on the floor cross-legged against a wall, side-by-side, watchful. Kel finished his circle with the incense, bringing it back to his point of origin. He carefully put the bowl on a table by the wall, allowing it to continue to smoke. He lowered himself to the floor, reclining next to the chair in which the little girl sat—numb and unseeing. He began taking deep, rhythmic breaths, slowly drawing in each breath consciously, holding it momentarily, and then exhaling. One...Two...

Lyria sat on the other side of the girl's chair, cross-legged like the shamans and began striking the drum. She used a steady beat—not too fast or too slow. Kel continued his deep, relaxing breathing. The sound of the drum at first filled his consciousness—then it seemed to be moving away from him. Slowly receding, it finally reached the very periphery of his hearing, and there it stayed...

CHAPTER 45

Kel heard birds and the wind singing in the branches of trees. He opened his eyes. The ancient forest stood before him, wild and dense. He was surrounded by it. Sunlight filtered through the leaves and branches of the trees, casting a translucent, luminous green radiance over the path on which he stood. The rocks and earth of the path were dappled with hints of sunlight and dense shade. The patterns of light and dark shifted, changing as the breezes moved the leaves and branches overhead. He looked up. He saw small birds flitting from tree to tree, calling in their distinctive voices to each other, and somehow also to him.

He was looking for someone, he realized gradually. There was someone waiting for him just a short distance ahead. He took a step forward. He heard the small, shallow stream to his right meandering off between the trees. He knew he must follow it—it would lead him to where he needed to be.

The stream was narrow and shallow—it was hardly a trickle of transparent water flowing quickly from some unseen source, heading for some unseen destination. He watched it, walking carefully along the bank, taking each turn as it happened. He noticed the stream gradually became wider, deeper. The sound it made was musical and soothing. Ahead, he saw the massive stone. It lay across the path by the stream, gray and impassive. It blocked his way but allowed the water to flow freely. He put one hand lightly on the rock for support, and stepped into the stream. Though wider than at its beginning, the stream was still shallow—it was hardly ankle deep as he stepped into it. He felt the cold water sliding over his moccasins, unimpeded by his intrusion. It took him four steps to pass the stone, regaining the path on the other side.

A short distance further he found his way blocked by a fallen tree. It was a very large tree, devoid of branches and he realized he'd have to climb over to continue on his way.

In the distance, the drum boomed.

He swung his left leg over the trunk, then his right leg, straddling and then passing over it. Climbing over it had been easier than he'd expected—he took that as a good omen. Again he began following the course of the stream, patiently following it—knowing it would eventually lead him, in the right time, to where he must go. Yellow and green light filtered through the trees, reflecting in the gurgling water to his right and illuminating an occasional, sudden butterfly.

The drum boomed.

It was only a little while until Kel found himself in the clearing. A short distance ahead, the familiar standing stone reared up—a dark monolith lit sharply by the sunlight that now had direct access to the Earth. The giant stone cast a black shadow across the ground behind it. Kel looked to his left, realizing someone was sitting on the ground near him—it was a little girl.

The blonde child sat immobile—eyes cast downward, hands folded in her lap, seemingly unaware of the wonders of the forest surrounding her or of Kel's presence. He looked at the child and somehow knew otherwise. The child was there—she was simply disconnected from the physical world by the terrors and pain to which she'd been subjected. Her soul wasn't gone it was simply in hiding. He walked slowly over to her, sitting cross-legged beside her in the warm sunlight.

The drum boomed.

Suddenly Kel heard something—a barely audible sound. There was a furtive movement in the forest that was barely detectable. He carefully scanned the far edge of the clearing, watching the tree line beyond the standing stone. Whatever was coming would show itself there. More sounds—a faint rustling movement through grass, the sudden sharp sound of a breaking twig. Kel was patient—when it was time, he would see. He looked again at the little girl. She was silent. He turned back to the forest and then he actually saw movement.

At first, he could see nothing more than a faint light—a white glow emanating from the dark, almost black-green background of the forest beyond the brightly sunlit clearing. As the diffuse white light drew closer, Kel saw that it had a shape—it was an elusive form moving delicately through the trees.

The stag stepped out of the last row of trees at the edge of the clearing. He was self-luminous—glowing white and pure against the darkness of the forest behind him. The great beast raised his head, staring at Kel. The shaman was awestruck. Though he'd seen the stag in his journeys from time to time, and even seen him occasionally in dreams since returning from The Green, when questioned, the animal always insisted that he wasn't one of Kel's totems—simply an observer of what was happening. Suddenly, Kel knew that was no longer true—the great animal and he were now one.

The shining stag looked at him with liquid brown eyes that seemed to see through him and into his very soul. To Kel, he seemed to know all of his secrets and desires. The animal's glowing antlers rose up to the heavens, forked and angled like captured lightning. Here there was power, Kel realized. Here was the presence of the Divine.

The drum boomed.

Suddenly the stag turned, shifting his gaze from Kel upward. Kel saw he was looking up toward the top of the standing stone. He followed the mystical animal's gaze as well. Something was sitting atop the stone—something that was tiny and bright. It was something that seemed to change color as it moved and danced: first purple, then red, then green.

Kel looked back to the stag. The giant animal looked at Kel for another moment, locking eyes once more, and then he nodded his head and turned back into the forest. Soon he was but a white glow amid the green, and then he was gone altogether.

Kel looked again at the top of the standing stone. He knew now what tiny creature was up there dancing in a rainbow of its own making. Suddenly the hummingbird descended toward them. It flitted down haphazardly on busy, buzzing wings. It flew directly toward the silent little girl, hovering in a magical array of shifting colors in the bright sunlight. It moved slowly closer, examining the child minutely. Then it moved forward once more and finally alighted right on the little girl's nose!

The child's eyes opened—she giggled, reaching out gently for the hummingbird. She scooped it gently into her hands, watching it flit about, watching the colors shift. It settled into the palm of her hand, wings cutting their eternal figure eights through the now still air. She turned and looked up at Kel and smiled at him.

The drum boomed.

The sound of the drum changed, Kel suddenly realized. It was booming faster now, signaling that it was time for him to return to the physical world. The little girl rose with Kel, looking up at him and taking his hand into her small one, smiling. She walked slowly by his side first to the edge of the clearing and then into the forest along the path Kel had walked on his journey to find her. She managed to pass both the giant rock and the fallen tree with the ease of childhood. She giggled again when the hummingbird flitted briefly in front of her eyes, seeming to communicate some wisdom only she could hear or comprehend. They walked out of the forest together.

The drum boomed.

Kel slowly became aware of physical reality—the hummingbird had flown back into the forest, the trees were fading. He began again, slowly becoming aware of his legs, his arms. Finally he opened his eyes and sat up. He looked at the chair, but the child was no longer sitting in it—she was standing in front of him. Then she said the first word she'd spoken in more than a year.

"Kel."

Kel stood, taking the child's hand. She was smiling at him. Everyone was silent—awed by what they'd seen. Kel went down on his haunches in front of the girl and asked, "What is your name, child?"

"Rosemarie," she answered timidly. "

Helen ran forward, hugging the child. Even Ma'hal seemed impressed.

"Kel? I saw him! I saw the white deer," the girl said with enthusiasm, "he's your friend, isn't he?"

"Yes, child," Kel answered, "he is a very powerful friend."

The girl looked up at Kel and asked, "Is a hummingbird powerful?"

"Oh yes," Kel responded, "hummingbirds carry remarkable powers of renewal and resurrection—why, I know of a little girl who was brought out of the darkness by one."

Rosemarie laughed, hugging Kel.

"Their power is in their delicateness," Kel continued, "the hummingbird passes lightly through the world bringing happiness and joy to everyone who sees her."

"That's what I wish to do," the girl said. "I want to make people happy."

Garn was watching carefully, holding his tongue. Ma'hal spoke first.

"This still means nothing," she said emphatically. "Even though Rosemarie is back, what was done to her cannot be undone. I still think we need to continue with our original plan. Now would actually be a good time to strike—the priests and police will not be expecting us."

Kel shook his head and answered her, gently, "Grandmother, hear my words. The Warbird to whom you have sworn allegiance these long years past craves blood—but She is a hard Mistress. She does not care what the source of that blood might be. That cloak of black feathers you wear blinds and confuses. She will take the blood of your women—the blood of this child—as eagerly as She will take the blood of priests, police, and politicians. Give over the cloak of black feathers and take back the coat of brown fur. Turn back to Bear Mother—serve the light rather than the darkness. Choose life over death. Take the spring and forget the winter. Reach for the sun and forget the ice."

The old woman looked at Kel—she seemed to be seeing him in a new light. She was confused.

"What say you?" Ma'hal asked Helen. "Is this your wish as well?"

The old woman looked at Helen and Rosemarie. Both children stood before her, radiant in their innocence.

The older girl said, "You named me yourself, Grandmother—you named me Bear, not Scald-Crow nor Warbird. I would choose life."

Rosemarie nodded silently.

Ma'hal's eyes filled with tears. She reached out, embracing both Helen and Rosemarie, whispering, "So is it over? Is it truly over?"

"It is," Rosemarie said. "Is Bear my last name too? I like it!"

Ma'hal laughed, saying, "Yes, child, your name is also Bear. You and Helen are sisters, you know—sisters in Light!"

Lyria put down the drum, walked to Kel, and gave him a hug—a 'Bear' hug she called it. Garn was watching Kel—he felt his grandfather's eyes on him.

Kel turned, smiling, and said, "I know now I cannot leave with you, Grandfather. My journey in this city is not over—there are people here that need help too. When you go back, you will be our tribe's shaman—I am not needed there. I have work to do here."

Garn smiled at his grandson, "There are two shamans in our village at this time already, Kel. I have seen it in journey when we were yet captives back in The Green. The tribes have been coming together because of the threat posed by the Cathedral and their raids. Now that threat is past, but I am thinking the villages will remain unified. Our home will be quite a bit larger than it was when we left it over six months ago!"

Lyria looked from Kel to Garn. "We're not going home, are we?"

Kel looked into Lyria's eyes and said, "We are home, my love. As time goes by, these women will need a healer—and a shaman, even if an almost-shaman. They may also need a protector—someone as fierce as an ice tiger. I cannot leave them, and I would you stay with me on this journey, my one true love. I need you with me. I need you to heal me."

Garn walked over to his grandson and Lyria. He put his arms around them both and said, "You have passed the test, my grandson. You are no longer an almost-shaman, as you called yourself—you are now truly a man of wisdom. You have passed your shadow walk!"

"I have? When?" Kel looked at his grandfather in surprise.

"You passed it just now, my boy! You have chosen duty over comfort—you have chosen to do what is right rather than simply what is easy. You saw a need and you filled it. You saw a soul in distress and you retrieved it. There is nothing more I can teach you."

Lyria reached up, standing on her toes and gave Garn a kiss on his cheek. She smiled at him and asked, "Does that mean we may marry?"

"It does, child," Garn said with a laugh, "your betrothed is now yours to take if you would have him. We'll set a date for the wedding, then prepare the ritual."

Dan looked at Sharrone—she smiled at him. "Isn't it wonderful? Our friends are being married," she said, dancing just a bit where she stood.

"Yes," Dan answered, "it's truly wonderful!"

Lyria grabbed Kel by the collar of his shirt, turned his head toward her and kissed him. As he returned the kiss, Lyria's lips parted. For the first time they dared to really kiss each other with the passion they felt. They both pulled back self-consciously, hearing the two young girls giggling behind them. They laughed as well, turned and hugged both of the young girls. They returned Kel and Lyria's hugs warmly.

"Why do you not all stay this night?" Rosemarie quickly seconded the invitation extended by Helen.

Helen looked to Ma'hal self-consciously. Had she taken too much on herself? Ma'hal considered for a moment, looking into the eyes of the newly reborn child, and agreed, saying, "It's now full dark anyway—stay this night and talk with us. I'm certain you have many strange and exciting tales to tell."

"Well, I'm going back to my office," Tom said, "I have things to do there, and I have a wife waiting at home. I would hate for her to find out I spent the night in a house full of unmarried women, especially with my arm still in a sling. Why, I couldn't even defend myself."

Everyone laughed at his comment, even Ma'hal. The old woman found she liked to laugh—it had been so long, she'd forgotten what it meant to be happy—to be joyful. Escorted by his friends, Tom walked down the steps to the street and his waiting automobile.

CHAPTER 46

Detective Olsen nudged his partner who was sitting, eyes closed, beside him in the dark steam-car. Hogan jumped, sitting up straight. He felt briefly guilty that he'd drifted off—still, after working a long shift, he wouldn't be too hard on himself for drifting briefly out of consciousness on this off-duty and very unofficial stake out. Both men picked up their telescopes once more, watching as a small gathering of people walked to the street and said their good nights to each other.

They were both surprised to see the steam-car pull from the side of the road with just the Journal editor inside. The others were apparently staying. They were walking back to the nest.

"Well," Detective Hogan said, "I think that pretty well wraps things up for tonight."

"I agree," his partner said, firing up the burner to get the steam pressure up once again.

"We found another nest of them—that's good. When the Bishop makes his move in the south, we'll be ready in the north to do his will."

Olsen laughed—vengeance could be such fun when very usable women were going to be involved.

"It's the will of the Redeemed God," Olsen reminded his partner piously. "I believe we'll take back the city from the unbelievers one day very soon, and the so-called 'free women' will become willing and humble servants of the Redeemed God!"

They both laughed, as the auto started moving. A quick U-turn and they were headed back to the police station, and then home for a good night's sleep.

* * * *

Kel and his companions sat for several hours with the former 'sisters in blood' discussing what the coming changes in the law might mean.

"I think that even most of the former supporters of the Bishop will see that to vote against establishing these laws now would be political suicide," Dan said.

Sharrone laughed, sitting with Rosemarie on her lap, and nodded in agreement saying, "I think their real religion, their god, is power—and their god has fled the Cathedral."

Garn answered with thoughtfulness, "This is true—but you must keep your guard up at least for the time being. Loss of power can turn quickly into thoughts of revenge. Though they have lost the city and flee into the south, you cannot know what they might be willing to do as a parting gesture."

That gave them all something to think about.

Changing the subject, Ma'hal turned to Lyria, "When will you wed?"

"Shortly, I hope," she answered with a smile, "Kel and I have traveled long and far together, yet we are apart. It is time for us to travel long and far together...together."

The women laughed with Lyria's joke.

Lyria then turned to Garn, a questioning look in her eyes. He smiled at her, "There are things that need to be planned, costumes that must be made. I expect, however, that the actors we will need are already in this room!"

Galv and Drog smiled. They knew they'd be included in the drama as would some of the women, should they be willing.

Helen looked at the three men of knowledge with a questioning in her eyes. Garn and Galv noticed the confusion in the young girl's eyes.

"Marriage is not just two people living together," Galv explained. "It is a spiritual binding of souls, blessed by God and Goddess."

"Our belief," Lyria said, adding to the explanation, "is that a true union cannot be made without such a blessing. The couple to be married is challenged—decisions have to be made, priorities decided. We will be tested before we can be one."

"The first test, since Kel was in training to be shaman of his tribe," elaborated Garn, "was that he finish his training before he would wed. This has now been accomplished by his decision to stay with you here in the Black City instead of returning to his home and family."

"But you've been traveling together long," Helen said, looking from Kel to Lyria, "you've gone from your home, to this great city, then into The Green to fight monsters! You've been together day and night for many months. Have you not slept together? Were you not eating, fighting, and running together? Through all that you haven't…"

Lyria blushed, "We have not, young one. That is our way—our word is sacred. Honor is more important than physical pleasure—we are bound by forces greater than our passion for each other."

"So then you are both still v…"

Again Lyria blushed as one of the other women quickly interrupted saying, "I think it's time for the young ones to go off to bed."

"I couldn't agree more," Ma'Hal said, grinning at Lyria. "It's time for young girls to seek their futures in their dreams."

With the historic grumbling and complaining that children have indulged in since the beginning of time, the four younger members of the group, including Helen and Rosemarie, filed out of the living room and trooped upstairs to their bedrooms. Helen took one quick, backward glance at Lyria and Kel—her childhood experiences making her wonder if any man would ever want her the way Kel wanted Lyria.

Ma'hal looked coyly at Kel, then said, "I expect you two will be wanting separate bedrooms for the night—is that correct?"

Garn laughed, and said, "We four shamans can sleep in the same room. We are your guests, kind lady, and we would not overly burden you."

"You are no burden," Ma'hal said. "You've freed us from a dark future—I can see that. I began this struggle so long ago with the very best of intentions. Still, women have died because of me, because I sought blood instead of reconciliation. Because helping my adoptive Clan wasn't enough—I needed personal revenge for something that happened decades ago. I am ashamed."

"Be not ashamed," Drog said kindly. "You have seen the path you were traveling and came to realize it was no longer truly your path. You had the wisdom to take the other road—there are many who would not have been able to do that, and I congratulate you on your wisdom."

Ma'hal smiled and lowered her eyes—it had been a long time since a man had complimented her.

The group sat together in the large living room, talking for a while longer, and then they too went to their rooms to sleep. Tomorrow was the start of an entirely new day—a day Ma'hal and the others were looking forward to. It would be their first truly new day in many years.

Sharrone had been asked by Helen to sleep in her room upstairs. She looked at Dan, explaining, and then ran her tongue over her upper lip slowly and suggestively. Dan took a step forward and Sharrone laughed, wagging her finger.

"No, no, you bad boy," she whispered to him. "One night without me will not harm you. Who knows—you might even think up new ways to show me how much you missed me when once again we can be together...together!"

He sighed, laughing at her wit while recognizing defeat. He turned to Galv and shrugged, saying ruefully, "I guess I'll be bunking with the men tonight."

One of the women showed them to their room and showed them where the bathroom on the first floor was located. The men would be sleeping downstairs.

Their room was large, and held six beds—it was almost like a dormitory. Kel looked around as he chose his sleeping place.

"I wonder how many women come here—how do they manage to feed them all?"

"I expect they come and go," Dan said. "Some will go back into slavery once their physical wounds are healed—a life of familiarity is what some seek, no matter the cost to themselves. Even some of those originally taken against their will may leave, going back to the streets, the narcotics...the Cathedral."

"I suppose that is true," Kel responded sadly, "still, I can see the merit of what they've built here. I want to help in this endeavor—it is a noble cause."

"And you shall," Garn said to his grandson. "You are beginning a new life too, you know, like the women Ma'hal and the others have rescued. You will soon have a wife—perhaps even children. I will share the news of what has happened and why you and Lyria decided to stay when I arrive back home. We will be leaving in four days or so, I expect."

"So soon?"

Garn laughed at that, saying, "Pela is waiting for me—we have been separated for more than six months now."

Kel smiled, remembering his grandmother.

"I will give her your greeting," Garn said, guessing Kel's thought. "She will be very proud of you, Kel."

"Well," Dan said, reclining on his bed, "I'll see you all in the morning."

Kel paused, and then spoke thoughtfully, "In the morning, I would like to go to the wharf to watch that crystal ship being loaded. I have heard of this mysterious cargo several times now and I want to see for myself what kind of machines the Bishop has ordered for use in The Green."

"We can do that," Dan said nonchalantly, "though we'll have to travel very early in the morning. Tom isn't here with his steam-car. Tell me, do you mind a bike ride?"

"Lyria is still alive," Kel said, "so I expect I will be relatively safe as well."

They laughed, and Dan turned down the lights. Soon they were all asleep.

CHAPTER 47

Dan and Kel were up just as the sun began to filter its light into the streets of the Black City. They dressed quickly, quietly. The rest of the men were still sleeping. Dan scribbled a note for Sharrone so she'd know where they'd gone. They slipped quietly out the front door.

Outside, Dan pushed the heavy bike a block before attempting to start it—no point in awakening anyone they knew. Then with a roar, they were off. Riding behind Dan, Kel quickly grasped the fundamentals of balance and turning. Forty minutes later, having traveled at a high rate of speed, they were in the dockyards. They rode slowly, the powerful bike grumbling and shaking beneath them like some wild animal straining to be unleashed. They stopped at one of the wharf offices. Dan stood the bike on its stand, and the two men dismounted.

They were informed, to their surprise, that three ships were leaving that day—mostly they'd be loaded with passengers and their belongings migrating south from Los Angeles and even from as far away as New Fresno. The wharf manager shook his head in disbelief as he talked with Dan and Kel—he couldn't imagine why anyone would be so foolish as to deliberately go that far out of their way simply to commit suicide by allowing themselves to be eaten alive by strange, giant animals and even stranger giant insects.

The man pointed out the three ships in question, so Dan and Kel again mounted the bike and rode to the first docking area. This ship couldn't be the one they were looking for—it was far too small. The gangplanks were already lowered to the wharf, and passengers were lined up, filing onboard slowly, following their Redeemed God and their dead Bishop into the unknown.

The second ship was berthed at a larger dock. It turned out to be the one they were seeking. This ship was a full-size steamer—the sides of the vessel, standing vertical from the water, looked almost like steel walls to Kel. At the ship's side stood two huge steel derricks mounted on great wheels that would have appeared right at home on the largest of steam locomotives.

The derricks were in the process of loading a series of heavy items into the hold of the ship. Kel and Dan walked casually down the dock, their footsteps thudding against the heavy wood planks. They got as close as they were allowed, having been stopped by a dock worker warning them of the potential danger of getting any closer. So there they stood and watched silently.

Two of the flatbed railroad cars on the siding that ran next to the giant ship were already empty—the great tarps that had covered their cargo were neatly folded and secured to the beds of the cars. It was obvious that loading had begun very early in the morning, probably at first light. The huge tarpaulins covering what rested on the third rail-road car were just now being untied and pulled to the dock by a dozen men. They pulled the tarps a fair distance from the railroad car and set them aside in a heap to be folded and stored for use later in the day.

Kel and Dan stared at what had been revealed on the flatbed car. What they saw was actually a little disappointing. They turned and looked at each other in surprise. The big mystery surrounding the cargo must've been someone's dream. It appeared there was noth-ing more sinister than a group of smaller than normal steam locomo-tives heading into The Green. They were probably going to be used as transport for the short runs the trains would make going from one of the small cities to another on the edge of The Green.

Workmen attached steel lifting cables around and under the mas-sive pallets upon which the small locomotives on the railway car were bound. With a grumble and a roar, the engines of the derricks surged to life as black smoke billowed into the air from two tall smokestacks. The cables tightened slowly—they strained and then the steam engine rose slowly into the air.

"Where are the wheels?" Dan made the observation, standing with his hand held to his brow over his eyes, shielding them from the sunlight reflecting from the unpainted steel of the gantry and the sur-face of the ocean beyond. Kel shielded his eyes as well, trying to see what Dan was talking about.

"I do not see any wheels," Kel commented, scanning the object that seemed almost to be levitating into the air beside the ship. "Per-haps this is but a part of the machine—perhaps the wheels may have been removed and are already aboard and stowed."

"That's possible, I guess," Dan said doubtfully, "but look at those odd objects on both sides of the engine—they look rather heavy and too well constructed and purposeful in design to be merely part of the incidental packing for the engine."

Kel examined the sections of steel to which Dan was referring. From where he stood, he could see two of them. They were long, rectangular objects lying tightly up against the boiler of the locomotive. They seemed to be attached to the engine itself—one was mounted directly in the rear. It was fastened to the side of the driver's cab, which seemed unusually long. The other one was attached near what had to be the front end of the steam engine—it was attached under the boiler and, folded as it was, it raised the front end of the machine from the pallet. Obviously there would be another such object on the other side of the driver's cab, hidden from them by the bulk of the machine.

Both of these odd objects had a wide disk-like device in the center with rods that seemed to extend into other rods of greater diameter. Dan recognized them as pistons. There were heavily sheathed cables or perhaps hoses running into the disks and laying closely along the sides of the straight parts, held in place themselves by massive steel brackets.

Protruding from the rear of the cab of the strange vehicle were two long, heavily constructed metal tubes. Kel could see they were lightly capped on the ends, the caps simply heavy canvas bound to the tubes by thinner canvas strips. He instinctively knew they must be hollow—there'd be no point installing caps over the end of a solid piece of steel. These two mysterious rods or tubes were attached to the back of the engine's cab area on either side by large steel balls that rode in sockets set into the machine itself giving the distinct impression that they could be rotated in any direction, probably powered from inside the cab. How, Kel wondered, with these long rods trailing behind the cab, could any cars be attached to allow this engine to become a train?

Interestingly, where large, open windows would have been on a standard locomotive's cabin, this engine had only small windows that were covered by heavy metal shutters. Hinged at the top, the steel shutters could be opened from the inside however far the crew wished—they looked to Kel and Dan like the shutters one might find on the windows of a house, or a fortress.

"Watch out there," a workman shouted.

Something on the other side of the engine slipped and came unfastened. Dan and Kel heard a metallic screeching and a heavy thud. Then they saw another long metal construction, like the two they could see on this side of the engine, swing downward suddenly to hang limply swinging back and forth. The bottom of the thing swung in the air about a foot above the dock. One worker barely managed to escape injury by jumping into the water when the object pivoted suddenly down with what looked like a great metal foot at its end. As the other workers scrambled to help their companion back out of the water, a realization struck Dan.

"Legs," Dan said, "they are legs! This is no locomotive—it is something that walks."

Kel nodded in silence, now understanding what he'd been looking at, and said, "Why would they want a walking locomotive?"

"It is not a locomotive," Dan whispered. "It is a war machine. The Cathedral is making war on The Green and its peoples."

They'd seen what they'd come to see. They mounted Dan's cycle, turned it around and headed back to the street. They'd have to tell the others what was happening, though what it actually meant, they couldn't say. How many of these devices were being sent south? They knew of at least three of them. How powerful were they? Kel believed they looked monstrously powerful. He imagined one of them standing on its legs—the steam boiler and cab towering at least thirty to forty feet into the sky! Not even the great beast he and Lyria encountered could match such a machine giant. Little Raven had been right, Kel thought; men had finally come to kill The Green.

They arrived back at the house just in time for breakfast. Tom had arrived just before them. After a hearty breakfast of eggs, bacon, and toast, the group sat drinking coffee together—this was a strange new beverage made from a plant found in The Green and only recently come north to Los Angeles. It had an interesting taste and seemed to awaken everyone as they sat sipping the hot beverage. The dishes were cleared from the table and they settled down to talk.

"So," Tom began, "you're to be married?"

Lyria smiled at Tom. "Yes, we are—in a few days when Garn is ready with the ceremonial objects and costumes."

"In that case," Tom said, "let me congratulate you, and be among the first to offer a wedding gift."

Kel and Lyria looked at each other—they'd thought being together was gift enough for their wedding!

"I've heard a rumor," Tom began again, "that says you aren't leaving us—that you've decided to stay. You say you have work to do here in the city, helping these women and others in similar circumstances to find themselves once again."

"That is right," Kel answered.

"Well then," the editor said, "you'll need a place to live, correct? A place where you can work and call home."

Again, Kel and Lyria hadn't thought about that.

Tom continued with a smile, "Since Dan and Sharrone have decided to move into their own home now that the threat to Sharrone has passed, I'm giving you the house where you've been staying since your return from The Green."

Kel looked at Lyria, then back to Tom, shock visible on his face.

"Also," Tom said with a grin, "I've bought, with the help of my old friend Mahrden, the six acres of open land surrounding that home. All of it is now yours—here's the deed."

He handed a rolled parchment to Kel. Kel took it, not knowing what to say. He could only look at Tom, dumbfounded.

Tom laughed merrily. "I've taken the liberty of adding some buildings to the property; construction will start today. You'll soon have corrals and barns for your three horses." He laughed aloud. "There will also be a small dormitory-style building in case the ladies here get an overflow of incoming women or children in need of your services. That should be enough room for everyone. You never know, as word of this spreads, we may see individuals coming here from other cities to find help and safety."

"Oh, Tom," Lyria said, tears forming in her eyes, "you are too generous!"

"I know," he answered with a grin, "but I generally do what I feel like doing, when I feel like doing it—and I feel like doing this right now."

He looked at his new friends, admiration in his eyes. "In my opinion," he said, "what you're helping to build is monumentally important, and you'll need the space to work and to live."

"Having the horses will help," Kel said thoughtfully. "We can teach injured and recovering people to ride and care for them—for some it could be healing—a nurturing experience. The horses will give them the love and gratitude only animals can show."

"I agree," Tom said, "and this little thing is what I can do to help you accomplish the great goals you have set for yourselves. I respect and admire you greatly."

"How can we ever thank you? This is far more than I had ever dreamed," Kel said, overwhelmed by the man's selfless gift.

"You can thank me through the hard work you do here."

Lyria turned to Sharrone. "When did you decide to move?"

"Oh, we've wanted to for some time, and you'll want your privacy—especially now that you and Kel will be spending a lot of your time together...together!"

Lyria blushed, and then laughed. She knew she wouldn't live that comment down for a very long time.

"Do you have a place in mind?"

"Yes, actually, we do," Sharrone answered. Grinning, she continued, "We'll be living in the house right in front of yours. Tom has given us what he called the 'guard house' for our very own now that the threat against my life is over. We'll be neighbors!"

Helen clapped her hands gleefully, saying, "Then we can visit, can't we?"

"Of course you can," Sharrone said.

"I like horses," Rosemarie said shyly, "at least, I think I do..."

"Our horses are spoiled rotten and very gentle—I am sure they will like you as much as you will like them," Lyria said with a laugh.

Kel and Lyria offered to help with the dishes and the offer was gratefully accepted. Around this house, everyone was expected to share the chores. While Kel and Lyria worked at the sink, scrubbing bacon grease and butter from plates, knives, and forks, Helen and Rosemarie stood by diligently drying them as fast as they were washed. Two other women helped by putting the dishes and silverware back into the cabinets. When they left the kitchen, Rosemarie was holding Kel's hand. Lyria smiled—she thought Kel would make a wonderful father...when the time was right.

Back in the living room, the three old shamans were deep in discussion. They were beginning to plan a wedding and there was much to be done. The others went out back to sit in the shade of the large trees growing there. Kel lay back in Lyria's arms, watching the two young girls chase butterflies with little success but much giggling.

* * * *

The next day Father Norville was tired—the day before had been a very long day. Now he needed to begin dealing with the museum curators and librarians. He knew it'd be a very tedious project. Still, it was necessary to convince the people of the city that things were really different and the reign of the Bishop was over. He felt certain that the laws discussed at the meeting two days ago would be passed. There was no way to stop it now, no matter who might try.

The first knock on the door was one of the younger priests. He looked in at Father Norville nervously, then said, "Your Grace, there's a Mister John Watson here to see you. He's the curator of the ancient cities collection at the Main Street Museum."

"Thank you," the priest answered, "show him in, please."

The young priest stood back, allowing Mister Watson to enter. He shook the priest's hand, settled into a comfortable chair and said, "Well, Father Norville, shall we get to work?"

The priest grimaced inwardly—it was going to be another very long day.

* * * *

Garn sat alone in the backyard of the Bear House. In the last two days, he and the other shamans had put together a wedding ceremony for Lyria and his grandson. Normally, these things took more planning, but with the help of two other men of wisdom, and the help of the women as well, they were going to be ready.

The wedding was planned for two days hence—Dan scouted several locations and found a perfect spot where they would be isolated, but not so isolated that it would be difficult to get there and back. Garn was impressed with young Hendrick's abilities and knowledge.

He was surprised when Dan took him and the other shamans to see the small, forested area he'd chosen for the ceremony. It was a perfect choice.

Sharrone spent much of that time with the women, occasionally going out on forays with one of the other women into the city. She was making her own plans for Lyria and Kel's wedding. She'd discussed this at length with Dan, and he was in complete agreement—this would be a wedding to remember.

With his friends and the talents of several of the women, they'd managed to produce the necessary costumes and props in just two days. Garn shook his head, smiling. He wouldn't have thought it possible. But he was glad they'd managed it. He missed Pela terribly, and he longed for the familiarity of his people—both the people of the Mastodon Clan in general, and more closely, the people from his own village. He wondered how much things might have changed. He'd soon know, he thought. He rose, walking back into the house. There were a few small details yet to be worked out with Mahrden before the wedding could take place—it was nothing that a little herb lore couldn't solve, and Mahrden was a real master in that arena…

CHAPTER 48

Lyria and Kel were beside themselves with eagerness—they'd waited so long and traveled so far to reach this moment! They left the Bear Clan's home in an auto with Dan driving. Kel and Lyria were in the back, while Sharrone rode in the front. The three shamans had left earlier to prepare the ceremony, accompanied by women of the Bear Clan who were eager to help their new friends complete their wedding ceremony.

Dan knew the route to the edge of the forested hills a little north and east of the city. The area was not really a forest, but a small region of dense growth as yet untouched by the city. It would be ideal for their ceremony, as it would not take long to get there or back, but it was isolated enough so there would be no interference from other people; the closest house was almost five miles away. Dan drove a short distance up the trail and parked by the other autos already there. Everyone else seemed to be gone—only Garn and Mahrden greeted them upon their arrival. Dan and Sharrone drifted away, moving up the trail and into the dark and mysterious woods.

Though it was not yet late, it was dark. The moon was almost full but little of its light filtered through the trees. The wind was cool—spring had finally arrived in the city. Kel and Lyria stood in the garb of the city. The city was now their home and with that came the necessity to become one with the city. Ahead, through the trees, they saw small glowing bonfires in the forest. Each fire, spaced far enough to let the darkness descend between them, illuminated the trunks of the trees in their immediate vicinity, giving the forest an ethereal glow.

Kel and Lyria were nervous—they had no idea what the Ordeal of Marriage might entail as it was subtly different for every couple in the tribe. They had both talked to newly married friends in the dim past of their before, but none had revealed the nature of the test—secrecy was one of the requirements.

Mahrden stood with Garn just behind the young couple. He handed each of them a cup of wine. "Drink," he said, "for the trials ahead may be easier if one's head is a little lighter."

Kel took the cup and drained it nervously. He watched Lyria do the same. The aftertaste came as a surprise. Kel knew where he'd tasted it before—in the Green Hyena before the man known then to him only as the magician had begun his magical show. The herbal infusion began to take effect immediately.

Lyria looked at Kel. He seemed to be glowing—a faint blue-green fire danced around his head. Mahrden whispered to them, his voice almost unheard. "You will see your spirits, young friends—look to each other."

Then Garn gently pushed Kel forward. Lyria stumbled after him. She noticed that they were bound together about their waists by a cord. The knots that bound them were simple bows, easily removed—but somehow she knew that to do so would be a mistake. They moved into the trees, and headed to the first bonfire. Kel took Lyria's hand, fearful of losing her in the darkness. They walked slowly, keeping to what seemed a narrow pathway. The forest was quiet—the only sound they could hear was the faint crackling of the fire as they drew near.

Someone approached Kel from the forest. It was a man, but he looked strange. Kel didn't know if it was the effect of the strange drug he'd ingested or if it was the man himself. The apparition stood well over six feet tall—his chest was very large—so large in fact that it pushed his head back so far Kel was looking at the bottom of his chin.

"Why do you want to be married?"

Kel, surprised by the question, answered, "Because Lyria is the woman I love and want to spend my life with."

The strange man laughed, then said, "But you are a young and handsome man with many talents. You could have any woman. You could have many women...why settle for just one? I certainly would not!"

"Then you and I are different, stranger. My love and my life are for Lyria alone."

The tall man huffed, turned and faded into the darkness.

Lyria knew Kel was talking to someone, but realized that someone was coming from the darkness toward her as well. She felt dizzy as the woman approached. Lyria stared. She did feel lightheaded as Mahrden said—could that be the reason the woman before her seemed so strange? The apparition before Lyria had outlandishly huge breasts.

Her blouse was bright red and fit tightly, and that was all she was wearing. She was naked from the waist down.

"Why do you want to be married?"

Lyria stammered, "Kel is the love of my life—I have chosen him!"

The woman laughed. "Surely you do not believe you are the only woman in his life?"

"This I do believe," Lyria said defensively.

The woman laughed again and answered, "He has been with me, you know…here." The apparition was touching herself between her legs. "He has been with women; surely you must know that!"

"I do not," Lyria said firmly. "Be gone from my presence, temptress!"

The woman laughed low, turned and faded into the forest.

Kel and Lyria reached the first bonfire. Garn and Galv were waiting there, offering them a skin of water. Kel took it and then hesitated.

"Is…" his tongue felt thick—it was hard to speak, but he continued, "Is this water clear? Or have you put more of the strangeness into it?"

Garn laughed, "The water is pure, my grandson. Drink."

Kel took the waterskin, handing it to Lyria. She smiled at him, taking a long drink. Then it was Kel's turn.

Suddenly Mahrden and Drog were behind them, urging them on. "The test is but begun, young ones," Mahrden whispered. "The elements speak—and you must answer."

Drog and Mahrden gently pushed the couple past the bonfire and back into the darkness. Ahead, they could see the next small fire.

Once again someone moved toward Kel. He turned to see, his head still reeling from the powerful chemicals coursing through his veins. A woman stepped out of the darkness. She smiled at Kel and he smiled back—she seemed…ordinary.

"Why do you want to be married?"

"Lyria is the only woman I could ever love," he responded.

The woman sneered, "Is that it or has she just gotten control over you? Could it be that she is fearful of spending her life alone? Could it be that any man would help her fill the emptiness?"

"That is not the case," Kel said firmly. "Lyria carries her own sword and knows how to use it!"

"But she depends on you so," the woman wheedled, "she is weak and insecure."

"You lie! Be gone, witch! You will not turn me from the light of my life!"

The woman chuckled, turned, and wandered into the darkness.

While Kel was so engaged, Lyria was again approached. A man was standing before her. He was an older man with a kindly face—a face that made one think of a favored grandfather.

"Why do you want to be married?"

"Since I was a child, I have loved Kel."

"And now he is abandoning his people—his tribe. Is that the action of an honorable man?

"Speak not to me of honor, old one," Lyria responded angrily. "Our tribe has many shamans. Kel is needed here in the Black City!"

"So he says," the old man said with a dry laugh. "Or is it that he is afraid that if he were to go home, he would not be the big man he can be here?"

"What are you saying?" Lyria hissed, her eyes flashing green for a moment.

"He may have no following where he should be—with his tribe. Are you sure he stays to help or does he stay out of fear that he won't measure up where people are familiar with the shamanic way?"

Lyria lunged at the man and felt the rope at her waist pull tight. She stopped. The old man was laughing now, fading into the darkness.

They moved on to the next bonfire. Around the fire sat several women of the Bear Clan. Everyone was watching them carefully—it made Lyria nervous. Ma'hal came to them, offering Lyria a waterskin. "Drink," the old woman said, "the water will purge you of your fears."

Lyria handed the skin to Kel after she had drunk deeply. He took a long drink, and then handed the skin back to Ma'hal.

They walked on toward the next fire.

A woman was approaching Kel. He turned toward her cautiously. What now? He stood passively waiting. She was heavily made up— her eyes lined widely with kohl, her cheeks and lips bright red with rouge. Her bust was gigantic.

"Why do you want to be married?"

"Because our kind is divided for love's sake—that we may come together once again in divine unity."

The woman laughed, "So you say! Look at me—I am a woman. Why not take me now? She does not have to know. I can work a magic that will make us disappear from her mind."

"I am not interested," Kel said.

"Yet you are always looking at other women," the apparition taunted. "Cease the cheating looks and take me!"

Kel backed away from the apparition, turning his head. When he looked back, she was gone—only the faintest movement into the trees remained.

Then Lyria saw a man coming toward her. He was smiling. When he spoke, his lips didn't move. She wondered why, and then decided he was wearing a mask.

"Why do you want to be married?"

"Because I cannot imagine a life without Kel."

The man smiled and spoke condescendingly, "But I imagine he could live quite well without you!"

"Speak plainly, creature of darkness."

"See? Anger already! Imagine living with the same man, year after year, growing old, wondering what you may have missed."

"I will miss nothing, night monster!"

"But you will always wonder, won't you? Would he have gone with those women in front of the Green Hyena had you not been there? How many women has he had, Lyria? How many has he paid for?"

"I know Kel—I have known him since childhood. Your black magic will not work on me, demon!"

The man laughed, turned, and walked into the forest without so much as a backward glance.

When they reached the third fire, there were benches for them to rest upon. When they sat, Helen came to them with a platter of meat and bread. "Eat," the young girl said quietly, "regain your strength."

"Thank you, Helen," Kel said, "the food is most welcome."

They sat there for almost fifteen minutes eating and drinking more water. Nobody was urging them on. Finally, they rose of their own accord and once again took the trail into darkness and discovery.

Once again a man approached Kel. He was extremely well dressed, wearing an expensive suit with cufflinks and watch chain that glittered in the waning firelight of the bonfire they had recently left behind. He wore a silk top hat—and his shoes were so highly polished, they glittered in the moonlight.

"Why do you want to be married?"

"Because Lyria's being sings inside of me—she makes me real."

"Real? I will show you what is real," the man said in a confidential whisper, "this is real!" The man was holding a small bag in his hand, offering it to Kel, who reached for it, then paused. The man laughed. "Come, Kel, do I look like a dangerous man?"

"I will hold my judgment on that question, sir," he replied.

The man chuckled, opening the bag. Into his left hand he poured a number of large gold coins. He jingled them teasingly. "You could make a lot of money, young man. You could charge people for healing them—for telling them their futures and their fortunes."

"Futures and fortunes are not mine to tell."

"But the people in this city won't know that. Many women will come to you—your power and your youth will attract them. They'll pay you to take them abed."

Kel recoiled in horror. "My knowledge is not to be sold on the street as a prostitute sells her body!"

The man sadly shook his head, putting the coins back in the bag. He handed it to Kel, and smiled.

The woman who approached Lyria was young and attractive. She had none of the outlandish physiology of the previous apparitions. Lyria wondered if the drug she'd ingested was finally running its course. She took a deep breath.

"Why do you want to be married?"

"I marry for love," she answered simply.

"Love? Don't make me laugh! Does your man marry for love? Look on him, poor child."

Lyria looked over at Kel. He was talking to a finely dressed man. The man just poured out a handful of gold coins—he seemed to be making a deal of some kind with Kel.

"He's selling his services," the apparition whispered in Lyria's ear, "he will be a rich man—taking money for magic."

"It is not so! Kel would not do that!"

"Look to the money, woman. What do you see?"

For an instant, Lyria looked at Kel scornfully—he'd taken the bag of gold.

"No," she said, "I do not believe Kel could do something like that and live. This is part of the evil dream you have woven around me."

Before the woman could reply, Lyria saw Kel open the bag and dump the gold coins to the ground. They tumbled, glittering in the faint moonlight. Then they changed. Halfway to the ground they suddenly became dark, many legged insects. They landed on the ground in a heap and scurried quickly into the forest. Lyria looked back, but the woman was gone.

They moved together toward the last bonfire. When they arrived, they saw Sharrone and Dan and all the shamans and several Bear Clan women. Some were still partly in their costumes. Everyone was laughing and smiling.

"Congratulations, Lyria and Kel," Garn announced. "Before the divine you have passed the Ordeal of Marriage—you have completed the Ritual of the Elements. You have run the elemental gauntlet and rejected all temptations and threats. This evening, in the eyes of all here present, and in the eyes of the divine, you have completed your marriage ceremony—you are now one!"

Kel looked into Lyria's eyes. They were sparkling in the firelight. They kissed to the applause of all present.

"Oh, Kel! I almost cannot believe we are wed!"

"You are me and I am you," he replied with a laugh. "What has occurred tonight cannot be undone by lie, greed, jealousy, or money!"

Garn laughed, "I expected a shaman of your standing to understand what was happening."

"Even so," Kel said, "with that strange concoction prepared by Mahrden, I was inside the journey. It is only now looking back that I can see the elements."

"What elements," Helen asked, "are you speaking of?"

"Why, the challenges. Air, Water, Fire and Earth—we have walked the very rim of creation and survived."

One by one the bonfires were carefully extinguished. They walked back down the trail to the waiting autos. Their next journey would be that of intimate love and discovery.

"We would like to come to your house before we go home," Sharrone said, giving Kel a quick glance. "Will that be all right?"

"I believe so," Lyria answered, glancing at Kel questioningly.

Kel took Lyria's hand, and said, "It will not be for long, my love."

"I hope not," Lyria answered happily.

"Don't worry," Dan said, smiling, "you'll be glad you took the time to do this!"

"We will?"

Sharrone looked at Lyria, smiled and said, "As a woman, I can say you will not regret the time."

"Well then, does this machine go any faster?"

"I am certain that it does," Dan responded, pushing the accelerator to the floor.

CHAPTER 49

It was already nine in the evening by the time they arrived at Dan and Sharrone's home. The two women sat on either side of Kel on the sofa. Dan walked into the kitchen, returning shortly with a bottle of wine. He set it on the table, corkscrew in hand. As he struggled with the cork, Sharrone looked at Kel and said, "Lyria told me that you have discovered a new totem animal. One day you must let me do an interview with you so I can publish your story—I think a book about what it's like to be a shaman would be fascinating."

"I would be willing to do that," Kel responded, "the way you write reaches people's souls. You have a rare talent, I believe."

"She also likes champagne," Dan said with a snicker.

There was a loud pop that made Lyria jump, and Dan went once more into the kitchen to get glasses for the champagne. He returned, placing the glasses carefully on the table. He sat across from them in one of the large stuffed chairs. He picked up the opened bottle and poured some wine into each of the glasses. Kel raised his glass, looking into it. "I have never seen wine so transparent, and with bubbles!"

Sharrone laughed, "It's called champagne—it's very good!"

Dan raised his glass. "I propose a toast to the newlyweds—may your love life be as adventurous as your day work."

They all laughed at that, touching glasses and tasting the champagne.

"It tickles my nose," Lyria said with delight.

Sharrone laughed, "That is not all it tickles!"

"So, Kel," Dan said, "before we leave you two to your own devices, tell us about your new totem."

"It is Stag. The funny thing is, I have seen him glowing in the forest from time to time as I journey—but when I would ask, he always denies he is a spirit guide for me. Then it seems he just…changed his mind, after The Green!"

Sharrone said, "Oooh! Stags are randy beasts!"

"Shar!" Dan looked at her in dismay, shaking his head. "Some of the things you say!"

She laughed, taking another sip of champagne. "I can blame it on the champagne tomorrow if I drink enough tonight."

She lifted her glass in a mock toast to Dan, taking another sip. She then looked over at Lyria, a sly grin on her face. "His totem may be a stag, my dear, but when the lights are low, you will believe it is a rhinoceros!"

"Sharrone!" Dan exclaimed—this time with a laugh.

Lyria looked at Kel, tipped her head and asked, "Rhinoceros?" Then suddenly she understood—she covered her face with both hands and buried her head in Kel's shoulder, blushing furiously.

"Well," Dan said, standing, "with that comment, I believe we should make our exit. Oh, by the way, we left a surprise for you."

"Really?" Lyria looked up from Kel's shoulder.

"You'll find it," Dan said with a smile.

Sharrone winked at Kel and then turned to leave. Kel knew what the surprise was—Sharrone and Dan had told him of the 'delicious recipe' as Sharrone called it. When the front door shut, Lyria looked questioningly at Kel.

"Surprise?"

"I think we should bathe first—then go looking. It has been a long day," Kel said.

"You are right, my husband," testing the words as she spoke them. They still felt new in her mouth. They walked down the hallway to the bathroom door together, holding hands. Lyria thought the feeling of holding hands with her husband was somehow more exciting than it had been before.

Lyria was carrying her new nightgown and was anxious to try it on. She opened the door, and Kel tried to follow her in. She laughed and gave him a quick shove, then slammed the door.

"Hey," he said in dismay, "we ARE married now, you know!"

"Yes, my love, I know," she responded through the locked door. "I will see you when I am finished."

Kel just stood at the door. *Well*, he thought, *that was sure a surprise!* He knew his bride had a mind of her own, which made him smile. If she hadn't, he wouldn't have found her interesting enough to court. There was nothing much he could do but wait.

Lyria didn't take a long time. When she opened the door, she was dressed very modestly in a voluminous bathrobe.

"How do I look," she asked, turning slowly in the hallway.

"You look…well wrapped," Kel said.

She laughed, taking one more slow turn. "And I am staying that way until after you bathe," she answered with a grin, "everyone knows about how dirty butter hogs can get."

"Right now the only dirty part of me is my mind."

"Well, maybe you can reach it through your ears, if you try hard enough."

She was still laughing when he shut and locked the door behind him. *Two could play that game!* Lyria playfully rattled the doorknob.

"It's locked," Kel called to her.

"I see that," she responded. "You *are* being difficult, aren't you?"

"Well," he answered after a moment's thought, "if I told you I was easy, you'd poke me in the ribs again for thinking I was looking at other women!"

"But whenever I poke you in the ribs, you ARE looking at other women."

"That is beside the point," Kel called back to her.

"I know what point you are referring to, you know," she said.

"Exactly how much do you know about that?"

"You will find out once you have bathed," she taunted. "Hurry up—I know one woman who is dying to have you look at her."

"I wonder who that could be," Kel responded playfully.

"If you do not know the answer to that question, you are certainly no shaman—with either stag or rhinoceros totems!"

She heard him laughing, and smiled, she loved to banter with him.

She walked into the living room and sat on the sofa, thinking about how very far they'd come. She knew of no one else in the world that had ever done and seen what they had done and seen together. That was the secret, wasn't it? She decided that it was 'together' that was both the secret and the answer.

She pulled her feet up onto the sofa, wrapping her arms around her legs, hugging herself. She was married now.

After what seemed an age, Kel finally opened the bathroom door.

He walked casually into the living room. Lyria looked at him in open-mouthed amazement, and then burst into laughter. Kel had done her one better. He was obviously wearing two robes—she could see the light tan of one covered almost entirely by a white one. And over the robes, he'd draped two massive bath towels. A third covered almost all of his head, draped to way past his shoulders.

Between giggles, Lyria said, "You look like a hill of snow!"

"I don't know. I don't feel nearly cold enough to be snow."

"I have an idea," she said, "leave the towels and the top robe here in case you need them later, and you can help me look for the surprise."

"I know about the surprise," Kel said smugly.

"How is it that you know and I don't?"

"I'm a shaman," he answered, "I know things!"

She laughed, watching him discard the ridiculous towels and the extra robe. She was anxious to find the surprise. Kel led her to the bedroom door. He put his hand on the knob.

"The surprise is right in here," he said, looking into her eyes.

"Show me," she said eagerly.

"You show me first," he whispered.

Lyria paused, and then let her bathrobe fall to the floor. The nightgown Sharrone had helped her pick out was sheer white silk—virtually transparent. It came barely past her hips, clinging to her curves. Kel ran his eyes down her form—seeing her nipples as they pushed against the silk. Kel saw that she was blushing.

"You are the most beautiful woman in the world, Lyria."

She smiled, lowering her eyes momentarily. Then she looked up at him; a playful grin on her face. "Now you show me."

Kel smiled, letting the robe fall from his body. He was wearing a thin deer hide loincloth fastened around his waist with a knotted cord. She looked at his body, which was muscular and firm. She put her hand on his bare chest, feeling the muscles ripple beneath his skin.

"You are so beautiful," she said in awe. "I never thought of men as being beautiful before, but you are."

She didn't finish the words. Kel took her gently into his arms. She raised her face to his, and they kissed. It was the first of many kisses they would share tonight.

She stepped eagerly into his arms, pressing her body against him. She felt her breasts rub against his chest through the thin material of her nightgown—felt her nipples becoming hard. The silk felt wonderful as it moved across her, caressing her breasts as a lover might. Kel put his hand on the back of her head, gently caressing her hair. He slowly ran his hand on down her back to where her slim waist spread gently into her hips. The feel of the silk was exquisite. He ran his hand over her backside. He could feel that she was muscular, yet incredibly feminine at the same time.

They traded breaths—licking each other's lips and tongues. Mouths touching, giving and taking pleasure simultaneously. Kel pulled gently away from her, a smile on his face. "I think now would be a good time for the surprise," he said breathlessly. She looked down at his loincloth as they separated. Yes, she decided, it would be more like a rhinoceros! She giggled helplessly, while Kel looked on, mystified.

After they'd regained their equilibrium, Kel opened the door to the bedroom, leading Lyria inside and closing the door behind them. There was a pallet of blankets and linens on the floor, making a padded, slightly raised platform. There were two shelves extending the entire length of the room. On each of the shelves burned at least twenty scented candles. They filled the air with a blend of floral scents. The flickering flames immersed the room in a dancing, golden light that seemed almost alive. Lyria looked up into Kel's eyes and saw fire there, though she could not tell if it was candlelight or something else.

She looked back at the shelves. In the middle of the lower shelf there was a small iron tripod supporting a ceramic bowl above one of the candles. She turned back to Kel with a questioning look on her face.

"That is the surprise," he explained. "One of the women Sharrone interviewed for her articles told her about this." He gestured about the room, and continued, "I am going to give you a massage, my love—an oil massage."

"Oil massage?"

"Sharrone said it must be experienced to understand."

"Did she experience it?"

"She told me she was so intrigued with the idea, that she let the woman she was interviewing give her a demonstration."

"She watched the woman give a man a massage?"

"No, she gave Sharrone a massage."

Lyria gasped, "What did she say about it?"

"She said it was delicious, but it has to be experienced, not described."

"Okay, what do I do?"

Kel took her by the hand, leading her to the raised pallet on the floor.

"The first part is simple, all you have to do is remove your night-gown, place it on the bed, then return here and lie down on your stomach."

She turned, and walked to the bed. Kel watched her as she took off her gown.

"You're watching me, aren't you?"

Lyria took a deep breath, turning to face Kel. She looked down at herself. Would he be pleased? She looked up at Kel who was standing transfixed. She walked to the low bed, sat down, and then rolled onto her stomach—waiting for Kel and what might happen next.

Kel walked to the iron tripod on the shelf, removing the bowl of warm, scented oil. He was nervous—what if he didn't do it right? Was there a wrong way? He had no idea. He put his nervousness aside though, walking to the low bed where his beautiful wife waited for him.

He set the bowl of oil next to her, kneeling beside it. He looked at Lyria, admiring the smoothness of her skin. The candlelight and the accompanying shadows accentuated every delicate curve of her body—the narrowing of her waist, the small depression, almost a dim-ple right at the base of her spine. He took a deep breath, and began.

He reached down and used the tips of his fingers to slowly spread the oil over her back and shoulders. He slowly ran his hands down her back on either side of her spine, stopping just above her hips. There, he applied pressure once more, gently kneading the muscles of her lower back with both thumbs.

Kel thought her skin was softer than the silk she'd discarded. He moved his hands again up to her shoulders and neck, kneading and rubbing the muscles. Now slowly down over Lyria's shoulder blades, moving his hands down her body and under her arms, but not quite touching the sides of her breasts. He felt her relax under his ministration. Her beauty and the feeling of peace that seemed to radiate from her entranced him.

He dipped his fingers into the bowl once more, allowing the oil to drip on Lyria's behind—watching in fascination as the oil spread and ran over her curves.

She shifted slightly, opening her legs a little.

He cupped her bottom in both hands and slid his hands down the insides of her thighs as far as he could reach. His hands moved up and down on her upper thighs—almost but not quite touching her in her most intimate place. She opened her legs a little further.

Now his thumbs were on either side of her womanhood. Up and down his thumbs moved, again not quite touching her directly. He wanted to touch her very badly, but he was determined to wait until the right time.

He moved his hands and ran them down the firm backs of her thighs—lingering a moment behind her knees, then down her calves. As he touched the backs of her thighs, Lyria squirmed. Before this night, he had no idea that he might be able to give her this much pleasure. He ran his hands up across her back, once again kneading the muscles in her neck and shoulders. He moved his hands down her sides again and this time allowing his fingertips to brush against the sides of her breasts. She gasped, and his hands were gone again, traveling once more to the base of her spine.

He pulled her legs slightly apart, running his hands down between them. He rubbed her along the tops of her thighs, though this time he touched her womanhood, briefly. She moaned in sudden pleasure. He paused for a moment, dipping his fingers once again into the oil. He let it drip onto her backside so it would run down between her legs.

Lyria squirmed as the oil ran down her body. The scents of the candles and the warm oil were overwhelming. Feeling Kel's gentle but firm hands moving over her body, pressing and rubbing and feeling her, excited her more than she'd imagined. When his hands slid between her legs, she shivered in delight and pleasure. It was almost impossible to believe that such feelings could exist in the mortal world.

Finally, she felt Kel running the flat of his hand between her legs. His hand stopped, fingers probing, and then moved on again. Her breathing was getting more rapid. Then his fingers opened her, pulling gently on her lips, as he rubbed oil over her most intimate regions. She relaxed, letting Kel do what he wanted. She gave herself over to him with a happy sigh.

She felt him probing gently at her womanhood. She knew she was the first woman Kel had ever touched—she couldn't imagine what he must be feeling, and still he was working only for her pleasure, and she loved him all the more for it. She'd heard stories of wedding nights when she lived in the tribe and some of them didn't sound very romantic. This was romantic!

There was a slight, brief sting of pain as she opened for the first time. She'd heard stories of that moment, but Kel's gentle, very patient timing had prepared her body, and now that part was over. Kel slowly pressed one finger, then two into her. She gasped as she felt him feeling the inside of her body, and felt herself opening as his fingers probed. He pulled his hand back, and then moved it forward again, rhythmically stroking her. She gasped again; surely he was as excited as she was.

He leaned over and whispered, "Why don't you turn over, my love?"

She rolled over onto her back, "Oh, Kel," she moaned, "I have never felt like this in my life." How could she have been so lucky to have such a fine and kind man in her life? And now, she realized once more, he belonged to her completely.

She lay back and closed her eyes as he dripped more oil over her. She felt each drop strike between her breasts and then run down her belly. He ran one hand slowly up to her throat between her breasts. She marveled at his control, and knew he wanted to feel her breasts yet he waited, ministering to her first.

He stared at her body, young and firm in the candlelight. He saw how her erect nipples cast their shadows across the darker skin around them. She was so beautiful, and he realized she belonged to him completely.

He dipped his finger gently into the pool of oil, allowing the tip of just one finger to move over her belly and into her navel. He saw her stomach muscles contract as he probed her there. At this moment, he only wanted to please Lyria and nothing more.

Lyria felt Kel's hands slowly moving up both sides of her body. Then, at last, she felt his hands very gently move up to the bottoms of her breasts, and gasped when she felt his fingers encircle her nipples. He slid his hands down her breasts once more, as he leaned over, gently kissing her on the lips.

Kel wanted to spend eternity touching her breasts, but he let his hands move down her body, moving to her womanhood. Her skin was so smooth under the oil—her shaved mound glistened in the candlelight—a surprise he hadn't expected. He pressed his hand against her, marveling at the roundness and firmness of her body. He pushed with his middle finger—touching ever so slightly.

Kel gently allowed his fingers to trace the contours of her womanhood, as Lyria raised her hips from the bed. Then his hands slid down and tenderly pushed against her inner thighs and she opened her legs even wider. Wave after wave of ecstasy coursed through her.

Another wave of pleasure struck her. There was no warning for this one; it hit like breakers striking rocks in a hurricane. These waves struck Lyria's soul three times before they abated. She was out of breath, overcome with emotion. She looked up at Kel, glistening in the candlelight. Tears formed in her eyes—tears of love and release.

It took a moment for Lyria and Kel to calm.

"Did you like the surprise, my love?"

"Oh, Kel," she breathed. "It is wonderful."

CHAPTER 50

"I have a surprise too, you know," Lyria said tauntingly.

"Really?"

"Really!"

"Tell me," he said.

"No," she answered.

"No?"

"No, I won't tell you—you'll like it much better if I show you."

"Oh, well in that case," he said, reclining on the bed, hands tucked behind his head, "show me!"

"What—right now?"

He stared at her speechless. She waited a moment, wanting to remember the one time Kel could not come back with a sly response to something she'd said. This, she realized, could be used in the future.

She laughed, saying, "Very well, relax and let me do all the work."

"I am told that is how married life is supposed to be," he said with a grin.

"Then I am worried about staying in the city," she said. "It's having a bad influence on you."

Their lips met and then parted. Now she had a new perspective on kissing—this was actually a sexual act as well. She allowed her tongue to run over Kel's lips and then let her tongue feel the inside of his mouth.

He rolled toward her as they kissed, drawing her body against his. He felt her delicious nakedness pressing against his body—the firmness of her breast against his shoulder. Then she touched him; feeling his chest and arms, and glanced down at the leather loincloth he still wore.

She snickered and said, "I believe Sharrone was right—about that rhinoceros thing."

He laughed, "But it's a very friendly rhinoceros!"

"Does he like to be petted?" She asked coyly, allowing her hand to feel the tautness of the leather, but not quite the object that made it so tight.

"Oh, I think he would love to be petted," Kel said, "especially his horn."

"His horn? You mean this?"

He gasped then as she suddenly rested her hand on him.

"Yes, that is what I mean," he said gasping for air.

"I don't know," she said, lifting her hand away, "it sounds like petting him might interfere with your breathing."

"Please," he begged, "interfere with my breathing!"

They kissed once more as her fingers felt for the knot that kept the loincloth around her lover's waist.

"Folks in the city say men are the stronger sex," Lyria said, "but I am not convinced."

"Me neither," Kel answered. "You know, you could prove that, don't you?"

"How?"

"By making me let you pet the rhinoceros on his horn!"

"Why didn't I think of that?" she responded just as the knot loosened.

She pressed her mouth against his once again, tasting his tongue, and gently biting his lower lip. She pressed her lips tightly against his, resting her left hand on his chest. She released him from the kiss, lowering her face to his left ear. Very gently she blew in his ear and then, with the lightest of touches, licked his earlobe. She used her hand to smooth the hair from his forehead and eyes. When he was properly distracted, she suddenly kissed his ear—feeling it with her lips and tongue. She then ran her fingertips over his lips and he gently kissed them. Now she was kissing his neck below his ear. She could see in the golden light that the fine hairs on his neck were standing up. She smiled, reassured that what she was doing was having the desired effect.

"Roll over on your stomach," she said.

He immediately complied. When he rolled, the leather that bound his manhood fell away. Then he was on his stomach, waiting. Lyria straddled him, pressing herself against him—feeling the tight muscles of his back and sides against her skin. She leaned forward and gently began rubbing his shoulders.

"I have not had any secret, private training from some other man, so I might not be as good at this as you are," she said.

"I did not have training," Kel protested. "I read a description on a piece of paper and Shar and Dan explained a few things that I did not comprehend and that is all."

"Oh, so there were two of them," she taunted as she ran her hands down his shoulder blades and over the sides of his chest. "I guess that makes it ok!"

"No," Kel said with a laugh, "but this is getting better by the minute!"

She smiled. All she wanted to do was to make her husband feel good. She leaned over a little farther so she could reach the tops of his shoulders, and worked the muscles there as well.

He sighed, giving himself over to his love.

She reached down and cast the leather that Kel had worn off the bed. She then began pressing her palms into the muscles of his lower back. He groaned.

"My love? Did I hurt you?"

"No—it feels wonderful! I had no idea what a massage could do."

"That makes me feel better," she said cryptically as she pushed her palms against his lower back, slowing moving toward his shoulders. She leaned into it to give more pressure.

"Why does that make you feel better?"

"It means you were truthful and you didn't have any special training," she retorted.

"I'm not going to live that down, am I?"

"Probably not!"

Then Lyria continued her pressing and pushing, and asked, "Does that feel good?"

"Oh yes, I can feel your breasts against my back, and I can feel the insides of your thighs on my bottom—how could it not feel good!"

"I meant the massage," she whispered in his ear, playfully nipping at it as she crawled up his body. She liked the feeling of their bodies touching completely—but then she sat up, turned around and straddled him, sitting once more around his waist, facing his legs.

As Kel had done for her, she began massaging his hips and upper thighs. Under her, she could feel him breathing, his chest rising and falling. She smiled. His legs were slightly parted. Between them, she could partly see his testicles in the deep shadows cast by the candles. She wondered what they would feel like. She waited, rubbing her hands down the backs of his thighs, kneading the muscles in his legs. She loved the feel of his strong thighs and the look of his firm bottom.

She slid her hands down the insides of his thighs. She saw him spread his legs a little more and heard him gasp. Each time she slid her hands down his legs her hands got closer to his testicles. She knew she was teasing him.

"Why don't you roll over now," she said.

When he was comfortably on his back, she straddled him at the waist, facing him. She leaned over him, allowing her nipples to lightly brush against his chest. She lay against him; pressing her mouth to his, taking and receiving in equal measure, another kiss.

"I love how you feel against me, my love," Kel said. "It feels like we fit together—as though we were made for each other."

She pushed herself up a bit to look into his eyes, and touched his chest, feeling the hair curl around her fingers. She touched one of his nipples gently, lightly rubbing it. She was astounded when it stiffened under her fingers.

"That is something I didn't know," she exclaimed.

"Well, I didn't either," he said. "I think you should try the other one just to make sure."

She laughed, reaching over and gently pulled on his nipple; running her fingers around it, then rubbing the palms of her hands over them.

Kel reached up, touching Lyria's breasts.

"All right," she said, sounding breathless, "enough of that!"

She slid back, spreading her legs to accommodate the width of his hips. She felt him pressing into the cleft of her bottom. She knew he obviously liked what she was doing. She leaned over, allowing his hardness to slide against her bottom.

She rose and turned to face away from him. Her thighs straddled his waist and his erection was right in front of her. She was amazed at how it just stood up like a tree—or a rhinoceros horn! She stifled a giggle—she didn't want Kel to think she was laughing at him.

Keith R. Mueller

She slid forward until her belly touched his erection, leaning forward a little, feeling the pressure of it against her belly. She looked down and saw that the skin was partly pulled back. She stared in fascination; never having seen a naked man before, much less one desiring pleasure.

She looked down again, and wondered about how it would fit inside of her. She touched her belly just above the tip of his manhood. She could feel herself getting wet inside. Then she reached down and touched him.

Kel felt her hand brush against him lightly at first, and then more firmly. It was like she was testing his body—unsure of what she should do. He was relaxed from the massage, and decided she could figure it out.

Lyria pressed his erection up against her body. She moved forward a little more, wanting him against her body. She reached down and gently rubbed it. She felt a slight spasm between her legs. Touching him was making her body respond as well. She leaned back, allowing her arms to support her. She pressed against him, rocking back and forth, allowing his manhood to open her. She pressed harder, rocking faster now, making Kel groan.

Suddenly she climaxed. It was completely unexpected in its suddenness, and she moaned deeply and loudly. She rocked against his hardness taking the pleasure as it came. Kel was slick from her pleasure as his erection rubbed against her. Then she climaxed again.

Suddenly she rose and turned to face him—a wild look on her face. Kel looked into her eyes, and saw green flashing in the blue. Now, instead of fear, he felt only love for his ice tiger. She straddled him again, pressing herself against him.

She opened herself with her fingers, rubbing the knob of his manhood and guided it into her womanhood. She rose, and settled onto him—driving his manhood all the way up into her body. She gasped as she felt him moving inside of her. She rose up and settled again, feeling the movement of him deep inside. She could only imagine how it must feel for Kel—she wanted so much to give him the same exquisite pleasure he'd given her.

Kel felt her engulf him, as she leaned forward, rocking against him—rubbing the inside of her body against his hardness. She held herself up with her hands sweat dripping onto his chest. He could feel himself deep inside of her. This was as close to absolute unity that was attainable in mortal life.

Then she climaxed again. Kel felt her pleasure running down his manhood—felt the contractions deep inside her body. Then he was there as well. She felt him jerk inside of her and sat upright. Her muscles squeezed against his hardness that swelled and throbbed inside her womanhood.

They were both locked in all consuming pleasure and both had the same thought, it was a moment of absolute connection, and absolute loss of individual identity. And in that instant, a revelation—the celestial dragons of legend dance to the divine music that is a mutual sharing of spirit and love. Then the thought faded, slipping back into the unconscious. Some of the mysteries of the divine were not meant for men to hold—like the pleasure they had just experienced, it could not endure and have life remain.

Lyria, exhausted, settled onto Kel's chest. He was panting as well. He knew he was still in her. He moved and she put a hand on his mouth, "Not just yet, I want to stay this way for a little longer."

So they stayed in each other's arms and fell asleep that way. They then passed into a deep and dreamless sleep, still joined, arms wrapped around each other—two individuals who were now and forever, one.

CHAPTER 51

Chirping of birds just outside their window woke Lyria early the next morning. She was now lying next to Kel, her left arm over his chest. She lay quietly, feeling the gentle, rhythmic rise and fall of his chest as he breathed. She smiled, remembering the night before—knowing their love would last forever. Outside, it sounded as though two birds were squabbling; the sound grew louder and Kel awoke. He inhaled heavily and exhaled. He opened his eyes. As his vision focused, he saw Lyria's face above his, smiling down on him. He smiled back, and propped himself up on his elbows.

"Now it will be me that suggests bathing," Lyria said with a smile. "I think we both need that!"

Kel put his hand on his chest—he felt the dried oil and perspiration, then nodded. Lyria removed her arm from around him and they sat up. Kel reached over impulsively, kissing Lyria. She returned the kiss. Kel yawned, stretched, and watched Lyria rise to her feet. The candles had burned themselves out in the night—only a small amount of light penetrated the heavy drapery. He looked at the candles thinking that though they had burned out in the night, his love for Lyria would burn like the sun for the rest of his life. He stood, and once more they walked to the bathroom hand in hand.

"I think we should bathe together," she said, "would you agree?"

Kel said nothing, but put his arm around her waist leading her into the bathroom. While Lyria ran water into the tub, Kel went quickly to the living room to retrieve the bath towels he'd worn the evening before—and the two bathrobes. When he returned, the water was steaming, and once the tub had sufficient water in it, she turned off the spigot and turned to Kel. "Shall we?"

"We shall," he responded.

Kel climbed into the tub. Lyria followed, sitting in front of him. The water was hot and it felt delightful against their skin.

"Wash me," Lyria whispered.

"With pleasure."

"That is what I was hoping for."

Kel found a soft cloth resting on the edge of the tub. He put it into the water, and then lathered it with soap. He began by washing Lyria's back. She leaned forward as he gently scrubbed her.

She leaned back into him as he washed her shoulders and neck, running his soapy hands over her skin. He dropped the cloth into the water. This was a job better done by hand.

Lyria's eyes were closed, but her mind was not. She felt Kel's hands as they slid down her body, turning in gentle circles, washing away the oil and sweat of last night's union. She felt his hands, slick with soap glide up and over her breasts, gently massaging her. She opened her eyes and watched, fascinated as his fingers worked their way gradually to her nipples. She knew he was watching her become aroused, and that made it happen all the quicker. When he finally touched her nipples they were already hard. He seemed to be spending more time washing her breasts than washing her back. Nothing pleased her more than knowing he enjoyed touching her.

Lyria sighed, too happy to even speak. Kel's hands moved downward, slowly. She opened her legs as he reached her womanhood. He ran his hands over her, worshipping her with his touch, gently scrubbing the oil and sweat away.

"Now," he whispered, "I am going to move around to face you."

She moved to one side so Kel could maneuver around her hip and legs, until he was facing her.

Kel slid his hands up Lyria's calves, running warm soapy water over her curves. The warm soapy water washed the oils from her body, leaving her skin feeling clean. He gently washed between her legs, massaging her but not entering her. He was bathing her now, and who might know what could follow next? But there was yet one secret she hadn't revealed. Was she ready?

Once the last of the soapy water flooded over her body. She leaned forward, turned, and gently pushed Kel into a reclining position, and said, "Though the stag is a mighty animal, he must remember to be ever vigilant for at any moment a tiger may leap out, pounce upon him....and eat him right up."

Lyria then picked up a pitcher of clear water that had been standing by their tub, and poured it over Kel's lower body, washing away the soap.

She set it down and said, "Tigers don't like the taste of soap!"

Then, before Kel could respond, she lowered herself. He felt her hair cascading over his body, tickling and stimulating at the same time. She kissed his belly near his navel and very slowly moved down, kissing as she went.

Kel gasped and started to say something, but couldn't finish as she gently lifted one testicle with her hand, licking and kissing it.

"It's heavy," she whispered.

"It holds the future," he responded.

"Well, one half of it anyway!"

She held his manhood in her hand, fingers wrapped lightly around it, slowly stroking him, and then kissed the tip. He inhaled sharply as he felt her lips moving over the skin. Suddenly she engulfed him with her mouth, which took Kel completely by surprise. He moved involuntarily back against the end of the tub, but she was just as quick.

Lyria, sensing he was close to release, raised her head, briefly looking Kel in the eyes she whispered, "I want to see it." Then she was on him again—one slow movement down, then up. She lifted her head again, looking at him, licking her lips seductively. "Will you show me? Kel, my love, I want to watch it happen."

She gasped in ecstasy along with her husband. Two people becoming one, she thought, climaxing together as we will do everything in our lives from now on—together. Afterward, she lay against him—head on his chest, both of them spent completely.

* * * *

They were sitting in the dining room eating breakfast in their bathrobes.

"When are Dan and Sharrone be coming over," Lyria asked.

Kel looked at his watch lying on the table—he was not yet used to carrying it. "They'll be here shortly, I believe."

"Then we must dress," she said, as they finished the last of the eggs and bacon and toast Lyria had prepared for them.

Lyria glanced at Kel, a smirk on her face. "Um…exactly how much butter did you put on your toast?"

"Not enough to be a butter hog," he responded.

"Good thing," she answered.

They were both dressed by the time they heard the auto coming up the drive. Kel opened the front door as the car came to a stop. Dan stepped out, moving to the passenger side to open the door for Sharrone. They both smiled at Kel as they walked into the house.

"So," Sharrone said, looking at Lyria, "are you happy?"

"There are no words for it," she replied, "the world is a lovely sunshiny place."

Sharrone laughed. Both she and Dan were now looking at Kel expectantly. He grinned, rising to his feet.

"You shall be my witnesses," he said to his friends.

Lyria looked at him questioningly. He reached into his pocket and withdrew a small box. Then he knelt before Lyria.

"What is this?"

She looked at Dan and Sharrone for an explanation but they were silent, smiling.

"Lyria," Kel began, "in front of witnesses I declare I have little in the way of possessions. The most precious thing I have is the certainty of my love for you. To me you are the Goddess made manifest."

He opened the box. Within, Lyria saw two metal bands that shimmered in the early morning light. Kel withdrew one, holding it so Lyria could examine it.

"Inside, right here," he said pointing, "is engraved my name. The metal is gold and silver—forged together as the steel of your sword is forged together. It represents the God and the Goddess—sun and moon. They exist in an eternal, spiral dance of love just as we exist within that same dance."

Lyria stared into Kel's eyes, tears forming in hers.

"I would like to place this ring on your finger, if you would allow me."

Lyria was weeping, and could only nod.

Kel smiled, sliding the ring slowly onto the second to littlest finger on Lyria's left hand. He held up the other ring, showing Lyria the inscription inside.

"This is your name, my love—and this," he handed her the ring, extending his own left hand toward her, "is my bond of love."

Lyria slid the ring on Kel's finger.

"Lyria," Kel said softly, "we have placed our flesh inside the eternal dance of love—the sacred love song of the universe. Will you sing this song with me for the rest of our lives?"

"Oh, Kel," Lyria said weeping, "I will be yours through eternity!"

Kel looked up at his friends—Sharrone was crying as well, and Dan's eyes were shining. He lowered his eyes again to Lyria, drawing her into his arms. She raised her head, kissing him passionately.

"I will love you till the sun burns dark—and then we shall reignite it with our passion," she sobbed.

"Are we going to have to come back later?"

Dan's unexpected remark made all of them laugh.

Kel and Lyria rose, and stood in front of their friends.

"Let me see, let me see," Sharrone said enthusiastically.

Lyria held out her hand so Sharrone could admire her ring.

"Oh, Lyria," she said, "it's magnificent!"

She looked at Dan, grinned, and said with a wink, "I am sooo jealous!"

She then turned back to Lyria and said, "Your husband had those made here in the city. Dan knows a jeweler of some skill he met years ago. Kel thought of this himself, you know. It's unprecedented, as far as I know!"

"When you do go back home to visit—and I am certain you will," Dan said, "you'll probably find you have started a brand new tradition for your tribe."

"He's started a brand new tradition here as well," Sharrone said, holding out her hand as though Dan was going to slip a ring on her finger.

"Alright, alright," Dan said, "if Kel has no objections, I will have two rings fashioned for us as well—but there is one thing you must do first, Sharrone."

"What is that?"

"Become my wife."

Sharrone gasped—they had been living together as free people— she thought Dan wanted it that way. "I can think of nothing that would make me happier than to become your wife!"

She moved into Dan's arms, kissing him. Kel watched for a

moment.

Lyria said, "Are we going to have to come back later?"

Sharrone and Dan looked up in surprise, suddenly bursting into laughter. They sat down to plan what they were going to do after this most perfect of days was spent.

CHAPTER 52

Kel was down on his hands and knees, gently patting the soft earth firmly into place with his hands over the small grave Lyria had just dug in the farthest corner of their new land. The sun shone brightly, nearly directly overhead by this time, and many birds were singing. It was a good day for a funeral. He then glanced at the nearby ash heap that had only minutes earlier been a funeral pyre. *Sun and fire,* he thought, *they are one—as Adria was one with the Mastodon Clan.*

Lyria stood silently with the spade still in her hand, solemnly looking down at the small patch of freshly turned earth. *How could a person be reduced to such a small amount of ash,* she thought in wonder, a tear sliding slowly down her cheek as she again wished Adria's spirit a quick journey to the Otherworld.

Kel quickly brushed the last of the dirt off his hands and gently put his arm around his wife comfortingly, drawing her close to him. He gently wiped away the tear from her cheek with his thumb, and smiled at her. She leaned into him, looking up at him with glistening blue eyes and a sad smile.

"She is finally at rest, isn't she, Kel? Really at rest?"

Kel nodded. "Yes, my love. She is at rest."

Lyria turned back to the little grave and spoke the prayer quietly.

Bless her, Mother,
She is Your child.
Bless her, Splendid Lady,
Young and wild.
Bless her Mother,
Take her back this night.
Bathe her in Your Otherworld light.
The field is quiet, her battle done.
Hold her, until her life's begun.

As Lyria wept, a small group of women stood respectfully waiting and quietly watching, some distance behind Kel and Lyria. Sharrone,

Dan, Mahrden, Tom, and the shamans were also there. Kel hugged Lyria and they stood for a moment longer, then turned to the silently gathered people standing behind them.

They walked slowly back to their group of friends—Lyria wiping the tears from her eyes with the back of her hand, the spade dragging in the dirt behind her. Wordlessly, Helen walked over to gently take the spade from Lyria's hands. She'd carry it back to the house. The women of Bear House who were accompanying them said nothing.

"It was rather nice of Father Norville to return Adria's body to us," Garn said softly. "I wonder if he may really be sincere, or if this is but another of many Cathedral ruses?"

"Perhaps he is sincere," Ma'hal said, "and perhaps he is not. Time and vigilance will tell us the truth of that question—though all the times now long past have not remembered the priest or his kind as being either caring or sincere to any but their own."

"With that I agree," Mahrden said.

Garn solemnly responded, "Adria has now come full circle—from the Light of the Spirit she came into the world and back unto the Light of the Spirit she has now returned. Her journey in this world is ended; what remains of this situation is now ours alone to handle."

"Still," Kel said, "whatever the priest's true motives might be, he nevertheless brought her back to us so we could perform her final rites respectfully according to our traditions and properly bury her—and for that, if for nothing else, we should be grateful to him."

Lyria nodded.

"There are those who'll question your mourning of a person such as Adria, you know," Ma'hal said to Lyria. "We've all heard the stories of the many terrible deeds she wrought in this city—and what horrors have been discovered in the park."

Lyria lifted her eyes defiantly to those of the old woman. "Then question my mourning of her they will," she responded firmly. "Adria was a child of our tribe, and nothing can change that—and though she tried to kill me, I believe that we could possibly have helped her and guided her to a healing had we the opportunity. Now she has been properly cremated and buried in the sacred tradition of the Mastodon Clan—whatever it was she might have done...whoever she might really have been, this was the right and proper thing to do. I care not what others may think of it."

"But she murdered people—even children," Helen said in a confused, trembling voice. Rosie took her hand, moving closer to the older girl.

As Lyria shifted her eyes to the young girl, her gaze softened, and she answered gently, "Adria was a woman held in thrall by strange powers she could neither comprehend nor control. Had none of this happened, it is entirely possible that Garn and the many ways of sacred magic could have helped her back into herself. But now…now we will never know if she could have been saved—if all those lives could have been saved…" Lyria wept, lowering her head.

"All those possibilities were gone forever when she left our tribe with the priest for the Black City," Kel said.

"Yes," Lyria responded with a nod, "and in the hands of the black priests she was as cruelly used as they cruelly used the women of the Bear Clan. Adria was as powerless to stop what was happening inside herself as a mountain is powerless to stop an avalanche. The black priests—they were in control of themselves and have always been so. So now tell me, who would question my mourning of this beautiful, lost child? Was it Adria or the priesthood that was truly the monster in this tale of horror?

To that they couldn't reply. Helen nodded silently, thinking over what had just been said, realizing that she'd just had an important lesson in perspective. She found herself admiring Lyria even more than she had before. She knew Lyria was a great warrior in her tribe, and in that moment of introspection and seeing—in that moment of clear light, she realized she'd found her own chosen path in life. She felt buoyant and liberated! She determined right then that nothing—not any power on earth, would stop her from convincing Lyria to teach her the way of the sword and the lance—the way of the warrior woman.

Slowly they made their way back toward Lyria and Kel's new home. The small crowd was silent—each person occupied with their own thoughts—at least for the moment. Rosemarie was gazing at the newly constructed but still empty corrals as they walked passed. "When will your horses arrive?"

Lyria smiled at the girl—the enthusiasm of youth couldn't be quelled even by a funeral. "In several days, I should think," she answered, looking questioningly at Tom.

"I think that's about right," he responded, "the corrals are already finished as you can see, and the barn needs only a roof. My workmen should have that finished by tomorrow night—all that remains to be done is put up the shingles."

Kel laughed. "It has been a quickly passing week, has it not?"

"That it has," Garn said, "and now my friends and I must prepare for our departure from this city."

"It is time," Drog commented dryly, "I hope my wife does not think I have left her for another woman."

"Imagine if she thinks you were kidnapped by a zeppelin full of women," Helen quipped. Drog shuddered in mock fear. "Now that is truly a frightening thought, young Helen Bear!" They all laughed at Drog's quick response as they entered the living room of the house for a final meal together.

After a leisurely lunch, the small group of friends sat together in the living room discussing the events of the past, and speculating on what path the future might hold for them.

Garn asked in a concerned voice, "Do you have any plans to keep watch over the Cathedral and their priests to make sure they are making good on their promises?"

Mahrden turned and looked at Garn. "We will keep close watch from the outside, of course. As for inside the priests' lair, the many scholars and museum people will be in there every day for many weeks to come—or, from what I hear, more likely for months or maybe even years."

"And if they see any…irregularities," questioned Ma'hal, "are you certain they will report them?"

Mahrden smiled and nodded, "Oh, I'm sure there are a few of them who'll be willing to tell someone about it—someone who'll then tell everyone in the city—and believe me when I say I have that on rather good authority.

"Tom tells me," the magician said, with a grin and a knowing wink, "that the black priests aren't the only ones with connections in and around the city—they are not the only ones with eyes and ears in unexpected and unsuspected places. And since I am one of his sources, it surely must be true."

"I hope that's truly the case," the old woman responded, "for I do not see a serpent changing its ways simply because it has shed its skin."

Everyone nodded in understanding. For the next several hours they talked and laughed of small things—things of no real import, such as the weather and the coming of summer once again. Punctuating the conversation and the liberal pouring of wine was the cheerful chirping of many birds in the flower garden growing in front of the house. The birds reminded them that even winter couldn't freeze out the spirit or dim the promise of a new year. What the coming year might bring was still to be seen.

It was nightfall before all of Lyria and Kel's guests had finally departed—the shamans not walking quite as straight or as steady as men of wisdom are usually expected to walk. The shamans left with Mahrden—who was just as unsteady on his feet. Dan, who'd had only a small amount of wine earlier in the evening, drove the women of Bear House back to their home in the center of the city. He knew he'd be driving them home, and he felt responsible for their safety.

He remembered his wild life on the streets of this city in his youth—back then he wouldn't have cared how drunk he was when he rode his steamcycle. He remembered even taking his beloved Daisy on the road when he knew he was in no condition to do so. He shook his head in disgust. Time and the responsible life as a tribal member, where people actually grew to depend on him, had changed him—and he was glad of the change.

Sharrone stayed behind with Lyria and Kel. When Dan had returned, he and Sharrone said their good nights and walked the short distance home. Dan laughed—he found he had to guide his intoxicated lady, chiding her for continuing to drink after he'd left—which of course she denied vehemently, giggling all the while.

Tomorrow promised to be a very busy day for everyone—the shamans would finally be bound for home, leaving by steam-train at mid-morning. There were yet a few things that had to be taken care of before that could come to pass. But, Kel realized as he yawned, all of that would be work for the early morning hours. He walked with Lyria toward their bedroom. She was already half asleep, leaning on his shoulder. He glanced at his watch. Though it was still quite early, they went to bed anyway, falling asleep quickly in each other's warm embrace.

CHAPTER 53

At the same time Adria's ashes were being interred, some many miles away work was also being done deep below the Cathedral.

"When do you want to break for lunch? According to the priest, we're halfway through their lunchtime already. If we don't go soon, we'll miss out completely."

"Scholarship doesn't win over hunger, my friend?"

The first man laughed, responding, "Only some of the time, Theo, my friend, only some of the time!" The three elderly scholars were standing in a dimly lit corridor in one of the many labyrinth-like sub-basements of the Cathedral. The hulking, basalt and granite building was over a thousand years old, and it had been added to many times over the long centuries as new materials—books, artifacts, and works of art—were brought in by visiting priests from far-flung city-states for safekeeping, as they referred to it. As the need for more storage space arose, the many basements and sub-basements grew deeper, their corridors longer—and their environment colder. Summer never seemed to reach this far below ground. Here, cold, dark winter prevailed eternally.

The scholars had spent the entire morning carefully going over the bookshelves lining both walls in the small room in which they stood. Some of the books were so old and so uncared for that they almost crumbled to dust when taken from the shelves. It was unfortunate that the priests of days long past hadn't thought to conserve these books. Who could say what important knowledge might be lost forever in the sudden fragmenting of paper, leather binding, and ink?

Even with the long neglect and destructive effects of time, even with the dust and the dimness of the light, it was hard not to notice the odd empty spaces here and there on the shelves. It was hard not to see the places where no books now stood yet were clear of dust, spider webs, and grime. It didn't take any kind of master detective to realize that books, or possibly something else, had been removed before the scholars had been allowed to examine the contents of the room. It was clear that the priests were lying. All three of the old men knew they'd have to tell someone about this once the day's work was finished.

The man who'd spoken about lunch slapped the front of his white lab coat with gloved hands, watching small clouds of dust rise up into the dim light. He coughed once, waving his hand in front of his face, attempting to disperse the dust he'd just stirred up. The other two men also were dusting themselves off as best they could under the circumstances, moving a bit with each pat and slap, trying to stay out of each other's—and their own—dust clouds.

One man began unbuttoning his lab coat, preparing to remove it. The others quickly followed his example. Once out of the long white coats, they were relatively dust free. All three men wore relatively inexpensive suits, and carried either gold-filled or sterling silver watches—the various museums and libraries of this city, and the other cities of the west for that matter, didn't pay well enough to allow for more. Still, these men were happy—they were doing what they wished to do with their lives—and how many in the Black City could truly say that?

They laid their lab coats on the makeshift table near the entryway—a simple board that lay casually across the seats of two chairs that were not quite the same height. The men were about to go up to the dining room when they heard a muffled sound in the next corridor.

The senior man paused and sighed—their two young assistants were always eager to press on around the next turn, even before the present area was completely scrutinized and catalogued. It was the nature of youth, he figured. He shifted the heavy books he was holding to his left arm, shaking the right one to restore the circulation.

"We're going to lunch now, Cooper…Justyn? Are you coming with us, or do you prefer the taste of dust and mold over nice, rare mastodon steaks, salads, and fine wine?" Emmett Johnson waited patiently for an answer. None was forthcoming. Instead, he heard more muffled scraping noises. He was becoming annoyed—enthusiasm was one thing, but ignoring lunch was something else entirely.

"Come on, gentlemen," he shouted impatiently, his voice rising. "They won't keep our repast warm if we arrive too late. They'll throw your lunch away." There was still no response. Emmett sighed again. "Theo, would you please go see what is keeping the youngsters? I don't know about the rest of you, but I rather like eating warm food—and eating it here, where it won't cost us anything."

Theo smirked, walking to the doorway that led into the corridor that crossed this one. "All right, Cooper…what's going on? We haven't all day, you know." He then walked through the doorway and turned to his left. Before him, the two younger members of his group were standing before a bookcase at the end of the short corridor. He stopped, hands on his hip, a bemused expression on his face. The two youngsters suddenly both squatted on their haunches in front of the huge cases.

The cases in this area were at least seven feet tall, Theo guessed. He looked up to the top shelves of one such case and knew they'd need some ladders after lunch to reach the topmost books—he'd inquire of that polite Father Norville when they met him in the dining hall in a few minutes. The young scholars remained where they were, squatting and looking intently down at the floor.

"Gentlemen…can it not wait until after we eat?"

"What's back here?" The question, asked by one of the young scholars squatting in the dim light of the basement, echoed against the stone walls. Justyn shivered in his lightweight suit. Even with his lab coat buttoned all the way to his throat, he was still cold—though summer was already in full glory in the outside world. He shivered again and dust fell from his hair, making a brief golden halo about his head in the dim light. That was to be expected, Theo reasoned as he watched, considering the nature of his work. The young man was staring at the base of the bookcase standing against the stone wall.

Theo returned to the other room to tell Emmett and Nycholas that the young men had apparently discovered something—a mystery. It was his opinion, however, that it was a mystery that could best be investigated after a good, hot lunch.

Emmett heaved another sigh, turning a rueful expression toward Theo. "That's probably true," he laughed, "but I'll go look anyway—we don't want to stifle the enthusiasm of youth, after all—and perhaps once we 'ooh' and 'ahh' over whatever they believe they've discovered, they'll come to their senses and realize how hungry they are."

With that comment, Emmett entered the room. He called out, "You said, 'What's back there?' What exactly do you mean by back there? Back where? Your description is woefully unscientific in its nonspecific vagueness, young man."

"Here, sir, just look at this bookcase—it seems to have been moved, and very recently, too," Justyn said loudly. "Just look at all the scrape marks on the floor." Emmett Johnson moved closer, the three large leather-bound tomes still clutched in his arms. Justyn held his lantern high, crabbing to one side, allowing the light to play fully across the floor. Emmett squinted through his dusty spectacles in the yellow light—yes…yes, it appeared to be true.

The marks the young men were pointing to clearly showed that something very heavy had been recently slid across the slate tile flooring—the marks very obvious, even in the wan light of the lantern. The odd marks seemed to end right in front of the bookcase—almost as if the case itself had been recently slid into its current position. The black-gray of the slate was clearly showing through the dust and grime of years that coated the rest of the floor, turning it a uniform brown.

Emmett set his books down on a bookshelf near him, and bent over at the waist to examine the marks more closely. Justyn was still squatting, touching the floor. The dirt and dust of ages was so imbedded and caked to the floor that he couldn't clear a spot with just his fingers no matter how vigorously he scrubbed them over the floor. He looked up at Emmett. "See? I can't even make a mark in all this grime, sir. Clearly, something very heavy was dragged along this area—and quite recently, if I may say so."

Emmett glanced at the books he'd placed on the shelf beside them to make sure they were secure, and then he squatted down next to Justyn to get a closer look at the mysterious marks. He groaned a bit as he positioned himself more comfortably on his knees, using Justyn's shoulder for an assist.

"If I didn't know better," Emmett said thoughtfully, "I'd wager that it was the bookcase itself that was moved."

"But that's silly," Cooper said, "I know that's what it looks like, but why would anyone move it now?"

"Nevertheless, look at the shelves, the books seem unusually dust free compared to those on other shelving, do they not? It's almost as if they were removed so the shelf would be lighter and easier to shift to its present position, and then they were replaced again."

"But why would anyone do such a thing?" Cooper looked questioningly from his mentor to Justyn and back again.

"Because Justyn's first question is still the best one—what's behind the case? I have an idea that if that case were moved once more, we would find a doorway into another room—a doorway the priests do not want us to pass through."

"This needs to be reported," Justyn said indignantly, "we should tell Father Norville immediately."

"No, we should not tell Father Norville about this," the older man whispered urgently, glancing left and right. "Do you think he wouldn't know of this? Do you not think he would've been the very person who ordered it to be so? No, we tell no priests of this discovery—but there are others who should know about this."

The three men, intent on studying the marks on the floor, didn't notice the bookcase right behind them beginning to lean ever so slowly toward them. All they might've heard was a muffled grunt, and a slight scraping sound. And even if they had, they wouldn't have had time to do more than turn their heads in curiosity—there would've been no time for anything else.

It might've been the added weight of the three heavy books the elder scholar had just placed so very near the front of the shelf. After all, the front legs of the bookcase, and probably the back ones as well, were probably rotten with age. The front left leg snapped suddenly with an audible crack. The older man turned in time to see the case falling toward him—to see the avalanche of heavy books tumbling through the air in a cascading cloud of dust.

He cried out, raising his hands defensively. Justyn and Cooper, taken by surprise as well, put out their arms in a vain attempt to stop the shelves' forward plunge—but the weight of the bookcase and the confusion of falling books overwhelmed their efforts. One shelf struck Emmett hard on the forehead and he knew no more.

Justyn and Cooper, both suddenly buried along with Emmett under a rolling cloud of thick dust, books, and crumbled wood, lived a little longer—they were younger and more fit—but the weight of the bookcase and the mountain of books laying atop them made it very hard to draw a breath, and that breath, once drawn, was filled with thick, choking dust. By the time Father Norville—who seemingly appeared from out of nowhere—reached them, they were both already quite dead. Theo and Nycholas were there in an instant as well, helping the priest in his attempt to uncover the three men buried beneath the clutter.

The three of them tried in vain to lift the heavy case, but it was too much for just the three of them. "Nycholas, go quickly to the dining hall and bring young, strong men," said Father Norville, "I'm afraid it will be too late…"

As he waited with Theo for additional help, the priest was worried—would this apparent accident impair the fragile peace he'd attempted to forge with the Cathedral's former enemies? He hoped not.

In just a couple of minutes, Theo returned with several priests and other museum researchers. They lifted the heavy case and shoved the books aside in an attempt to save the men, but none had survived. The men who helped excavated the bodies quickly carried them upstairs into the Cathedral proper where the light of the afternoon filtered through stained glass windows, filling the building with a divine and colorful radiance. There, the dead men were laid gently on the hard, wooden pews.

"We must notify the police and that newspaper editor immediately," Father Norville said, sweat carving clean paths through the grime on his face. "I'll go call him at once."

He turned to another priest, Father Anderson, and smiled inwardly as he saw the dust on the old priest's jacket. As usual, the spy-priest was not wearing priestly attire. "Help them clean the bodies, would you, Father? At the very least, we should make them as presentable as we can."

"Yes, Your Grace," the old priest said with a nod and a smirk, "I'll see to it."

Father Norville quickly climbed the stairs to the Bishop's office—*my office,* he reminded himself. He sat back in the Bishop's big leather chair—*my chair,* he reminded himself. He took a deep breath and exhaled slowly. He picked up the receiver, listening for the line to open.

CHAPTER 54

"I see," Tom said when he'd heard the priest's story of the accident and the deaths of the three victims. "Would it be possible for me to see the site of the accident?"

"Of course," Father Norville said in a conciliatory tone, "I was actually hoping you'd say that. This is truly a terrible thing, and there are many that are waiting for any excuse to begin their war against us once again. I am hopeful we can avoid any conflict with the citizens of Los Angeles."

"So am I. I'll come right now, if that's all right."

"That's more than all right," the priest enthused. "I'd like you here as soon as possible—you can interview the rescuers yourself, if you wish. We've already called the police—they're sending investigators as we speak."

"Can you keep everyone there until I arrive?"

"Certainly," Father Norville said, "we're ministering to the bodies of the victims now—cleaning them up as best as we can. The police have also asked me to keep everyone who was present here until they arrive. No one will be going anywhere."

Tom grabbed his hat and jacket and headed out the door of his office, one arm still fumbling for an elusive sleeve on his coat that seemed intent on evading his best efforts to find it. He shouted over his shoulder as he hustled out the door of the pressroom for someone to call for a driver to bring a vehicle to the front. He was through the lobby in seconds and opening the front doors of his building.

By the time he'd descended the steps and reached the street, there was a steam-car waiting at the curb with a driver behind the wheel. He climbed quickly into the back seat, giving the driver the address, and the car, already at full steam, hurried away from the curb and out into the mid-afternoon traffic. He was already planning a new front page for this evening's edition.

TRAGIC ACCIDENT IN
DEEP BASEMENT OF CATHEDRAL
A tragic accident occurred early this afternoon in one of the many

ancient basements of the Cathedral. Three levels below ground, in an area seldom visited even by the priesthood, toppling the case on three unfortunate museum employees—the names of the victims will be withheld as a courtesy until their relatives have been properly notified.

We can say at this time that these men were in the employ of the city museum and were part of the group invited by the Cathedral to examine, catalogue, and reference the many books and artifacts that have been stored there in secret for many centuries.

The editor of this paper, Thomas Leatham, personally inspected the site of the accident shortly after it happened, and it appears that this was nothing more than an unfortunate accident. The bookcase that collapsed was at least five or six hundred years old and the wood was quite rotten. This editor is actually surprised that it had stood as long as it had.

It is thought by this editor, and others investigating at the scene, that the extraordinary movements and sounds of investigation and re-search in recent days caused the aged and worm-ridden case to col-lapse. When the bookcase was finally lifted from the victims, the en-tire floor was covered in a think layer of dust and dirt that must have accumulated over many centuries on the shelving as well as on the fallen books themselves.

In fact, there was so much dust present that the floor was not vis-ible save for where the feet of the rescuers had disturbed the dust. The police have informed this paper that their investigation also proved this to be simply an accident and nothing more. There is no reason for anyone not to believe this to be the truth, backed by hard facts and diligent investigations.

The next morning dawned clear and cool in the city. Kel arose early, dressed quietly, and prepared breakfast for Lyria and himself. He heard the birds of summer merrily singing to each other as he worked. He was already missing his grandfather almost more acutely now than he had right after his kidnapping—how that could be baf-fled him. Still, he was determined to stay in the Black City to help the women of the Bear Clan and any others who might need his help as time went on. He sighed as he walked into the bedroom to awaken

Lyria. He found her already up and dressed when he opened the bedroom door.

She greeted him with a long, passionate kiss, her arms wrapped tightly around his waist, and then asked, "What have you been doing while I slept?"

"Come into the kitchen, my beautiful wife, and I will show you."

Lyria was proud of her husband as they walked into the kitchen to share their breakfast. Garn was right, she realized—Kel was truly a man of wisdom now. His choice to stay here in Los Angeles rather than to return to the Mastodon Clan and their family and friends had been the right choice—though by far the hardest to make.

When she'd seen Rosemarie awaken from her dark retreat with Kel's assistance, Lyria knew that her husband had done something spectacular—something that was almost divine. Perhaps, after a little time, they would be able to travel home for a visit to renew connections with their tribe and friends. She thought briefly of her many girlfriends and the sometimes entertaining, sometimes annoying Mart and Geog…long-time friends of Kel's who could only make decisions by arguing with each other. She smiled at the thought. For now though, she knew they had important work still to do here in the Black City.

Kel was still washing the last of the breakfast dishes when the knock came on the door. Lyria opened it to find Tom, Dan, and Sharrone standing there. She invited them inside with a smile. As they were sitting down in the living room, Kel walked in from the kitchen, apron around his waist and towel draped casually over one arm.

Sharrone looked at him—then turned to Lyria, saying, "You've trained him well, woman. And quickly too—I believe he'll be fully domesticated in no time at all."

Kel laughed, turned, and tossed the dishtowel back into the kitchen. He pulled off the apron, then turned back and saw that Tom had brought with him a copy of the morning paper. Tom unfolded it and read aloud the article he'd written about the accident at the Cathedral. He looked at his friends. "This is the second run of this story—it also ran in last evening's edition."

Without hesitation, Kel asked, "You think this accident was actually deliberate?"

Tom looked at Kel, smiled, and then slowly nodded his head. "Though I could find no hard and fast reason for it to be so, my instincts continue to tell me that there's something missing—some small piece of the puzzle that we haven't seen. The books scattered about in the room seemed to be nothing more than old history books containing commonly known facts and works of fiction—none of this would be something one would think Father Norville, or anyone else for that matter, would feel compelled to hide and protect with murder—especially considering the new and still rather fragile peace he's just brokered with the Bear Clan and others in the city."

Lyria asked, "Then why would the priests risk the new peace in that way? What would they have to gain?"

"I don't know," the editor said with an angry shake of his head. "Everything in the article I just read is the absolute truth—even the police investigators found nothing extraordinary at the scene—nothing criminal—and these were coppers with no connection at all to the Cathedral or the Bishop. In fact, several of them were just as suspicious as I when all was said and done. They didn't trust their eyes either—after a while, in any kind of investigative work, one's instincts must be acknowledged. I don't know…maybe I've been working too long against the Cathedral's way of doing things and have become so suspicious that I'm seeing hidden causes and sinister motives where none truly exist."

"Or maybe the priests removed something before you got there—a book or an artifact," Lyria offered. "I cannot find much trust in my soul for the priesthood—and I have known them for a much shorter length of time than you have."

Tom snorted. "I can understand why! Still, with no actual proof, we can't risk upsetting the new peace. What if it turned out we were just seeing things in the dark? What if we're simply seeing monsters under our beds like frightened little children? Would we truly want to be responsible for the potential bloodshed and chaos that could ensue if we made charges and accusations against the Cathedral that were unfounded? I, for one, don't think so."

"I agree," Dan responded. "I'm certain that you or Mahrden will eventually hear something through your various connections that'll lead you one way or another. In the meantime, we can only wait and watch—and listen."

Sharrone nodded. "I'll talk with Ma'hal and we'll begin talking to the street women in the city. Men, even priests—especially priests—often confess things to women they want to impress more easily than they would to almost anyone else—far more easily than they would to other men…even under torture. This is especially true in the immediate urgency of their lust. Eventually someone will hear something one way or the other. Then we can take appropriate action."

At that, the conversation turned to this morning's upcoming departure of the shamans. Kel thought of the trunk he'd taken so long ago from his friend Llo. He smiled as he thought of Llo—their village blacksmith and artisan who forged and fashioned items both practical and decorative throughout the year for trade at the yearly summer gathering of the tribes.

He commented on the trunk, and Dan smiled, saying, "I know of what you're speaking—it was moved with the rest of your belongings and your horses before the attempt on your lives. I'm sure Mahrden will be glad to bring it to the train station with him."

Tom retrieved his pocket watch from his vest, opened the lid, and then closed it. He rose, saying, "Well, folks, it is, unfortunately, that time. We must meet our friends at the station one last time, and then we must part from them."

It was almost ten in the morning by the time everyone had arrived at the train station. The magician brought the trunk of trade items Llo had given to Kel, as was promised. It didn't seem possible to any of those present that so much time could have passed so quickly. Only one object had been removed from the chest so far—a beautifully articulated metal eagle Kel had left with the corpse of a young boy slain, along with his parents, by bandits.

Now he opened the trunk once more, searching for something else he'd seen on that terrible day on the other side of the mountains when he and Lyria had found and buried Noria's slaughtered family. He reverently lifted out the small bundle he was seeking, setting it to one side. He closed the lid and nodded to the porter to load the box aboard the train. As the porter grunted under the weight of the box,

Kel put the small linen-wrapped object into his right jacket pocket.

The huge black locomotive stood huffing patiently like some large domesticated animal awaiting word from its master to move on down the rails, dragging its burden behind it. Smoke stained the sky as the locomotive huffed and snorted.

Kel hugged his grandfather. "I have found you only to lose you once more," he said, tears making his eyes bright.

"But I am no longer lost, my grandson," the old man said with a smile. "I will be just a short way down the road. It is even a shorter distance, as Hawk flies. One day soon you will come to visit us—remember, I am a shaman—I know things."

Kel laughed, "And so we shall come to visit you—and soon I hope. Once we have everything in order here, I think we will be able to leave for a short period of time. You know, I've always wanted to ride inside one of these iron monsters!" Just then the whistle of the locomotive sounded. Kel and Garn both laughed. They hugged once more.

"The iron serpent is calling me," Garn said laughing. "I do not think I should keep him waiting—he seems fierce!"

"I suppose not," Kel said, laughing as he reluctantly released his grip on his grandfather's arm. Now it was Lyria's turn to hug Garn one last time—she wished him a quick, safe, and happy journey. "Thank you for marrying us," she said with tears in her eyes. "I love your grandson more than my own life and I would surely lay that small thing down for him should it be necessary."

"I know you would, my child," Garn answered fondly. "I could never have dreamed a better woman to look after Kel. And your life is no small thing, child—I do not know why, but I believe there are life and death decisions yet coming in your life. Life and death decisions that will stand for many, not just you and Kel."

Lyria laughed. "I am a warrior. What you say is not a prediction—it is simply a statement of fact." They laughed together one final time, and then they released each other. Garn walked the short distance along the rails, his tribal moccasins crunching in the gravel that lined the railway, and climbed aboard the train car. Drog and Galv were already aboard, looking out the windows at their new friends standing beside the train.

They were anxious to leave, yet at the same time they were sorry they were going. It was the nature of the event, they realized—the nature of life itself. Garn joined them shortly, waving to his grandson and Lyria and the rest of his new group of friends. Miles might separate them, but still they would always be united in friendship and love.

The steam engine whistled once more as the wheels began turning and the railroad car began rolling, slowly at first, then progressively faster down the track and ultimately out of the Black City. In just a few short minutes, the locomotive was just a black spot receding quickly into the distance, leaving only its trail of black smoke in the sky to show where it had been.

Lyria, Kel, and the rest stood for a short while watching the train as it gradually disappeared into the hazy distance. Then, reluctantly, they turned to their waiting automobiles to begin their journey back into the city and their new lives. Kel gently patted the bundle in his pocket and smiled. This object, he was certain, Llo wouldn't mind him taking. The articulated eagle had been given in death. This object, he patted his pocket again, would be given in life.

CHAPTER 55

Two days later, as Tom and Mahrden had promised, a steam lorry arrived towing an enclosed trailer. Kel and Lyria heard its arrival and walked out front. Dan and Sharrone joined them. The truck squealed to a stop, and with a final huff of steam, the engine quieted, and the driver's door opened.

Mahrden, smiling broadly as he stepped from the lorry, was greeted by the small group. Before they could finish their greetings, they were interrupted by a snort from inside the trailer.

"Morning?" Lyria's inquiry was met with another snort and the sound of hooves stamping impatiently on a wooden floor. She ran to the back of the trailer, and Kel ran to catch up to her. By the time he'd arrived, Lyria had already opened the latch and was attempting to lower the hinged rear panel of the trailer that would also serve as a ramp.

Kel laughed as he helped her lower it the last few feet to the ground. Lyria and Kel led the horses out of the trailer into the bright sunlight, the horses shaking their heads and switching their tails. Lyria was laughing in delight as she gently stroked first one soft muzzle, and then the next.

The horses' coats gleamed in the sunlight. They had obviously been well cared for. Morning took a step toward Kel, gently nudging him with her nose. He put his arms around her neck and gave her a hug, kissing her on the tip of her nose. When Dan and Sharrone arrived, they patted the horses on their necks and flanks, as well.

Mahrden helped them lead the horses to the corral and the newly finished barn. The horses went eagerly—happy to be reunited with their humans. Once they were inside the corral, Dan and Kel poured some grain into the wooden trough and the three horses began eating heartily, knowing they were finally home for keeps.

Dan stood with his arm around Sharrone as he turned to Lyria and Kel. "There is something that still must be done—it is something I have let go far too long. Raven knew of it. My beautiful Sharrone knows as well, as I have told her. Will you help me?"

"Daisy?" Lyria's single word caused Dan to sob aloud. Sharrone hugged him tightly—she was crying too. "Though I've never met the woman," she said quietly, "I'm certain that we would've been friends in life. We cannot just let her memory fade from the world without a testimony to her life and her bravery."

"I've ordered a stone," Dan said. "It'll be ready this afternoon. Will you go with us to pick it up and take it to its home?"

"We would be honored to do so," Kel said, emotions almost overwhelming him as well. "We will eat a meal in Daisy's honor, and then we will do this for her."

They ate their lunch silently for the most part. Once in a while, as memories popped into his mind, Dan would relate a story about his life with Daisy—some were humorous and made all at the table laugh. He told them of her frantic search one time for her special fountain pen—as it turned out, it had been in her handbag all the time, nestled safely beneath a lace kerchief. Other stories were more serious. He spoke of her passion for life, and her unselfish caring for the small, injured animals her neighbors and friends would bring to her from time to time for healing.

Lyria looked at Sharrone and saw only compassion and love for Dan reflected in her eyes—no hint of jealousy betrayed itself in her sad smile. Lyria was impressed that this woman felt only sorrow for the death of another woman Dan had deeply loved. After all, if Daisy were still alive, Sharrone might not have ever met Dan—and surely would not have captured his heart.

The sky was deeply overcast as they left the stonecutter's shop in the center of the Black City. Kel helped Dan lift the heavy stone into the back of the vehicle. Dan and Sharrone sat in the back seat while Mahrden drove. Lyria and Kel sat silently beside him in the front. It was a somber journey, made even darker by the glowering gray sky. As they turned into the cemetery, rain that was really more like a fine mist began falling. Lyria looked silently at Kel. There was nothing to say, but his eye contact was comforting nevertheless.

Mahrden drove slowly through the open iron gates and down the winding dirt path to the back of the cemetery where the unmarked grave waited. He pulled off the path onto the gravel shoulder, parked, and everyone exited the steam-car. Mahrden carried an umbrella over Dan and Kel as they carried the stone between them. Lyria and Sharrone shared another umbrella. They walked silently through the cool mist to their destination.

Dan knelt beside the grave, his tears mingling with the rain. Sharrone knelt at his side. He reverently unwrapped the linen covering from the stone as Kel knelt beside him and helped him lift the stone into place. The carving on the stone simply read, "Daisy Hargrowve. She lived and died for love." When the stone was firmly placed on the grassy plot, Sharrone opened her large handbag and removed three flowers from a paper wrapping—daisies she had picked that morning—and gently laid them on the headstone, patting them sorrowfully.

She was crying with Dan when suddenly the sun came out of the overcast for just the briefest of moments, illuminating the grave in a brilliant shaft of sunlight. The daisies glowed briefly like small suns—seemingly lit with their own internal fires. Then the clouds again closed the sky. They walked back to the car in silence. As they drove away, Dan said, "I wish Raven could have seen this."

Kel responded simply, "How do you know she has not?"

* * * *

The next morning, Ma'hal, Helen, and Rosemarie arrived with two other women to see the progress on Kel and Lyria's home and how they were settling in. The girls were especially eager to see the horses, so Lyria led them to the corral as the rest followed behind. Mahrden, taking his time, walked slowly with Ma'hal, holding her arm.

The young girls eagerly ran forward until they were within thirty feet of the corral and there they stopped. Though they'd seen horses many times in the past, it had always been from a distance. The horse standing by the rails of the corral seemed much larger than those other horses for some reason. They walked more slowly now, trailing slightly behind Lyria.

Faithful Morning snorted, bobbing her head in greeting. She surveyed the children with placid brown eyes. Lyria was talking to the horse as they approached. She reached into her bag, taking out three apples. She kept one, giving the other two to the girls. There was a slight commotion in the barn and Fog and Mist suddenly appeared in the door, looking in their direction. They came trotting over, knowing there would be a treat in store for them as well. Kel stood in the doorway of the barn, smiling as Lyria and the girls gave an apple apiece to the horses. Morning gently nudged Rosemarie with her nose.

The girl giggled, "Her nose is wet!"

Lyria laughed and gently moved the girl forward, standing behind her, so she could pet the horse. Morning lowered her head, calmly accepting the small hand of the little girl on her forehead.

"When can we ride?" Helen asked. "Will you teach us?"

"I certainly will," Lyria responded, "but for now it is lunch time and I believe there is some food waiting for us back at the house."

After a leisurely lunch, Dan and Kel cleared the dishes as the women sat in the living room with Mahrden discussing what the days ahead might hold in store. When Dan and Kel returned, the subject under discussion was once again the Cathedral, their sudden change in attitude, and the unfortunate and very mysterious accident of a few days ago.

"As Dan can tell you, our rather loose confederation of people is quite good at gathering secrets," Mahrden was saying. "If the accident was not an accident, we'll find out."

"In the meantime," Dan added, "we must be vigilant and watchful. What Garn said about the possibility of revenge on the part of the priesthood of the so-called 'Redeemed God' must be taken at face value."

"I have found it curious, upon reflection, that Father Norville was so quickly on the scene of this so-called accident," Mahrden said. "He is the chief priest of the Cathedral at this time, standing in for the Bishop, no less. Yet he was the first one on the scene, three floors below ground—arriving even before the dead men's companions, who were standing in the very next corridor, only a dozen feet away—it strikes me as odd. How could he have gotten there so fast?"

"I have thought that myself," Dan said with a nod. "How could he have arrived so early and conveniently to call for help?"

"I've been talking with Tom," Mahrden said. "If you've no objection, Ma'hal, we think there should be guards placed at your home at least for the short term."

"I think we can take care of ourselves," the old woman said firmly. "I want no men staying in my house."

"I understand," the magician said, nodding. "Then how about this—we'll rent one of the houses just down the street…there are three currently vacant. Our men will stay there in shifts. We'll watch, and we'll walk about on the street from time to time—but if you have trouble, you have only to call on the phone or even shout loudly from an open window—we can be inside your house in less than a minute."

"That is acceptable," the old woman conceded. "Thank you for your concern for our well being and your consideration. Remember, though, that we are armed—make sure your men tell us clearly who they are before they enter."

Mahrden laughed. "I shall certainly let them know."

As they were preparing to depart, Kel remembered the small bundle still in his pocket. He smiled as he withdrew it. He walked over to Rosemarie, knelt in front of her, handing her the wrapped object.

The little girl smiled and said, "What is this?"

"This is something that was made by an amazing man who lives very far from here. I am certain he wants you to have it."

She looked at him quizzically, and then opened the bundle. She stared for a moment, a smile lighting up her face. Gently she lifted the small piece of jewelry to show the others.

In her hand was a finely made chain of the finest silver, and suspended from that chain was a copper hummingbird with an inlay of malachite for its chest. The copper wings and head of the tiny bird had been heated and oiled repeatedly so the metal shone with iridescent reds, purples, and blues. Rosie looked up at Kel and leaped into his arms. Everyone laughed as she gave Kel a 'bear hug'—the term now popular among all the women of the house.

"Now I can wear my hummingbird," the girl said happily.

"Yes, you may," Kel answered. "She will always be with you, little one. She is your protector and adviser. Listen for her words—she will not guide you astray." Kel set the girl down on the floor once more. She turned quickly, asking Kel to attach the chain around her neck. She then pranced around the room, displaying her jewelry to the women present. Ma'hal approached Kel, hugged him, and said, "You've restored her soul, young man. You've restored all of us."

"You have restored yourselves," Kel responded. "The only thing I did was show you where the door stood."

Ma'hal smiled, giving Kel another hug.

* * * *

After the visitors had all left for the day, Lyria looked at Kel.

"That was a very kind thing you just did, my love."

"I would not have been able to do it had not Llo included that piece in the trunk for us to take with us so very long ago. It is almost as though he…knew."

"I have been thinking as well," Lyria said, smiling slyly.

"About what?"

"About animals…"

"Animals?"

She took him by the hand, leading him toward the bedroom. "Yes…animals. Like—oh, say, stags and rhinoceros?"

"Oh," Kel responded with a smile, "those kinds of animals…."

CHAPTER 56

"So what do you think?"

The old man in tattered clothing leaned forward and said, "I think we need to be very cautious now. That little incident in the basement could've easily gone very badly—if they'd seen the rope."

"I realize that," Father Norville said.

"It was very fortunate," Father Anderson continued, "that I was following them—watching in what direction they were going. If we hadn't moved that case, and if they'd found that door..."

"But they didn't find it—and they didn't know you were standing in that doorway behind the case," Father Norville interjected, laughing. "That part of the Cathedral is beyond their finding now."

"See to it that it remains so," the old spy-priest said warningly, "we cannot afford any more mistakes now."

"That section of the basement has been completely cleared of the museum people," Father Norville snickered, "and we've moved all the books to a safer location for them to study. The area of the accident is now considered to be far too dangerous for further exploration at this time—besides, there's no longer anything to interest them there. They are quite happy to sit in better light, looking at books that nobody but them will ever read. And we've told them that they can re-enter the area after our engineers have proclaimed it safe, if they so desire."

Father Anderson laughed. "And they accepted that?"

"Absolutely. We should have no more problems with museum people."

Anderson then asked, "So how is that search the Bishop has sent us on faring? Are we still on a wild swan chase?"

"Progress is slow, Your Grace, we have only a handful of men who are trusted enough to do the looking. We're also not exactly sure of what we're looking for."

"That's the damnable part of it," the old priest said with a nod. "Still, if it's the will of the Redeemed God, we'll find it."

"Then, as once before, we will be the hand of God—we will wield the mighty sword our ancestors wielded so very many years ago. We will bring the unbelievers to their knees in the name of the

Redeemed God!"

"Or to their graves," the old priest said with a dry chuckle.

"We must proceed at all speed," Father Norville said, slamming his fist on the desk. "The Redeemed God has a brighter future in store for His faithful than living with monsters in the reeking swamps and diseased jungles of The Green."

"We're controlling The Green," Father Anderson said with confidence. "Vast amounts of very exotic lumber are now headed to our fine city. The sale of it will buy the help we need for this endeavor, and the other construction job. Even the unbelievers—nay, especially the unbelievers—are paying for the search that will end in their destruction. It is almost…poetic. There are currently three Trimotives in place in The Green for the protection of the cities there, and two more are under construction in Atlanta—plus the new, fast battle zeppelins are nearing completion as well. We will dominate The Green on land and in the air."

"By the way," Father Anderson continued with a crooked grin, "I've been meaning to ask you—have you seen what the young, dark-skinned half-human girls of the southern regions look like?"

"I have not," Father Norville said.

"Well then," the old priest said, rising from his chair, "come with me—I have a real treat in store for you—they have feathers!"

"Feathers?" The young priest quickly rose from his seat, turned down the gaslight jet, and eagerly followed the old spy-priest out of the Cathedral, down the front steps out into the darkness.

* * * *

It was also dark when the locomotive made a short stop, seemingly in the middle of nowhere. With the engine chuffing somewhere up ahead of them, the shamans climbed down the three steps from train to the earth. The porter looked questioningly at the three men as he struggled with their luggage.

"It will be all right," Garn reassured him, "we are home. You need not worry about our well being."

The porter looked about himself fearfully—it was not his passengers' wellbeing he was concerned about. He looked around again, suspiciously—as though expecting a pack of dire wolves to descend on all of them right there by the tracks. By the time he was back aboard and the train was rolling once again for its next stop, Atlanta, not one dire wolf had put in an appearance. Even so, he breathed a sigh of relief to be once again moving through this God-forsaken wilderness toward real civilization.

The three shamans watched the train as it receded into the night. The sound of approaching hooves attracted their attention. They turned, looking out into the darkness.

"We were told there'd be three waiting for us," a voice said in the darkness. There was a spark, and then a flame as a torch was lit. Vorth, the appointed war-band leader of the gathered tribes grinned at the three shamans.

"Vorth! If any would know of our arrival, surely it would have been you," Galv chortled. "How have you been, my old friend?"

"We are better now that you all have returned," the warrior said with a smile. "Pela has missed you, Garn…"

"And I her," he answered. "Shall we be on our way?"

"That is why we brought a wagon," Vorth commented dryly, "so the old men can ride in comfort, and also bring their belongings with them."

"Right now," Galv said, "I will take any transportation to return to my tribe and my people."

"Then climb in, seers," Vorth said, "and we will be on our way."

Then they were moving. Drog and Galv were seated comfortably on rolled cushions of straw wrapped in linen. The trunk of objects, given so long ago to Kel sat behind them, giving them something of a backrest. Garn chose to sit at the end of the cart, with his legs dangling. That was when he heard the familiar voices of Kel's childhood friends, Mart and Geog. He laughed happily as he listened to them arguing with each other.

"I told you we should have put at least three more seats in the back of the wagon, Geog."

"This is good enough," his friend responded from the darkness, "there is plenty of room for everyone."

"But what if there had been all five of them returning, Geog… then what would we have done?"

"But there are not five, Mart—count them. I only see three… though it is dark—maybe I am just not seeing as many as you see!"

"Well…there might have been five…" Mart retorted defensively, feeling himself gradually losing the argument. He hated that feeling.

"Then our seers' advice would have been faulty,' Geog continued. "Four separate shamans told us on four separate occasions to expect three returning travelers, not five."

"But look at Garn—he must now sit with his legs hanging out the back of the wagon," Mart responded.

"We have ridden in wagons in that manner many times in our lifetimes," Geog retorted defensively, knowing that he'd already won the discussion, as he preferred to call his dealings with his friend. He smiled smugly in the dark.

"Yes, Geog—but that was when we were but seven summers of age!"

"We are not yet so aged that dangling legs pose much of a problem, youngsters," Garn interjected. "There is room in the wagon for me—I like riding this way, and have since I was young."

"Garn speaks the truth," Galv added with a laugh. "Why, we had to outrun fierce dragons when we escaped The Green. We are thankful we still have legs to dangle!" With that, Galv slid down from his seat and joined Garn at the end of the wagon, and Drog quickly followed him. The three of them sat now at the back of the wagon, looking smugly up at Mart.

Though he couldn't see him clearly in the dark, Mart knew Geog was grinning at him—almost as though he thought he'd actually won the argument. Mart knew he had, but only with the help of the rescued shamans. That meant it wasn't actually his loss; his friend had help in his argument. Nevertheless, Mart knew it was time to change the subject.

"Lyria and Kel are not among those returning," he commented.

"No," Garn responded, "but do not fear, they are well. Tomorrow we will tell the village of our journey—what we saw and what we fled from."

"Why can you not tell us tonight?"

Garn laughed. "I said I will not tell the village this night, oh young and impatient Mart. I have not seen my lovely Pela in six months, and I long for her companionship after all this time. But you, my fine young man, and these with you, shall hear our tale as we travel back to the village."

Mart laughed. "That is more like it!"

And so, Garn and the other shamans told their story of wonder and fear—of loss and gain.'

Mart and Geog were silent regarding the attack on Garn's wife. They knew Garn had no knowledge of the assault committed on Pela by a vengeance-seeking Adria. They knew he should hear about the attack from his wife in her own voice—and for once, both men decided to keep their council.

And so, the shamans began the daylong trek back to their homes and families. The shamans were all glad to be going back home after all this time, wondering how life in the tribes had changed with the great gatherings they knew were happening. Garn was concerned about Pela—they'd not been separated since the days of his Shadow Walk all those long years ago. He was very anxious to see her—to hold her once more in his arms. He smiled at the thought.

CHAPTER 57

"It's been days now and we've heard nothing—nothing at all. I'm worried, and I don't mind saying so." Tom looked up at Mahrden. They were sitting together in the editor's office. It was night once more, and the lights were dimmed. They were again reviewing the police report describing the so-called 'accident' in the Cathedral basement—futilely looking for the sixth time for some small thing—some little fact they might have previously missed.

They were also sharing a bottle of wine. Almost inaudible, the rhythmic thrumming of the printing presses made a subtle backdrop to their conversation. Tom took another sip from his glass, shaking his head in disgust, almost hoping that intoxication might bring insight. It didn't seem to be working.

"We must find a way to get back inside the Cathedral," the magician said. "We've got to see the accident site for ourselves—and it must be sooner rather than later—they may have already covered their tracks. But guilt always leaves its footprints, if one looks closely enough." He slammed his fist on the desk. "There must be a way we can get someone of our own inside the Cathedral."

"There is one way," Tom said with a smile. "Speaking in…a relative way, that is."

Mahrden looked at his friend suspiciously. "A…relative way?"

"Yes, certainly," the editor smirked. "I have a relative that could easily get in there. He's a scholar affiliated with the museum and with the library. He's a top-flight investigator, and an interesting man. I'll send for him and let's see what he thinks of the matter."

"I can think of no better alternative," Mahrden said with a shake of his head. "If this man is as good as you say, this may be our only chance of ferreting out the truth."

"I can't think of another one either. But this I can say with complete confidence—if there is something to be discovered there, something hidden or disguised that we might have missed, no matter how small or how well hidden—Adrian will be able to discover it and understand it."

"Adrian?"

"Why yes, my cousin Adrian Buffington. If he cannot help us, there is no one who can."

"Well," Mahrden said with a grin, "what are you waiting for— call the man right now."

Tom laughed, picking up his phone. "He's in San Diego right now," he explained, "it may take a while for him to finish up down there before we can get him to come up here."

"All the more reason to call him right this minute," Mahrden said with a firm nod of his head. Tom quickly placed the call.

"Hello, Adrian, it's me. What do you mean, 'Who's me'? It's your cousin Tom. Yes? Really? So you've already heard about the situation? That's what I'm calling about." There was a short pause as Tom listened. Then he laughed. "You've been expecting my call? So, you think we can't handle this by ourselves?" Another pause, followed by another laugh. "Well, you're right, Adrian, we can't handle this by ourselves."

As he hung up the phone, Mahrden said, "Well?"

"He has a few loose ends to tie up in San Diego," Tom answered, "and then he'll come up here. It might be a couple days, at the most, he said. He also said he'd clear his way ahead of time with the museum staff so he'll have all the proper identification and certifications he'll need to get into the Cathedral with the other museum people by the time he gets here."

Mahrden responded, clearly impressed, "You're right, my friend, this Adrian Buffington is an interesting man."

Tom laughed. "You have no idea. More wine? No point in having to pour any of it away."

"Pour it into my glass then," the magician said, "I can put it to good use!"

* * * *

"By the Redeemed God! She fought hard, didn't she? Much harder than I would have thought possible." Father Norville chuckled, holding a raw bison steak over his swelling eye as he reclined in his chair after they'd returned to the Cathedral. They were back in his office after a two-hour interlude in the warehouse on the waterfront where all the half-human girls brought up from the south were kept until they could be tamed—at least somewhat tamed.

Father Anderson guffawed. "I told you you'd need to hold her down. She's only half human, after all, and you know how strong some animals can be when they're cornered."

"And I suppose, technically, she was cornered—wasn't she?"

"Like I said," Father Anderson repeated, grinning, "I told you to hold her down."

"I was holding her down," the young priest protested with a laugh, "just not hard enough, I guess. I would never have thought someone so small and young could hit that hard."

"Did she think that was a problem as well, Father Norville? That it wasn't hard enough?"

Norville laughed at the taunt, "Ow, don't make me laugh—it makes my face hurt."

"So, do you think she was she worth it? I mean was she worth the expense of dragging her here all the way from the jungle? I understand they had to kill most of her tribe before they could even reach the young ones."

"I would say so," Father Norville enthused, "but I could tell she's still pretty new at this sex thing, isn't she?"

"Well, she's still pretty young, you know…but don't worry about that, we'll get her broken in real good before we put her into the corral with the other rides."

Both priests laughed, sharing a bottle of wine in celebration. Their compatriots in the south had captured several new girls who were now on their way to salvation—and on their way to the secret underground pleasure house run by the Cathedral. This was a pleasure house that was reserved for their most wealthy and exclusive clients—men, and some women, who would never tell the press or the police what went on there. The wealthy and influential simply had too much to lose.

* * * *

The wagon and its escort rode into the village very early the next morning. The sun was barely over the horizon as they passed the first dwellings. The shamans were surprised at the changes they beheld. No longer a small tribe of a few dozen, this was now a village! Wooden structures and tents covered the ground and dozens of cook fires sent their wisps of white smoke into the air. They rode down the center road—now there was little else it could be called—to the central meeting space of the tribe.

"If I did not know this was my home, I would not have recognized it," Garn commented.

Vorth laughed. "There have been many changes, wise one—some not as pleasant as others, I fear."

Garn glanced at the warrior, but before he could question that statement, he realized he was in the village common. He stared in disbelief at his tribe's once familiar gathering spot. Now, the wooden benches stood twice as tall as they'd been the last time he'd seen them—and they were rapidly filling up with people eager to hear of their adventures since their disappearance.

Garn looked around anxiously, searching for his beloved Pela. He wasn't disappointed. She was standing beside the fire, along with the wives of the other two shamans, smiling up at him as they climbed from the wagon.

"My beloved," he whispered, and embraced his love. Until now, he hadn't realized how much he'd missed even the warmth of her body held against his.

"I have missed you so, my darling," she whispered in his ear. "I keep making breakfast for two," she quipped.

Garn laughed, responding, "I am ready to eat that breakfast now, my one true love."

"Well…you can't," she laughed, "you must first tell our people gathered here of your adventures."

"No, I must not," he responded. "Evening is time enough. We three need to be with our families this day. We've told the tale to Mart and Geog and the others. They can relate it in the village common, and this evening while Mart and Geog are still arguing about what we said, we will tell the story in our words. Have you made breakfast?"

Pela laughed gaily. "No, I have not—come home with me, my love, and you can help me." Garn and Pela walked hand in hand back to their home, realizing as they passed through the doorway, that it was now once again a home.

Breakfast was quickly prepared—Pela had almost forgotten how much help her man had been. Now it was even more important. She told him of the attacks and killings that happened shortly after Kel and Lyria had departed. She told him of her dream of animals slain, only to realize too late that the animals she'd seen in her dream were in reality the four slaughtered shamans' totems.

She told him of Adria's predations—and the deranged girl's nearly lethal assault on her. Garn was shocked—he had no idea that any of this had occurred.

"Adria is dead, my darling," he explained, "inadvertently dead by her own hand. She took many with her—many innocent lives, including women and children. But tell me, my love, how are you now feeling?"

Pela laughed, attempting to lighten the mood. "Oh, I am fine now—that happened a while ago. With the help of fellow healers and shamans, I am almost fully recovered."

"Almost?"

"Yes, almost. My right arm is no longer as strong as it once was, and sometimes I have a difficult time remembering someone's name. It is most embarrassing. But—I have been told this from very reliable individuals—most of the strength in my arm will return eventually, and I can see that my memory is getting better every day."

"That is well," Garn said, a worried tone in his voice.

"Oh, do not worry—it's going to be all right. Um…by the way… what did you say your name was?" Pela's mischievous grin gave her away.

Garn laughed, taking her into his arms. "Come with me—dance, my love—winter's been so cold this year. Give me your warmth, my summertime love."

And so, as the wood stove in the kitchen was heating up for breakfast, Garn and Pela danced. It was a slow dance; they moved together to music that had been played long ago. They were dancing their wedding dance—remembered from over fifty years before.

And so, the story continues. *After: The New Earth III: Journey into Legend — coming soon.*

Night descends across the wild lands south of the glacier, drawing its soft velvet blanket of sleep over the shamans and their families, once again united—and over warrior, healer, and farmer. Night also descends across the city-state of Los Angeles, The Black City of the West, drawing its soft velvet blanket of sleep over the citizens. And they sleep—but for some it's a fitful sleep, a sleep filled with nameless dread, and dark red shadows hinting the possibility of war.

The black priesthood sleeps soundly, both in this city and far to the south in their new walled cities built by slaves on the rim of the primal jungle. They sleep soundly with the smugness of the righteous—with the smugness of the saved. Their towering war machines, hissing and clanking, stand guard through the night and patrol the darkness. But the darkness hides many things.

The Bishop and his fanatical followers have attempted to fraudulently use the fabled image of the Celestial Dragons—legendary beings who, it was said, brought the universe into being. They intended to use a captive dinosaur to help them frighten and dominate the world—to give them ultimate power. Now that plan is in ruin. Their city has been burned and their people slain.

But something else is happening that they cannot foresee—for now The Green is awakening, and a different mythic legend is emerging. This ancient legend is now only spoken of in children's nursery rhymes and tall tales. But unlike the Bishop's fraudulent Celestial Dragon, this is a very real power that has awakened. It is a power not felt in the world of men in an age—a power now undreamed of in the philosophies of the black priests.

In the midst of this great power stands a young human girl who was once called Noria but is now Raven—a girl horribly used by the Bishop and his kind, but who has now come into her own. If the black priests want to wield the power of a legendary past, they need to beware; that power is coming for them. And if the priests want war, they'll have a war they could never have imagined.

ACKNOWLEDGEMENTS

I would first like to thank my wife; though she's now gone from me, she taught me a great deal about 'drive' and self-starting. I also want to thank my English teachers, both in High School and College, who taught me grammar, spelling, and the attention to detail needed to write. Also, I want to thank my Editors, Sherry Folb and Holly Chapman who have worked very hard getting this book ready for publication. I want to thank Kathryn Lucas for her fine artwork. And finally, I want to thank that inscrutable power which has placed so many people and events in my path to teach me empathy and expand my awareness of the human condition.

ABOUT THE AUTHOR

Keith Mueller was born in Tucson, Arizona, and is a graduate of the University of Arizona with degrees in art and art education. He served six years in the US Air Force as a firearms instructor and competitive shooter on the Air Force pistol team at Lackland AFB, and later as an instructor at the Air Force Academy. He's had an interest in metaphysical studies, shamanism, ancient cultures and religions since the late 1960s, personally practicing some of these disciplines. Though he's had an interest in writing for many years, retirement has allowed this interest to finally manifest in this book series.

CPSIA information can be obtained
at www.ICGtesting.com
Printed in the USA
BVHW03s0857071018
529254BV00007B/1/P

9 781641 369695